'Masterful storytelling at its finest, be prepared for a late night'

Maria V. Snyder, *New York Times* bestselling author

'A first-rate sword-and-sorcery tale, with intriguing characters, that moves at a quick pace' *Booklist*

'*Shadow's Son* is easily one of my favourite books of 2010'
Fantasy Book Critic

'When Sprunk gets going, he writes with an energy that has to be experienced to be believed . . . a thoroughly entertaining read' *Graeme's Fantasy Book Review*

Also by Jon Sprunk from Gollancz:

Shadow's Son
Shadow's Lure

SHADOW'S LURE

LuRe

Jon Sprunk

The right of Jon Sprunk to be identified as the author
of this work has been asserted by him in accordance with
the Copyright, Designs and Patents Act 1988.

First published by Pyr®,
an imprint of Prometheus Books,
59 John Glenn Drive, Amherst, NY 14228-2119
www.pyrsf.com

First published in Great Britain in 2011 by
Gollancz
An imprint of the Orion Publishing Group
Orion House, 5 Upper St Martin's Lane,
London WC2H 9EA
An Hachette UK Company

This edition published in Great Britain in 2012
by Gollancz

1 3 5 7 9 10 8 6 4 2

A CIP catalogue record for this book
is available, from the British Library

ISBN 978 0 575 09606 6

Typeset at The Spartan Press Ltd,
Lymington, Hants

Printed in Great Britain by Clays Ltd, St Ives plc

The Orion Publishing Group's policy is to use papers
that are natural, renewable and recyclable products and
made from wood grown in sustainable forests. The logging
and manufacturing processes are expected to conform to
the environmental regulations of the country of origin.

www.jonsprunk.com
www.orionbooks.co.uk

This book is dedicated to my wife and son,
the twin centers of my universe;
and to the family and friends who enrich our lives every day.

O God of earth and altar,
Bow down and hear our cry.
Our earthly rulers falter,
Our people drift and die;
The walls of gold entomb us,
The swords of scorn divide,
Take not Thy thunder from us,
But take away our pride.

G K. Chesterton, 1906

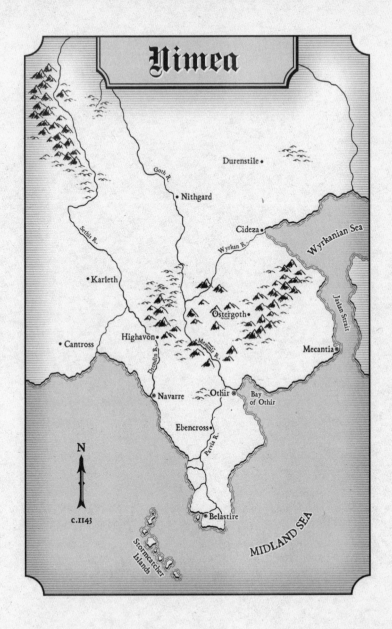

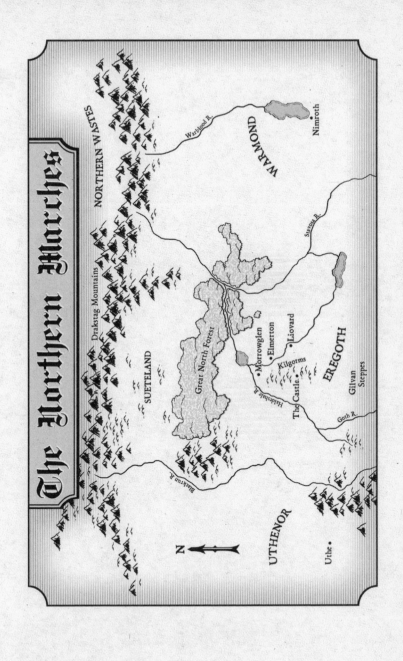

The Northern Marches

NORTHERN WASTES

Drakstag Mountains

Wartfred R.

WARMOND

Nimroth

Savron R.

SUETELAND

Great North Forest

Morrowglen

Elmerton

Liovard

Kilgorms

EREGOTH

The Castle

Haldshiek R.

Goth R.

Gilvan Steppes

Blacktrun R.

UTHENOR

Uthe

N

PROLOGUE

A bitter north wind blew off the moors.

It sliced through Keegan's thick winter cloak and shirt as he handed over his sword to the gate-wardens. Faint moonbeams cast deep shadows across the weathered ramparts and frost-rimmed towers of Aldercairn Keep. When the sentries were satisfied, he and his band were allowed to enter.

They passed between the close walls of the tunnel running under the ancient gatehouse, and Keegan didn't breathe easy until they emerged in a courtyard on the other side, where another pair of guards opened the door to the inner keep. Bright light flooded across the snow at their feet. Tromping after his comrades, Keegan entered.

Heat from four great hearths wrapped him in a sweltering embrace as Caedman, their war leader, led them to a table at the end of the hall. Keegan loosened his cloak as he took a seat under an open window and glanced around. This was his first peace-meet. Warriors and house-carls sat shoulder-to-shoulder. Their deep laughter shook the timber walls. At the other end of the hall, a long table sat on a riser above the rest. The five men at the high table were adorned with silver and gold. Their white fur mantles gleamed in the firelight.

One of Keegan's comrades gestured to a venerable man

wrapped in a black bearskin cloak in the center seat. 'That's Old Jevick.'

'The Allastar thane?' Keegan asked.

'They say he hasn't stepped outside of this big pile of rock in years.'

Keegan took in the banners hanging on the walls, the rows of trophies, and the roaring hearths. 'I don't blame him. This is a good place for an old man to rest his bones.'

As a cupbearer set down a double-handful of mugs before them, a loud thump echoed from the high table. Heads turned as Thane Jevick pulled himself to his feet.

'Welcome, sons of Eregoth.' His voice was shaky, but deeper than his years suggested. 'I have called this peace-meet to discuss the troubles that plague our lands.'

Keegan looked around and saw heads nodding. Farms had been burned to the ground, men killed, and women and children taken away. Everyone knew from where the troubles came. He and his comrades had decided it was time to do something about it, and Caedman had brought them here to find out if anyone else felt the same.

The pounding of five hundred fists filled the hall as the aged chieftain returned to his seat. One by one, the other thanes introduced themselves. This took some time, as each attached numerous titles and accomplishments to his name. The last thane was a powerful figure. Flame-red braids hung down his leather breastplate.

'Many of you know me. I am Comarc of the Ragarson clan.' He rapped his knuckles on the table. 'And I won't bore you with the long list of my deeds.'

More fist pounding resounded. Everyone knew of the exploits of Comarc Ragarson and his Red Riders. His had been the driving force behind their country's march to freedom, but that had been years ago, before Keegan's birth. Would the Ragarsons ride again?

Thane Comarc looked around the hall. 'But I will be the first to speak. We fought and bled to free our country. But now the ravens of war have come scratching at our windows again.

2

Darkness lies heavy over our lands. And Liovard sits at the heart of it!'

There it was, spoken plain for all to hear. Keegan shifted on his seat as the assembly fell silent.

Taelish, the thane of the Nuodir, stood up. 'You speak as if we can change things, Comarc. But this peace-meet is a waste of time. Clan Eviskine has grown too powerful. We must make an accommodation with them, or risk losing what we have left.'

Comarc spat on the table and ignored the pointed look it earned him from Jevick. 'You Nuodir can go kiss Eviskine's lily-white arse if you like, but the Ragarsons will fight to our last breath!'

A mighty roar shook the hall as a contingent of men jumped to their feet and pounded on the tables. The other thanes at the high table exchanged concerned glances behind Comarc's back. One voice rose above the tumult.

'Why fight alone?'

Old Jevick peered into the crowd. 'Who speaks?'

The hall had quieted, but the looks cast in the direction of their table couldn't be called friendly. Keegan swallowed the last of his ale as his captain stood up.

'I am Caedman Du'Ormik, son of Londain.'

Murmurs spread through the hall. Old Jevick turned to speak with the other thanes, but Comarc didn't wait.

'I've heard of you,' the Ragarson chief said. 'Most of my fighters cannot decide if you're a hero, or just a lucky fool. But only a clan thane has the right to speak here.'

Bench legs screeched as two men from Keegan's band stood up and threw back their cloaks to reveal white mantles underneath. Tongues wagged at the sight.

'He speaks for Clan Indrig,' Thane Samnus said.

'And for the Hurrolds,' Thane Obern added.

Comarc snorted. 'I see you've brought a pair of yapping dogs with you. Too bad they're squatting at your heels instead of sitting up here with their rightful peers.'

'Go frig your mother, Comarc,' Samnus said. 'I'm here

to make sure you don't run off with the women when the talking gets fierce.'

Comarc laughed. 'I see you, Du'Ormik. Speak your mind.'

Caedman looked around the room. 'I asked why we should fight alone. If every man stands only for his own hearth and clan as we've always done, then we'll be split apart and killed, and our families taken as chattel.'

Keegan didn't know what chattel was, but it sounded bad.

The Nuodir thane threw his cup to land with a clatter somewhere on the floor. 'I've heard enough. These fools are the reason Liovard burns our villages and chases off our people.'

'If we unite,' Caedman said, 'we can defend ourselves and perhaps win a lasting peace for our country, like the one promised years ago when our fathers and uncles rousted the Nimeans.'

Every man in the hall was on his feet now, banging and shouting to be heard. Keegan couldn't tell what most of them were saying, in favor of Caedman's idea or against. The thanes at the raised table yelled alongside their men. Comarc bellowed something about the debt of Eregothic blood being repaid a hundred times over, but Keegan lost the gist of his argument in the clamor.

A noise had caught his ear, faint at first, but it grew to a keening howl. Men quieted as the ceiling timbers shook. The flames in the fireplaces flickered and threatened to go out as shrieking winds blew down the chimney flues. Keegan looked around, but everyone was absorbed by the chaos ripping through the hall. Then the doors of the hall shook. The impact echoed in Keegan's chest. Chairs fell over and table legs groaned as the warriors turned. Outside, a wolf howled.

A whisper rose from the crowd. 'The Hunt!'

Keegan swallowed. With the second blow, the doors burst open and a crowd of intruders with gleaming steel in their fists rushed into the hall. Everyone stood gaping as the interlopers pushed through their ranks, shoving the clansmen back. Keegan climbed up on the table for a better view. The intruders towered over the warriors in the hall, with pale eyes

4

glaring from under bestial helmets fashioned like wolves' heads. They carried axes and hammers of dark iron and broad shields. Keegan knew them at once from stories he'd heard from his father.

Northmen.

Keegan watched them with awe, but then another entered the hall, and a sick feeling uncoiled in his stomach. Clad from crown to foot in a shell of black steel, the new arrival stood even taller than the other Northmen. Keegan clenched his hands into fists. He knew this one from stories, too. Wherever he appeared, people died. The clans called him the Beast.

A pair of figures entered behind the steel-skinned giant. The man had a narrow build and a lean face with features some might call refined, and he wore enough gilt to bury a prince. But it was the woman beside him who stole Keegan's attention. The way she moved, and the curves under her sheer black gown, made his blood boil. Her skin glistened like wet silk. This was no ordinary woman. Upon her arrival, the hall fell into perilous silence.

Preceded by the Beast, the man and his lady walked arm-in-arm down the center of the hall, and the clansmen fell back before them. Those who did not move quickly enough were smashed out of the way by the Northmen. In that instant, Keegan understood who these people were. The man had to be Erric Eviskine, the Duke of Liovard. And that meant the lady at his side was . . .

The Witch. Sybelle, Queen of the Dark.

Keegan looked away from her eyes, not daring to meet them again even from this distance. The heels of the duke's polished boots clacked on the floor until he and his paramour came before the thanes.

'Eviskine.' Comarc Ragarson's mouth twisted. 'This peace-meet is for patriots of Eregoth.'

The duke clasped the gold pommel of his sword. 'Who dares to say I am no patriot?' He turned, and the large medallion around his neck swayed. 'Am I not thane of one of the oldest clans?'

5

Mutters circulated through the crowd, but no one dared to speak up, not even Comarc, though he and the other chiefs glared back and forth. Then another voice spoke. Keegan's stomach shrank as Caedman pushed through the crowd.

'I name you traitor, Eviskine,' Caedman said. 'Even if no one else has the stomach to do it.'

The duke made a half-smile as if he'd heard a poor jest. 'Jevick, it seems your house is infested with vermin.'

'I am a free man of Eregoth,' Caedman said. 'Again I name you a traitor. A traitor to this land, which you have sown with blood and fear. A traitor to your own people by the company you keep. While others fought and bled for their country, you rolled over like a whore and let the enemy in.'

The lady laughed. For a moment, it seemed to Keegan that time stood still, and all he could hear was the cool melody of her voice. Then the moment was gone. He coughed into his sleeve. The back of his throat tasted like a burnt copper penny.

'Come, Erric,' she said. 'I told you they would be intractable.' The duke shook his head at the high table. 'I would have saved you. Remember that.'

Keegan watched with an uneasy feeling as the duke and lady departed. They halted on the threshold and turned around. Keegan expected some parting words, some base insult. Instead, the witch whistled. The candles and hearth fires went out, plunging the hall into darkness.

Shouts echoed off the walls, punctuated by screams and the wet smacks of cleaving steel. A strange blue light flashed above Keegan's head. What it illuminated below was like a vision from Hell. The weaponless clansmen used table legs and eating knives – anything they could find – as they fought for their lives, but the axes of the Northmen rose and fell like threshers' flails, reaping a harvest that washed the floor in blood. Nor three paces away, a warrior was cut down by a Northman. Keegan went for his belt knife, but the killer moved away to find another victim.

Samnus and Obert led the band into the mayhem after

Caedman. Keegan started to go after them, but remembered his war leader's words from before they entered the keep.

No matter what happens, Keegan, you must survive. You must tell the clans what you've seen and heard this night, or we are all lost.

Keegan located Caedman in the fray. Dark patches of blood matted the war leader's leathers as he fended off the attacks of a Northman with his bare hands. Then Samnus and the others arrived and bore the invader to the floor. Keegan smiled, until the crowd parted as if drawn back by invisible strings, and a tide of dread filled his chest.

The Beast approached.

Steam rose from the giant's armored hide as he strode toward Caedman. Keegan yelled a warning to his comrades, but it was swallowed by the cacophony. Then the crowd surged, and he lost sight of the fighters. A moment later he glimpsed a body on the floor. It was Caedman, laid out on his back like a dead man. Bile flooded the back of Keegan's throat as he stumbled down from the table. He couldn't catch his breath. The air was thick with the stench of blood and sweat. He turned, looking for a way out, and spied the window above his head. He leapt to catch the stone sill. As he pulled his upper body over the ledge, his shoulders caught in the narrow casement. A frantic wriggle broke him free from the stone's embrace, and he pushed into the empty space beyond.

Keegan landed in a snowbank. A sour taste coated his tongue as he heard the cries from inside the keep. Then he was up and running across the frozen fields.

He didn't look back.

SHADOW'S

Chapter
ONE

LURE

Caim drew in a breath and held it. The bow shaft creaked as he pulled the string back to his ear.

Forty paces away, the target turned his head, but then went back to his meal. Caim measured the distance again, allowing for wind and a slight difference in elevation. The temperature had dropped to near freezing with the sun's setting, which would affect the arrow's flight.

'Still playing around out here?' a voice whispered in his ear.

Caim shivered as Kit passed through him, and then she was beside him. Her hair gleamed like quicksilver in the dying light.

'You're going to shoot without giving him a chance?'

'Don't—' he said as she leaned across his field of vision to look down the arrow.

The mark glanced up again. Caim's hands were cramping from the cold, the bowstring biting into his fingers.

'—move,' he breathed.

But it was too late. The stag gathered its legs and leapt away between two leaning evergreens. Snow from dislodged branches showered over its trail. Caim ducked away from Kit and tracked his quarry's movement through the thicket. Time slowed. In the space between two heartbeats, he found the target and shot.

The arrow spun in a tight spiral as the stag emerged from the trees, hooves churning in the deep snow. Caim leaned forward as the arrow and its target collided. The stag's high-pitched squeal startled him when the missile punched into its side. The arrow struck high and behind the foreleg. The stag foundered, but then it took off through the snow. How long could it run? By the brightness of the blood running down its tawny coat, the shot had punctured a lung.

Caim fumbled for his quiver as he ran after it, but the stag raced like lightning through the snow. In another few heartbeats, it would be gone. His breath burned in his chest as the creature passed behind a thick bole. What emerged on the other side nearly caused Caim to stumble in his tracks. It had the rough size and shape of the stag, but its coat was silky black like the fur of a jungle cat. Two slender horns of bone-white ivory rose from the back of the narrow skull. A twinge ached in Caim's chest, and the stag returned, galloping away through the snow. Without thinking about it, he reached out to the shadows gathering in the trees around him. The stag snorted as a ribbon of darkness fell over its face. It slid in the snow, just a momentary hitch in its gait, but that was enough for Caim to draw and fire. The second arrow went high. He shot the third almost without aiming. It looked like it was going to veer wide until the stag blundered into its path. This time the animal fell.

When Caim caught up, the stag was kicking weakly on its side. There was no sign of the strange transformation it had undergone. Caim drew one of the long *suete* knives sheathed in the harness at the small of his back and put the animal out of its misery. He tied its legs together while bright red blood pumped out into the snow.

Kit floated at his side and watched the animal's last throes. 'Did you see the way it looked at you? It was the saddest thing I've ever seen.'

Kit continued to chatter as Caim dragged the carcass in the direction of his camp. He hadn't known what to expect when he decided to come north. Eregoth loomed in his memory like a half-forgotten nightmare, but the last Nimean outpost was six days behind them and they hadn't seen another living soul since. Of course, he traveled cross-country, avoiding anything more established than hunting trails. Game was plentiful; he wouldn't starve if he could manage to keep from freezing to death. But he hardly slept anymore, and when he did the dreams were waiting for him, worse than before. And he saw things, too. Shadow things, like what happened with the stag. They appeared without warning, day and night. Ever since Othir.

'You're passing it,' Kit chided over his head.

Caim stopped beside a screen of brush. Through the canopy of tree branches, the sky was a sheet of cobalt. The moon hung low, a slender sickle among the evening's first stars. He dropped his prize and knelt down to clean it. With the bloody meat in hand, he kicked snow over the carcass and tromped through the undergrowth.

His camp was a lean-to and a fire pit, which had gone out in his absence. Once he got the fire going again, he spitted the meat and set it over the flames. Then he cleaned his hands in the snow and settled back against the tree supporting his impromptu shelter.

Kit appeared before him, standing in the fire. Her arms were folded across her chest, a bad sign. Caim took a deep breath to prepare for the onslaught.

'What are you doing?' she asked.

'Waiting for my supper.'

'You know what I mean!' She waved her hands over her head. 'Why are we here?'

'You know why, Kit.' He broke a pair of semi-dry branches in half and tossed them into the fire. 'You were all in favor of this before.'

'When?'

'Back in Othir. You heard me explain it to Josey. You didn't have any objections then.'

'Yes, I did. I just didn't voice them.'

He turned the spits. 'Then you forfeited your chance.'

'I'm voicing them now! Look at you. You're half frozen,

living like an animal. And you don't have any idea what you're searching for. Do you?'

Caim grunted, but it came out like a clearing of his throat. *When was the last time you agreed with anything I did, Kit?* But she was always there, every time he fell down, even if sometimes it was only to throw salt in his wounds. 'I'm tired, Kit. Let it go.'

She floated over to sit beside him and leaned against his arm. Ghostly tickles raised gooseflesh under his leathers. 'Why don't we go to Arnos? Just the two of us, down to the Midland shore. Bright beaches, clear waters. By the time we get there, it would be warmer—'

He scooted away from her. 'Cut it out, Kit.'

'Fine.'

With a last glower, she vanished. No sparkles, no glitter. Out in the gathering darkness, an owl hooted. The air seemed colder when she was gone. What was he trying to prove? That he didn't need anyone? He'd spent most of the first week after he left Othir looking over his shoulder, hoping Josey had ignored his admonition not to come after him. Even after he stopped looking back, that didn't make his decision to continue north any easier. The encounter with Levictus was still fresh in his mind.

The wind died down for a moment, making the sorcerer's next words resound like thunder crashing over Caim's head. 'She dwells in the peerless realm of her ancestors, beyond the veil in the Land of Shadow.'

The Land of Shadow. Children's nonsense. But it wasn't. Caim reached out his hand and called to the darkness. A patch of shadow appeared in his palm. It came with hardly any effort. The shadows. The stag. His dreams. What else was changing?

Caim gave a mental push and the shadow slid away. After giving the spits another turn, he ducked inside the lean-to, where his few possessions were pushed against the canvas wall. On top of the pile lay a long bundle wrapped in burlap.

11

He reached inside and pulled, and the sword slid clear of its housing with a whisper. The black blade reflected no shine from the firelight. It had lain in the ground behind Kas's cabin for almost twenty years, yet showed not the least sign of tarnish.

Where did you come from?

As if in answer, a tremble slithered up his arm. And then the night came alive. The sky lightened to milky gray. The trees stood taller and shed their shady cloaks, and the snow gleamed beneath him like a blanket of Stardust.

Caim thrust the sword back into its scabbard. When his hand left the hilt, his vision returned to normal. With a grimace, he folded the burlap over the end and shoved the entire thing under a blanket, where it made a conspicuous hump. He pulled over the bulging satchel. Under layers of spare clothes, he found a narrow book bound in a black cord. It was Archpriest Vassili's personal journal, given to him by Josey. There had also been papers for safe passage, but he'd burned them. From what he had seen journeying north, any document found on his person tying him to the new empress would do him more harm than good. If things had been bad in Nimea before the Church's downfall, they were worse now. There was no law beyond the length of a sword's blade. The nobles squabbled over land rights while the commons stole off to become brigands.

Caim cracked open the book, and a square of parchment slid out onto his lap. He held it up. A capital letter J was stamped in gold wax over the fold. A letter from Josey, tucked where he would find it. Was it a plea for him to come back? Or a warning to stay away and never return? He shoved it in the back of the book.

The lines on the book's smooth vellum pages were penned in Vassili's cultured hand. He read a page or two each night. So far he hadn't found anything useful, mostly passages about the archpriest's early days as a praetor in Belastire.

Caim touched the key-shaped pendant, another gift from Josey, under his shirt as he flipped through the pages until something caught his eye.

12

Eighth day of Atrius, 1123

We have arrived in Othir after fourteen days on the road. Despite the speed of our passage, I was the last of the conclave to arrive, a fact which shall no doubt be used against me.

We were received at DiVecci in the afternoon. Just as I suggested in my treatise, the Inquest has been expanded several times beyond their original . . .

The next couple words were indecipherable. Then:

The oubliettes beneath the castle stink of river water and are bursting with prisoners, many of them imperialist agitators, but one caught my attention. Something about his eyes. I have decided to return tomorrow and inquire about him.

Hearing the sizzle of dripping fat, Caim lurched forward and caught the meat before it fell into the fire. He peeled off strips with his teeth and hissed as he gulped down the steaming flesh, then turned back to the journal. The text went on to tell how Vassili liberated a young man from the torture cells beneath Castle DiVecci and decided to keep him as a ward.

The prisoner's name was Levictus.

By the time Caim finished the page, the sun had gone down. He put the book away, tossed another couple of branches on the fire, and crawled under his shelter. As he lay there, gazing up at the stars through gaps in the canopy, Josey intruded into his thoughts. What was she doing? Was she safe? Had she forgotten about him? But the more he thought of her, the more he knew he'd made the right decision. She was an empress now, and he was a penniless freebooter without a home or history.

His last thoughts, as he drifted off, were about Kit. He regretted the way he had spoken to her. Promises of making it up to her lulled him into an uneasy slumber.

Caim could tell he was dreaming by the phosphorescent tint of the starshine and the springy softness of the grass underfoot. He stood beside a split-rail fence as tall as his chest. Beyond it stretched a long yard of tar-black earth. He was eight years old again. Small. Scrawny. Weak.

The fence rail was coarse under his palms. A big man knelt in the center of the yard. Caim's breath remained trapped in his lungs as he looked upon his father. Over him towered a cloak-shrouded scarecrow. Moonlight illuminated the face of a young Levictus, with a midnight blade in his hand. The scene played out as it had a thousand times before. The blade swooped down. Caim bit his lip to stifle the scream. He wanted to run away, but he could only stand and watch as his father crumpled to the ground, the familiar sword's hilt protruding from his chest.

Levictus turned, and another figure came into view, garbed in a black cloak like the wings of a giant bat. A cold finger of dread scratched down Caim's backbone. He started as a dry branch snapped beneath his foot. The figures looked toward him from across the yard.

A sharp pain pierced his right ear. Caim tried to let go of the rail, but his hands wouldn't obey. Shadows swirled as the figures melted away into the night, leaving his father alone in the yard. Caim wanted to go to him, but his head hurt so much. He focused on his fingers, willing them to let go. His arms shook with the effort.

Just . . . let . . . go . . .

A titanic roar jerked Caim awake, to find a huge shape looming above him. Massive jaws studded with fangs opened beneath a snub nose. Tiny eyes peered from under tufts of dark fur. Caim started to lift his arms, but the bear's plate-sized paw knocked him sideways.

Rocks gouged his back as he skidded over the hard ground, and another roar filled his ears. He reached for his knives, but his right arm was pinned underneath him. The fingers of his left hand were stiff with cold, but he made them curl around a hilt and pull it free. As the animal lurched over him, Caim thrust upward. The knife's point struck hide as hard as old

14

timber, and the air rushed from his lungs as clawed paws came down on his chest. The bear's jaws gaped wide, spewing the stench of rotten meat into his face. Caim freed his trapped arm in time to wedge it between his throat and the bear's teeth. The jaws slammed shut on his forearm. Spots of light danced in front of Caim's eyes as he stabbed repeatedly into the animal's side, but he might as well have been chopping down a tree with a spoon. Growls pierced his skull as he was thrashed from side to side. Biting back on his fear, Caim reached out to the shadows. He could feel them lurking around the edge of the camp, but he couldn't summon the momentary calm he needed to call them. The spots began to swirl as his free hand swept back and forth across the ground, searching for . . . for . . .

I'm going to die.

With that realization, the terror receded long enough for him to detect a familiar feeling in his chest, a tugging he'd felt before. Then a horrific screech split the night, and a long, low shape rose above the bear's rugged shoulder. Blacker than the night sky, it clove to the darkness. Wide, lambent eyes gazed down as its mouth closed around the bear's neck.

The bear roared and threw Caim away. He rolled over several times before crashing into the base of a tree. He tried to sit up and sucked in a short breath as a sharp pain erupted down his leg. He lay still, gasping in the snow, as the two beasts rolled across the ground, clawing and biting at each other. The bear's struggles grew weaker by the heartbeat; its attempts to dislodge the huge shadow slowed until the great animal finally collapsed in a heap.

A cold dread settled in Caim's stomach as the shadow beast released the bear's throat and stared at him from atop the shaggy corpse. Then it climbed down out of sight and disappeared. Caim craned his neck, but there was no sign of it. The pressure in his chest faded.

Caim reached up to touch the side of his face. His fingers found a warm slick of blood and the loose flap of his earlobe attached by a thin membrane. With a grunt, he tore off the skin and dropped it in the snow. His body hurt all over. His forearm throbbed where the bear's teeth had shredded his jacket sleeve and the flesh underneath. Lines of blood dripped down his hand to stain the snow. A darker pool was spreading under his left leg from a set of long parallel gouges.

Moving slowly, Caim crawled past the carcass to the remains of his fire. He blinked back the darkness from the edges of his vision. He couldn't afford to pass out. Even if he didn't freeze, he would bleed to death before morning. The warmth of the fire pit felt good against his face and hands. Working quickly, he shoved his knives into the bed of coals. Then he sat up, wincing, and pulled open the gashes in his pant leg and sleeve. Blood poured from both sets of wounds. He pulled the first knife out of the fire and slapped its glowing red tip against the raw meat of his thigh. Blazing pain shot straight to his brain. For an instant he was back on the roof of the palace in Othir. Josey's face hovered over him, saying something, but he couldn't hear a word.

Reality returned as he pulled the cooling blade away. The stench of burnt flesh clogged the back of his throat. The leg wound was blackened and puckered, but most of the bleeding had stopped. Before he could think it through, Caim pulled the second knife from the coals and placed it across the two larger bite marks on his forearm. The pain wasn't as bad the second time, or maybe he was getting numb to it. When he was through, he slumped back on the ground.

Stars twinkled overhead. Save for a low buzzing in his head, the night was quiet. He wanted to close his eyes and sleep, but he fought it off and started crawling. He snagged the straps of his gear as he passed the wreckage of his lean-to. Dragging the bundles, he pushed onward into the night. If he kept moving until morning, he might survive. If his wounds didn't reopen while he crawled. If he wasn't visited by any more uninvited guests.

If. If. If.

With the buzz droning in his ears, he took it one painful inch at a time.

SHADOW'S LURE

Chapter
Two

Standing by the clear glass window, Josey plucked at the lace cuffs that encased her wrists. Her suite at the top of the imperial residence was a series of connected rooms larger than the entire top floor of her old house. This parlor was her favorite place to come and be alone. A vase of fresh amaryllis filled the cloistered air with a delicate scent. Pale rectangles of sunlight reflected on the parquet floor. Master-pieces in oil and bronze hung on the walls.

She reached into a small pocket sewn into her skirt and took out a square of parchment. She unfolded it and counted the rows of hatches drawn on the page. Forty-one, one for every day Caim had been gone. It seemed longer than that – weeks longer. Some part of her had believed he would return before now; another part whispered he was never coming back.

Hearing footsteps out in the foyer, Josey stuffed the paper back in her pocket. The door opened, and a servant appeared, dressed in a blue doublet and hose with a griffin stitched over his heart in gold thread. He held out a steaming porcelain cup on a silver tray.

'Tea, Your Majesty?'

It smelled divine. Josey started to accept, but a twinge in her stomach reminded her that breakfast had not settled well. With a shake of her head, she sent the servant away. She took out the parchment and smoothed it on a sideboard table. She was about to fold it back up when Fenrik entered, carrying a long teakwood box. Her foster father's manservant had aged dreadfully over the past months. His internment at Castle DiVecci during the recent troubles had turned him into an old man before his time. His hair had gone from gray to white, and his back bowed like a withered tree trunk. He set the box down on the table, opened the lid, and stood aside.

Josey went over to him. 'Please, Fenrik. You should have had someone else carry this.'

'I can pull my weight, my lady. Always have, always will.'

'I know. It's just that I worry about you.'

Fenrik made a show of looking abashed. 'Your father. The earl, I mean. He would have been proud to see you finally come into your own.'

She smiled at him, then eyed the open box. A sparkling array of stones nestled on a bed of ivory silk. A necklace of sapphires and another of sea-green emeralds, three pairs of earrings, an assortment of rings and bracelets. Resting in their midst was the crown. Interlocked golden circlets formed the base of the diadem, sweeping up into nine delicate points. The whole thing was encrusted with enough precious stones to feed the city for a month. She reached out with one hand, but stopped before touching it.

'Allow me.'

Fenrik whisked the crown out of the box before she could protest and settled it upon her head. Josey glanced into the mirror set in the lid of the box. The image that looked back at her was a stranger, far too regal and serene to be her. She wasn't sure she liked the change.

'What's that?' he asked.

Josey followed his gaze to the parchment in her hand. She folded it up and slid it into her pocket. 'Nothing, Fenrik. Just a reminder.'

The door opened again, this time admitting a gentleman with a balding pate, one of the court's many secretaries. 'Your Majesty, the court waits at your pleasure.'

Squeezing Fenrik's arm, Josey bid him good-bye and

followed the secretary, her long skirt swishing. Two guards in burnished armor waited in the hallway outside. They fell in behind her as she walked down a winding staircase to the ground floor.

When they reached the door to the Grand Hall, the secretary looked to Josey, but she held up a hand for him to wait. Her stomach was uneasy again. The crown felt like it wanted to slide off. She took a deep breath as she reached up to adjust it. *Just breathe, Josey. It will be fine.* When Josey got the diadem balanced, she nodded to the secretary, and he held open the door with a bow.

Although she had grown accustomed to the opulence of palace life, Josey's pulse still quickened each time she entered the Grand Hall. The elaborate tapestries, the vast marble floor, the graceful pillars rising to the domed ceiling – they filled her with reverence. Yet ghosts also lingered in the vast chamber. The bloodstains had been removed, but in her imagination she could still see the spots where the assassin Ral had kicked over boxes holding the severed heads of the Elector Council. And when her gaze strayed too high, the paintings depicting the glories of the True Church illuminated above brought her back down to solid ground. She might be empress now, but her rise to power had not been easy, or without bloodshed.

Sixteen ministers of the Thurim – less than a third of the officials who'd held the post when her father reigned – stood upon her arrival. They were old men, nobles for the most part, but two were elected by the common people of Othir. That had been one of her more progressive ideas.

Josey ascended the dais where the Elector Council's thrones had been replaced with a gaudy eyesore of mahogany and teak decorated with golden studs over every conceivable surface. The palace staff had retrieved it from some cellar storeroom where it had sat since the overthrow of her father and restored it here. She sat down with all the grace she could muster on the seat as hard as an old stump and forced herself to smile.

Hubert stepped to the foot of the dais and made a deep bow.

'Majesty,' he said, loud enough to be heard throughout the hall. 'Have we your leave to begin this day's proceedings?'

When she assumed the throne, Josey hadn't much of an idea what an empress actually *did*. Presented with a host of questions, from whom to appoint to various administrative posts left vacant when the Church officials who had been running the country were removed, to how to raise a new police force to enforce her laws now that the Sacred Brotherhood was disbanded, Josey had turned over much of the daily operations to Hubert, her new lord chancellor, so that she was free to consider larger matters of state. Or so she had told herself.

'Yes, Your Grace,' she said. 'In one moment.'

Hubert had started to turn away, but halted in midstep. Josey flicked a glance toward the offensive ceiling paintings and tried not to meet the mournful eyes of the Prophet hanging on his noose.

'When will the ceiling be restored?'

Hubert cleared his throat. 'We have not yet acquired an artist, Your Majesty.'

'Why not?'

Hubert turned to the long desk he shared with the new Keeper of the Imperial Treasury. Ozmond Parmian cut a fine figure in his fashionable white suit.

'It is a matter of funds,' Ozmond said, 'which are somewhat lacking at the moment, Majesty. Revenues from the outlying provinces have been late in arriving, while the cost of raising, training, and barracking the City Watch, combined with the new measures put in place to assist the poor—'

Josey lifted a hand. 'I see. Your Grace, you may proceed.'

With a nod, Hubert faced the ministers, and Josey settled back in her seat. At first, she had looked forward to these meetings, anticipating the chance to enact policies that would improve the lives of her subjects, but it had become apparent after just a few days that only her presence was required, not her voice. While she sat in the excruciating chair, her ministers heard from petitioners and judged their cases. After a short recess, she would be paraded through a series of smaller meetings where she was also encouraged to smile and say little. In short, she was treated like a painted doll.

While Hubert intoned the day's agenda, Josey played with the heavy ring on her fourth finger. Her father's signet. The large carbuncle had been reset onto a new band sized for her hand. She ran her fingertip over the smooth facets. *How many emperors have worn this before me? What would they think if they saw me sitting here now?*

Hubert talked about the unrest across the empire. It seemed that in the absence of the Church's authority, some of the nobility took the opportunity to revisit old grudges upon their neighbors. This had escalated into a handful of tiny wars. Every day the Thurim debated options to suppress the violence, but so far they hadn't actually done anything. Then something Hubert said caught her attention.

'What was that?' she asked.

He looked up from the scroll he was reading. 'The western territories, Majesty. Lord Ulbrecht of Cantross writes with news of banditry along the border and asks for assistance in quelling the problem.'

'Any news from the soldiers I sent north?'

'Ah, not as yet, Majesty.'

'Lord Ulbrecht commands a fortress in the town, does he not?'

'Yes, Majesty. I believe so, but he says in his letter he does not possess sufficient soldiers to impose order beyond the town walls.'

'This makes how many reports of brigandry along the western border?'

'This is the fourth this month, Majesty.'

Josey tapped the arms of the throne with her fingernails. Cantross was near the border in a lawless stretch of land where her writ meant very little. Still, the people living in that territory were her subjects. She had a duty to them. 'We will send a company of troops to his aid.'

'Majesty, we have a shortage of—'

'Draw up a list of those lords who have made war within the empire's borders without Our consent. Demand from each a levy of soldiers, armed and equipped for a campaign.' A warm glow heated Josey's cheeks as she spoke. 'If we deprive the fractious nobles of their weapons, they will have nothing with which to harass each other.'

The corners of Hubert's mouth quivered as if he wanted to smile, but did not dare. 'That is one idea, Majesty. But might I ask what we shall do if they refuse?'

'Any who refuse will be stripped of their lands and titles, and branded an enemy of the crown.'

That got the ministers talking. Someone *tsked* at her pronouncement, but nobody protested outright. A few actually nodded, possibly because their lands were the ones under attack. Josey smiled to herself. 'What's next?' she asked.

Hubert hesitated, and then reached for another scroll. 'There is the Akeshian problem. The war in the east continues without respite, now going into its seventh year. The enemy has made advances into the southern continent. That, along with their seizure of imperial trading colonies in Altaia and Sulene, has given them firm control over the eastern Midland Sea.'

All pleasant feelings left Josey. The war in the east was something she had inherited from the previous regime. Although there had been tensions between the two empires for as long as anyone could remember, it had never flared into war until the Church came to power with its persecution toward all who would not bow to the True Faith. She had seen the reports from the Treasury, read about the battles, the investitures, the list of towns won and lost. Sixty thousand men dead and countless more maimed at a cost of more than two million gold soldats, leaving Nimea on the brink of bankruptcy. All for nothing, as far as she could see. It was something she had argued with Hubert about in private. Although he shared her view of the war, he argued it was popular with the people and the nobles. Josey caught her fingers twisting her signet ring and forced them to stop.

'Ministers of the Thurim, in the name of peace and mercy I put before you a call to end this senseless conflict.'

There was silence. Then someone coughed, and that broke the floodgates. Voices rose throughout the hall, some of them violently. Josey squirmed on the throne.

'Good lords and ladies.' She tried to be heard above the noise. 'For too long this war has clouded the empire's conscience! It has destroyed families and sown discord throughout—'

No one was listening. Josey looked to Hubert, but he was too busy watching the arguments to notice. One of the people's ministers, Lord Du'Quendel, stood up on his chair and clapped for her over the crowd of wizened heads. Josey gave him a small smile, hoping his enthusiasm would spread, but that did not seem likely. After a few minutes, a loud bang got the attention of enough people to quiet the din, and a petite woman in a long hunter-green dress made herself heard. The ministers quieted as Hubert announced her.

'The Lady Philomena shall address the court.'

The only woman on the Thurim, Lady Philomena looked a fragile figure among the ministers, but as she strode to the center of the hall she assumed a stance more like a battlefield commander than a wilting flower. Her dress was designed for austerity and plainness, and did nothing to accentuate her shape. She was older than Josey by several years, but was not an unhandsome woman; she had classic features and bright golden hair wrapped up in a bun at the back of her head. She might have been stunning if not for the pinched firmness of her mouth and the way her eyes bulged as if she had bitten into something sour. Josey didn't know much about the lady – something about a wealthy husband who had died this past year, bequeathing to her his title and an enormous fortune. And Josey recalled something else as she glimpsed the golden circle brooch pinned to her breast. Lady Philomena was an ardent supporter of the Church.

Philomena got right to the point. 'It would be a grave error to send envoys to the empire of Akeshia with terms of surrender.'

'Terms of peace, my lady,' Hubert interjected.

'One and the same to those savages. To show weakness would only encourage further aggression.'

'But we will not know that,' Josey said, 'unless we try to make an accord with them.'

The lady lifted a delicate, plucked eyebrow. 'It is a holy war ordained by God, received by His Holiness the prelate, and executed by the will of the Faithful.' After a moment, she added, 'Majesty.'

Josey ground her teeth together. The Church had been willing to bleed the empire dry when it held power, and now this woman wanted her to continue the same insane policy. It was beyond ludicrous. She started to speak, but Hubert jumped in before her.

'I beg your pardon, my lady, but the continuation of the war in the east is no longer viable, things in the realm being as they are.'

'All things' – Lady Philomena looked directly at Josey – 'are possible through the Light.'

Josey tried to bite her tongue and failed. 'What does the Light say about the thousands of young men who have died overseas and will never see their homeland again?'

'Sacrifices made in the name of the True Faith are never in vain. As the Holy Writs say, those souls now dwell in glory at the right hand of the Prophet.'

Josey grabbed handfuls of her skirt to keep herself under control. Fortunately, Hubert stepped in just in time to prevent another eruption.

'Thank you, milady,' he said. 'The empress will take your words under advisement.'

Josey glared at Lady Philomena's back as the woman returned to her seat.

'Anything else, Lord Chancellor?' she asked, dreading the answer. She just wanted to get out of this hall.

'Duke Mormaer has asked for an audience.'

Josey stifled a sigh. Her forehead had begun to throb. 'Very well. Send him in.'

At Hubert's command, the guards admitted the next petitioner. Mormaer was an ample-sized man, bordering on stoutness. His wealth was displayed with many jewel-encrusted rings and a heavy gold chain around his neck from which hung seven huge emeralds. A footman in black livery marched a pace behind him. The duke stopped at the first step of the dais and presented a shallow bow that seemed to say, *You may stand above me, but only a trifle.*

'Duke Mormaer of Wistros, Margrave of Ebencross,' the footman announced.

Mormaer turned so as to face both the ministers and the throne. His dark eyes were half hidden under untamed, black brows that came together over a spongy nose. His lips were pressed together like battle lines.

'Majesty,' his deep voice rumbled through the hall, 'and councilors of the Thurim. Twice I have come before this court to present my petition, and twice been sent away without an answer.' He held up a roll of papers clenched in a hairy fist. 'I come this third time to be heard, or to return to my lands with the message that our empress cares nothing for the welfare of those who live beyond these walls.'

Josey didn't know what this was about. This was the first she'd heard of any petition. But she didn't intend to allow any man to barge into her palace and make demands.

'Duke—'

'Duke Mormaer,' Hubert interjected. 'We have reviewed your petition most carefully, but feel it might be premature to raise that particular subject.'

Josey looked at Hubert, wishing he would turn around and see the look of shock that must be written on her face, but all his attention was focused on the petitioner.

Duke Mormaer shook the papers again. 'It is the will of the nobles of this realm. What matter could be more important?'

Josey wanted to know, too. As Hubert reached for the papers, she stood up. Everyone rose from their seats, even Lady Philomena, although she did so with a languor that suggested she was only acting under duress. Trying to hide

25

the stiffness in her posterior, Josey descended the steps of the dais.

'Your Majesty—' Hubert started to say.

She cut him off with a firm shake of her head and took the papers from Mormaer's hand. She opened to the first page. Her stomach tightened as she read the scrawling script. The sensation worsened as she flipped to the next page and read the list of signatures attached. They went on for six more pages and included the names of significant families from every province of the empire.

Willing her insides to settle, she read the top of the first page again.

In the interest of the continued peace and prosperity of the realm, we, the signed, call for Her Imperial Majesty, Empress Josephine Corrinada I, to be wed before the turn of midsummer and begin the production of a line of heirs in a timely fashion, so as to ensure . . .

It went on to suggest a list of eligible suitors, starting with three names she recognized by their surname. The sons of Duke Mormaer.

Josey couldn't believe what she was reading. *Who are they to demand . . . ? How dare they? Begin the production of a line of heirs in a timely fashion!*

'Duke Mormaer.' She struggled to control her voice. Hubert watched with concern, but she charged ahead. 'You will explain yourself and' – she thrust the papers at him – 'this!'

Mormaer regarded her with a bland expression, as if he couldn't be bothered to acknowledge her ire. The duke appeared about to say something, but Josey turned away.

'This audience is finished. Lord Chancellor, attend me.'

Without waiting for Hubert, she crossed to the exit. Everyone bowed as she and her bodyguards left the hall. As the chamber doors closed, Josey leaned against the wall. The ache in her head throbbed so that she could hardly see straight. Composing herself, she walked down the hallway to a small parlor room decorated with lace curtains and dainty furniture. She slammed the door behind her and started to pace across the thin woven carpet. By the time a soft knock sounded, her anger had worked itself into a blistering fury.

'You!' she shouted as Hubert stepped into the room.

He quickly shut the door and stood with his arms at his sides.

Josey wanted to kick him. Instead, she resumed pacing. 'First, you push me into a corner like a holy icon while you and the other ministers make decisions about *my* realm. Then you allow me to be ambushed by that . . . that *man* who proposes to breed me like a prize cow!'

'Yes, my lady.'

'Yes?' She stopped pacing. 'Yes, what?'

'Mormaer has a valid point, Your Majesty.'

'You can call me Josey in private, Hubert.'

'Your Maj—'

She propped her fists on her hips. 'Josey.'

'All right. Josey. Duke Mormaer is many things, but he is no fool. He is within his rights to raise this issue.'

'Then you had better explain it before I have you tossed in the moat.'

'The palace doesn't have a—'

'Get on with it!'

He cleared his throat. 'You must marry, and you must do it soon.'

She snatched a peach from a basket by the window, took a bite, and then thought better of it. Not seeing a place to put it, she placed the fruit back in the basket.

'Oh really? I thought I was empress. I didn't know I had to contort my life to suit the desires of my advisors.'

'Cinattus the Younger wrote that to rule a nation is to be the servant of the people.'

'Then Cinattus can damned well marry one of Mormaer's sons!'

She huffed while Hubert admired the floor. Finally, she relented with a nod. 'I understand, but I won't take advice from the likes of Mormaer.'

27

'He is very powerful, Majesty.'

'He's a great, bloated hog!'

'That, too.' Hubert cleared his throat. 'And there is another matter.'

He opened his hand. In the center of his palm sat a small ivory cameo carved in the likeness of a woman. 'Lord Du'Quendel sends this with a request for a private audience.'

Josey took the plaque. 'Du'Quendel. From Belastire? What does he want?'

She knew of the Du'Quendel family, though only by reputation. They were a very old noble dynasty. Not so wealthy or powerful as they once were, but still respected.

'I believe he wants a more meaningful position here at court.'

She saw the problem. Lord Du'Quendel wanted a higher rank, but had done nothing to distinguish himself for such an honor. However, the throne could not afford to insult his family. Josey ran her fingertips over the face on the token. The edges were darkened and the face marred by tiny cracks, as if the piece had been kept in a dirty niche for years or burned in a fire . . .

The fire.

The cellar in the earl's house came back to her, and a row of thirteen ivory plaques, one for each member of her foster father's secret society. This was either an exact replica, or . . .

'Empress, is something wrong?'

'No, I'm fine. It's just—'

Josey handed back the cameo and turned to the window. Outside, dark clouds gathered in a steely gray sky. The first snows of winter were expected any day. Expectations. They were a tricky thing. *You have to face the fact that he may never come back.*

'I'm tired of waiting, Hubert. Tired of the court and the problems.' She sighed. 'Give Lord Du'Quendel what he wants. Take care of the details, but I don't want to see him. I don't want to see anyone.'

'I shall inform the court. But what of the ball? Shall I postpone it?'

Josey rubbed her forehead. She had forgotten about the ball in honor of her coronation. It had sounded like a good idea when it was presented to her a month ago, but now with all the problems in the realm it felt callous and wasteful.

'When is it?'

'Tomorrow evening, Majesty. After your meeting with the Arnossi delegation.'

'I suppose it's too late to call it off. Very well. Please send up a report of the day's judgments and whatever else you need me to sign.'

'Very good, Majesty.'

She thanked him as she walked to the door. Flanked by her guards, she trod the lonely corridors up to her apartments.

SHADOW'S LURE

Chapter
THREE

C aim shifted in his cot as sunbeams stabbed his eyelids. He didn't want to get up. It had been ages since he'd slept so well, but an empty belly and an intense need to use the chamberpot nudged him awake. *I wonder if there's any eggs left in the coldbox.*

His thigh itched. He scratched at it, imagining fried eggs with a slice of ham, but the itch persisted. With a groan, he opened his eyes and discovered he wasn't in his apartment in Othir. He blinked against the sunlight shining between the gaps in the dingy gray boards of the peaked roof twenty feet above him. Then he remembered. His apartment building had burned down months ago. Where in hell was he? A barn?

He sat up. Tight bandages bound his arm from wrist to elbow. He smelled a pungent odor coming from the wrapping; not putrefaction – thank the gods – but an earthy smell. Some kind of poultice.

Following the itch, Caim pulled away the old blanket to find he was in his smallclothes. He nearly jumped when he saw the throbbing shadow wrapped around his thigh, sucking at the wound through a layer of bandages. He grabbed for it, but the thing slipped through his fingers and vanished into the shade under the hayloft. Checking the injury, Caim saw a little seepage, but it wasn't as bad as he'd feared. A line of tenderness itched down the right side of his face. He fought a pang of nausea when his fingers encountered a missing chunk from his earlobe the size of his thumbnail. The skin was still raw to the touch, and there were some scratches down his cheek, but otherwise his face appeared intact. The rest of his body was bruised and battered, but he thought he'd be able to walk if he tried.

Now that he was awake, he began to remember. He had crawled from his camp, hurting and bleeding, through the snow. He didn't know how long he'd endured, fighting off unconsciousness. Finally, he reached something resembling a road. He seemed to recall a small face peering down at him, or maybe he'd been dreaming. The next thing he knew, he was here. His gear lay in the straw a few feet away, his knives in their sheaths beside the long bundles of his sword and bow, and his satchel.

A noise rustled off to his side. Caim rolled over and gasped at a sudden spasm in his leg. He drew a knife and spun around with the blade extended. A small boy stood in the doorway. Caim let out a slow breath and lowered the weapon. The kid watched him for a moment with large brown eyes and then ran off. *Good move. He's probably off to fetch his brothers.*

Caim gathered his clothes and was in the process of easing them over his wounded body when footsteps approached. He managed to pull up his pants and buckle on his *suete* knives before the door opened. A big man filled the doorway. He wore a simple smock and breeches of rough homespun wool. His work boots were worn and spattered with mud. He took off a wide-brimmed hat and wiped his forehead with the back of his other arm.

'You mend quick,' the man said. 'Didn't expect you'd be up and walking for a couple days yet.'

Caim pulled on his shirt. 'Is this your barn?'

The man nodded.

'Thank you for letting me stay.' Caim lifted his bandaged arm. 'And for this. I must have looked in pretty bad shape.'

'I've seen plenty worse. The sheep are always getting into something or other.'

Sheep. Right.

Talking made Caim realize how thirsty he was. 'Could I have something to drink? Some wat—?'

The man bellowed over his shoulder. 'Tarn, fetch him a cup from the barrel.'

Lifting the satchel jarred Caim's lower back. Breathing slow through his nose, he slid the strap over his shoulder along with the bundles. The walls tilted a little as he took the first couple steps, but righted themselves before he reached the doorway. Stepping out into the daylight, Caim shaded his eyes. The sky was a flawless sapphire blue. The barn was situated a score of paces off a snowy road. There was also a small farmhouse and an animal coop. He didn't see any sheep, but the smells of livestock were pungent.

The little boy ran up, a sloshing clay cup in his hand. Caim accepted it and drained it all at once. The ice-cold water tasted better than wine. Caim thanked him and returned the cup.

'More?' the boy asked.

Caim was tempted, but wanted to get moving before he wore out his welcome. Already the boy's father was eyeing him a little too close for his comfort. Next would come questions, most of which he didn't want to answer. These seemed like nice folk. The best thing he could do was leave them alone.

Caim reached inside his satchel. 'I've got money. For your trouble.'

The man looked down at the coins in Caim's hand, and then shook his head. With a smack of his lips, he said, 'Wasn't no trouble. But it'd be best if you moved on, now that you're well.'

Caim nodded and put the money away. As he turned toward the road, the door of the house opened, and a woman appeared. It was hard to guess her age, younger than him maybe, but not by much. She brought over a bundle about the size of a bread loaf and handed it to him. Still warm, it smelled divine. With a nod and a glance at the boy standing behind his father, Caim departed.

It wasn't until he was down the road that Caim realized the herdsman had been afraid. Nor just anxious, but deep down afraid. He understood. The world was a rough place, especially out here in the hinterlands. And strangers with swords meant trouble.

The trail was bumpy compared to the smooth, straight roads of the south, and every impediment was magnified by his condition. Rocky protrusions and patches of ice lurking under the snow made for treacherous footing. He settled into a stiff, shambling gait that didn't hurt too much. He wasn't going to win any foot races, but it was better than crawling.

It took his leg about a mile to loosen up to the point where he could take a real stride, but he kept it slow, not wanting to aggravate his injuries. His back was sore already, and his arm throbbed a little. If he'd been in Othir, he would have holed up somewhere comfortable – Madam Sanya's came to mind – and convalesced. He was daydreaming about a soft feather bed when the humming returned. It wasn't painful, more irritating than anything, but it bothered him not to know what was causing it. He was feeling his head for bumps when Kit popped up beside him.

'Morning, sunshine. You look awful. Feeling any better?'

He squinted at her through the dazzling sunlight. Kit was wearing a teal dress with a scandalous hemline. She skimmed along through the air, her bare toes not quite touching the snow.

Caim tugged at the sleeve of his injured arm. 'I'll live. Where have you been lurking?'

Kit bent down to study his injured leg, and in the process her skirt lifted another couple of inches. He looked away.

'Scouting, like you always tell me to do.'

'No need to put yourself out. I mean, there's no need to feel guilty.'

She popped up to her full height, fists resting on her hips. 'So this is my fault?'

He flicked his bloodied ear. 'Not at all. I mean, you could have warned me that a man-eating bear was about to—'

33

'Whose bright idea was it to dump the body of a poor, defenseless deer right next to his camp where any old creature could smell it?'

'I wouldn't have,' he said, 'if I'd known you were sleeping on the job.'

'Sleeping! As I remember, you wanted to be alone. Anyway, you survived. So stop complaining.'

Caim stepped into a rut and clenched his teeth as a stabbing pain shot up his leg and through his lower back. He stopped in place, and Kit's expression transformed in an instant. She rushed closer to his side, and electric tingles ran up his thigh.

'Are you all right? Can I do anything?'

He waited until the pain subsided to a tolerable throb. Then he took a step. When he didn't fall down, he started off again. Nice and slow. Kit kept pace with him, chattering like a doting mother. It was almost sweet, for about a minute.

'It's okay, Kit. Take a step back, will you?'

'Fine. Don't accept my help.'

'I'm all right. Really. Tell me what you found up ahead.'

Kit floated past his head. 'That's what I was going to tell you. There's a house a little way up the road.'

A sinking sensation pulled Caim's stomach. He had avoided habitations for most of his journey, only stopping when he needed to resupply or when the desire for news from Othir overrode his instinct for self-preservation.

'Well, more like a bunkhouse, actually,' she said. 'But it's better than sleeping in a snowbank.'

'Is it safe?'

Kit brushed her fingers through his hair. 'Safe enough for a big, strong man like you.'

Caim ducked his head away. This wasn't like Kit. Sure, sometimes she was flirty and crazy, but she'd never been so demonstrative.

She drifted back a few paces. 'You're acting strange. Did that bear rattle your brains loose?'

He quickened his pace, though it caused him pain. He kept expecting Kit to pop up in front of him. After a minute or so, he stopped and looked back. She was gone. He considered saying something, knowing she would hear him wherever she had gone, but he just kept walking.

He climbed low hills and passed stands of scrub. The air was still and crisp, thick with the promise of more snow to come. The trees along the road thinned after a few hundred yards and gave way to a vast prairie. The table-flat Gilvan Steppes stretched from horizon to horizon under the limitless blue sky. He vaguely remembered crossing this land as a child; these plains had seemed like an ocean of nothingness to a boy of eight. As he looked out across the distance, he wondered if he was making a mistake.

What choice do I have? Keep living without knowing?

The trail broadened under his feet until it verged on becoming a true road. Low sod roofs sprouted on the prairie, farmhouses by their looks. A quarter of a candlemark later, he came to a dirt lane flanked by thick hedges. Three young boys stood along the road, kicking at snowbanks. They wore crude rag shoes and coarse jackets that came down below their knees but failed to hide their dirty shins. One of the boys caught sight of Caim and shouted to his fellows, who all turned to watch him. Caim pulled his hood down and continued on his way. His chest constricted as old fears returned, brought on by long periods of solitude. He didn't spot the slanted roof ahead on the road until he was almost upon it.

This was obviously the bunkhouse Kit had seen. It sat alongside the road. A split-rail fence enclosed a yard and two small outbuildings behind the main house. A thin ribbon of smoke rose from the single brick chimney. Caim adjusted the strap of his satchel and checked his knives.

There was no gate in front, so he followed the uneven path of stones up to the main house and pushed open the weather-beaten door. The dim interior swallowed the daylight as he stepped across the threshold. The smoky air stung Caim's eyes. The front room took up most of the ground floor. Its walls were bare timber joined with wattle. Two scarred wooden pillars supported the low roof. There were no windows, and no bar either, just a doorway covered by a sheet of dingy canvas leading to a back room, possibly the kitchen. Two long trestle tables occupied much of the floor. Five men sat around the first, smoking from clay pipes and drinking. By their simple clothing and muddy boots, he took them for farmers or ranch hands.

Three men occupied the second table. Two could have been brothers. Both were large and rawboned, though one had long blond hair, and the other black as pitch. The man sitting across from them was a head shorter. A sharp chin protruded from the confines of his hood, which he kept pulled down. All three wore buckskin instead of wool and carried weapons of a sort. Boar spears leaned against the table beside the larger men; their companion had something hidden under his cloak, maybe a sword or a truncheon. The two larger men looked up with dark, sunken eyes as Caim entered, and just as quick went back to their business.

The canvas sheet was shoved aside, and a man emerged from the back. By the wooden mugs in his hands, he was the proprietor. He had a sagging chin and a dark port-wine stain down the side of his neck. His eyes were deep-set with many folds underneath, but in their depths lay a kernel of toughness, the same as his customers, as though they were all chipped from the same quarry.

When he'd served the drinks, the owner regarded Caim with a sour expression. Caim stood as straight as he could manage and tried not to advertise his injuries. His face itched all of a sudden, but he kept his hands by his sides.

'You the innkeep?' Caim asked.

The man wiped his hands on his shirt, which was covered in grease spots. He glanced at Caim's torn ear and said, 'What do you want?'

'A hot meal and a room for the night if there's one to be had.'

'We've no boarding.' The owner waved a hand at a seat at the end of the table nearest the meager fireplace. 'But I'll bring you something to eat.'

Caim crossed the room and leaned his bundles against the wall. The heat from the fireplace lapped against his back as he sat down. He closed his eyes, imagining the warmth creeping into the marrow of his bones. By his best reckoning, he was roughly twenty leagues north of the Nimean border. If he had succeeded in following a northerly track, and if his injuries allowed him to maintain the pace, that would put him in Liovard, Eregoth's largest town, in a few days.

The three men sitting together seemed to be arguing, but Caim couldn't hear their words. Then the larger two stood up. Taking up the spears, they went out the door and left the smaller man alone with a trio of cups. Caim leaned back and closed his eyes, minding his own business. The last thing he wanted was trouble.

The sound of shoes scraping over the floorboards dragged his eyelids open. A woman had come out of the back room to bring him a flattened bread plate covered with brown stew and a wooden mug. She didn't meet his eyes, but that didn't surprise him; he knew he looked bad, and probably smelled worse. When she started to turn away, he cleared his throat. She hesitated, but gave no other indication she'd heard.

'I'm heading to Liovard. Can you tell me how far it is?'

The woman shrugged. She was about the same age as the innkeeper, with the same tired features of someone who had been driven hard on the wheel of life.

'Orso!' she yelled over her shoulder. 'How far to the city?'

The innkeeper looked over from the table of farmers with a scowl. 'Two. Maybe three days on foot.'

Caim nodded to the woman. 'I'm trying to find a place.' He dredged the name from the dreams of his earliest years. He wasn't even sure it was right. 'Morrowglen.'

'Soja!'

The innkeeper beckoned her, and the woman shuffled away. Her employer, or husband perhaps, cast an ill look at Caim.

'We've no boarding!' he grumbled before following the woman into the back.

Caim settled in his chair, and winced as his sore back rubbed against the slats. The other guests had paused again to watch him. He returned their gazes until, one by one, they went back to their cups. The cloaked man never looked up.

Caim stared at the steaming pile of runt potatoes and carrots on his plate. The heat at his back, so delicious just minutes ago, was oppressive now. He took a sip from the cup and almost spat it out. Pieces of millet floated in the bitter beer. He started to put it down, but then took another slug.

The sound of hoofbeats outside almost caused him to spit it out. On the road, horses meant rich people or soldiers, and either way it spelled trouble. Caim placed his hands on the tabletop. There was only one way out unless the back room had an exit. The other patrons cast glances around at the sounds from outside, but otherwise stayed as they were when the door slammed open. Caim eased his chair back out of the light of the fireplace.

A group of men in damp leather armor and steel caps entered and stamped the snow from their boots. Five in number. No uniforms, but they wore enough hardware to make sure everyone knew they meant business. Then a sixth entered, wearing a steel cuirass over a mail byrnie; his riding boots were muddy from the road.

Soldiers. Just what I don't need.

Everyone in the room bent farther over their drinks at the sight of the new arrivals. All conversation stopped. The crackle of the fire popped loud in the sudden silence. As the soldiers took seats at the table, pushing the farmers down to make room, the innkeeper hurried through the curtain with fistfuls of foaming mugs. He nodded as he set them down, but by the downward curve of his mouth he was anything but glad to see his new guests.

'Good day, my lords.'

One of the soldiers, the largest, tossed a couple coins on the table. 'We need something to eat. And fodder for our mounts. See to it.'

The owner bowed as he collected the money, and then

departed back through the curtain. There was a ruckus in the back, accompanied by the sound of breaking clay, and the soldiers laughed to each other. Their captain sat with his back to the wall and minded his cup. He looked younger than the rest. Even without his armor or the expensive cavalry sword with its wire-wrapped hilt at his side, Caim would have guessed him to be the leader. He held himself a little apart from the others and had more of a care for his appearance. Likely he was some minor lord's fourth son, reduced to serving in the army for self-advancement.

While the soldiers drank and spoke among themselves, the cloaked man at Caim's table stood up and headed toward the door. It looked like he might make it without incident until one of the soldiers called out.

'Ho there!'

The caller stood up, as did one of his brother soldiers, while the rest watched on. The officer did not stir, but he looked up over the rim of his mug. The cloaked man kept walking.

Big mistake.

The soldiers on their feet moved to intercept him, and the others were rising now, too. The farmers bent over their table as if minding their own business, except for one. Older than the rest, he was downright ancient, with a full white beard that hung down to his navel. Of them all, only he dared to raise his head and watch.

One of the soldiers grabbed the cloaked man's arm and yanked him to a halt. 'Where you off to?'

The other trooper snatched back the hood to reveal a youthful face with a hawkish nose, topped by a mop of unruly black hair. He couldn't have been older than sixteen or eighteen. The soldiers grinned at each other.

'What's this?' the first asked. 'He looks a little young to be out wandering without his mother.'

The cloaked youth looked away, but said nothing. By this time, the big soldier had come over. Still holding his mug, he grabbed the boy by the hair and forced his head back.

'You with the army, boy?'

The first soldier poked the youth in the kidney. 'Speak up, boy. We're talking to you.'

The big soldier threw back the boy's cloak and whistled as he reached down. He drew out a sword and held it up. It was a northern short sword called a spatha, with a straight blade and a narrow guard. This one had a bronze hilt and a dull steel blade that showed the dents of a blacksmith's hammer.

'You better be explaining yourself,' the big soldier said.

The officer came over. 'What have you got, Sergeant?'

The sergeant dropped the sword to the floor where it rattled with a hollow clang. 'A deserter is my guess.'

'Is that true? Are you a deserter from His Grace's army?'

'Leave him be!' the oldster sitting at the table yelled. 'He ain't harming nobody.'

The officer gestured, and the other three soldiers hauled the farmers to their feet and shoved them against the wall. The old man protested, and was cuffed across the mouth, which only made him curse them more roundly.

'Shut him up!' the sergeant shouted. 'Or tickle his ribs with something sharp.'

One of the soldiers drew a dagger from his belt.

Caim sat back in his chair, feeling the ache of his wounds. This was going bad, fast. He thought the soldiers would just give the youth a hard time, but the mention of desertion had changed his mind. He didn't know Eregothic law, but a man could get hanged for that in Nimea. And most of the executions were summary judgments on the spot. But this wasn't his problem. He could remain here in the shadows, with luck pass undetected, and be on his way. But what would Josey say? Would she tell him he'd done the right thing? In his imagination he saw the disappointment in her eyes.

All right, Kit. Where are you?

The officer reached over and pulled aside the collar of the young man's shirt. A filigree of knotted blue lines was tattooed on the boy's shoulder in the shape of three circles bound through the center by a fourth. Caim didn't know what that signified, but the sergeant pounced on the boy all of a sudden, yanking his arms behind his back, while the other soldiers drew their swords. One farmer turned around, and was slugged in the face with a steel pommel. He dropped to the floor, blood streaming from a mouthful of broken teeth. The old man cursed at their oppressors. Caim reached behind his back. He had seen enough.

As the troopers herded the boy toward the door, Caim stood up. His leg burned like red-hot hooks were shredding the flesh. He drew his left-hand *suete* knife. Every head turned as he slammed its point into the wooden tabletop.

'Let him go.'

A soldier with a drawn infantry sword started toward him. Caim turned the ruined side of his face toward the firelight. The soldier drew up quick. *Not quite what you expected to see in this backwoods inn, eh?*

The sergeant hollered, 'Yanig! Stop ogling the bastard and put him up against the wall.'

The soldier took another step. That was all Caim needed. He jerked the *suete* free from its wooden prison. The soldier gasped and dropped his sword as the knife's edge sliced across the back of his hand. As he pulled back, Caim lashed out again. Once, twice, thrice, and the soldier fell back, disarmed and bleeding from holes through his light armor. Messy wounds, but nothing vital. He'd live if they got him to a chirurgeon.

The other pair of soldiers guarding the patrons charged over. Caim drew his right-hand knife and yanked the other from the table. These soldiers showed more sense, coming in side by side. One held a cavalry sword with a long blade; the other had just a mean-looking dirk, but he carried it like he knew what he was doing. Caim caught the sword with a stop-thrust and bit back a curse as his leg buckled. He remained upright and fended off a slash from the knife-man, and responded with quick cuts that sent both soldiers reeling back. Caim let the men limp away. His forearm stung, and the strain of maintaining a fighting stance made his lower back tighten into knots. He was afraid he would fall over if he tried to move. What were his options? Surrender?

Tiny voices whispered in his ears. When the remaining soldiers advanced, he didn't have to call for the shadows. They came on their own, and the light from the fireplace suddenly cut out as if a wet blanket had been thrown over the flames. One soldier stopped in midstep. His mouth contorted in terror as a shadow dropped on his head and oozed down his face. The others shouted and swiped at the air as an avalanche of shadows fell from the ceiling. Behind them, the officer drew his sword.

Caim took a step. His leg burned like hellfire, but it held. Every step was agony as he crossed the room. The shadows followed him, crawling along the floor, across the walls, over the struggling soldiers. He could feel them watching him, waiting . . . for what? The patrons had fled. The back room was quiet.

Caim stopped in front of the officer. Up close, he looked even younger, but he stood his ground even as his men groaned and bled on the floor. *Brave little shit.*

'Get out,' Caim said. 'And take the others with you.'

The young officer looked at the *suete* knives. 'We'll be back. With more men.'

'Then bring shovels and a priest.'

Caim dismissed the shadows, sending them back to the corners of the room as the officer gathered up his men and herded them toward the door. They watched him with haunted eyes as they passed out the door. At least they were alive. Their voices murmured in the yard, followed by the muted thunder of retreating hoofbeats. Caim noticed the cloaked youth's sword was gone, too, vanished from the floor where the soldiers had dropped it. *You're welcome, whoever you were.*

Caim dragged himself back to his table, where he found a cloth to clean his knives before putting them away. For a moment, he felt the desire to inflict a real massacre in this place. His gaze went to his father's sword against the wall. Flexing his right hand, he sat down. The stew had congealed into a gooey mass, but he ate it anyway. While he tore off hunks of the bread platter and shoveled them into his mouth, the innkeeper pushed through the curtain with his wife at his back. Caim got the impression they weren't particularly glad to see him still here. The innkeeper looked around as if he half expected the soldiers to come charging back any moment.

'Erm,' he said. The woman prodded him. 'You'll have to be moving on now. We don't want trouble.'

Funny. That's what I said. And where did it get me?

Caim paused with a shovel of cold mush halfway to his mouth. 'You've already had the trouble. It's gone.'

'They'll be back,' the woman said from behind the innkeeper's elbow.

He pushed his cup toward them. 'Another beer.'

At a nod from her husband, she took it and went back to the kitchen.

'Please,' the innkeeper said. 'Leave us in peace.'

Caim chewed his food. He wanted to be angry, but he understood their position. Those soldiers would be back, probably at the head of a small army. These people would be lucky if this shack was still standing a few days from now.

He pushed back from the table and stood up. His leg complained with a sharp twinge, but it obeyed. He dropped a handful of small coins beside his plate.

'Before I go,' Caim said, 'I need directions to Morrowglen.'

'Never heard of such a place.'

Caim held the innkeeper's gaze for a moment, and looked past him as the curtain to the back room parted and a man walked into the room. The shadows noticed, too. Caim's skin prickled with the silent mews of a thousand tiny shadows, but the newcomer didn't resemble a soldier. Rawhide buskins peeked from under the great bearskin that cloaked his sturdy frame. Pushing back his hood to reveal a mass of silver-gray braids framing a weathered face half hidden behind a long beard, the man glanced around the shambles of the room. Then he sized up Caim with eyes as pale as a frozen lake.

'I know the way.'

The innkeeper looked about to say something, but then

lifted both hands as if to shoo them out the door. Caim nodded and picked up his gear. The older man was already heading out the front.

Outside it was snowing again. As the door banged shut behind them, Caim watched his guide head down the road, northward. Caim reached up to scratch an itch on his face, but stopped his hand before it reached his bloodied cheek. *It's not too late to go back to Othir.*

Caim started off through the snow.

SHADOW'S LURE

Chapter
FOUR

Sybelle stood over the rack of broken vials littering the floor. The tinkle of breaking glass did nothing to soothe her nerves. For three days she'd been attempting to contact her agent in the south, but the oily scrying pool remained blank. It could only mean one thing.

Her sanctum sanctorum was a wide chamber in the heart of her temple. It pleased her to think of it as *her* temple. Although she had not laid the stones for the vast basilica, she was responsible for its reconsecration. The shadowed recesses of the vaulted ceiling comforted her.

Calmer, she crossed the stone floor to a shelf on the wall. She took what she required, then went to a tall object standing in a corner, covered in a pale sheet. She swept away the cover from the lidless sarcophagus carved from a single piece of volcanic stone. Nestled within were the mummified remains of a three-thousand-year-old warrior who had lived in an empire that had once spanned the known boundaries of this world.

Sybelle sat cross-legged upon the floor before the withered cadaver. First, she opened a vein in her wrist and spilled a portion of blood into a pan. After sealing the cut with a Word, she cracked open three stone jars and sifted their gritty contents through her fingers, one by one.

'*Adulai nocet e'sulphruka,*' she whispered. 'By heart and

45

lungs and soul, appear before mine eyes. Het Xenai, I conjure thee!'

Shadows flickered as a combination of odors met her nose, of dust and sand and endless night. The blood in the pan disappeared as if sucked into an invisible mouth, and a draining sensation came over Sybelle. A sigh, as coarse and dry as mummified bones, filled the chamber.

'Speak, Witch.'

'Great warrior, I seek to reach into the land of the dead and contact a departed soul.'

'Ask.'

'Bring me the shade of my servant Levictus.'

Though there were no windows in the sacred chamber, a wisp of a breeze tickled the back of her neck. A pallid light glimmered in the air. It flickered several times before coalescing into a shape roughly the size and manner of a man. Sybelle recognized the scarred face.

'Levictus.'

After a pair of slow heartbeats, he answered in a hollow tone. 'Sybelle.'

'Tell me how you came to die. When was the hour? Where the place?'

'Dead?'

'Yes.' She resisted the urge to curse him. It would do no good in the land of shades. 'Tell me how you died.'

'I was killed . . . not long ago.'

She frowned. Before his disappearance, Levictus had contacted her to ask for additional strength, which she had provided at great cost to herself. Levictus had been her most important tool in the southern lands. Not the most reliable – the sorcerer was as unstable as any Brightlander – but his role was crucial to her plans. For him to be killed at the apex of his power was no small matter.

'Who was it?'

'The night was so dark. No moon. So beautiful . . . We fight.'

She dug her fingernails into her palms, marshalling her self-control.

'Who? Who did you fight, Levictus?'

The shade paused for a few heartbeats. Then his rasping voice warbled across the void.

'The scion.'

Her bosom heaved as the words echoed across the ethers between life and death. Upon granting his boon, she had required one task of her servant. That he kill one man. A very dangerous man.

'Did you slay him as well?' she asked.

Mumbled words whispered from the portal.

'Levictus! Did you slay the scion?'

'He was defeated.'

Sybelle released the breath she had been holding. *Thanks be to the Mother Dark—*

'But something . . . interfered. I die. *Shinae* . . .'

Sybelle hissed between parted lips. *Shinae* was a dark metal native to the Shadowlands. She had gifted the sorcerer with a pair of *shinae* knives during his visit to Eregoth, years ago, but what was he talking about? She needed more answers. Yet he was fading before her eyes. She reached out to take hold of the spirit directly and wring the truth from its spectral voice, but it slipped through her psychic grasp. She lunged after him, but the withered shade of Het Xenai reappeared, gazing at her with vacant holes.

'Bring him back!' she demanded. 'I was not finished.'

The ancient warrior's sigh was a gust of wind over a cold desert plain. 'The shade has passed beyond my sight.'

Invectives flew from her lips. The warrior's spirit wavered and departed, back to its eternal sleep. She brushed the charnel dust from her hands and arose.

This was unforeseen. For almost two decades she had been assembling her power. Levictus was supposed to blaze the trail. Now her plans were unraveled, and her Master was unforgiving. She threw the sheet back over the sarcophagus, its paleness reminding her of the snowfields on the day she emerged from the gateway to step onto these cursed lands. Her father – her liege – had stood before her under the alien blue sky that burned her eyes, and lifted up his hand.

'From this land,' he said, 'we shall forge a new empire.'

Despair had welled up inside Sybelle as she gazed out upon the blankness of the bare ice and stone and the foul light rising in the east. They were exiles, outcasts in a world that was but a hollow reflection of the one they had left behind.

She reached out to catch her father's arm. 'We should go back. We could make peace—'

He struck her, and she fell upon the icy ground. She lay there, feeling the sting of his hand, which she knew and hated.

'No,' he said. 'We must make our destiny in this world now, or be crushed by it.'

His fist closed, and there was a terrible crash. Sybelle looked back to see the path behind them swallowed into an icy crevasse. The gateway was gone. They were marooned here.

Sybelle pulled her gaze away from the covered sarcophagus. That had been a long time ago, but the pain was still fresh. She had left behind a life of luxury and privilege, and in return been given only hardship and an endless litany of demands. Nothing in this world had been able to assuage the betrayal, not even the birth of her son, Soloroth, who had never seen the onyx skies of Shadow, nor walked upon the pallid shores of its midnight seas.

Steadying herself against a stone pillar, Sybelle went to an alcove in the wall. She took down an elaborate orichalcum box and opened the lid. A bed of fine golden powder lay inside. She took a pinch between her fingers and held it up to her nose. Inhaling the sweet powder, she was instantly rejuvenated. She took another pinch before putting the container back.

Sweeping a curtain aside, she traveled down a narrow passage of dressed stone to a doorway. The beat of pounding drums echoed from beyond the portal. Splinters of ruddy light throbbed in time with the rhythm.

She emerged into a vast hall filled with a throng of sweating, writhing, groaning bodies. The sweet heat of their passion seeped into her flesh and warmed her chilled bones. The smells of blood and sex swept the dusty attar from her lungs. Sybelle closed her eyes and let the energy of the ritual fill her. Since coming to these lands, she had tried to civilize its savage inhabitants. For four years she had worked to eradicate all traces of the True Church. She was shocked to find so many men – and even women, who should have known better – willing to die for their idols. Yet once she and Erric took the city and exterminated the Light-worshipping cult, Sybelle had had a change of heart. Why deny the people an outlet for their baser natures? So she'd devised a new sect to venerate the Dark, with herself as the earthly incarnation of Mother Night. Those who came to worship here gave of their blood and their bodies, infusing the temple with a power that lapped at her soul like an ocean of ambrosia.

Glowing braziers sat along the walls. A company of men and women in various stages of undress cavorted under the lurid light. A haze of blue smoke from a forest of water-pipes clouded the air. Golden bowls filled with ruby wine were placed about the chamber, from which the people dipped their cups and drank or poured the contents over their lovers. Grunts and sighs echoed from the vaulted ceiling while blind musicians played. Near to her entrance, a black basalt throne sat upon a raised platform. Two smaller thrones were placed before the platform. In one of them, the Duke of Liovard slouched, puffing on the end of a water-pipe while a lithe slip of a girl hunched over his lap. Her golden locks rose and fell in time with the music.

Sybelle took her place beside the duke and shooed away the vixen servicing him. The pipe slipped from Erric's lips. Then he relaxed as she took his manhood in hand. While coaxing him onward, Sybelle observed a knot of glistening bodies on the floor. Amid the tangle of graceful limbs, two rugged men lay upon their backs, drinking from silver cups as they enjoyed the comforts provided by a flock of young beauties.

'How fare our guests from Warmond?' she asked.

The duke made a final groan and slumped in his chair. Sybelle pressed herself against him as she wiped her hands on his pant leg.

He took a deep breath and let it out, deflated. 'They seem satisfied. Although they mentioned a need for assurances about the firmness of my control over the clans. Something about rumors that have reached the ears of their liege.'

'Just as I told you.' She traced a tiny scar running down the cleft of his chin. 'The death of the thanes was not enough. You must move quickly to consolidate your gains.'

He caught her hand and nipped at her fingertips. 'We agreed to wait for Arion's return. His report will tell us how go the activities along the border.'

Sybelle pulled away. 'I grow tired of waiting.'

'Your distaste for my son does not sit well with me, Sybelle.'

She bit her tongue before she said what she really thought of his son. Antagonizing her paramour would only make him less biddable.

'I think only of your future. I helped you secure the greatest city of the north. Will you not trust me to guide you to your rightful place?'

He grunted and reached for a cup beside his chair. Sloshing the wine on his stain-riddled shirt, he took a sip.

'My soldiers are overextended as it stands now, love. It will take months to raise a new levy and train them, and weeks more to relocate them.'

'Then use the mercenaries I have secured for you.'

'I don't trust them. Their commanders show me no respect.'

'They respect only strength, my lord. Show it to them – send them out to do your bidding – and they will give you the honor you deserve. The honor due to a king.'

He eyed her with a peculiar expression, like a man woken from a disturbing dream. He blinked and the look faded, replaced by his usual jaded gleam.

'Still, I would rather wait for Arion. When I know all is well in the south, I will feel more agreeable to do as you suggest.'

Sybelle stared at the duke, debating how hard to press him, but the sweet ecstasy of the temple chamber made her unable to sustain any true ire toward him. Against her better judgment, she let the matter pass.

She stood up. 'As you will, my lord.'

'Where are you going?'

The sorrowfulness in his voice was like a knife down her spine.

'Stay and enjoy the fete.' She bent down to kiss him. 'I shall join you later.'

Sybelle turned away as Erric reached for his pipe and signaled a servant to fire up another cube of kafir resin. She wasn't thinking of the duke, or even the emissaries she had invited to forge a pact that would eventually unite the Northlands under Erric's banner. Her thoughts were focused on a man who had thwarted her designs in another direction, a man who should be dead, and the plans intended to remedy the situation.

SHADOW'S

Chapter
FIVE

LURE

Josey twisted the ring around her finger as she stood outside the ballroom doors. The imperial palace had three ballrooms, but this one – the largest – was reserved for state occasions. The strains of the orchestra tugged at the pain in her temples. She had cancelled her audiences again today, taken a ride through the imperial grounds, and even tried her foster father's remedy of ground fennel root mixed in diluted wine, but nothing had relieved the headache. And now she had to contend with this infernal pageant.

Forty-two days. This morning when she woke up, she had been seized by a stranglehold of panic when she tried to conjure an image of Caim in her head and found herself grasping for details. It was the little things that she couldn't remember, like the pattern of scars on his hands, and the smell of his sweat. She'd spent the morning locked in her bed-chamber and called off the ball at least four times, and each time relented.

Josey took a deep breath that threatened to burst the seams of her bodice. *Might as well get it over with*.

At her nod, two footmen opened the doors. A wave of sound and light washed over her. Dozens of lords and ladies in elegant attire promenaded about the room. Crystal mirrors reflected the light of a thousand candles, and their soft glow lent the ball an air of otherworldliness. For a moment she forgot her anxiety and let the music carry her inside.

Everyone stopped and bowed at her entrance. The musicians stopped their song and began to play the imperial anthem. Josey smiled to everyone as she swept through the room. *This isn't so bad. Why was I so concerned?*

Hubert came over to stroll beside her. 'Put your hand down,' he whispered below the level of the music.

She nodded to an older lady in a purple-and-white gown that resembled the plumage of a strange bird. 'Why?'

'Because.' Hubert inclined his head to a pair of older men in military uniforms. 'You look like a farm girl on her first trip to the big city.'

Awkward warmth crept into Josey's cheeks as she lowered her hand. 'I'm a little nervous, all right?'

'No need to be. You look enchanting.'

She brushed her hands down the panels of her gown, chartreuse in tabaret with a lace décolleté. 'Well, thank you, Your Grace, but I don't feel it. My head hurts, these shoes are killing my feet already, and maybe I would know what to do if you had been around today to coach me.'

'I was working hard on the behalf of your empire.' Hubert nodded to an aged duchess of some middling territory. 'I have written to your rambunctious nobles, but I don't expect a reply for some days. Perhaps longer, as they weigh their options.'

'Send another message. Command them to appear and answer for their offenses.'

'Yes, Majesty. And there is something else. I believe I have an answer to the Akeshian problem.'

'Really?'

'You've read the reports about food shortages across the realm. Last year's harvest was abysmally meager, and with anarchy running rampant through the central provinces and the troubles on the border—'

'I understand, but how does this tie to Akesh—?' She grinned at him. 'You want to offer the Akeshians a trade agreement. Food in exchange for peace. Very clever, Lord Chancellor.'

'Actually, Lord Parmian devised it. His plan makes perfect sense. Akeshia is swimming in grain, so they get rid of their surplus for a hefty profit. We receive the food we need and a chance at building a new relationship. Everyone benefits.'

'Except for the Church.'

'True. The hierarchs will not be pleased to see an end to the eastern crusades. There is also the matter of convincing enough ministers to support it, and then where to obtain the funds to pay for the grain.'

Josey took a cleansing breath. 'I'm sure you and Lord Parmian will work out the details. Thank you, Hubert. This is the best news I've had in weeks.'

She hesitated before asking about the thing plaguing her mind, but then plunged into it regardless. 'Any word from—?'

'No.' He dropped voice even lower. 'Nothing yet. I have sent additional riders north, but none have returned so far. I will come to you the moment I hear anything.'

She hadn't expected more than that. Still, she could not help but be a little depressed. 'Thank you, Hubert.'

He started to bow, but his gaze wandered away to focus on something behind her. Josey turned and laughed in delight.

' 'Stasia!'

Josey met her friend with an embrace. Pulling back, she admired Anastasia's lavender gown, which fitted her slender frame like a second skin. Waves of golden curls framed her doll-like face.

'You look—'

'You look—' Anastasia said.

They melted into each other's arms with laughter. Behind Josey, someone cleared his throat, and she let go.

Anastasia made a graceful curtsy to Hubert. 'Duke Vassili.'

He returned with a low bow. 'Lady Farthington.'

Josey looked from one to the other. *What's gotten into – Oh!*

She raised her eyebrows, and Anastasia's smile deepened.

'Lord Chancellor,' Josey said. 'I believe the Lady Anastasia is here unescorted. Would you do her the honor of a dance?'

A crimson stain spread across Hubert's face. 'Ah, Majesty. I should . . . I mean, I would if Your Majesty . . . That is to say—'

'Oh, it's just a dance.' Josey grabbed his hand and placed it under Anastasia's arm. 'There. Off you go.'

A warm feeling glowed in Josey's chest as she watched them walk onto the dance floor. Anastasia had been devastated by Markus's death, so much so that Josey hadn't had the heart to reveal all the cruelties she'd suffered at his hands. Now it appeared that 'Stasia was over the past.

While the couple danced, Josey felt she was being watched. Looking through the crowd, her gaze stopped on a man staring at her from across the ballroom. Her first impression was that he was quite handsome. Almost *too* handsome. Rings of inky black hair. Tanned skin. Dark eyes with long lashes. He smiled, and Josey couldn't help smiling back. She wanted to know his name. She looked for Anastasia, who would probably know him on sight, social butterfly that she was, but she was still dancing with Hubert.

While Josey greeted people, looking everywhere *except* the direction of the handsome man across the room, a dry voice spoke behind her.

'Your Highness.'

Josey turned around to be confronted by Lady Philomena in a hideous, high-necked gray dress. The lady bobbed an inch or two, but her head never bowed. Her eyes were like small glass beads painted with a patina of disdain.

Josey waited for her to say something. Then, as the moment stretched into an uncomfortable silence, she felt the touch of other eyes upon them. *Pretentious bitch. She's making a scene, just staring at me.*

Finally, when Josey couldn't take it any longer, Lady Philomena spoke.

'That is an interesting gown,' she said. 'It brings to mind the dress I bought for my maid last Yuletide.'

Josey gathered two handfuls of her skin into her fists to keep from punching the lady in her aristocratic nose. She tried to think of a scathing reply, but Philomena glided away before

55

anything came to her. Josey looked around to see who might have overheard, but everyone in the area was involved in their own conversations. Which meant, of course, that they all had heard. *Hang that woman!*

Moisture stung the corners of her eyes, but Josey held up her head as if nothing had happened. People did not meet her gaze as freely as before. Or perhaps that was her imagination. She fought the urge to look around for Anastasia, but she really needed her best friend.

Then a man sidled up to her. Lord Du'Quendel, dressed in a smart suit of black with silver trimming. A thick gold chain garnished with tourmalines was draped around his neck.

'Your Majesty,' he said. 'Allow me to say how honored I am to become your new Master of Luminaries.'

'Uh. Yes, Lord Du'Quendel. The honor is mine.'

'And may I introduce a new addition to your court.'

The nobleman turned to reveal a man standing behind him. Josey swallowed as she saw a smile of brilliant teeth set in a bronzed face. Inky black ringlets of hair. *Oh heavens! It's him!*

She tripped over her own feet as she tried to stop and turn at the same time. The man moved with effortless grace to catch her with a grip as firm as stone, but gentler than she expected. She couldn't stop staring into his eyes.

'Pardon me, Majesty.' His voice was like pure silk.

She extricated herself. 'Thank you, sir.'

Lord Du'Quendel cleared his throat. 'This is my cousin, Lieutenant Dimas Walthom of Your Majesty's Light Horse.'

Josey had a hard time catching her breath. The room had become overly warm in the past few moments. 'Are you enjoying the ball, Lieutenant?'

He leaned closer. 'To be honest, Your Majesty, I am not much for this sort of thing. But here, in your presence, I cannot bear the thought of leaving.'

Josey's feet didn't want to move. Then an image insinuated itself into her thoughts, of her and Caim walking in the gardens a few weeks ago, surrounded by leafless trees. She blinked as the soldier said something.

'I'm sorry. I was somewhere else for a moment.'

His smile was easy. Practiced. 'Wherever it was, I am glad you returned to me.'

Josey glanced away. Whatever she had felt a moment ago, it was gone now. She wished Anastasia would find her. Then Hubert was beside her, nodding to the two lords as he offered his arm. She took it with relief.

'We're ready, Majesty,' he said.

'Thank you, Your Grace.' She turned back to the other men. 'Lord Du'Quendel. Lieutenant Walthom, it was a pleasure to meet you.'

The lieutenant bent his head, but his eyes never left her. 'The pleasure was mine. Perhaps we shall speak another time.'

'Another time,' she said as Hubert led her away.

'Thank you,' she whispered. 'Your timing is impeccable—'

The bottom dropped out of Josey's stomach as she realized where they were going. The musicians put down their instruments and departed the stage. It was time for her introduction. She'd had a few remarks prepared, but now she couldn't remember a single word to save her life. Swallowing, she tried not to show the dread oozing up as Hubert escorted her through the crowd.

He climbed the stage first and helped her up. As Josey turned to the assembly, her stomach twisted to the point where she thought she might be ill. A servant appeared with a silver platter, and Hubert handed her a gold chalice. The people in the crowd held crystal glasses filled with wine.

Hubert raised his glass. 'Lords and ladies of Nimea, good gentles, I present to you Empress Josephine.'

Josey forced herself to smile as she lifted her cup to the crowd. Looking out over their faces, seeing them watching her, she couldn't think of anything to say. She considered taking a sip of wine to stall for time, but thought it would appear rude. These were her people. They wanted to hear from her.

'Good people,' she began.

A shout from the other end of the room made a few heads turn. Hubert craned his neck to see.

Josey tried to go on with her speech. 'We thank you, one and all, for attending—'

A loud crash startled her. Cold wine from her cup spilled down her gown. Hubert jumped down from the stage, leaving Josey alone. On the floor, everyone faced away toward the main doors. Wiping at her bodice with her hands, and only making the mess worse, Josey couldn't see the source of the commotion. Then a shout rang out.

'Death to the usurper whore!'

A man ran through the crowd straight toward the stage. Josey froze. People backed away, and she didn't blame them when she caught sight of the man. He had the look of a madman, with great bulging eyes that focused on her like a coursing hound on a hare. He was dressed in some type of uniform. It took her a moment to realize it was the livery of a palace servant.

Josey backed away, fearing the man was about to leap upon the stage to assault her, but he stopped at the foot of the platform.

There, raising his left fist into the air, he shouted aloud, 'Long live the Church of the True Faith! And death to the usurp—'

His words were muffled under the press of several large guardsmen. Hubert reappeared. He blanched when he saw her.

'Majesty, are you . . . ?'

Josey looked down at the stain spreading across her bosom. 'It's just wine.'

'Thank goodness. Perhaps we should retire in light of this.'

The crowd buzzed as the agitator was dragged away. Few people were paying her any attention, and those who did wore unreadable expressions. Josey couldn't tell if they were relieved to see the man go, or sorry.

'One moment, Hubert.'

Josey held up her cup as she raised her voice. 'Some of you

don't know much about me. Most of you, in fact. But I want to remedy that in the coming days.' She cleared her throat, not sure where to go from there. Then she recalled something her foster father had once said to her. 'Nimea was once a nation of culture and gentility, a nation who welcomed her neighbors and grew prosperous through mutual benefit. Those days can return. They *shall* return. To Nimea! Long may She stand.'

A couple of glasses went up. Scattered responses arose, and gained strength as more and more people took up the call. After a moment, the entire assembly repeated the toast.

Hubert watched with wide eyes. Then he turned to her and bowed. 'Majesty.'

Taking his arm, Josey allowed herself to be led down from the stage. Guards surrounded them as they walked out. Behind them, music began to play over the thunder of applause.

Anastasia found them in the corridor. She rushed through the hedge of soldiers and hugged Josey, heedless of the wine stain. 'Thank the Light! I saw everything. Are you all right?'

'I'm all right. Just a little shaken up.'

Josey looked to Hubert over Anastasia's shoulder. She expected him to say something, but he appeared to find the floor tiles of great interest.

'It's a travesty,' Anastasia went on. 'The Imperial Guard should have put better precautions in place.'

'Everything is fine, 'Stasia. It was just someone seeking attention.'

'But the things he said!'

Josey put on a smile. 'It's nothing. Will you stay at the palace tonight?'

'I would, Josey. I mean "Your Majesty". But Father will be expecting me. He hasn't been well.'

'I understand.' Josey gave her another hug. 'Come see me tomorrow, will you?'

'Of course.'

Heaviness descended over Josey as she watched her friend

depart. Hubert was watching, too, but his expression was more sublime.

'Well?' she asked.

'Majesty?'

'What did the two of you talk about?'

He ran a finger across the bridge of his nose. 'Ah, nothing of import. She talked a bit about the decorations and the music. She liked the music most, I believe.'

Josey shook her head. 'Decorations and music? You're impossible, Hubert. Do you know that?'

'So I've been told.'

'I'm exhausted. Is there anything else I need to do tonight?'

'No, Majesty.'

'Then I bid you good night, Lord Chancellor.'

Still shaking her head, Josey walked away. The climb to her apartments seemed interminable. Her bodyguards took up positions outside as she entered. A shadowed chamber greeted her. The curtains had been drawn, but the hearth was unlit. Faint light flickered across the wide expanse of the foyer.

Calling for Amelia, her evening chambermaid, Josey crossed the cold floor. She reached a round table where a single candle dripped wax into a silver reservoir. Where was everyone? Perhaps her maids had not anticipated she would return from the ball so early.

As Josey approached the doorway to her bedchamber, a warm current of air brushed her face. Smells of dust and old leather tantalized her nose for a moment. She started to call out again, but a sliver of apprehension gave her pause. Why was it so quiet? Amelia wasn't the type to fall asleep on her duties. Josey took another step, but stopped when a soft sound reached her ears, a metallic click from behind her.

Fists balled against her sides, Josey turned around, but the darkness beyond the candle's feeble glow was unfathomable. She was tempted to call for her guards, but what if it was the maid returning from some errand, or her mind playing tricks? A yelp raced up her throat as a hand closed on her arm, but the scream sputtered and died when a familiar face emerged into the light.

'Fenrik!' Josey shivered as the pent-up fear drained out of her. 'You scared me half to death.'

With a stiff nod, the manservant walked her to the inner doorway. Her nightgown had been laid out on the bed, and there was a fire in the fireplace.

'Fenrik,' she said. 'Would you ask Amelia to—?'

Then she saw the blood, a rivulet of deep scarlet, trickle out from beneath her bed. Josey watched it run across the hardwood floor to the edge of the Hestrian rug and sink into the plush fibers. She gasped as a bony forearm smashed across her throat. She tried to scream, but nothing came out. She scratched at the arm with her free hand. Strips of skin, feverishly hot to the touch, came loose under her nails; the muscle and sinew underneath were like stone. Josey struggled, but couldn't break free.

As her lungs burned, she gave up clawing at the gnarled arm and plunged her hand into the folds of her skirts. She searched frantically until her fingers found a smooth handle. She tugged the knife free from the sheath hidden under her petticoats. Too desperate to care where she aimed, Josey plunged the knife over her shoulder. The first thrust met only air, but the next collided with something solid. Fenrik shuddered behind her as she yanked on the handle. When it came free, an acrid stench like rotting meat clogged her nostrils. She thrust again, and the arm around her neck let go. Shoved hard from behind, she was propelled across the room. She turned with her back to the wall.

Fenrik hunched in the middle of the floor, silhouetted against the hearth's glow. His left eye was sliced open where her knife had found its mark, but not a drop of blood spilled from the ruined socket.

'Stay back!' she shouted as he took a step toward her. 'Help!'

He shuffled forward with small, quick steps. She cried out as he lunged. Her knife connected with his breastbone and slid along his ribs. Without so much as a gasp, Fenrik grabbed her by the neck with one hand and slammed her against the wall. The back of her head struck stone, and white spots filled her vision. A balled fist rose above her. She watched it out of the corner of a teary eye. She almost welcomed it. When it fell, the pain would end. But some part of her refused to surrender. Then Caim's words tumbled through the drifting confines of her mind.

When you're faced with danger, don't wait for an opening. Strike hard and fast, because you won't get a second chance.

Josey wrapped the fingers of both hands around the hilt of her knife. As the fist reached its apogee, tears filled her eyes. *I'm sorry, Fenrik.*

With a hard upward thrust, the knife's point pierced through the bottom of Fenrik's jaw and up through his mouth. Still, his grip on her throat did not slacken. Her eyes lost their focus as the room began to spin.

Then, the world tilted as Fenrik's hand was jerked away. The knife clattered on the floor, but Josey only cared about the fresh air filling her lungs. Her sight cleared, and she saw Fenrik sprawled on the floor, her bodyguards hacking at him. With horrifying slowness, he crawled across the floor, even as the soldiers continued their brutal assault on his body, until he reached the wall.

Where is the blood? The thought battered her brain. *He's supposed to bleed when they cut him.*

Light filled the bedroom, and Josey sobbed in relief at the sight of Captain Drathan, the leader of her Imperial Guard, arriving at the head of more soldiers.

'To the empress!'

But Fenrik had reached the wall. Like a spider, he scuttled up the stones to the window and thrust open the shutters. Captain Drathan lunged, but he was too late. Fenrik leapt.

Staring at the empty windowsill, Josey fell back against the wall. Her hands shook as she folded them across her chest. A bitter taste curdled on her tongue.

'Gone.' Captain Drathan turned toward her, his features constricted in a tight scowl. 'Are you hurt, Majesty?'

Josey shook her head, but could not find her voice. She pointed to the bed. One of the guardsmen lifted the ruffled skirt. Josey's neck felt like a block of wood as she turned her head. With a heave, the soldier pulled a long, spindly shape from under the bed. It was Fenrik, his features frozen in death, blood dribbling from his throat.

Josey shook her head as a shudder took hold of her. Then she was on her hands and knees heaving up the remains of her supper. She closed her eyes, but could not block out the sight of his pale face.

SHADOW'S LURE

Chapter
SIX

The snow let up as Caim limped along the narrow country lane after his guide. The sun was in its last throes, but there was enough daylight to make another mile or two.

They had been marching for the better part of three candlemarks. His injured leg was stiff; his back protested every step with sharp twinges. His guide hadn't spoken since they left the roadhouse, but he kept a manageable pace. Deep ruts carved the road's frozen mud. A blanket of white covered the steppes, broken by stands of pine and spruce and occasional outcrops of bare gray rock. The deepening azure sky seemed to stretch forever, marred only by a handful of wispy clouds along the horizon. Almost invisible in the sea of blue, a black-winged bird soared overhead.

The old man turned off the road to cut across the open countryside. Caim eyed the snow for a moment and then followed. The ground beneath the thin crust was uneven, forcing him to slow his pace. They walked along the bottom of a long depression that Caim realized was an old riverbed. It wound northwest through the steppe. Caim was so absorbed minding his footing he almost walked past his guide when the old man stopped by a line of pine trees. In a clearing beyond their laden branches, a herd of caribou passed by. They were graceful creatures even in the deep snow, like the stag he had shot.

'Are you going to take one?' Caim asked in a low whisper.

His guide shook his head as he watched the animals for a few moments more. Then he started off again, his boots crunching through the snow. Caim tried to stay abreast of the old man, but soon fell behind again. After another half a mile, the guide stopped beside a tall hemlock tree. The lower branches had been chopped away to create a small hideaway. Caim didn't see how he had found it; this tree looked the same as any of the other evergreens around. But he was grateful to duck out of the wind just the same.

The guide dropped his rucksack by the trunk of the tree and hunkered down over a cold fire pit. As the guide began making camp, Caim sank down on the bed of pine needles, too tired and sore to lend a hand. The man muttered something about being back soon and tromped off through the under-brush.

Caim had just closed his eyes when a soft glow pierced his eyelids.

'Caim.'

He opened one eye. Kit levitated over him, just a few inches from his face.

'What?'

'You just can't resist the urge to play hero, can you?'

'What's wrong now?'

'What were you thinking back there?' She floated down to lay beside him. 'Taking on five men by yourself. And for what?'

He wanted to laugh, but it was too much effort. 'Kit, for as long as I've known you, you've been tugging me toward the straight and narrow.'

'That's preposterous.'

'How about that time in Brevenna when I nearly killed that palfrey racing Kevan? You hounded me until I swore to never treat another animal like that again.'

'And you forgot your promise riding to save your precious mud-woman, didn't you? Rode that poor horse to death.'

'I didn't forget. I had to do what needed doing.'

'I know.'

'Kit, what's wrong?'

The crunch of snow interrupted their conversation as the guide returned with a bundle of sticks under his arm. Without looking at Caim, he knelt beside the campfire and fed it smaller branches until the flames grew into a blaze. Caim inched closer to get at the warmth. When he glanced over at Kit, she was gone.

'Figures,' he said under his breath.

'What's that?' the guide asked.

'Just thinking aloud.'

Caim introduced himself and offered his hand.

The guide took it with a firm grip. 'I'm Hagan.'

Caim got a better view of his guide as Hagan set a battered pan over the fire. His face was creased and pitted like an ancient boulder. The silver bristles of his beard were matted and stiff. His only weapon was the long knife on his belt, a double-bladed seax.

Flames licked up the sides of the pan as Hagan dumped in a lump of meat. Bacon, by the smell. Caim's stomach reminded him he hadn't eaten much today. They sat in silence as the meat cooked. When Hagan deemed it ready, slightly on the rare side but Caim wasn't in the mood to be picky, he scooped out portions in two tin cups.

The fire snapped and popped as they ate. Caim wolfed down the food and licked the juice from his hands. Hagan, when he was finished, reclined against the tree trunk and ran his fingers through his beard.

'You're from the Southlands,' he said.

'Calanth.'

The lie came easy. Trust was a fragile thing, especially for a man in his former line of work. *Former? So it's decided then?*

'Those blades you wear.' Hagan gestured down toward Caim's side. '*Suete* knives, aren't they?'

Caim reached back and drew the left-hand knife. He held it up so the light reflected off the long blade. He still remembered the day he had claimed them off the body of a mercenary in Michaia. At the time, he'd had no idea they would become so much a part of him.

'I haven't seen a knife like that in a long time. Not since the war.'

Caim believed him. The Suete rarely left their highlands far to the north in the lee of the Drakstag Mountains, and when they did it was to make war.

Hagan tossed another stick in the fire. 'Mind if I ask what takes you up to Haldeshale?'

Caim put the knife away. Haldeshale was a region that had bordered his father's estate. 'I have family in Morrowglen.'

'Maybe I know them. I've been all around these—'

'I doubt it.' Caim bit his tongue. He was exhausted and not thinking straight.

Hagan pulled a pipe from his coat. It was a nice piece of craftsmanship, carved from a light yellow wood and polished to a shine. He filled the bowl with a pinch of dry leaves – wild talbac by the rich green color – and lit the bowl with a stick from the fire. He didn't give any sign that he suspected anything.

There's nothing to suspect. That was true enough. It had been more than seventeen years since he left Eregoth, an orphan and a fugitive.

'Maybe you do,' Caim said. 'My father soldiered a bit, under the baron.'

'The old lord of Morrowglen?'

'I suppose. I heard his name was Du'Vartha.'

Hagan took a long pull from his pipe and blew the smoke up into the tree branches. 'That's a name from the old days. It reminds me of a story. About a nobleman who went north to fight in a great battle, and returned with a Fae wife.'

Caim nodded and tried not to appear too interested. 'I never heard that one.'

'It happened not so long ago, during the empire's crusade

into the Wastes. The lord was injured on the battlefield and struck senseless. When he awoke his army had moved on, but such were his wounds that he could not follow.'

Anxiety stirred in Caim's belly as the old man talked. He felt like he knew how this tale was going to end.

'He managed to crawl away,' Hagan continued. 'Into an old, old forest where he thought to spend his last hours in this world. But just as he was beginning to lose hope, someone found him. A maid, alone in the woods. Day after day, she tended to him and cared for his wounds. In time, when he was able to ride again, he brought her back to his homeland, and she became his wife.'

Caim listened to the crackle of the fire as he digested the tale. Is that what they said about his parents? His mother was a Fae wife? His memories of his childhood were mixed up and fragmented. He knew his mother had come from a foreign land, but not which one.

Caim caught the old man watching him. 'Nice story, but I don't see how it could be true. A great lord like that, it doesn't make sense his army would leave without making sure he was well and truly dead.'

Hagan shrugged. 'Like most tales, it's hard to know where the truth leaves off and storytelling takes over. But that's how it was told to me. Lots of folks around here respected the baron. Du'Vartha, I mean. Even though he was a foreigner.'

Caim looked up. 'He wasn't from Eregoth?'

'No, from down your way. Nimea, or so I heard. It's not uncommon. Eregoth is a tapestry of clans and families from all over. The Du'Ormiks came from the south, too, long time ago.'

Caim ground his teeth together. His father was Nimean? Why hadn't he ever heard about that? 'Any stories about why he came north? The baron, that is.'

'He was an exile. Some kind of trouble back home, before the war. Came up with some armsmen and made a deal in Liovard for a plot of land and assurances of peace.'

'But that didn't last long.'

Caim meant it for himself, but Hagan nodded.

'True enough, but in the end it wasn't the clans that came for Du'Vartha.'

'How's that?'

Hagan glanced out at the darkness beyond the circle of their campfire. 'What do you know about recent troubles in Warmond and Uthenor?'

'Not much. Talk of fighting reached us in Nimea, but not the details.'

'Perhaps I shouldn't say any more.'

'I'd appreciate it if you would speak your mind. I'm a stranger here, but even I can see that things are amiss. The people at the roadhouse were afraid.'

'There's good reason.' Hagan looked into the fire for several heartbeats. 'But it's getting late. We'll need our strength for tomorrow.'

Caim's hands itched. 'What were you doing at the tavern?'

Hagan tapped the ashes from his pipe and settled against the tree trunk. 'Looking for someone.'

'Did you find him?'

When Hagan didn't seem inclined to talk further, Caim lay back and closed his eyes. But even tired as he was, sleep eluded him. He watched the play of the shadows cast by the firelight on the branches overhead. Pockets of deeper darkness peered down at him from the spaces within. After a time, he fished inside his satchel for Vassili's journal. With the book propped on his chest, Caim skimmed through the pages until a line caught his attention. He went up to the top of the entry.

Thirteenth day of Sorrob, 1126

 It has been more than two months since my apprentice departed to the northern marches. I am anxious to learn whether my efforts in those lands have been for gain or ill. If the northern lands cannot be tamed, then all this effort and treasure have been for naught, and there will be a reckoning within the Council. Yet that may also work to my advantage.

The entry went on about Vassili's personal agenda for two pages before Caim found another name he recognized.

Levictus has returned.

I have grave misgivings about the northern campaign, even more than before. The countryside is awash in uprisings, and the governor's militia dares not muster beyond the walls of Liovard. Perhaps more disturbing, the stories of evil happenings in the outlands seem to have some basis in truth, though Levictus could find no direct proof. His distant gaze upon me as I write this is evidence enough. I intend to request an audience with the Holy Office today.

Caim set down the journal. Eighteen years ago, the north was in disarray, and the political winds were shifting. In the chaos, few would notice an assault against a foreign lord. And less would care. As Caim tried to imagine what those times must have been like for his mother and father, images of the old dream flashed through his head. Of Levictus standing over his father's corpse. And behind the sorcerer, a great mountain of darkness.

A low droning sound intruded upon his rest. Caim tried to ignore it, but the buzzing persisted, and a feeling developed in his stomach. Like he was being watched.

Caim's eyes snapped open as he stood up. The night was full upon the land now, its darkness blanketing the forest. Throwing his cloak around his shoulders, he slipped the sword into his belt and left the shelter.

Beyond the firelight, the buzz grew louder. Caim stalked the sensation in a slow circle until he faced the northern horizon. He didn't see anything moving on the bright, snowy plain, but the feeling never left him. There was something out in the darkness. He stood for a few minutes more, until the cold and the mounting pain in his leg forced him to move. He turned to find a figure standing behind him. It melded so perfectly with the darkness he almost didn't see it. By its petite outline, his first thought was it might be Kit. Then it hissed and flew toward him.

Both *suetes* flashed in Caim's fists. The figure raised a slender hand. He slashed, but the blades cut through nothing. The campfire shone through the thing's parted fingers as it clawed at him. He leapt back, cutting again and again, but the thing paid no attention to his defenses. When the smoky hand touched him, a lance of freezing cold speared through his chest. The knives fell to the ground as his muscles spasmed.

As the specter reached up with its other hand, Caim struggled for his sword. He fumbled with the burlap covering until his fingers found the sword's cool pommel. A jolt ran through his hand, jangling his nerves, as he drew the blade. All at once, the bizarre paralysis left him, and the night came alive in amazing clarity. He jumped back as the hands – suddenly become skeletal claws – reached for his face. Caim swung, and a new pain cut through his shoulder as the sword connected.

He drew back the blade, expecting another attack, but the figure was gone. Caim turned in a slow circle. The sword trembled in his grip. A faint scent snared his attention. Warm and sweet, it was familiar in a way he could not pinpoint, like the ghost of a memory. It continued to tantalize him even after it faded into the cold night air.

With a mumbled curse, Caim gathered his knives and headed back to the camp. He stooped under the tree branches to find Hagan awake. The guide was tending the campfire.

He glanced up as Caim entered. 'Stay near the fire. Safer here.'

Caim sat down. His chest ached like a spike had been pounded through his breastbone where the apparition had touched him. The camp-fire blasted him like a furnace, but the flames could not touch the chill lingering inside him.

'What was—?' he started to ask, but he didn't know what to say. What had he seen? It had seemed more like a dream than reality.

'There's things out there.' Hagan cocked his head toward

the outside. 'People who go wandering in the dark sometimes don't come back.'

Caim leaned back against his satchel. The adrenaline was draining out of him, suppressed by deep exhaustion. His eyes shut of their own accord. As he let his chin droop, he remembered where he'd smelled that scent before. It had surrounded him as a child, an invisible blanket that made him feel safe when he was hurt or afraid.

The smell of his mother's hair.

Arion's boots clacked on the stone tiles as he strode through the palace corridors. For a day and a half they'd ridden hard back to Liovard. He didn't know how Yanig held on, punched full of holes as he was, but the army doctors said he'd gotten to them just in time. Okin hadn't spoken a word since they left the roadside inn. He'd survived the attack by those little black creatures, whatever they had been, but an unnerving look had taken over his eyes, as if he'd glimpsed damnation and couldn't forget it.

Arion passed a servant carrying a silver ewer. A livid bruise darkened the boy's eye. Arion smacked his gauntlets into the palm of his hand. He'd hoped things would improve while he was away, but they had only gotten worse. The sentries at the gates lounged in their guard shack, drinking and playing cards. The stables where he left his horse were filthy, with no grooms in sight; he'd had to brush his mare and put her in a stall himself. Worst of all, he knew the root of these problems, but could do nothing about it.

His father's mistress.

Just the thought of her made him want to punch the wall. His life had been easier before she arrived. It was a little more than two years ago since she had appeared in the midst of a cold winter night, she and the Beast and his Northmen. The people called her a witch, and Arion could see why. Not only had she convinced his father to embark on a campaign to take the city and declare himself duke of Eregoth, recently there had been rumors she was urging him to take the next step – to conquer all of the northern states and take up the mantle of king. It was beyond madness. Whereas Eregoth's clans had lived in uneasy peace since winning their freedom from Nimea, now there was open warfare. Add to that the covert raids they were launching across the southern border, and even he was ready to suspect witchcraft.

If things don't change, the entire country will collapse around our ears. If father won't get rid of the witch—

The doors of the great hall opened before him. Arion remembered this chamber from years ago when his father had brought him to the city as a boy. Then, the castle had been a place of light and laughter where thanes discussed their disputes without rancor or bloodshed. Those days were gone. Half a dozen men slouched at a table that looked ridiculously small in the vast chamber. The brilliant banners that had covered the walls were gone, revealing sooty wooden panels and bare windows looking out onto a smoke-smudged sky.

The lean man with graying sideburns sitting at the head of the table glanced up and wobbled to his feet. 'My son returns!'

Arion could see at once that his father was drunk, or befuddled by the noxious herbs he smoked. The others at the table, his captains, nodded and grumbled their greetings. Arion tried not to show what he was thinking when he saw the old warriors, some he had known since boyhood. Once they had been a proud lot, fiercely protective of his father. Now they sat around this hall, draped with chains and jeweled rings, like a pack of toothless old lions. Some couldn't even meet his gaze. His father was a sick man, but no one said anything. *Can you blame them? They're afraid to lose their place at the table.*

As Arion embraced his father, he smelled strong spirits and the stink of days-old sweat. His father's clothes were soiled and wrinkled. His laugh was a pale whisper of its former self.

'Tell me everything, Arion. Did you see Hamock? How do the men look?'

Arion brushed a dead fly off the bench as he sat down. 'The

73

men are well, and Commander Hamock sends his regards. But something happened on the ride back, Father.'

The duke chuckled, and it turned into a cough. A servant rushed forward with a cup. The duke guzzled it down. Setting the cup aside and mopping his tangled beard with a grimy sleeve, he sighed.

'Father,' Arion said. 'Do you remember the first time we came to Liovard together?'

The duke stared off into the distance for a moment. Then he nodded, slowly at first, but with growing vigor. 'It was the Feast of Saint Olaf. You were just a boy.'

Kulloch, the oldest of his father's captains, rapped his hairy knuckles on the table. 'I remember that day. Allarand held games, and you won the sword match, Your Grace.'

For a moment, Arion saw a glimmer of his father's old self, the powerful man who had defeated a host of rivals to take the reins of their clan. Then a voice filled the hall, and the duke slouched back in his seat.

'*Majesty.*'

The captains looked down into their cups. Arion gripped the table as Sybelle came around the throne to perch on his father's lap.

'We must all address His Majesty as he is due,' she said. 'For someday he will be king.'

Arion wanted to hurl the words back in her face. King? His father barely controlled the lands just a few leagues from the city walls, but she filled his head with dreams of conquest and glory.

Arion focused on his father. 'I was trying to tell you. On the way back we stopped at a comfort house along the road and had some trouble with the locals. We caught an insurrectionist – he had the mark. But another man interfered with our arrest.'

The duke snorted. 'Did you string him up as an example?'

'We tried to take him into custody, but he escaped. And not before he cut down my men.'

'One man defeated your entire entourage?' Sybelle's throaty laughter clawed Arion's spine.

His father grinned as he pounded the arm of his throne. 'You were drunk again, Arion! And you tried to molest some of my commons, and one of them showed you the useful end of a spade. Ha!'

Arion's grip on the tabletop tightened until he thought he would break his fingers. 'I know what I saw. Brustus is no slouch with a blade, and Sergeant Stiv is stronger than any two men in the company, but this stranger was fast – faster than anyone I've ever seen. He toyed with us like we were children. And then something happened.'

As Arion remembered, his stomach clenched. 'The inside of the house became as dark as night. And there were these . . . things . . .'

Sybelle pushed away from his father. 'What kind of things?'

'I don't know how to explain them, except that they seemed . . .'

He would have stopped there. Every eye was on him, magnifying his shame. But Sybelle leaned closer. Her gaze burned into him.

'It seemed like the darkness shattered into pieces and came to this man's aid,' Arion said. 'Like they were his pets, or guardians.'

A couple of the captains chuckled. His father just looked away.

Arion struck the table with his open palm. 'Ask the others if you don't believe me! Better yet, go down to the infirmary and see what those things did to Okin's face. It doesn't matter. Stiv and I are going back out to find this man.'

The duke rubbed his lips. 'That's out of the quest—'

'An excellent idea,' Sybelle interrupted. 'You should find this person and bring him to justice. Lord Soloroth will accompany you.'

Arion shoved himself back from the table. 'I don't need any help from your demon spawn—'

'Careful.' Sybelle raised a finger. The dark irises of her eyes reflected no light. 'Soloroth holds his honor as dearly as you. Erric, as you have heard from your progeny's own words, the maneuvers in the south are well under way. It is time to consolidate your control of this land. We cannot strike southward until our flanks are secure.'

The duke reached for his cup. 'As you say, Sybelle. It is time for Eregoth to bow to one master. Wine!'

Arion stood up. Without a word, he turned away.

'Son!' his father called. 'Come and we'll have supper. A feast to celebrate your return. We'll broach a cask of wine . . .'

But Arion kept walking, out the door and down the empty hallway. And the witch's laughter followed him.

SHADOW'S LURE

Chapter
SEVEN

Caim awoke to the smell of wood smoke and opened his eyes to see Kit floating above him. Her long, silver hair hung loose about her shoulders.

'Good morning, sunshine.'

Caim opened his mouth, and then closed it. He hadn't expected her back in such a good humor. It made him suspicious. But now wasn't the time to get to the bottom of it. Knowing Kit, she would let him know why when she was good and ready.

Hagan bent over the fire pit. His pan nestled in the embers, giving off an aroma of sizzling meat. Beef this time. Caim pushed away his blanket and took stock of his condition. His leg was stiff, but it felt better than the day before. His face didn't hurt as much either. When he probed the area around his ear, flakes of dried blood came away on his ringers. The gouges in his back weren't as deep as he'd feared. *Good thing, or I'd be crippled.*

When he reached over to put on his boots, a jolt ran up his right forearm. Pulling up his sleeve, he peeled back the bandage. The flesh underneath was torn like his leg wound and sore to the touch. He pulled off his shirt and started ripping it into strips.

When he had rewrapped his arm and donned a fresh shirt from his pack, Caim scooted up to the fire. The morning was bitter cold. Holding out his hands to the warmth, a memory came to him of another bitter winter, of him and Kas sitting across the table in their ramshackle cabin, shivering over plates of beans and mutton while a blizzard wailed outside. He could see the old soldier's grim smile as he joked about people someday finding their frozen bodies.

Hagan held out a steaming cup. '*Cha?* Not strong enough by a fair measure, but it'll warm you up.'

As Caim took the cup, Kit brushed against him.

'I already checked for poison,' she said. 'But he's a good man. You can trust him.'

Caim almost choked on the hot, bitter liquid. If this was weak, he didn't want to know this man's idea of a proper *cha*. Still, it was hot, so he drank until the cup was empty, whereupon Hagan filled it with browned meat from the pan. They ate in silence. More snow had fallen in the night. It covered their tracks and made everything look new and clean, as if he had dreamed the apparition that attacked him. He would have liked to ask Kit about it, but while Hagan looked rather old, he didn't seem hard of hearing.

They washed out their cups in the snow and packed up. Grabbing his gear, Caim walked out from under the tree with only a slight hobble. Hagan didn't wait for him, but started off toward whatever landmarks he used to guide his path. Caim was content to trail behind. It wasn't like he was going to lose the old man out here in the wilderness. While he walked, Kit kept pace with his strides.

'Where have you been?' he asked her in a low whisper.

'Right here. I was watching you sleep.'

'I mean last night.'

'Why? Did something happen? Did the old guy try to cut your throat in the night?'

'Of course n – I thought you said I could trust him.'

Her laughter rang like a chorus of bells. 'I'm just teasing. He's a good egg.'

'Good egg, eh? Well, to answer your question, yes, something did happen last night.' He told her about the strange apparition and how it vanished into the night.

'That's odd,' she said. When he gave her a strained look, she asked, 'What?'

'Well, for a start you could tell me what it might have been.'

'Do I look like a ghoul hunter?'

Caim sighed and shifted the bundles on his shoulder to a new position. 'Don't get pissy. I just asked a question. It's just that you're . . . you know . . .'

'What? Fae?'

'Yes, as a matter of fact.'

Hagan turned his head to the side as if he'd heard something, and Caim dropped his voice ever lower. 'I figure you would know more about this stuff than me.'

'Not without being there to see it myself, or getting a better description than what you've told me so far.'

'I didn't get a good look at it. The darkness seemed to, I don't know, gather around the thing.'

'Well, that's interesting, but what I was going to say . . .' She paused until he nodded for her to proceed. 'I was going to say maybe I don't know any more than you about such things.'

'What is that supposed to mean?'

'If I had to guess, I'd say it sounds like something from the Shadow.'

'Our guide says people disappear a lot out here.'

'So you'll be careful?'

'That's why I keep you around.'

She floated closer and put her arms around his neck. 'I thought it was because you couldn't resist me.'

'Go see where we're going.'

Her teeth snapped at the end of his nose. 'Fine. Be that way.'

Then she was gone. The sky had lost some of its color and now glimmered with an icy grayness. The breeze was slight, but with the exertion of hiking he didn't mind the chill. In all, Caim felt like he was finally heading in the right direction. But within a candlemark, he started to slow again and pulled down his hood over his eyes. They kept traveling cross-country and stopped at midday to share a cold meal of bread and cheese provided by Hagan.

As the afternoon waned, Caim began to wonder where they would make camp. Hagan surprised him with an invitation.

'My home is close by,' he said. 'Just past the next stand. You're welcome to stay for the night.'

Tempted by the idea of sleeping under a roof, Caim assented, and Hagan adjusted their path a couple points westward. As the sky darkened, a ridge appeared before them. Denuded trees sprouted from its snowy slopes. At the base of the hill stood a small cottage. Tufts of grass showed through the snow covering the low roof. Squares holes covered by hide panes served for windows.

Hagan pushed open the solid plank door and stood aside for Caim to enter. The inside of the cottage was a single open room. It reminded him of Kas's cabin. Three small beds sat against the walls. A fire burned in a round hearth in the center of the floor, surrounded by a bench of fieldstone. The place smelled of smoke and old leather. Wooden beams crisscrossed the ceiling, hung with herbs. A young woman turned toward the door as they entered. The first thing Caim noticed was the way the firelight glimmered in her amber-brown eyes. She was quite pretty, with a pert nose, and copper-hued braids draped down her shoulders.

'Daughter, we have a guest.' Hagan stomped his boots to shake off the snow. 'Caim, this is Liana. Seat yourself by the fire and take the chill off.'

Caim set down his burdens and pulled a chair over to the hearth. Liana grimaced as she maneuvered around her father to take a stack of plates down from a shelf and set them around the homemade table. Caim watched the girl out of the corner of his eye. He doubted she'd seen her twentieth summer yet. Twice, he caught her glancing in his direction. He smiled after the second time, and she pulled her father aside. Snippets of their conversation reached him.

'. . . is he?'

'Mind your . . . guest . . .'

'. . . don't even know . . .'

'. . . the proper respect.'

Liana brought over a bowl of warm water and a cake of hard soap so they could wash. Caim was embarrassed when his hands turned the water brown, but Hagan didn't appear to notice as he splashed his face and dried off with a cloth. Hagan dragged the only other chair up to the table and sat down. Caim got up to offer Liana his seat, but she swept by without looking at him and pulled out a three-legged stool for herself.

The meal was a simple affair, round loaves of bread hot from the hearth-oven, ash-roasted potatoes in the skin, and strips of chewy meat that were probably rabbit. Hagan worked his way across his plate like a lumberjack felling trees. Liana pushed around her food, but little made it into her mouth. Caim devoured everything they put in front of him. After a time, he had to stop or risk splitting his insides. It was with a satisfied sigh that he sat back in the chair.

A row of clay figurines stood on a shelf above Hagan's head. Caim recognized the major deities of the north – Nogh, Saronna, Sirga, and Father Ell. All outlawed since the coming of the Church. Beside the pagan icons hung a sunburst medallion on a nail, which struck Caim as strange. Stories of the crusade that had brought the True Faith to Eregoth were legendary for their carnage and viciousness on both sides. Yet both faiths were represented here, side by side under the same roof. Caim would have liked to know the reason behind it, but he wasn't curious enough to offend his hosts by asking.

Hagan pulled out his pipe and a pouch. 'So, your father was a soldier.'

Caim plucked at the whiskers on his chin. Why keep lying? Who was he trying to protect? The air in the hut felt stuffy. He wished his host would prop open one of the flaps over the windows.

'I'm sorry, Hagan. I didn't tell you the truth before. My

father . . .' He took a breath, unable to believe what he was about to do. 'My father was Baron Du'Vartha.'

If the old man was shocked, he didn't show it. He combed his fingers through his beard and nodded as if he dined with nobility all the time. His daughter glanced up for a moment, and then dropped her gaze again.

'Liana, clear this off, won't you?'

With a sharp glance at her father, the girl threw on a knitted shawl and carried the dirty tableware outside.

Hagan lit his pipe from a candle and took short puffs. Looking at him, secure in his home, surrounded by a growing cloud of smoke, Caim saw a different side to his host. There was an air of gravity about him, like a magistrate at his tall bench.

'It's said none survived the attack on Du'Vartha's manor. Not even the animals in their pens, all dead by fire or sword.'

Caim put both hands on the table, palms down. A rivulet of sweat ran down his spine. 'I survived. And so did my mother.'

The old man leaned forward, and the top of his shirt gaped open to reveal a bronze torc around his neck. 'I never heard that, and I know just about everything that happens in these parts.'

'What *do* you know about what happened?'

Hagan took another pull at his pipe. 'Not much more than the tale I spun for you before. The baron made no secret that his wife came from the north, but she didn't look like any Northman bride. Dark features, night-black hair. Eyes deeper than the sea. Some said she was a witch.'

Caim thought back to the woman at the prison gate.

Hagan coughed into his fist. 'When the empire took the clans over the mountains to make war in the north, men came back with tales of all manner of unnatural things they'd seen. And now with the witch in Liovard—'

The door of the hut slammed open. Caim spun out of the chair, both knives leaping into his hands. Two cloaked men stood in the doorway. The first was tall with big shoulders and a double-bladed axe held in one hairy hand. No logger's tool, the axe was made for hewing down men. The smaller man behind him clutched a sword. Both men were hooded, revealing little except that the bigger man sported a dark beard down his chest while his comrade was smooth-shaven.

Caim edged toward the wall where his bundles sat. Then he recognized the short sword in the smaller man's grip by its poor-quality steel and flimsy guard. He had seen it before. At the roadhouse. The thin-shouldered youth.

The men stumbled sideways as Liana jostled them from behind. She gave them both hard looks as she pushed between them with an armful of plates. The big man recovered first and pointed his axe at Caim.

'We're here for you, outlander.'

Hagan stood up. 'What is the meaning of this? This man is my guest.'

'Don't get involved, Father.' The smaller man pushed back his hood to reveal a slender face topped by the same mop of pitch-black hair Caim had seen at the hostel.

Hagan looked over. 'This is my son. Keegan.'

Caim lowered his knives. 'I saw him at the roadhouse, though he didn't stick around to see how it all ended.'

Up close, Hagan's son was a solid young man in his early twenties. His hands were small, with long fingers, more delicate than Caim would have guessed on a country lad.

'Never mind me,' Keegan said. 'I saw what happened at Orso's and told Ramon. He thought we should follow the stranger.'

'What were you doing there?' Hagan asked. 'I told you I didn't want you going there anymore.'

'Ask him how he took down five of the duke's soldiers, Father,' Keegan said. 'Not to mention Lord Arion his self.'

A sinking feeling hit Caim in the stomach. The duke's son? *Oh, gods. Kit, what kind of shit-storm did you let me walk into?*

Hagan pounded his fist on the table. 'Keegan, I will not—!'

Keegan pointed his sword at Caim. 'Father, if you were more concerned about your people, and less about the honor of your house, you'd wonder the same thing.'

Liana came over holding a damp rag. 'You're always looking

at things the wrong way, Keegan. If he fought Lord Arion as you say, then how could he be working for the duke?'

'It might have been a trick.' Keegan looked to the big man. 'To make it look like he was on our side.'

She clicked her tongue. 'Sounds like an awful lot of trouble, and no little risk, just to catch some blueflies like you and your friends.'

'I gave the order.' The other man said, still watching Caim. 'We've been hearing about spies sent by Liovard to search us out. If he's one of them, we'll deal with him.'

'Stop this foolishness,' Hagan said. 'You'll not harm a guest under my—'

'It's all right.' Hands by his sides, Caim took a step toward the men. 'You want to know how I got out of there alive? It's because those soldiers talked when they should have fought.'

He took another step. 'And they fought when they should have retreated.'

A third step put him within reach of the axe. 'And because, for all their size and bluster, they were piss-poor fighters.'

The big man watched him with a stony expression. Sweat beaded along Keegan's hairline. His pupils were wide with . . . fear? Anticipation?

'Caim!'

Kit appeared beside the door. 'Men with torches and weapons outside. Lots of them!'

Caim clamped his jaws shut before the questions spinning through his mind could escape in front of these people. He didn't want to risk hurting Hagan's family, but he didn't fancy a trip to a dungeon cell, or a gallows.

Kit hopped up and down. 'They're surrounding this place. Maybe it's time to call your little friends?'

Caim didn't even consider it. He wasn't going to unleash the shadows inside this house. But what were his options? The thought of running on his bad leg was almost worse than rotting in a cell. He made up his mind. The look on Kit's face was worth the cost to his ego as he let his knives drop to the floor and raised his hands.

'All right. I'll go with you.'

The big man grabbed Caim and spun him around, and Keegan produced a coil of hemp rope.

As they bound his wrists behind his back, Caim said, 'Bring my things.'

Keegan picked up the satchel and slung it over his shoulder, but he left the knives and bundles where they lay. Caim started to object, but the big man prodded him with the butt of his axe.

'Move.'

Hagan sat down in his chair with a deep sigh. Liana had gone over to stand beside her father, one hand upon his sloped shoulders.

As Caim was ushered past them, he said, 'Thank you for your hospitality.'

He passed through the doorway, and the light of a dozen torches shone in his eyes.

SHADOW'S LURE

Chapter
EIGHT

A draft blew down on Josey's neck as she tried not to be sick. Around her stood the members of her war council accoutered in their fine ball regalia, with capes thrown hastily over their shoulders as they answered her emergency summons. The reason was laid out on the table before them.

Poor Fenrik.

After the attempt on her life, Josey had waited in a salon with her maids and a team of bodyguards as the palace grounds were scoured. Now the notables of her court gathered in the armory hall where the remains had been brought for examination. Candlelight reflected off the weapons and polished coats of armor that hung on the walls. Looking down at the body, Josey couldn't believe that Fenrik, a man she'd known and trusted her entire life, was dead. But she still didn't understand how, after his escape, his body had appeared under her bed. She felt like she might be going insane.

'Drained of blood, you say?' Lord Du'Quendel asked through a scarf pressed over his nose and mouth.

Hubert wore a rapier at his side, the first time Josey had seen him wear the sword since . . . *since Caim's bogus funeral.*

'That is correct, my lord,' Hubert replied.

Standing at Josey's side, Anastasia shook her head. 'It's terrible.'

Duke Mormaer reached over and turned the corpse's head to the side, revealing jagged wounds on the throat. They looked like the marks a beast might make tearing into its prey. Lord Du'Quendel gasped and pressed his scarf tighter to his mouth. Josey bit down hard on her tongue to keep her stomach from rebelling; she was still a little queasy, and this examination wasn't making her feel any better.

'And what of the man who interrupted the empress's coronation ball?' the duke asked.

Josey looked to Hubert. The agitator had been hustled out of her sight, and she'd not heard anything about him either.

'He is the son of a minor family,' Hubert said. 'And, no surprise, an ardent supporter of the Church. We are in the process of determining if he had any help from the palace staff, but it appears he was alone and not involved in the attempt on the empress's life.'

'Thank the Light,' Anastasia said.

'I trust, Lord Chancellor,' Duke Mormaer said, 'that you will be fervent in your quest for the truth of the matter.'

'Of course, Your Grace.'

'No torture,' Josey said. Then, as both men looked to her, she said, 'I do not condone it, Lord Chancellor, not for this or any matter. Do you understand?'

'It will be as Your Majesty commands.'

Josey glanced back to the body, the flesh pale as ivory. She remembered the way Fenrik had looked at her as he attacked, like a crazed rabid beast. Now his eyes were closed in a peaceful demeanor. His clothes were rumpled but whole, save for the torn collar. No sign of the gashes she had made with the knife now sheathed once again at her thigh. No sign of the ghastly wounds inflicted by the guardsmen as they drove the manservant away. It was like the whole thing had been a dream.

Captain Drathan cleared his throat. By his sweat-slicked hair and the shadow of stubble on his face, he had not slept since yesterday.

'We searched every foot of the grounds and found nothing

amiss,' he said, his voice gruffer than normal. 'There is no sign of anyone falling from Her Majesty's chamber window. Nor did the sentries posted outside notice anything out of the ordinary.'

Duke Mormaer slapped the corpse upon the forehead. 'Did this just appear out of the air, Captain?'

Before Captain Drathan could answer, Josey snapped, 'Be so kind as to unhand my servant, Your Grace.'

Mormaer lifted his hand from Fenrik's white-haired pate. He started to say something, but a voice called from the entry-way.

'If you would, stand away from the body!'

Everyone turned to where a man stood beyond the door sentries. He was short and wore a brown overcoat several sizes too big. That, combined with a frumpy blue-brimmed hat and big shiny boots, made him look like a barker from a carnival show. He started to enter the chamber, but the soldiers blocked his way. He stopped short of their poleaxes and looked past them.

'Who let this man into the palace?' Hubert asked. 'Guards, escort him out.'

The man in the hat stared at the sentries as if daring them to try. He reminded her of someone, but Josey couldn't place where she might have seen him before. She stopped the guardsmen as they moved to obey.

'Wait.' Josey pulled free of Anastasia. 'Who are you? How did you get inside the palace unescorted?'

He made a bow, doffing his hat to reveal a circle of rust-red hair. Returning his hat to its rightful place, he answered, 'I am Hirsch, adept of the Enclave. I have come to see the empress.'

Josey looked to Hubert, who lifted both hands as if to say he had no explanation.

'I am Empress Josephine. What is your business here?'

'I have been sent to assist you in this dire time.'

The man – the adept – pulled a scroll from inside his sleeve and held it out. Josey wasn't sure what to make of this. With a nod, she instructed one of the guards to bring her the scroll.

Hubert moved to take it, but she waved him aside. She was tired of being treated like a piece of the palace décor. The wax seal that bound the scroll was stamped with a sigil she didn't recognize, an owl clutching a rod and a sheaf of papers in its talons. Josey broke it open. The message inside was written in stark black ink.

> Empress Josephine,
>   In accordance with the enduring pact between the Empire of Nimea and our Benevolent Society, the Enclave of the Unseen offers to Your Person the service of this adept, Hirsch Red-Hand, for as long as Your Majesty should require it. We desire nothing in exchange save for the continuation of the proprieties and conditions agreed upon by our forebears.
>   In Highest Regard,
>   High Magus Threptos

Hubert looked up from reading over her shoulder. 'Enclave of the Unseen, eh? An apt name for an organization we know nothing about.'

Josey held up the scroll. 'What does this mean by the "enduring pact" between us?'

Hirsch scratched the end of his pug nose. 'The accord was created three hundred years ago between the Enclave and the Empire. For generations, our order has served the rulers of Nimea, but the recent regime was . . . prejudiced against me and my brethren. We have remained out of sight, underground you might say, until the day we could once again step into the light. It is the sincere wish of my superiors that, with your assent, that day has come.'

While Josey pondered the statement, Mormaer leaned both hands on the table.

'Bona fides from an imaginary society are worthless. I suggest that this man be taken into custody and interrogated concerning tonight's events.'

'It is because of tonight's events that I am here,' the adept said.

Josey stared into his eyes. By all the stories she'd been told as a child, that was the wrong thing to do with an adept, but she wanted to see if there was deception in his gaze.

'How did you know?' she asked. 'No one outside this chamber has been informed of the attempt on my life.'

'The cabalists of my order see far, lass. Little that happens within the city walls is hidden from us.'

Not sure how to take that, Josey gestured for the guards to stand aside. Hirsch came over to the table, leaning between Du'Quendel and Mormaer without giving either noble so much as a glance.

'A close friend?'

'He was in my father's employ.' Josey glanced at Hubert. How farseeing was this adept if he couldn't tell a servant from a noble of the court by dress alone? 'I have known him my entire life.'

Hirsch bent down and peeled back one of Fenrik's eyelids. 'Male. Sixty-three years of age.'

Josey almost bit her tongue at that. 'How did you—?'

But the adept kept on talking as if he were the only one in the room. 'Contusions at the left carpal spur. More along the sixth rib, right side, and up through the sternum. Serrations at the neck juncture.' He stuck his forefinger into the throat wounds. 'Two digits in depth.'

Anastasia averted her eyes as Hirsch moved around the table, not bothering to look up to see who he was jostling. Duke Mormaer stepped out of his way with a frown. The adept whispered something under his breath as he placed a hand on Fenrik's chest. Then he stood up straight as a flagpole and rushed over to Josey. Like everyone else, she was so surprised by this sudden flurry of movement that she just stood there as he grasped her by the arm and pressed two fingers against the underside of her wrist.

Hubert grabbed for the adept. 'Unhand the empress!'

Hirsch hissed a word and Hubert fell back against the table, his face frozen into a mask of terror. When the guards raised their weapons, Hirsch gazed deep into Josey's eyes.

'Did it bite you?'

His tone was harsh, almost commanding, but there was concern in his eyes, true apprehension for her welfare. With her free hand, Josey held the advancing soldiers in abeyance.

'No.'

'Are you sure? Even a scratch—'

'No,' she repeated, firmer this time. 'Why? What did you see?'

Hirsch let go of her arm. Hubert recovered enough to put himself between them. Josey was touched by the gesture, but if the adept meant to harm her she felt certain no one in the room could have stopped him.

'Tell me,' she whispered. 'What did you see?'

'Your man was killed by a *voldak*, a creature of the Shadow that survives on human blood. This body must be burned at once.'

Josey looked around the table. Everyone's face was marred by confusion. A year ago she would have laughed at those words, but she had been through a lot since then. She wanted to think she had grown up.

'How do you know this?' she asked.

Hirsch pointed to the neck wounds. 'The *voldak* injects a paralytic toxin with its bite when it wants to kill, and then drains the body of blood. But certain contagions can also be spread by means of the monster's saliva, so precautions must be—'

'God's breath!' Duke Mormaer said. 'Enough of this farce. Take this man away before we're all bewildered by his words.'

'No,' Josey said. 'I believe he is telling the truth.'

'Are you a seer now as well, Majesty?'

'I am your liege, Your Grace. As such, I expect you to believe *me* when I say I saw my manservant stabbed repeatedly before he leapt from my chamber window. Only to find the same man, moments later, dead on the floor of my chamber.'

Their gazes remained locked for a moment, and then Duke Mormaer turned on his heels and strode out of the chamber. Josey looked to Hubert.

'Burn the body.' Then she said to Hirsch, 'Does that solve the problem?'

'Yes, but it's only the tip of the tower. You remain in very serious danger.' Hirsch gestured to Fenrik as a pair of guardsmen hoisted the body. 'Your servant was chosen for his advanced age and his access to your person, but the *voldak* is still at large.'

A hollow pain yawned in Josey's chest, as if her heart had fallen down to her stomach. She had been prepared for any answer, even the prospect of treachery within her household, but not the thought of her friends dying for their proximity to her. She looked to Anastasia. *I must send her away to somewhere safe.*

Hirsch placed a hand over his chest. 'I offer my protection to your person in the name of the Enclave, until such time as the killer is caught.'

Josey didn't know what to do, but the sincerity in his eyes convinced her.

'I accept,' she said.

Ignoring the streaks of blood on the table, she sat down. She wanted a glass of wine, perhaps several.

'Your first task, Master Hirsch,' she said, 'is to tell us everything you know about the assassin, and how we can stop him from killing again.'

Chair legs scraped against the floor tiles as the remaining members of the council seated themselves. The adept pulled back Mormaer's chair and sat down.

While he began his lecture, Josey signaled to one of the guards. All of a sudden she was famished.

SHADOW'S LURE

Chapter NINE

Caim pitched forward as a stray root snagged his toe. With both hands bound behind his back, he would have fallen if not for the men holding him upright.

They had been marching for some time now, first across snow-covered fields and then along a hunting trail through woods that turned out to be deeper and more extensive than he first assumed. The trees grew taller than Caim had ever seen before, some more than ten times his height. Masses of black briars with finger-long thorns made travel in a straight line impossible. In the distance rose the dark outlines of hills against the starry sky. If they were the southern tip of the Kilgorms, that would put him roughly southwest of Liovard.

His captors were fifteen cloaked men, including Keegan and his large comrade. Kit flitted among them, peering under their hoods and occasionally darting ahead. Every so often she returned to report her findings, which weren't much. They were local men, which he had already guessed. None of them wore anything heavier than a thick woolen jacket, but each man held some type of implement in hand, however, whether it was a simple truncheon or a rusty thresher. The big man, Ramon, was their leader, although how Kit discovered that when the men hardly spoke was a mystery to Caim.

A light appeared through the trees ahead. Small and flickering at first, it grew brighter as they traveled, even as the path became more uneven, sometimes disappearing altogether for a few yards before it reappeared. Another few minutes brought the party to a wide clearing lit up by three bonfires. Sturdy boles as wide as a man's height surrounded a patch of ground seventy paces across.

His captors ushered Caim to the center between the fires and surrounded him. Most of the solemn faces watching him were bearded and sun-bronzed. They wore their hair long, some in braids. Their garb was wool and buckskin. These were men of the earth who toiled for their bread, not soldiers, and certainly not practiced killers. Keegan stood in the circle. In the firelight it looked like the youth was poking himself in the leg repeatedly with his sword. While Ramon pawed through his satchel, Caim tested his bonds. The cord was rough hemp; strong, but it had some give to it.

'What are you going to do?' Kit whispered from above him, like she thought these men might overhear.

Caim shot her a glance instead of replying and noticed something odd. At first he thought it was a trick of the light, but then she moved to hover before him and the effect remained the same. She appeared less solid than normal, if that word could be applied to Kit. Faded. Caim bunched his hands into fists behind his back. Another damned mystery, as if he didn't have enough trouble on his plate.

Ramon dropped Caim's bag on the ground. His cloak hung open, revealing a white fur mantle draped across his shoulders. 'Who are you?'

Caim looked the big man up and down. 'You tell me. You seem to think you already know.'

'Feisty little shit, ain't he?' another woodsman said. 'Sounds like one of Eviskine's Nimean lapdogs by the way he talks.'

Caim recognized the man and his boar spear from the roadhouse. He had long hair, black as pitch, and a strong, square chin.

The other spearman from the roadhouse stood beside him. 'Maybe he's a priest sent by the Church to help us.'

The black-haired woodsman smacked his fellow in the back

of the head. 'The Church and its priests can go fuck them-selves! They ain't never done us no favors, unless it was holding out their hands for an honest man's coin.'

'Coins, he has.' Ramon held out a hand. Gold and silver glittered on his palm. 'Enough to buy Glynburn Abbey. All Nimean mint. Did the duke send you to sniff out our where-abouts?'

As the woodsmen leered at the coins, Caim relaxed his shoulders. 'I'm done answering questions until I know who's asking them.'

Ramon pulled out his great axe and set the head on the ground between his feet. 'You already know my name. Ramon, thane of the Gilbaern clan. The rest of these lads are my men. Now, answer my question before I kill you where you stand. Are you a spy for Eviskine?'

'I'm from Nimea,' Caim replied. 'But I am no man's spy.'

'He's lying,' a slack-jawed man said. 'You can see it in his eyes.'

Caim fixed the man with a glance. 'Insult me again and I will not forget it.'

The hung-faced man took a step forward, a wooden mallet in his hands. Ramon shooed him back in line.

'You shouldn't provoke us. We deal swiftly with our enemies.'

Caim chewed on his tongue. These men were obviously serious, but for all their dedication, they were an undisciplined lot. Yet they carried themselves like men spoiling for a fight.

'What are you waiting for?' Kit asked.

Caim didn't know what was happening to her – Kit's voice was softer now, barely audible over the crackle of the fires – but he had his hands full.

'Who is this Eviskine?' he asked.

'He's the fucking Duke of Liovard,' the dark-haired hunter growled.

Ramon scowled, and a scar down the cleft of his chin dark-ened. 'Enough games. Keegan says you bested a dozen of the duke's best men, but I say he ran before the first drop of blood was spilled. I say you never killed any soldiers.'

Caim met the big man's gaze. He'd faced down his share of bravos before. His first few months in Othir had been consumed with a constant stream of challengers who wanted to test the newcomer. It wasn't until he put a fair number in the ground that the rest learned to avoid him. In his peripheral vision, he spotted a shadow entering the clearing. Alone, it undulated across the snow. He hadn't called it, not exactly, but it had come to him just the same, as if sensing his dilemma. Caim flexed his hands inside his gloves. He hadn't come this far to fight a bunch of woodsmen, but he also didn't want to end up in a shallow grave in the forest.

'You're right,' Caim said. 'I didn't kill any of the soldiers at the roadhouse.'

He yanked his hands apart. The rope held for an awful moment. Then his fingers slipped through. At the same time, the shadow leapt up to land across Ramon's eyes. The big man shouted, reaching up. Caim spun around behind Ramon and kicked the back of his knees. The axe fell from the big man's fingers as he tumbled forward. While the others watched, Caim grabbed their leader in a chokehold. Ramon clawed at his face, but his fingers found nothing to grip. Caim looked around the circle. The woodsmen might have overwhelmed him if they all rushed in together, but they held back.

Caim released Ramon and stepped away. At his silent command, the shadow disappeared. Ramon snatched up his axe and lurched to his feet. He raised the weapon over his shoulder. Caim didn't move.

'Don't!'

A slender figure pushed into the circle. It was Hagan's daughter, with Caim's bundles slung over her shoulder.

'Li!' Keegan shouted. 'What are you doing here?'

'He's done nothing to deserve this, Keegan,' she said. 'He saved your life, and this is how you treat him?'

'Be quiet!' Keegan hissed. 'He bewitched Ramon. We all saw it.'

Liana snorted. 'I saw Ramon fall for a child's trick. Some dirt in his eyes. Nothing magic about that.'

'Well?' Caim asked Ramon. 'Are you going to strike me down?'

Anger smoldered in his eyes, but he lowered the axe. 'I will not kill a man until he's proven to be our enemy.'

Caim shivered as an eerie noise buzzed in the back of his head. All of a sudden, a heavy weight dragged at the center of his chest, sucking the air from his lungs.

Kit, her faded eyes wide with foreboding, shimmered before him. 'Caim!'

'I feel it,' he whispered as loud as he dared. Something was happening. Was it tied to Kit's fading? He had no idea, but it seemed a good bet. He said to Ramon, 'You have to leave. Now.'

'If you mean to threaten us—'

'I'm not threatening you.' Caim took a deep breath. He'd felt this way before, back in Othir when he first met – 'Something is coming. If you stay—'

A distant howl broke the stillness. Heads turned as the baying was joined by another, and then a third, all coming from the east.

'The Hunt!' someone said, but Caim wasn't sure he heard right.

'Ermin!' Ramon said. 'Go take a look.'

The woodsman didn't move at first, but a harsh glare from Ramon sent him running off toward the trees.

'What is it?' Caim asked.

A hoarse cry cut off Ramon's reply. Branches snapped as something staggered out of the forest. It was the woodsman, Ermin. He stared at them, his face rigid in the firelight. Then he fell over, the haft of a spear buried in his back. Yowls cut through the night as a line of huge shapes erupted from the trees like a pack of wolves running on two legs. But these wolves carried great wooden shields and steel weapons.

Several of the woodsmen backed away at the sight of the wolf-men racing toward them. Ramon lifted his axe and stood his ground. Caim launched himself at the girl. Keegan pulled his sister away, but Caim slapped the youth's sword aside and reached under Liana's cloak to slip his *suete* knives from her belt. A huge shape reared against the firelight. In trying to protect her, Keegan had pulled his sister into the path of a marauder. A wolf's head, with fierce eyes and sharp fangs, perched on the barbarian's head. Ivory trinkets clacked from a cord around his neck – human teeth.

The barbarian swung a war axe with a gray crescent blade. Gritting his teeth as all of his injuries cried out, Caim yanked Liana out of the weapon's path. Quicker than a cat, the barbarian reversed his momentum and nearly took off Caim's head with the backswing. Caim pushed Keegan and his sister back, putting himself between them and the bestial warrior. The barbarian brought his axe down in a swift overhand chop. Caim felt the wind of the blade's passage on his face as he leaned out of the way. He sliced open the wolf-man's arm from wrist to elbow, but the barbarian acted like he didn't feel a thing, swinging his shield as he spun around. Caim jumped back.

The clash of weapons echoed through the clearing. The barbarians had the look of reavers from the north, relentless warriors who raided and pillaged at will, leaving little behind but corpses and burnt-out shells. Ramon stood toe-to-toe with a wolf-man, both of them screaming as they swung their axes with abandon. Liana and Keegan had drifted away from the melee.

Caim grunted as he blocked another attack. Though his leg protested and his forearm burned, he threw himself into a roll that carried him behind his foe. Pushing aside his pains, he slashed with both knives as he came to his feet. His left-hand *suete* got caught up in the wolf-man's shaggy cloak, but the other blade pierced his lower back. Dripping spittle from his beard, the barbarian whirled with a ferocious chop. Caim ducked under the swing. His left-hand *suete* ripped open the barbarian's middle, spilling blood and entrails down the man's breeches. Yet even as the Northman fell to his knees, he grabbed Caim by the arms and tried to pull him to the ground. A crack to the side of the head with a knife pommel put him down.

Breathing hard, Caim looked around. Several bodies lay on the ground, but many of the woodsmen had escaped. Bestial screams echoed from the trees. There was no sign of Ramon, although his corpse could have been among those scattered around.

Caim found his satchel on the ground as he limped over to Keegan and Liana. The youth held out his sword like a talisman. The girl clutched two long bundles to her chest, his sword and bow, still in their wrappings.

Caim took back his possessions. The buzzing in his head persisted. 'You two all right? I see you managed to stick around this time.'

The muscles in Keegan's cheek twitched. 'I'm no coward.'

'That's too bad. I was starting to think you were the smart one in this bunch. Come on.'

Caim didn't wait, but took off. Keegan and Liana stuck to his heels. He didn't know what he was going to do with them. Get them back to their father, he supposed. The problem lay in eluding pursuit with the youths in tow.

The trees on the other side of the bonfires loomed like a company of silent sentries. Caim glimpsed a flash of metal among the underbrush a split-second before something hurtled out of the darkness. He dragged Keegan and Liana to the ground as the missile zipped over their heads. Five men in steel helms and leather coats emerged from the trees. One was clad in mail. Caim recognized them as he climbed to his feet. The soldiers from the roadhouse and the duke's son. *What are they doing out here?*

Caim looked over his shoulder as the soldiers advanced with drawn weapons. Keegan was helping Liana up and almost stabbed her by accident. Clenching his jaws, Caim reached out to the shadows. They swarmed out of the trees like a plague of locusts. One soldier with wild, yellow locks turned and ran back into the woods. The others pummeled themselves with their fists as the shadows slithered inside their armor.

Caim called off his minions before they killed. For a moment, they remained as if testing him, but then left with sullen slothfulness.

The duke's son stood alone as his men writhed on the ground. When Caim approached, the young noble slashed the air with his sword. Caim blocked it and punched him flush in the nose. The duke's son fell on his back in a jingle of mail links.

Caim kicked the lordling's sword away and crouched over him. The point of his knife hovered over the young man's eyes. *Do I let him live, and possibly have to face him again, maybe at the head of an army? Or kill him now and get it over with?*

The buzzing in his head had gotten worse. No matter how he tried to ignore it, the droning remained nonetheless. The duke's son looked up without expression. With a frown, Caim touched the man's throat with the tip of a knife. Then, he stood up and beckoned to the siblings. They stepped around the soldiers and joined him under the trees.

'What are we going to do?' Liana asked.

'Hide,' Keegan said. 'Wait for them to leave, and then I'll take you back home.'

'I'm not going back!'

'Yes, you are!'

Caim ground his teeth together. Somewhere nearby, Kit was probably laughing her ass off. Shouts echoed through the surrounding forest.

'Quiet!' he whispered. 'Hiding is a good idea. Do you know someplace nearby?'

Keegan chewed his bottom lip for a moment, until Liana hit him. The youth rubbed his arm and glared at her. 'The hills. There are places they won't find us.'

'Secret places,' Liana added.

Caim considered the idea. Getting to higher ground was a good plan, as long as they didn't starve or freeze to death. For now, he'd have to trust these people.

'All right. We'll—'

The words caught in his throat as a sudden pressure expanded behind his breastbone, squeezing the air from his lungs. Fighting the pain, he motioned for Keegan and Liana to go ahead. They looked at him for a moment.

'Go on!' he growled.

Keegan led his sister away through the trees. Caim waited until they were gone before he turned around. Something moved beyond the bonfires on the other side of the clearing. Then he saw it, a black pillar emerging from the space between two tree trunks. The pressure in his chest throbbed as a figure stepped out onto the snow.

The warrior was huge. His thick arms swung like tree trunks as he strode into the clearing. A cloud of shadows clung to him like a cloak ripped from the night sky. Yet it wasn't the intruder's size or the company of shadows that slowed the blood in Caim's veins, but the armor that encased him from crown to foot – plates of black steel with scalloped edges that seemed welded to his body. Caim had seen that style of armor before. In his dreams, the night the soldiers came to kill his father.

Caim froze as the visored helmet turned in his direction. Before he realized what he was doing, he started back into the clearing. He stopped himself. The shadows crowded around his feet, their touch colder than the winter air, while long-buried emotions roiled inside him. He had come north to find some clue related to his mother's disappearance, and the gods had sent him this darkly shining gift. He wanted to go out there and peel the armor from the giant's body, and then go to work on the flesh underneath until he got some answers.

Two Northmen entered the clearing. They looked like children beside the armored giant. One tossed something into the nearest bonfire. Caim saw it just before it fell into the flames. A severed head.

He let out a slow breath. He wasn't in any shape for another fight. Cursing, he jogged back among the trees in the direction of the siblings. His leg ached, worse than it had in days, and

101

his arm hurt so much he wanted to cut it off. How fast could he move with two kids hanging on his apron strings? Not fast enough. The Northmen would be on their trail with a vengeance. Unless they were distracted.

Caim gathered up the shadows around him. They whispered and crooned in the trees overhead. Taking a deep breath, he sent them back toward the clearing.

Through the canopy of branches, the horned moon emerged from behind a bank of clouds. Its rays cast silver halos around ice crystals hanging in the trees. Caim pulled down his hood and concentrated on keeping his footing.

It was going to be a long night.

SHADOW'S LURE

Chapter
TEN

Sybelle gazed down at her lover reclining on the bed, and thoughts of murder turned in her head. He slept like a man half in his grave, drunk on rich southern wine and kafir and sex. So fragile, this life he clung to. She could extinguish it as easily as putting out a candle. Somehow, that made her love him all the more. She bit down on her tongue.

I will not love him anymore. I will not!

He stirred, his lips pursing as if to kiss her, and the murderous thoughts fled. As she leaned down to meet his mouth, an icy tentacle caressed her ankle. Turning away from the bed, she opened a shadow door, and stepped through . . .

. . . onto the cool stone floor of her sanctum. Shadows flocked to her as she went to the pool.

The waters were in flux. Leaning over the low retaining wall, Sybelle saw bodies on the snow amid puddles of congealing blood. So it was no surprise to her when a great helmet filled the pool. Flecks of moonlight glinted from its black metal, but no light intruded upon the narrow eye slits. Soloroth had been taken from her not long after he was born to be raised by his grandfather, and she hadn't seen him again until he came of age. By then his eyes – as dark as her own – had become empty. The eyes of a stranger.

'What did you find?'

'The information was accurate.' His voice echoed through

the cavern. 'An unlawful gathering took place here, but the area is now under our control.'

The view shifted to a nearby body. The man had been split nearly in half at the waist – Soloroth's handiwork, no doubt.

'All were slain?'

'A handful escaped. My wolves are in pursuit.'

His wolves. With a hiss, Sybelle slashed her fingers across the water's surface where the helmet loomed. 'I told you to eliminate them completely!'

The slits of his helmet remained fixed upon her across the intervening distance until the waves stilled. 'They will be found.'

'There is something else. What is it?'

'There was a *shivalar* among the outlaws.'

A shadow walker?

'Impossible. There are no *shivalar* in this—' A wayward thought froze the words on her lips. She swallowed. 'The scion?'

He stared at her without answering. She had known it might come to this after she communed with Levictus's shade. She could send Soloroth after the target, but it would take him into unknown territory. Still, if he succeeded . . .

Sybelle's heart almost stopped as a deep tone echoed through the sanctum. A summons.

'Find him,' she told Soloroth. 'And kill him.'

'There is another matter. Lord Arion wishes to return to the city.'

No surprise in that. She wished she could allow Soloroth to eliminate the duke's whelp while he was at it, but Erric adored his son and that tenderness was a useful vulnerability.

'Convince him. Tie him over a horse if need be, but bring me the scion's head.'

As the helmet disappeared into the pool's depths, the chime rang again. At a pass of her hand, the waters became as smooth as glass, and another image appeared. Sybelle bowed her head.

'Master.'

'Have your forces crossed yet into Nimea, Sybelle?'

No greeting. No words of affection. His voice was hard enough to shatter an empire, and perhaps rebuild it anew. Though she would have preferred to lie, she dared not.

'No. There have been delays with—'

'More excuses! My agents report the Nimeans are divided against each other and ready to topple at the slightest excuse.'

She flinched at his anger, and at the mention of other agents in the south. She had believed she was his only emissary in this part of the world, and cursed herself for not suspecting otherwise.

'I serve as best I am able with the tools at hand, Master. And now that the cold season has set in—'

'The weakness of these Brightlanders has corrupted you, Sybelle. My own daughter, reduced to a mewling babe spewing pretexts and justifications.'

'No, Master.' She dared to meet his eyes. They were shimmering jewels set deep in his face under ominous brows, reflecting nothing back to her. 'Plans are moving according to your dictates.'

'Tell me.'

Sybelle bowed her head once more, the picture of perfect obedience as she told him about the massacre of the clan chiefs, and how under her supervision Erric was moving to pacify the region.

'I mistrust this alliance you have embarked upon, Sybelle. These Brightlanders do not think as we do. They do not understand power. End it.'

Sybelle swallowed as she scrambled for an argument to salvage what she had built here. When she first joined her father in exile from the Shadow, she had shared his vision for the conquest of a new domain. But matters changed when he sent her to Eregoth. First there was the unspeakable business with her sister. Then she'd found Erric, and her ideas about what was possible in this world had altered.

'I believe this can still work to our advantage.'

She trembled as the words left her mouth. Testing her

father's indulgence was a dangerous gambit. He cared for her, she knew, as much as he cared for anything or anyone, but the risk lay in measuring those depths.

'Explain.'

'Though the duke is weak as you say, his people are loyal. Much time would be lost if we deposed him now. I can manage him. He will do whatever I instruct. Soon this land will be under our full control, and thereafter we will expand into Nimea.'

She waited with downcast eyes for his response. She thought of Erric and the life she wished she could have with him. A normal life. And perhaps another child, one not so brooding and distant as her son. A child she could love and teach—

'I see through you, Sybelle. You spend too much time in the pursuit of your appetites.'

'Master, I—'

'Be silent.'

Her hands curled into fists within the wide sleeves of her gown, but she held her tongue. Evil thoughts percolated inside her brain, dreams of a day when she would supplant him.

'Sybelle, Sybelle. My dark angel. Sorceress without peer.'

She tensed. When her father handed out praise, people died.

'Impress me, Sybelle.'

She was careful to hide her smile.

'Impress me with swift victory,' he said. 'My other captains are enjoying success on their fronts. I would not wish to see you fall behind.'

'I will make every effort. You will see. I shall prove myself still your most potent weapon.'

'I hope so. For your sake, Daughter.'

She froze in the act of looking up. As the image dimmed within the pool's water, those last words lingered between them. She experienced a moment of panic, but calmed herself. Not even *he* could read her thoughts. Still, she would pressure Erric to make more advances, to win more victories she could claim as her own. So far, she had been content to hide behind the throne and pull the strings, but perhaps she had erred too far on the side of prudence.

Sybelle turned away from the pool, and the shadows flocked to her, cooing as they pressed their small bodies against her skin. She walked to the passageway leading to the temple. Her next move would be a bold thrust, enough to pacify her father and bring her one step closer to her ultimate aim. If she could not change what was, she must prepare for what would be.

Her mind awash with plans and stratagems, it occurred to Sybelle that she had failed to mention the scion to her father. An oversight? No, she didn't want her father involved. She didn't know on which side he would come down.

The corpse's ice-blue eyes stared up at the sky. Looking down, Arion wondered if such eyes were common among the barbarians. This was the first dead Northman he'd ever seen. They had seemed so indestructible, until today.

He turned to Stiv. The sergeant still lived, but it was hard to look at him. Horrid coin-sized wounds covered his face, even through his thick beard. When they were through with this fool's errand, would they envy Yanig, lying in a bed with a yard of stitches in his body?

'How do you feel?'

The sergeant dabbed at his face with the end of his cloak, 'Like a damned fool. We should have known to bring crossbows. Shot the bastard from a hundred paces.'

Arion glanced away. For the sake of his honor, he had put the lives of his men at risk. He didn't know why the man in black hadn't killed them. Twice they'd been at his mercy, and twice been allowed to live.

Okin sat beside a bonfire, staring into the dwindling flames. He had screamed when the demon bats – the little pieces of darkness – fell upon them a second time. At least Arion thought it had been Okin. *Maybe it was me.*

Bodies were strewn across the snow, most of them outlaws.

Is that what they are? He'd been taught to believe that criminals ran when confronted, rather than stand and fight, but he didn't know what to think anymore. Not about this, and not about what he'd seen in the south, where his father's raiding parties sacked defenseless villages. He only knew he didn't want to be a part of it anymore.

The stomp of heavy boots brought him around as the Northmen returned to the clearing. They numbered just twenty, but each fought like a grizzly bear. Their leader, Garmok, was a vicious hulk of a man who laughed as he killed.

The Beast stood before the trees, looking in the direction the man in black had run off. His Northmen moved around the clearing, stabbing the cold bodies, hacking off limbs and unspooling entrails. Arion looked away. It wasn't until he heard stifled groans that he understood they were killing the wounded, friend and foe alike.

'Lord Soloroth!' Arion shouted. 'We should take prisoners.'

The Beast turned. A rumble echoed from the mouth slit of his helmet. 'We pursue the one who escaped.'

'I told you. You can go after them if you like, but my men are injured. We're returning to Liovard to report to my father.'

The Beast did not move, but something in his stance made Arion want to grab for his sword.

'We give chase. Those who cannot keep up . . .'

A shriek sounded from the other side of the clearing, followed by a wicked chortle. Arion's hands trembled, but whether from fear or rage he could not say. Instead of answering, he helped Stiv to his feet, and together they assisted the others.

As Garmok led the barbarians northward, followed by their dread master, Arion waited behind. They'd left their dead without so much as a prayer to see them into the next world. *How can you defeat men who don't even fear the gods?*

Arion tried not to think about it as he focused on putting one foot before the other.

SHADOW'S
Chapter
ELEVEN
LURE

Kit sighed as the sunshine penetrated her body. A cool breeze rustled the grass beneath her hair and bathed her in smells of willow and sweet water. She looked up into the lavender sky. Then a note of agitation entered her brain. Something was wrong. It took a moment for it to sink in.

She was solid again.

Kit sat up in a short dress that left her legs bare. A ruby-red stream drifted past her toes. Beyond the stream, and all around her, stretched a forest of small, cyan trees. Ashen clouds wafted in the distance. She put a hand to her mouth, not trusting her eyes. *It can't be!*

She was home.

How could this have happened? The last thing she remembered was floating above Caim as he argued with the other mud-men. While she waited for Caim to kill them, she investigated the surrounding woods. Something hadn't felt right. She recalled feeling a little odd, like there was a rope around her waist, pulling her away from the firelit meadow. She had tried to fight it. Then more mud-men arrived, and everything went dark.

Kit stood up and swayed for a moment. After being weightless for so long, the sudden drag of the ground upon her body was disconcerting. As she found her balance, a high, piping voice caught her ears. Kit froze, knowing it at once.

'Kitrine! Kitrine, there you are!'

Kit turned to see her sister, Dahlia, running across the sapphire lawn. She almost tripped, and Dahlia caught her with a contralto laugh.

'Kitrine, what's the matter with you? Mother and father are waiting.'

Kit's stomach flipped over and she clutched onto her sister, who felt more real than, well, anything she'd known in the last twenty-odd years. Tears formed in the corners of her eyes.

'Dahlia, how long have I been away?'

'Away?' Her sister kissed her on the cheek. She smelled of ginrose and papucorn blossoms. 'Silly! Where would you go? Come on. It's already past midday, and Mother made tarts just for you.'

Kit pulled back, confused. This didn't feel right. She'd been gone for a long time. Why was Dahlia talking as if she'd never left? *Unless I didn't. Unless it was all just a dream . . . No! I was in the Brightlands with Caim. It was real!*

But here was her little sister, tugging on her hand. Laughing, Dahlia ran ahead toward a gentle hill that rose from the trees. A small palace sat upon the tor, its argent walls glistening in the sunlight. Kit started to follow, but her steps slowed as something tugged at the back of her mind. She looked over her shoulder, to the stream and the dark clouds on the horizon. There was a brief flash in the distance. A storm was coming. *Why do I feel so strange?*

'Kitrine!' Dahlia called. 'We're all waiting for you.'

Kit wanted to follow, but a quiet dread held her back, a feeling that she was missing something. A rugged profile appeared in her thoughts. Caim! She had to get back to him. Kit took a step toward the stream.

The sky turned dark. A cruel wind erupted from nowhere and knocked her to the ground. The trees bent over. Kit winced at the sounds of snapping branches. Fighting through the tumult, she crawled another step. A tear ripped down the center of the sky, filled with angry thunder-heads. Kit shouted as an invisible force snatched her up.

The roaring wind battered her to the ground. She coughed as grit flew up her nose. Hacking it out, Kit turned away from the brunt of the cruel gale and opened her eyes.

There was no sky overhead, no sun or moon, no mountains or hills in the distance, only roiling masses of black storm clouds all around. But this was no dream. She knew this place. She'd been here once before, when she answered the call of Caim's mother. This was the Barrier, the netherworld between the Shadow and the Brightlands. And the place where she had been – or thought she'd been – was far away. Standing up, buffeted by the powerful wind, she tried to forget the mirage of her homeland. From what she recalled of her last journey through this place, she wasn't glad to be back. Things lurked in the hazy mists, things even a Fae had reason to fear.

A glimmer of light made her turn around. A vertical disk of light split the grayness a dozen strides away. It was a gateway between worlds, one of the many that permeated the Barrier. Something moved within the circle of light. She saw a face.

Caim!

With a surge of exhilaration, Kit threw herself at the portal, then gasped as she slid down its unyielding surface. Her hands pawed at the glassy plane where the opening should have been. She shouted and beat on it with her fists, finally stopping when the pain became too much to continue. Then she sat down and buried her face in her arms against the harsh wind. She didn't know what was happening, or why she was here, but this portal wasn't going to grant her passage. She had to find another. As she looked around, trying to determine the best direction to go, a low growl rumbled in the haze. Kit gathered her legs under her.

A long black shape appeared, prowling low to the ground. Kit moved away, but there was nowhere to hide. She had no weapons. Here, as solid as a mud-woman, she was struck by an awareness of her own vulnerability. Then she straightened up. She recognized this creature, although she wasn't sure that was a good thing.

Kit held out a hand to Caim's shadow monster.

She didn't know exactly what the creature was. She wasn't an expert on the Shadowlands; her people tried to avoid that gloomy place whenever possible. Of course, Caim never believed her. He always assumed she was keeping things from him. Well, sometimes she did, but only for his own good.

The shadow beastie stopped a couple paces away. It looked bigger than the few times she'd seen it before, or perhaps she was just more conscious of its size now that it could conceivably kill and eat her. *Don't think about that. Think good thoughts! Nice doggie!*

She clucked her tongue and reached out to entice the creature, but it just looked at her. *This is just like Caim. To get me thrown into this horrible place, and then send his pet along to make it more unpleasant.* She stamped her foot, wishing she could chew him out right now. Or kiss him.

What? Stop it, Kit! Keep your mind on getting out of here.

She needed to get back before Caim, and maybe the shadow doggie could help. She tried to get its attention with a friendly wave.

'Hello! Looks like we're both stuck here, huh? At least it's nice to see a familiar face. . . .'

She stopped as the creature faded from sight. One moment it was there, the next it was gone. *How annoying! It just left me standing here.*

What would she do now? Kit turned in a slow circle, hoping to see something that might point her in the right direction. The glowing portal shimmered as if mocking her. She scratched her head. Her back of her scalp tingled like little fireflies were dancing in her hair. She turned her head, and the tingling shifted, now coming from the opposite direction as the portal. What did that mean?

Kit chewed on her bottom lip. She could remain here and

wait for the portal to work, which didn't seem to be getting her anywhere. Or she could strike out and hope to find another way back. As she considered, a third option entered her mind. She could go back home. It would be a simple thing. Just a step and a moment's concentration, and she would be back in the Fae for real this time. To see Dahlia and the rest of her family again. In all these years she'd spent with Caim, she never once considered it, but now . . .

She thought of the azure moons shining in the emerald-green sky, the cool sea-blue grass along the banks of the lazy Seludon where she used to lie, alone, and dream of a more exciting life. *Isn't that why I answered the call on the wind? Excitement. Adventure. And someone to share it with.*

But even as she imagined the wonders of the homeland she'd left behind, the tugging intensified. *Caim needs me.*

As the resolve quickened inside her, Kit put her back to the frustrating circle of light and set off to find whatever was pulling her. With every step, images of Caim played in the back of her mind. And from those memories arose the fervent hope that her love would survive until she returned.

SHADOW'S
LURE

Chapter
TWELVE

Caim kept his eyes on the rising ground ahead of him where Keegan and his sister made their way up the hillside. He saw them clear enough in the darkness, but the youths had to be navigating by instinct. He hoped they knew where they were going, because he didn't have a clue.

Caim stopped beside a leaning pine and scratched his aching forearm through the sleeve as he looked back the way they'd come. The snow glowed with a ghostly luminance. There was no sign of pursuit, but he wished he knew where Kit had gone. She was always flighty, but he'd never seen her fade out like that. But her absence wasn't the only thing bothering him. The marauders who had attacked the woodsmen's gathering stuck in his head like a bad dream. More than fierce, they had been almost bestial. And the huge fighter . . .

Caim's hands clenched and unclenched at his sides. He knew what he had seen. The black armor, the cloak of darkness – they screamed that he was in trouble up to his eyeballs. Caim continued up the slope, which became steeper as they got higher. The siblings had gotten a couple hundred yards ahead of him. A face peered back. The girl. She had come out here for him. He hoped she didn't end up dead because of it.

Caim caught up to them on a narrow shelf of ground that wound around the hill toward its northern face. Keegan hugged the sheer face of bare stone and kept as far as possible from the hundred-foot drop on the other side. The path was short and ended at the mouth of a small cave. Keegan ducked inside without hesitation, and Liana followed.

Caim stood at the entrance for a moment to let his eyes adjust to the new level of darkness. With the sharp clack of steel against stone, a tiny spark burst into view. On the second strike, the spark caught and light blossomed. The cave extended about fifteen feet or so into the hillside. The roof was right above his head. Although not cozy, it was, he had to admit, an excellent hiding place, provided no one stumbled upon them. He didn't want to think about trying to fight his way out of here.

While Liana joined her brother at the back of the cave to tend the fire, Caim sat down and stretched out his legs. A knotted muscle throbbed in his thigh, and another one higher up in his hip, but it was his arm that bothered him the most. It itched like he had a hornet buried under the skin. He rolled back his sleeve and pulled back the bandage, and hissed as fresh air touched the wound. The skin around the bite punctures was swollen and purple. Rivulets of yellow pus ran from the holes as he prodded the site. He started to roll down his sleeve, but Liana stopped him.

'Let me see.'

'It's fine.'

'Just give me a look.'

He sat back and let her have his arm. With a light touch, she probed the wound, causing more pus to ooze.

'Where did you get these?'

'A bear.'

She reached behind her back. 'Getting bit by a bear is supposed to be good luck.'

'And how many times have you been bit – ouch!'

While he was talking, she had produced a small knife – very sharp – and ran its blade lengthwise across the holes. He started to grab for her, but she pointed the knife at his face. Despite the grime and the sweat, she was beautiful.

'Don't be a child. I have to get the bad humors out or they'll

115

spread to other parts of your body, and then we'll have to cut off your arm.'

Caim leaned back against the wall and tried to ignore the fiery jolts shooting up his arm. The smell was worse than the pain.

'So why have you come north?' Liana asked.

'I needed a fresh start. There was some trouble back home.'

'So you chose Eregoth? In winter?'

'I know. I—' He almost said he had forgotten how cold it got up here, but stopped himself. 'I may have made a mistake.'

'A woman,' Keegan said.

Caim looked over. 'What?'

'The trouble,' he said. 'It was over a woman, right?'

Liana pursed her lips. 'No, I'm thinking maybe the woman *was* the trouble.'

Caim shook his head at their guesses, and winced when Liana slapped his leg.

'I'm right, aren't I?

'If we're asking questions, I notice you and your father live pretty far out of the way.'

'Is that a question?'

'Isn't it dangerous out here?'

Liana bent down over his arm. 'We used to live on the steppe. Papa is loreman of the clans. He keeps our stories and songs, and teaches the young. It seemed like he was always on his way to or coming back from someplace new. Sometimes we'd go with him. When mother died, we moved out to the hills.'

Keegan kicked a stone into the fire. 'That's enough, Li. He don't need to know our whole history.'

'All right,' Caim said. 'Then tell me what happened back there. You can start at the point where your friends kidnapped me. That was your doing, right?'

'Ramon gave the order.'

'Ramon's the big guy with the white cape, right? He's your leader?'

When Keegan shrugged, Liana huffed at him.

116

'Is that why he wasn't at Aldercairn? He leads the Gilbaerns now?'

'Thane Sigmer died in his sleep. Ramon was chosen the next day.'

Liana finished rubbing Caim's arm and rooted through his satchel. He helped by fishing out a semi-clean shirt, which she ripped into long strips.

'You spoke of problems in Liovard,' Caim said. 'Starting with the coming of this duke. I take it you and your friends don't much like him.'

Keegan pulled a small bundle wrapped in cloth from his pocket. Inside was a wedge of cheese. He broke off a piece and tossed it to Liana; she offered a piece to Caim, but he shook his head.

'He's taken everything short of our lives,' the youth said. 'And he'll come for those soon enough. The Eviskines were nothing more than horse thieves until a couple years ago. Then the duke's father died, and Erric took over the clan. The next summer they came down and took the city. A moon ago, a council of thanes was called to make a plan. Eviskine killed them all.'

Caim flexed his wrist. Liana's new binding was better than he could have done. 'But you escaped?'

Keegan finished his cheese and brushed off his hands. 'Caedman – our captain – asked me to go, so I went.'

'Caedman Du'Ormik was a good man,' Liana said. 'Now that he's gone . . .'

'He's not gone.'

She turned to her brother. 'But you said everyone at the peace-meet was killed.'

'Aemon and Dray found me at Orso's. They heard from Vaner that Caedman was taken alive. The duke is keeping him at the prison.'

'Does Ramon know that?'

Keegan shrugged. 'Probably. I never got the chance to ask him.'

Listening to them and trying to get a sense of this land

117

which had once been his home, there was something else Caim wanted to know, but he wasn't sure how to ask it without revealing too much about himself. *But who else is going to tell me?*

'Who was the warrior in black?'

'The Beast.' Keegan tossed another stick in the fire. 'If you want to know about that one, you should first start with the *darghul*. She was at Aldercairn, too.'

'You never told me she was there,' Liana said. 'Keegan, we have to tell Papa.'

Her brother shook his head. 'We can't involve him, Li.'

'But, Keegan—'

Caim was ready to knock their heads together until he got a straight answer. 'What's a *darghul?*'

Liana glared at Keegan as she answered. 'An evil spirit.'

'What? Like a demon?'

Keegan pulled his cloak up around his shoulders. 'She looked like the queen of the damned in the flesh. And her eyes. When she looks at you, it's like seeing your own death.'

Caim wasn't sure he believed any of this, but he asked, 'And the giant? This Beast.'

'He and the Northmen came with the witch. None can stand before them.'

'Caim did,' Liana said.

Keegan scowled at her over the flames. Then he pulled his hood up over his head.

'I'm tired.'

With a shake of her head, Liana held out a hand to Caim.

'Give me your coat.'

'Hmm?' He realized she wore only the smock under her cloak. 'Oh, here.'

He pulled off the leather jacket, careful not to jar the bandages around his arm, and made to settle the garment around her shoulders. Instead, she retrieved a small sewing kit from a pocket and set to mending the tears in his sleeve.

Caim scratched his thigh. 'One of the men at the clearing

said something odd before the Northmen arrived. What is the Hunt?'

'It's an old legend. Pa told it to us often when we were little. It gave Keegan nightmares.'

There was a grunt from the other side of the fire, but Liana continued.

'Every winter, during the longest nights, a pack of wolves comes down from the mountains to hunt, led by their master. A man with skin like coal. Anyone caught out of doors must run until daybreak or be torn to pieces.'

Caim thought of the barbarians with their wolf-pelt head-dresses and the giant in black armor. 'The Master of the Hunt'.

Gentle snores echoed from the back of the cave as Liana moved closer to the fire. Caim retrieved a whetstone from his satchel and set to work on his blades. The scrape of the steel over stone was like a draught of cool wine, releasing the tension in his shoulders and neck. Its rhythm lulled him into a peaceful trance where nothing existed except him and the blades and the play of the shadows across the ceiling. Sleep would be a long time coming, but he had gone without its succor on jobs before. He had everything he needed right here.

Stone and steel and shadow.

SHADOW'S LURE

Chapter
THIRTEEN

Caim winced as frigid needles penetrated the pores of his face. Holding his breath, he rubbed the snow over his forehead, across his cheeks, and – gently – around his sore ear. His hands came away with flakes of scabbing, but no fresh blood. Satisfied, he rubbed his hands in the snow and picked up the meal cake that was his breakfast.

He had forgotten how peaceful the forest could be. Rising between the snowy hilltops, the sun lit up the valley below in shades of gold and orange. Fingers of white mist wended through the carpet of trees. Birds twittered, and small creatures scampered through the underbrush. They'd hiked farther last night than he realized, at least four or five miles, much of it over rough terrain. To the north, the chain of peaks extended as far as he could see. Beyond them lay the Great Forest, running all the way to the Drakstag Mountains. When Caim was a boy, Kas had told him stories about how he and Caim's father had journeyed over those mountains and into the forbidding wastelands beyond. A fool's crusade, he'd called it. Among the memories of Caim's childhood, that one sparkled like a polished jewel.

He looked down at the open pages of Vassili's journal in his hand, but put it away after reading the same paragraph three times. He couldn't concentrate. His thoughts kept running to last night and the fight at the clearing, the warrior in black armor. *Keegan called him the Beast. What did that mean?*

He didn't know, and he had no clue what to do next. At least Keegan hadn't tried to stick a knife in him while he slept. That had to count for something. But he and his sister would probably be better off without him. *Right up until they run into another band of wildmen.*

Leather soles scraped across the ground behind him as Keegan emerged from the cave. Tugging on the cuffs of his coat sleeves, the youth looked scruffier than last night. Caim ran a hand across his whiskered chin and thought the same could probably be said about him. He put away the journal.

'I need to get to Morrowglen. I'll pay whatever you think is fair.'

Keegan came up beside him and kicked a stone down the loose talus. 'I think Ramon still has your money.'

Caim didn't mention the stash of coins tucked in a false pocket the woodsmen hadn't found.

'Anyway,' the youth said. 'We can take you as far as Liovard. After that, you're on your own.'

It was as good a deal as Caim expected to get. 'Fair enough.'

'I figure the duke's men have given up by now, but we'll head north for a few miles anyway before we angle east. Just to be sure.'

Keegan turned back to the cave. 'Come on, Li! We're freezing our asses off!'

She came out and gave Caim a quick look before following her brother down the narrow shelf. Caim picked up his bundles and went after them. Liana walked with an easy stride. Her face looked freshly scrubbed, and her hair was tied up in a handkerchief.

Caim patted the stitched sleeve of his jacket. His arm was still a little sore, but not as bad as last night. 'Thank you. Good as new.'

'You get into a lot of fights.'

It wasn't a question, so he didn't answer. She looked back, and her gaze went to his cheek.

'What did that? It doesn't look like another bear bite.'

Caim touched his cheek and remembered the scar, and the black knife that had caused it. 'A fight. Long time ago.'

'I hope you won.'

'I'm still breathing.'

'So, you have trouble with women.' She smiled at him. 'And a lot of scars. Are they related?'

'Some of them.'

'What did you do back in the south? Let me guess. You weren't a shoemaker.'

'No,' he answered. 'I . . . cleaned up messes.'

She laughed out loud. 'What? You were a housemaid?'

Keegan looked back over his shoulder. 'He's a hired sword, Liana. He kills people for money.'

She looked at Caim, all humor gone from her face. Caim waited. This had happened so many times before it was almost second nature to him. He met someone who seemed to enjoy his company. Then they found out what he did for a living, and their attitude changed. Josey had been one of the few to accept him for what he was, warts and all, and it hadn't been easy with her, either.

Liana hurried to catch up to her brother. Caim filled his lungs with cool forest air and let it out. It didn't matter what they thought of him. Soon he would be done with them, and they could go back to their lives.

Keegan led them down into a saddle between the hills. Though steep in places, the descent wasn't difficult. Keegan and Liana exchanged occasional whispers, but Caim didn't pay much attention until their tones began to rise. Before long, their conversation erupted into a hushed quarrel. He couldn't make out what they were saying except for his name, Liovard, and something about a castle. After a time, the siblings let off their arguing and focused on the hike. The forest thinned as they traveled north, and they made good time down through the narrow valley. They reached its lowest point just after midday and stopped in the shade between two tall pine trees to eat. Lunch consisted of whatever they could pool from their

122

collective stashes, which wasn't much. Caim provided a pair of hardtack rolls and his last strip of jerky. Liana collected water and a double handful of wild strawberries. Keegan lay on his back, looking up at the sky.

When he had swallowed his last bite, Caim asked, 'How far is Liovard?'

Keegan didn't look at him.

Liana glanced between them. 'Half a day's walk. Once we get clear of the woods, you should be able to see its walls.'

When Caim stood up there was barely a hitch in his step. He flexed his injured forearm and felt a twinge. It still hurt, worse than before. When they reached the city, he would look for a cut-man.

Liana also got to her feet, but Keegan was slow to move. Yet once he was up the young man set a brisk pace, this time angling to the northeast. As Keegan marched out ahead, Caim found himself walking beside Liana again.

'I'm sorry about back there,' she said. 'I didn't mean to pry into your life. It's none of my affair what you do. You saved my brother and me. He might be too thick-headed to thank you, but I'm not.'

'It's all right.' A thought occurred to him. 'Are there settlements out this far?'

'A few timber camps. Not much else.'

'No villages?'

A shadow crossed her face as she dipped her chin toward her chest. 'Not anymore. There's been a lot of fighting around these parts. Pa says it's spread all across the country. Most people have left, or were driven away. That's why Keegan joined with—'

'Shut up, Li,' Keegan said from ahead of them.

Liana bent closer to Caim. 'He doesn't like anyone talking about it, but most of the menfolk have gone. Those who don't join the duke's army usually find themselves on the end of a rope sooner or later.'

Caim recalled the fight at the clearing. He'd assumed the soldiers were after him, but if they had come for the woodsmen . . . then he could just walk away. There was nothing holding him here. Except for the Beast.

'Did I hear something about a castle?' Caim asked. 'Is that where Ramon's men hole up?'

Liana started to nod until Keegan stopped and spun around.

'Gods be damned, Li! We don't even know anything about him. He could be—'

'A spy,' Caim finished for him. 'I know, but suppose I'm not. Suppose I'm exactly what I told your father, a traveler trying to find his home.'

'Doesn't matter. You're a stranger. We don't know you and we don't trust you.'

Keegan glared at his sister before resuming the march. She jogged to catch up to him. Watching them, Caim's estimation of Keegan rose. The boy was young and largely ignorant of the world outside these parts, but he was tougher than he looked. If he ever got the chance to grow up, he might make a name for himself, but Caim didn't think the chances of that were very good.

Of course, the same could have been said about him once.

The sentries outside the prison house snapped to attention as Sybelle stepped out of the shadow gate. The sky was darkening into twilight as the solar disk slid beneath the horizon. This was her favorite time of the day, when the light gave way to the inevitable dark.

Sinking deeper into the folds of her snow leopard coat, she swept past the guards and through the iron gates of the prison. It was a massive structure that resembled nothing so much as a colossal stone block studded with small windows. The chamber inside the gates resembled a fortress barbican more than a foyer. This seemed to be the standard form in old Nimean construction. Whatever it lacked in aesthetic appeal, she admired its efficiency. A long corridor with rows of doors extended beyond the entrance. One of the nearest doors opened as she entered, and a uniformed man with slick, black hair exited. He rushed forward to greet her.

'Lady Sybelle, it is my personal honor to receive you. I am Chief Warden Lormew.'

His tone was unctuous to the point of being disgusting, but there was something about the man that intrigued her. Had she the time, she might have been tempted to take him back to whatever little cell he called home in this foul-smelling pit. She offered her left hand, which he took and kissed.

'We did not expect you until tomorrow,' he continued, 'but I have put everything aside to assist you myself.'

'Take me to the prisoner.'

With a nod, the chief warden led her down the corridor. A set of large metal keys jangled on his belt. Misery exuded from the cells they passed and washed over her like a shower of warm oil. She reveled in it. She had been in an evil mood for the past few days. Last night, after enduring one of her tirades, Erric had left their bed to find other sport. She knew the reason her emotions were running beyond her control; Soloroth hadn't returned, or even bothered to contact her. Had he found the scion yet? The frustration of not knowing gnawed at her insides.

The warden ushered her up a flight of stairs at the end of the corridor. They passed other levels where groans and cries murmured from behind closed doors. The warden stopped on the landing at the sixth and highest floor of the prison, where he opened a door and held it open for her. Sybelle stepped into a corridor lined with cells. Guards armed with bronze-capped truncheons walked up and down the hallway. One noticed their arrival and hurried over.

'The prisoner has been moved to the interrogation chamber as you ordered, sir.'

The chief warden turned to her with his oily smile in place. 'This way, my lady.'

For a moment, she thought he was going to offer his arm to her, and she wondered for a moment whether she would have taken it or ripped the flesh from his bones at the temerity.

However, the chief warden kept his hands to himself and trotted down the corridor like an eager puppy. Perhaps he was looking forward to this encounter as much as she.

The interrogation chamber was located behind a heavy door at the end of the hall. Iron braziers full of burning coals sat in each corner, making the small room too bright for her tastes. Sybelle made a gesture and their radiance dimmed. Two burly guards stood by the back wall, upon which hung an assortment of metal instruments: whips, hammers, pinchers, hooks, thin iron rods, and such. The sight of them made her tremble.

Warden Lormew extended his hand. 'Your prisoner.'

A man hung from thick eyebolts in the ceiling. Stripped to the waist and hooded, he was suspended by his wrists so that his powerful arms were twisted up behind his back. His shoulders were swollen and distended from all his weight hanging on them. Burns and lacerations crisscrossed his torso. Sybelle smiled at the sight. The rush was more potent than sex.

She walked up to the captive and ran a hand along his ribs, and felt the slick of sweat and blood. His chest expanded as he took in a deep breath, and then released it in a long, slow exhalation. It was measured and controlled, not like a man condemned, but one who had to know what awaited him.

'Leave me,' she commanded.

Warden Lormew cleared his throat. 'Lady, for your protection we should—'

'Now.'

At a look from their boss, the guards clomped out of the room. Lormew went with them. Sybelle waited for a time – fifty heartbeats or more – before she plucked the sack from his head. While the captive blinked, she studied his features. He had been beaten recently, by the bruises puffing his eye sockets. His lips, full for a man, were split in several places. A line of dry blood ran down his neck from his left ear. Still, beyond these scrapes and cuts, he appeared as strong as the night he was seized. A bull of a man. Then he looked at her, and she glimpsed the intelligence behind his sky-blue eyes.

126

'I am Sybelle. I hope the warden and his men haven't been too harsh with you.'

When he gave no answer, she reached out and caught his chin. Prickly stubble rasped against her palm. Muscles and sinew bunched under her touch as he tightened his jaw. She ran her fingers down his neck to his shoulder. The flesh was tight and hot under her touch. Her fingertips continued down to the blue circles tattooed over his heart.

'But I must know where your compatriots hide,' she said. 'Tell me and I will grant you a swift death.'

It was a lie, of course. She intended to wring every last delightful ounce of pain from his body before she allowed him to expire. The captive glared straight ahead as if she wasn't speaking. Sybelle frowned. She could stomach many things, but to be disregarded infuriated her. The circles of ink on his chest mocked her. With a thought, she channeled the energy of the shadows until the tips of her fingers glowed red-hot. Without warning, she pressed them into his flesh. Streamers of smoke rose with the intoxicating scent of burning skin. The captive growled and shuddered as she dragged her fingernails back and forth over his chest, and down across the nipple. The insufferable tattoo was obliterated under a mass of oozing flesh. When she pulled her hand away, he collapsed as far as his bonds permitted. She listened for a moan, or even a sigh, to show that she'd gotten his attention, but there was nothing.

She cupped his chin with her other hand. 'You know what I am, do you not?'

His eyes drilled holes in her face.

'Yes, I see you do, Caedman Du'Ormik. I do not care about you or the reasons you fight. I only want to know where to find the rest of your kind. Tell me what I want to know and this—'

She dragged her fingernails across his face. The straps holding him aloft quivered as he tried to break free, but they held.

'—will end,' she finished.

The prisoner growled, bloody spittle drooling from his sliced lips, but he did not speak, not even when she slapped him, over and over, making his blood fly with every blow. When she stopped, her chest rose and fell in short gasps; her hand stung, and delicious beads of anguish rolled off the prisoner.

Sybelle licked her fingers as she considered him. She could employ the tools arrayed on the walls, but it would be a waste of time. The man had resigned himself to death. In his eyes he was making a sacrifice for the greater good, to secure the safety of his comrades. The idea was foreign to her way of thinking, but she understood how it worked. If time were not an issue, she would enjoy breaking him for the sheer sport of it, but her Master's words were never far from her mind. To fail was to die, and she intended to live long past the conquest of this land.

Sybelle leaned forward and grasped him by both sides of the head. He tried to pull away, but she had opened herself fully to the shadows. Their strength flowed through her hands to hold him as if he were a babe. She forced his face upward so she could stare into his eyes. His fury rolled over her in tiny palpitations. Despite herself, she laughed. They were beyond games. She had tried the gentle way. Now she would take what she needed.

Ribbons of darkness uncoiled from her lips and vanished into his mouth. He tried to jerk away, but she held him steady as the sorcery did its work. It took only a moment. Then he slumped in his bonds. His chest rose and fell in a regular rhythm as if he were sleeping. Sybelle peeled back his drooping eyelids. The pupils had widened to twice their normal size.

Sybelle stepped back. The captive's gaze followed her. He was hers now. The power of the shadow had infused him, taking by force what he would not volunteer.

'Now,' she said. 'Tell me everything.'

SHADOW'S LURE

Chapter
FOURTEEN

Keegan heaved his upper body over the side rail as the wagon crossed the bridge. As globs of spittle fell down into the dark waters of the Ascander River below, he was reminded how much he hated riding in the back.

The three of them – him, Liana, and the foreigner – had come out of the woods near Shireman's Way. By a stroke of good fortune, a farmer hauling winter wheat had been driving along the lane just in time to give them a ride. As much as he despised it, riding was faster than walking, and less suspicious. He worried about how they were going to get into the city. The main gates closed at daybreak; after that, those who wanted in or out had to pass through a smaller postern gate where there was more scrutiny.

With a groan, Keegan sat back and tried to make himself comfortable. On the other side of the wagon bed, Caim reclined against the backboard, legs pushed out in front of him among the bushels, as still as the statues on Liberty Way. *He never gets sick or tired. He must be a warlock, the way he took down Ramon, and then that Northman. But what does he want?*

Keegan couldn't get what he'd seen at the roadhouse, and again in the woods, out of his mind. It wasn't natural, the way the darkness responded to this stranger. *Like it knows its own kind.*

Caim reached under his cloak to rub the small of his back. *So he's human after all.* Keegan started to smile, but then Caim looked over. One look from those stone-dead eyes set his stomach to churning again. He would be glad to be rid of this man. He needed to find his friends, those who survived. He could still hear the shouts and screams of the fighting, reminding him of the slaughter at Aldercairn. Once again, he had run and lived while others died. The shame of it burned in his chest.

The wagon slowed as the farmer – Henrick? Heddick? – clucked his tongue and shook the reins. Keegan craned his neck around. The high gray walls of the city blocked out the horizon. A muffled croak issued from the front seat. Keegan looked up to see Liana with both hands clasped over her mouth, her eyes wide. He followed her gaze to a line of poles erected on the side of the road. A cold lump formed in his stomach as he saw the charred remains chained to the stakes and smelled the stench of burned meat. He held a sleeve over his nose and tried to make out their features as the wagon passed the gruesome display, but the corpses were little more than blackened cinders without faces or hair. Bloated crows cackled as they feasted on roasted flesh.

'What was their crime?' Caim asked.

The farmer spat over the buckboard. 'No need for a crime to find yourself shackled to a stake around here, son. Some days, just breathing seems like enough reason.'

Keegan nodded, glad for an excuse to look away. 'He's right. People are put to death all the time in Liovard, for any excuse. The duke doesn't care as long as his coffers are full. But they were probably priests, all the same.'

'The duke has a problem with the Church?'

'Why? Are you one of those sun-worshippers come to civilize us ignorant barbarians?'

Liana shushed him. Keegan opened his mouth to argue, but shut it again. He wasn't in the mood. He just wanted to get to their uncle's place. Caim had gone back to staring at nothing. A moment later, he grunted. Keegan looked over, but he didn't elaborate. *A strange man.*

The wagon rolled to the back of a short queue. Ahead, soldiers searched a hay wain, even going so far as to plunge their spears into the bales of straw. Keegan swallowed and looked to Caim. Of course, he didn't look concerned.

When their turn came, the soldiers made everyone get out of the wagon. The trooper in charge, a fat corporal with brown stains down the front of his uniform, ordered them all to lift their hands as he struggled to get out of his flimsy seat, which shook under his bulk like it wanted to collapse at any moment. Keegan braced himself to run as the fear of discovery surged through his limbs. Caim and Liana, however, raised their arms without hesitation. While some of the soldiers patted them down, others pawed through the farmer's produce, all under the corporal's suspicious gaze as he stood scratching his arse during the proceedings. A soldier walked over to Keegan.

'Lift your arms!'

Keegan glanced around. He didn't see any archers on the wall, and he was confident he could outrun any of these overfed bastards in their heavy armor, but people inside were expecting him. Swallowing his ire, he raised his hands over his head.

The soldier patted his sides, his back, around his belt, and down his legs. The knife in his left boot was found and held up.

The corporal eyed the weapon. 'What's that for?'

'For eating, your lordship.'

The corporal scowled at him, hard enough to make Keegan consider a mad dash for safety. Then the fat man spat into the mud at his feet.

'Mind your tongue, boy. Or you'll be missing it.'

Keegan nodded and tried to look scared, which wasn't much of a stretch. Caim, Liana, and the farmer had all been searched and cleared. At a nod from the sentries, they climbed back into the wagon. The corporal squinted at Keegan, and then let him join them. As they rolled past, the soldier who had confiscated Keegan's knife flipped it back to him.

'It worked!' Liana whispered when they were through the gate.

Keegan slipped the knife back into his boot. 'Of course. They're as dumb as rocks.'

'Is that why you almost pissed your britches?' Caim asked. Then Keegan saw the faint hint of a smile tugging at the corners of his mouth.

'Go sod yourself!'

The wagon coasted to a halt under a huge stone arch straddling the road. Keegan didn't like looking at the edifice, erected by the Nimeans to commemorate some big battle up north back in his father's time. It made him feel small, which was something he wrestled with on a daily basis anyway. Everyone climbed out of the wagon. Caim shook hands with the farmer, and coins passed hands. Keegan thought he saw the shine of silver, and hoped he was mistaken. One silver plate was more than the man probably earned in a month. It would make him suspicious, but Caim didn't appear concerned as he knelt down beside the wagon and retrieved several items, including their weapons and the mysterious bundles he carried. The soldiers hadn't come close to finding the cache hidden under the wagon bed. Keegan wondered what Caim would have done if the weapons had been found. *Probably something very unpleasant.*

Keegan accepted his sword back, thrust it under his cloak, and took Liana by the elbow. 'Good fortune to you,' he said with a nod.

Caim returned the gesture as he slipped the long bundles and bag over his shoulder. He looked just like a normal traveler, except for the nasty scabs down the side of his face. And his eyes.

'Wait.' Liana yanked her arm free. 'We can't just abandon him here in the street, Keegan.'

'We have someplace to be, Li. And so does Caim.'

'Where will he stay? He doesn't know anyone.'

'I'll find someplace to bunk down,' Caim said.

'No,' she said. 'You can come with us. I'm sure our uncle

132

would let you stay for a couple days, at least until you get on your feet. And you shouldn't be going off on any expeditions until you've had proper time to heal.'

'Li!'

Keegan looked around. Passersby paid them little mind, but the duke's spies were scattered throughout Liovard like fleas on a dog. His sister was going to land him in trouble with her big mouth. He thought of the blackened bodies on the stakes.

By a stroke of luck, Caim shook his head. 'I need to be going. You two be careful.'

Keegan grunted. They should be careful? He knew this city better than any foreigner would. Warlock or not, Caim was the one who needed eyes in the back of his head.

Liana reached out to put a hand on Caim's arm. 'If you change your mind, the shop is in the south ward. Turnstile Lane. Look for a sign with a hammer and two nails.'

Caim nodded. 'Farewell.'

Keegan started walking. It was too damned cold to stand around. If his sister didn't want to follow, that was her problem. *Would serve her right to get lost out here.*

He reached the corner to turn toward the south ward and looked back. Liana was still talking to Caim. Then, as he watched, the foreign killer shook his head. Liana turned and walked away.

When she caught up to him, Keegan asked, 'What was that about?'

She didn't meet his gaze. 'Nothing. I'm cold. Let's go.'

Shrugging his cloak higher around his neck, Keegan headed toward their uncle's store. Whatever was going on with Liana was her own fault. What was she thinking, following after him in the woods, and now practically begging Caim to come with them? The girl had gone crazy. And he was stuck with her, at least until he could figure a way to get her back home.

Keegan sighed as he tromped through the streets. His responsibilities never seemed to end. But it was good to be back in Liovard again. Although he'd been raised out in the sticks, he loved the feel of the city. Its busy streets, the tall buildings with their roofs sheathed in black wooden slats instead of rotting thatch, the energy of the people as they passed by. When they got rid of the duke and his cronies, he wanted to live here. He could run an ale hall, or a stable. He was good with animals.

He glanced back at Liana, who trudged a few steps behind him, lost in her thoughts. As usual. She never had any dreams, at least none she cared to share with him. She was the most boring person he'd ever known, except maybe his father. Like two bumps on the same log.

As he stepped around a stinking brown puddle, Keegan's gaze was drawn to the east side of town where the prison house was located. He couldn't see it from here, down by the riverbank, but he wondered how Caedman was doing, or even if he was still alive. His shame returned. He couldn't change the past, but maybe he could make up for it.

Keegan looked around for a food vendor to take his mind off his guilt and spotted a group of men pushing through the street ahead. They wore coats of iron scales and carried enough weapons to start a war. Freeswords. Foreigners by their look, Hveklanders or Warmonds. It didn't matter which; they were both bad news.

'Come on, Li.'

He turned down a side street to avoid the armored men.

'I'm coming,' she replied.

Caim watched Liana walk away. She was only trying to help, but he needed to cut his ties with them. And Keegan seemed to know where he was going.

Caim looked down the street in the opposite direction. He needed a physician, and then someplace he could warm up and get a decent meal. As he started walking he was glad for the dwindling sunlight; it would make moving around easier. He passed a group of young men in heavy wool coats and caps – maybe laborers heading to their favorite watering hole – and decided to follow them.

The city looked different than he remembered; it had loomed so large and forbidding in his memories, and the reality was disappointing. Othir could have swallowed Liovard whole and still had room for a couple more courses. The architecture was an odd mixture of northern and southern styles. The city was laid out like two-thirds of a wheel, with a bare hillock bordered by the river filling the missing space. Atop the tor stood the citadel, a stone fortress dwarfing everything around it. He recalled seeing it when he was a boy. Back then, its concentric walls and square towers had seemed so remote, like the moon or a different world, impossible to reach. Lesser buildings in red and gray stone tumbled down the hillside and surrounding land, intermingled with wooden homes and shops. All in all, the city gave an impression of past glories imposed by distant Nimean emperors. Combined with the antipathy he had received from Keegan's people, it gave him something to think about.

Many of the stalls and shops he passed were already closed or in the process of shutting for the night. Few windows showed any light, and those that did were covered by heavy shutters. Even the noises of the city were muted. An odd stall was still open. Three venerable women in quilted shawls with handkerchiefs over their heads sat under a blue awning, chanting to the beat of small metal drums. Caim remembered something about the ritual from the months he'd spent living on these streets. The chanting was supposed to fight off evil or give good luck. As Caim stood watching, a man in a simple undyed robe ducked under the awning and gave the women a copper penny. Then he sat while they played and chanted for him. Caim moved on.

As he walked, the smells of the city filled his lungs. He'd missed them and the feeling of firm stones under his feet, the high walls around him. He would enjoy sleeping on a bed again instead of the ground, but sleep was the last thing on his mind. This city had an undercurrent; he felt it the moment they passed through the gates. It was a sensation he knew from his days in the south, the feeling of terror. It nipped at the back of his mind.

Caim crossed a broad thoroughfare, the bumpy cobbles underfoot changing to broad blocks with worn channels from the passage of countless wheels, and stopped at an intersection of two streets. On the opposite corner stood a pile of broken masonry covered by a blanket of unsullied snow. The ends of burned timbers and long pieces of twisted iron protruded from the wreckage. Caim glanced down the street, but this was the only building he could see that had been demolished and left in its ruined state. He crossed the street for a closer look. Pieces of splintered wood hung from the doorway's broken hinges. Stone shards covered the ground. He kicked one over with his toe and discovered it wasn't stone, but a piece of dusty, yellow-stained glass. He took another look at the building as a whole, trying to fill in the missing details with his imagination. It had been a church.

Caim studied the structure as he walked past. He had become so accustomed to churches and holy grounds being sacrosanct that seeing one in ruins was disconcerting, like coming across an open grave in the middle of the street. He didn't see any signs for barbers or medicine shops, but spotted the bright lights of a tavern. Deciding a good night's sleep would have to do for now, he pushed open the front door. Instead of a taproom, the entire ground floor of the building was open, filled with long tables and benches. Serving boys and women came up from a staircase in the back carrying double handfuls of tankards and trenchers of food. The smells made Caim's mouth water.

The crowd was a rowdy mix of hard-drinking lower-class types, as well as a smattering of soldiers. No, not soldiers. Mercenaries. Caim could tell by their haphazard appearance and the variety of dialects shouted across tables.

When no one came over to see to his needs, he stopped one of the scullions. With a jerk of her sharp chin, she indicated he should find his own seat.

'Do you rent rooms for the night?' he asked, trying not to

shout, but having trouble hearing himself over the din of the patrons.

'I'll send the master of the house over to see you,' she said, and hurried away.

Caim waited for a few minutes. He was about to find a seat when a young man ambled over. He was dressed rather sharply, with a leather vest and fine trousers tucked into knee-high boots. Caim would have taken him for just another patron until he introduced himself as the proprietor.

'How can I help you, sir?'

'Is it always this loud in here?' Caim was thinking about trying to sleep with this racket going on under his room.

The young owner gave him an appraising look. 'It's Holbermass Eve, sir.'

Already? Holbermass was fourteen days before Yuletide. Caim counted the days in his head and found he had missed a few. The year was almost over.

'I'll take a room and a bath,' Caim said. 'Followed by a hot meal.'

The owner named a price. Caim didn't bother haggling, but just paid it, whereupon he was passed off to another serving girl, who led him to the back where another staircase climbed to the second floor.

A candlemark later, he returned to the ground floor freshly bathed, shaven, changed, and feeling almost human. If anything, the tavern was fuller than when he went upstairs, so he had to look around to find an open seat against a wall with a good view of the entire room. He wound up taking the end spot at a table full of young people, men and women no older than Josey, if that, drinking and laughing. He leaned back as he sat down, trying to keep his face out of the light as much as possible. The shadows tickled at the edges of his perception, but he kept them at bay. The last thing he wanted was to draw attention.

A girl brought his dinner, mutton on the bone, a loaf of brown bread large enough to choke a mule, and a mug of what smelled like the same barley beer he had gotten at the roadhouse. He tossed her a couple pennies as he tore into the food. The fare wasn't fancy, but it tasted like heaven after so long on the road. He even stomached the beer.

His fingers were stiff as he ate, and the forearm began to itch. He had changed the dressing after his bath, but the wound was still oozing. He needed to find a chirurgeon to take a look at it. *Tomorrow.*

He had almost finished the platter when a table near the middle of the room fell over on its side. Benches scraped as men jumped to their feet. Steel flashed and someone yelled, and everyone backed away as two men grappled amid puddles of spilled beer. One wore a vest of iron rings, the other a coat of boiled leather. Holes appeared in their armor and leaked blood as they punched at each other with short daggers. All the while, their comrades shouted and laughed at the spectacle.

Caim waited to see what would happen. While the others at his table stood up on their seats for a better look, most of the room cleared out. The owner stood well away from the brawl, frowning as his profits ran out the door. Caim debated staying put, but after another minute of watching the mercs brutalize each other, he got up and went to his room. He gathered his things, few as they were, and pulled the black sword from its wrapping. The weapon felt right in his hands, like a part of him. He bared several inches of the night-black blade and ran his fingers across the pommel, down the hilt to the cross-guard. *It's only a sword. Nothing more.* Yet the quiet hum in his fingertips when he touched the metal told him otherwise. He shoved the weapon back into its housing. Adjusting the straps on the scabbard, Caim slung it across his back before he picked up the other bundle and left.

The outside chill was refreshing after the heat of the tavern. The light was fading. The moon was a golden fingernail paring over the city skyline. A heavy crash resounded from inside, and Caim started walking. He had paid for the room, but he didn't feel like sleeping someplace that might get raided by the authorities or burned down around his ears by a bunch of angry drunks. He would find a cheap flophouse and in the morning seek out a guide. Or not. Either way, he was leaving the city tomorrow.

Slush splashed under his heels as he crossed another avenue – it must have been the South Road leading out of the city – and entered another neighborhood. When he left the tavern Caim hadn't much of an idea where he was heading, but with every step he found himself going deeper into the sorrier sections of the city. Though less ornamented, the buildings in this district were taller, some reaching as high as six stories, their upper floors leaning out over the street to shut out the sky. Down at the street level, the darkness was nigh absolute. It reminded him of Low Town in Othir, except everything here was built of wood and wattle, even the shanties. And, of course, there were no people on the streets. Even in the darkest hours, there were always a few people out and about in the Gutters: bully boys, smash-and-grabbers, sailors from the docks. Here, the quiet was eerie, like he was the only soul alive in the entire city. He reached back to loosen his knives in their sheaths and almost called for the shadows before he stopped himself. He was getting too comfortable with them.

He passed a cobbler's shop, quite unremarkable with small frosted windows and a black wooden placard over the door in the shape of a boot, but it perfectly matched an image he'd had stuck in his head for a long time without realizing it. Past the shop, Caim turned left at the next intersection on instinct. The street that opened before him could have been torn from his memory. Rows of narrow tenement houses lined each side, jammed together like toy soldiers in tight formation. Each house had a front stoop or a patio on the street. In his mind's eye this neighborhood was clean and prosperous, but the image before him was quite different. Mounds of garbage piled between the homes. Low shadows slipped between the heaps, dogs rooting through the refuse. Feeble lights in a few of the windows over the street showed that people still lived here despite the conditions.

Caim strode down the middle of the street. Some of the doorways were occupied by blanket-covered lumps. A tiny fire burned in one brick archway beside a drowsing white-haired man with a dirty beard. Caim stopped outside a building with a large blue door, its round bronze knocker green with verdigris. Four windows faced the street. The shutters had all fallen off except for one stubborn panel on an upper window. No light showed through the grimy panes. The place looked dead, like no one had lived here for years.

Caim kicked aside a lump of snow-covered trash and ascended the uneven steps. The front door swung inward with a low whine. Darkness pooled inside the doorway. Odors of wood rot and mildew pulled him inside. He stood on the threshold as his eyes adjusted. A hallway extended all the way back through the tenement. Doors branched off to either side, and a rickety staircase led upward to more darkness. Smears of charcoal marred the cracked plaster walls and ceiling.

Caim peered through the doorways as he passed down the hallway. The first door was closed. Inside the next was a sparse room, containing only a loveseat with ripped cushions and a rocking chair in a corner. Broken bottles and scraps of dingy blankets littered the floor. The stench of excrement was choking. Caim went to the stairs.

The steps creaked underfoot, loud to his ears. He climbed them with caution, listening for sounds of occupation, but the place was deadly quiet. At the top, a faint gleam of moonlight filtered through the dirty windows at either end of the hallway, illuminating dark streaks and piles of trash on the floor, and the shadowed doors of three apartments.

Caim stepped to the middle door. Long scratches gouged the varnished wood. The bronze handle was loose and unlocked. Standing out of the way, he nudged it open. Trash and broken furniture covered the floor of the front room. Slivers of yellow light showed a narrow hallway on the other side and outlined a door at the far end. Caim slipped into the corridor. So much had changed over the years, but he still remembered how the place used to look. The lime-green walls, now besmirched with marks and holes, had been clean ivory white. There had been a long blue runner down this hallway and a quilted blanket hung over the now-bare left-hand wall.

Before he reached the door, it swung open, spilling light into the hallway. Caim tensed to see a figure standing in the doorway. It was short and heavyset like a toad. The figure took a step. Something tapped on the hardwood floor, and a creaky voice screeched.

'Out!'

By the sound, the voice belonged to a woman, and an old one at that. Caim stood his ground. Warm air wafted from the room beyond, carrying with it a strange blend of sweat, crabapple, and sour wine. He stood up straight and kept his knives out of sight.

'I won't hurt—'

'Get out!'

Caim winced as her voice carried through the apartment. If there was anyone else in this building, they would have heard her. He didn't need any unwanted attention. He started to back away down the hall. Then she stepped after him and pointed a long object at him like an impossibly long finger. A cane.

'Challen? What are you doing here? Your mother will be—' She sounded confused, but then the shrillness returned. 'You broke my teacup!'

Caim remained where he was.

'Come on!' she snapped before he could say anything. 'You're letting in the cold.'

Caim followed at a respectful distance as she turned and shuffled back inside. He stepped into a cramped kitchen. A rickety table sat against the near wall. Three dirty glass jars sat on a shelf above the table; two were empty, the third was two-thirds full of dead roaches. On the other side of the room were a cast-iron stove and a battered coldbox. The light came from the stove's feeble flame. A stack of papers, leaflets by the look of them, sat on the floor beside the fire pan.

The old woman jabbed her cane at the table's sole chair. 'Sit.'

141

While he obeyed, she went over to the stove and fidgeted with a dinged teapot. She wore a shabby housecoat that didn't look thick enough to keep a dog warm in this weather, and a pair of what he took to be woolen boots at first; but then he realized with a closer look that she had old shirts wrapped around her feet.

Caim took off his gloves as the old woman poured two cups and brought one over to the table.

'Mind you don't break this one,' she said.

Caim nodded and sniffed the tea. It smelled awful. He set it aside when she turned around. Traces of memories tugged at the back of his mind. Everything was recognizable, and yet not quite right. The stove, for instance, had been in the corner once where the coldbox now stood. The walls were cracked pea-green plaster, but splotches of a darker color peeked from under the peeling strips of paints. Brown? Yes, he saw it clearly now. This had been their apartment, his and Kas's, when they lived in the city.

While Caim looked around, the old woman perched on a wooden stool. She looked like a bird hunched over her cup, shoulders bowed and the sleeves of her coat drooping from her spindly arms.

'Everyone says old Ida is losing her mind,' she said. 'But I still remember you and your father. What was his name?'

'I don't think I am who you think I am.'

'Such a handsome man he was. A bit scary at first, but he had the heart of a kitten. Used to come over some nights when you were sleeping. We'd sit right here and talk until dawn. Very nice man.'

'A lot has changed around here. The city feels . . .'

Caim wasn't sure how to finish that statement. In this neighborhood, which had once been a flourishing community full of life and well-being, the dogs outnumbered the people, and probably ate better. It was as if the entire city was . . .

'Dead,' she said.

Caim sat back in the chair. Yes, that was what he'd felt, like he'd been walking through a graveyard, every building a charnel house holding naught but the dead and their care-takers.

'What's happened?'

'Happened?' Her thin shoulders rose and fell. 'They've all left, or gone down to Arugul's dark realm since *she* came. All the good ones dead. And those that stayed behind have been sucking this town dry like a pack of ticks on a dead hound. The duke don't see it. My husband gone. My sons gone, too. And this' – she shook her cup at the walls and ceiling – 'this is where I spend my last days.'

A talon of cold slipped between Caim's ribs to prick at his heart. 'Are you talking about the duke's witch? What do you know about her?'

The old woman gave a sharp laugh. Her eyes, which had looked glassy a moment before, stared at him intently. 'You shouldn't have come back, child. Dark's been waiting for you.' Then she coughed into her balled-up hands.

'What did you say?'

The old woman's coughing fit lasted several moments as Caim tried to get her attention with no results. Finally she waved him away.

'Ida doesn't go out at night anymore. It's not safe for an old woman on these streets. The shadows.' She wheezed into her cup. 'They're always watching.'

The hairs at the nape of Caim's neck stood up. He knew what she meant. He could feel them watching him, too. This city was infested with them. The scabbard on his back quivered. Or maybe it was his imagination.

The old woman swayed on her seat, mumbling to herself. Caim set a stack of silver coins on the table as he got up and left the apartment. He'd seen enough. There was nothing here but ghosts and memories, a few good, but more than enough bad ones to drive him away. He missed Kas. And Kit and Josey. Hell, he even missed Hubert.

Caim dropped down the stairs two at a time, heedless of the creaking protests of the boards and the twinge in his thigh. He understood this city now. There were no great mysteries to be solved; just living, breathing, dying people, and he knew where he fit in among them. He wouldn't wait for morning to leave. If he couldn't find a guide, he would make his own way. But first he had to do something.

Shadows scattered as he emerged from the tenement's front door.

Kit huddled behind a pillar of black-veined stone in a field of weathered stalagmites. She couldn't stop shivering as the wind lashed her bare skin. She had been so long out of the flesh that every stimulus down to the most minute sensation set her off, and nothing in this never-realm could be considered gentle.

The presence returned, gliding past her in the mists. She had first noticed it a few candlemarks ago. Or was it a few days? There was no day or night here, only endless nothing. The first time she'd thought it was Caim's shadow pet, come back to annoy her again, but as she stopped and waited for it to appear, the presence took on a predatory quality. The disturbed miasma of clouds made her nervous; she'd built up the terror in her mind until she had no choice. She fled.

She'd escaped the feeling that time, but it had returned. Ducking her head, Kit ran until she found someplace to hide. That's when she came upon this strange formation of rocks. She didn't know why they were here, but she was grateful for them.

Caim, please give me a sign. Show me how to get back to you.

There was no answer, nothing but the gray haze and the vast, approaching presence. The prickliness was stronger now, growing with every step she took, but she had no idea how far away it might be. And what would she find when she got there? A trap set up to ensnare Fae-folk caught in the Barrier? But what other choice did she have?

The mists parted, and Kit ducked as a long shape like the fluke of an enormous fish sliced through the murk over her head. She couldn't control the tremors racing through her body as the presence crashed over her. It was gone a moment later, but the next time it might not be content to pass by. She pressed her chest against the hard stone.

A rumbling snarl cut through the howling winds. Kit sat up as a long, low shape emerged from the storm. She threw her arms around its broad neck and hugged it tight. The shadow beast indulged her for a pair of heartbeats before leaning away.

'I'm so glad to see you!' Kit wiped away the tears in her eyes. 'Don't go disappearing on me again. You hear?'

The creature blinked, and then it looked in the direction the monster had gone.

'I don't know what to do. I'm afraid.' Kit looked over her shoulder toward the source of the tingling. 'I think there's someplace I need to go. It might be a way out, but I don't know. What do you think?'

The shadow pet blinked at her. Kit looked into the mists. She had to make a decision before it was too late. *You can do this. Caim wouldn't let some overgrown fish stop him.* She glanced back to the shadow dog-thing. When she nodded, it nodded back. *Okay. That's my cue.*

She took a step toward the tingling, and the presence returned, approaching fast from behind. Kit froze beside the stone pillar as the mists billowed around her. The shadow beast yowled. Kit blinked. It almost sounded like the thing was trying to tell her something . . .

With another yowl aimed at her, Caim's pet dashed in the other direction, straight at the impending monstrosity. Kit tried to call out, but the shadow beast disappeared into the gloom before she got the chance. A titanic bellow shook the ground. Kit slapped her hands to her ears and fell back against the pillar, but the presence lessened. It was leading the monster away! *Go, Kit. Now's your chance.*

With a sob, she pushed off from the rock projection and ran into the mists, following the sensation.

SHADOW'S LURE

Chapter
FIFTEEN

The carriage lurched as one of its wheels struck a pothole in the road. Josey held onto her seat to keep from pitching into the laps of her companions. Hubert grimaced and shifted about for a more comfortable position.

'This may be a bad idea, my lady,' he told her for the tenth time since they'd left the palace.

Hubert sounded like he had caught a cold. The lantern lighting the carriage's cabin made him look pale, which only heightened the effect. The adept, Hirsch, watched from the corner of the seat, but made no comment. Josey wasn't sure what to think of him. At the council meeting she'd learned a great many things, among them that the adept liked to hear himself speak. But even after a lengthy explanation about the Other Side and how it impacted magical affairs here in their world, she could scarcely remember anything he'd said except for one salient detail. Her unknown assailant was very dangerous, virtually unstoppable by blade or venom, and completely devoid of human sentiments. Beyond that, Hirsch carried himself with an air of diffidence. Josey knew little of sorcery, but she had witnessed enough around Caim to be wary of it and those who walked its twilight paths.

'Your objection is noted,' Josey said. 'But I refuse to be a prisoner in my own palace. Now, can we please talk about something else before I go mad? Have we heard any news from the north?'

Hubert's eyes slid toward Hirsch and back to her. Josey motioned for him to continue.

'Nothing official,' Hubert said. 'The envoys we sent to the border have not returned, but that is not surprising. This time of year the roads are nigh impassable.'

'But unofficially?' She knew better than to ask how he could have received information faster than the imperial courier system. The lord chancellor's office had its ways.

'Excuse me.' Hubert took out a handkerchief and wiped his nose. 'Unofficially, three dispatches have reached my office.'

Josey almost threw herself at him. 'Three? What did they say?'

'If Your Majesty would prefer a private conference . . .'

She clutched her hands together on her lap to keep from throttling him. 'Go on, Hubert! For Phebus's sake.'

'Very well. They had nothing good to say. Little more than rumors, really, but two of the three mentioned a squabble among the nobility of Eregoth.' The way he said 'nobility of Eregoth' with a slight inflection showed how little he thought of their aristocratic brethren to the north. It wasn't an uncommon prejudice among the peers of Othir, as she had discovered of late.

'What sort of squabble?'

Hubert cleared his throat. 'A bloody one, from the reports. More than a score of tribal chieftains were slain. Executed, if it can be believed.' His voice trailed off. 'And there was mention of strange goings-on.'

'Strange how?'

Hubert's gaze slipped over to Hirsch. 'Sorcery.'

Josey struggled to keep her face calm, but her insides felt like they were being sucked into a dark hole in the center of her stomach. Executions and sorcery in the north, and Caim had walked right into it. Some part of her hoped he had sensed the danger and was now on his way back to her, but she knew it for a foolish wish. The man she loved would die before backing down from a challenge, and that possibility terrified her more than anything.

'What of the troops we sent?' She almost tacked 'after Caim left' onto the end of the question, but caught herself.

'No word yet, but they may be delayed. The mud, you know.'

Josey didn't want to hear about mud, but Hubert was only doing his job, and under very trying circumstances. Still, sometimes she felt like she had less control over her life than when she was just the daughter of an elderly earl. It was beyond frustrating. Her stomach rumbled. She should have eaten before they left, but as always her preparations for public display took longer than anticipated.

'And the western territories?' she asked, knowing she would regret it. *I might as well receive all the bad news together.*

'Also not good, Majesty.'

This time there was genuine concern in his voice. *For nameless people on the edge of the realm, but not for Caim?* Josey tamped out the thought as soon as it popped into her head. Every living soul within Nimea's borders was her subject. She had to care for them all.

'Go on,' she said.

'We've received messages from various towns. Bandits have struck all across the region. Farms have been burned, livestock slaughtered or stolen. The provincial lords fear they'll face a famine come spring if matters are not rectified before the planting season.'

Josey wanted to bury her face in her hands. 'Where is all this coming from?'

'There is some speculation that a foreign power could be working behind the scenes. Financing the brigands, providing them with arms and safe havens. We have no proof of this, but . . .'

'Who would be—?'

She already knew the answer, or enough suspects to make a short list. Nimea was surrounded by countries that would benefit from her misfortune. Arnos had the motivation, but that nation would have to be running supplies by sea, a risky proposition in winter. And the merchant-lords of Illmyn were known to dabble in international politics when they saw an opportunity to tip the scales of trade in their favor. The ambassadors from both nations had been curiously absent from her court.

'Find me some proof. Then I can act.'

Hubert nodded. 'And there's another problem.'

'What else?'

'A watch post in Low Town was attacked last night. Two watchmen were injured and some prisoners escaped.'

'Here in Othir?'

A furious seed of anger bloomed in Josey's belly. Border problems were nothing new; she'd heard her foster father speak of them since she was a little girl. But an attack against her peacekeepers was unacceptable.

'I want all patrols doubled,' she said. 'The same with the guards at all posts throughout the city.'

'For how long, Majesty?'

'For as long as it takes to get my city under control, Lord Chancellor.'

'That will be an expensive undertaking.'

She threw up her hands. 'Has the realm suddenly become impoverished?'

'No, but—'

'I have every confidence in you.' A thought occurred to her. 'If we're short of money, go to the merchants. They'll suffer the most if crime and injustice run rampant.'

'I suppose we can try.'

Throughout the exchange, Hirsch had volunteered nothing. It was a little unnerving. Josey started to say something to the adept, but a sound from outside caught her attention. Above the clack of the team's hooves, a susurrus had arisen. She pushed aside the lace curtains, and a bracing gust of wind blew through her hair. Candles glowed in the windows facing the Processional. This was her favorite time of year. Soon there would be snow on the streets and rooftops, converting the entire city into a winter paradise.

Something flew past the window. Josey tumbled back into her seat as it thudded against the side of the cabin. At the same time, her brain registered the speeding object. A melon, thrown at the carriage. Someone had tried to hit her!

She peered out the window. A crowd of people lined the street beyond the pikes of her mounted bodyguards. Josey started to wave until she heard the chant coming from the mouths of her subjects.

'The empire is dead! Long live the Church!'

Josey froze, stricken by the words. Then she saw a picture scrawled on the side of the building above the crowd, of a woman wearing a crown, and beside her was drawn a downward facing hook like a claw. The demon's horn, the mark of a blasphemer condemned by the True Church to eternal exile in this world and the next. Hubert took Josey by the arm and eased her back into the seat. She was numb. It was like a horrible nightmare.

Hubert closed the curtain. 'I told you it was a bad idea to venture out tonight, Majesty, but you insisted.' He smiled when she glared at him. 'The people are a rambunctious lot. They just require time to get to know you better.'

'They *hate* me.'

'Nonsense. They simply don't understand the complexities of governing. In time, they will come to love you as their imperial matron.'

Josey wasn't sure she liked the idea of being anyone's matron, nor did she enjoy the professorial tone Hubert had adopted, but she got his point.

'It's the Church, isn't it? I've deposed them and now they're turning the people against me.'

Hubert made a face like he was biting into something sour. 'There have been reports of priests giving sermons against Your Majesty's reign.'

'What are they saying?'

'The actual wording is not impor—'

150

She stared at him.

'Some have threatened the Prophet's wrath upon those who support the . . .' He cleared his throat. 'The "usurper-whore." '

Josey sat back in her seat. She pinched the back of her hand to keep the sting in her eyes at bay. The carriage swayed as it slowed to a halt. Apprehension gripped Josey for a moment until the footmen jumped down from the roof and she realized they had reached their destination. Hubert stepped out first as the door opened, and he turned to offer her a hand.

As she climbed down from the carriage, Josey pushed aside her sadness and allowed a ribbon of excitement to flutter in her belly. She hadn't been to the Kravoy Theater in years, but it was every bit as impressive as she remembered. Flambeaux flickered in the scores of arched windows piercing the massive circular wall. The Kravoy had been built during the height of the empire, when art and culture flourished. Hoping to foster such a revival during her reign, Josey had commissioned a season of performances.

A multitude of people awaited her. When Josey emerged holding her fur-lined cloak about her shoulders, they surged forward as far as her line of bodyguards would allow. Here, at least, the reception was mixed. For every catcall issued from the throng, a hearty 'Hail to the empress!' resounded.

A loud grunt from behind her ruined the moment for Josey. She turned as Hirsch, standing on the top step of the ladder, craned his neck to survey the theater.

'This will not do,' the adept said over the crowd. 'Not at all.'

The carriage rocked as the adept clambered down the steps. He looked around as if he couldn't find the gate, which was right in front of them, festooned with bouquets of fresh flowers.

Josey swallowed the smile that wanted to play upon her lips. 'You do not enjoy the theater, Master Hirsch?'

'You cannot enter this . . . place.' Hirsch scowled at the theater. 'No, no. I forbid it!'

151

All jocularity dropped from Josey's mood. Gasps erupted from the nearest citizens, and Hubert's mouth fell open.

Josey frowned. 'Master Hirsch, I do not like your—'

But he rode over her words with another grunt. 'It's too big. Impossible to defend. Why, it fairly begs anyone in the vicinity to attempt any manner of larceny. No, no. This is out of the question. We must leave at once.'

'*We* are not leaving,' she said. 'But *you* are. Captain Drathan!'

The leader of her bodyguards stepped up and made a sharp salute.

'Escort Master Hirsch back to the palace, Captain. And confine him to the guest wing.'

The officer gestured for a pair of his men to come forward as he turned to the adept.

Hirsch stared at Josey. 'So be it. I wash my hands of this evening's fiasco.'

With another grunt, he walked away. Josey watched them depart, the adept leading the soldiers away into the night. Was she making the right decision? She twisted the imperial signet around her finger, feeling its weight. She couldn't back down now. Josey glanced around at the faces surrounding her. Her subjects. *I must lead with strength, not weakness.*

Josey turned to Hubert, who had watched the exchange with a frown. He clearly wanted to say something, but wisely did not. She hooked his elbow before he could change his mind, and they entered the theater arm in arm.

The atrium was a tribute to the imperial age of Nimea, with a massive colonnade supporting the ceiling five stories above their heads. Luxurious fresco murals of the city provided the backdrop for the scads of attendees who lined the walls as she passed. Josey waved and nodded to everyone as if this was the grandest moment of her life. In a way it was. Since taking the throne, she had seen more of the inside of her palace than of the city beyond its walls. She knew less of her people – their habits and preferences – than she cared to admit. Of all the things Caim had shown her in their time together, it was that the city, and the entire country, consisted of more than just nobles and prefects and exarches, that the life-blood of her realm were the common men and women who toiled every day to provide for their families.

Caim. There he was again, infiltrating her thoughts even though he was a thousand leagues away. Did he ever think of her? Josey shoved aside the wistful feelings and concentrated on her presentation, her walk, her wave – all the things Hubert had drilled into her during their long preparation. She thought she was doing pretty well until she caught his glare out of the corner of her eye.

'Rarm dun,' he murmured under his breath. 'Rarm dun!'

She frowned, and then noticed her arm swaying above her head. *Arm down!* She pulled her hand back down beside her face, waving from the wrist. *Turn and wave to the other side. Now nod, but not too much.* Like a pair of dancers, they crossed the atrium and went up a flight of carpeted stairs to the balcony level. An usher bowed low before leading them into the imperial box.

Josey settled into the center seat, which was fashioned into a miniature throne, but was more comfortable. *Thank heaven.* Hubert took her cloak and hung it on a hook while four bodyguards took up positions, two inside the box's curtained entrance and two outside. While listening to the strains of the orchestra tuning up, Josey looked around. The imperial box was the highest seat in the house, directly before the stage. Lesser boxes fanned out to either side. Many of their occupants turned her way. Her gaze swept across the men and women in formal attire as Hubert, sitting at her right side, pointed out a few he thought she should know.

'There is Lord Rodney, the Viscount of Wessenax, with a young woman who is *not* his wife. And in the next box over is Percival Heinley. His family isn't noble, but he's one of the richest men in the kingdom. Inherited a string of silver mines from his father. Now *there* was a true bastard in every sense of the word, though it's said he had a fine eye for horseflesh.'

While Hubert ran through the litany of names and ranks,

Josey leaned over the balustrade. Numerous alcoves sur-rounded the floor beneath the box seats. Aisles ran from these recesses down to the main seating. Besides the alcoves, there were exits on both sides of the stage. She estimated there were four hundred people in the audience below. She ought to have felt safe. Instead, a bud of anxiety was lodged in her bosom.

A pair of familiar faces in a box across the theater caught her attention. Lord Du'Quendel and Lieutenant Walthom sat with a pack of other young men in military uniform. Before she could look away and pretend she hadn't seen them, Walthom stood up and made a formal bow in her direction. Lord Du'Quendel hastily did likewise. She started to raise her hand out of habit. *Oh heaven, Josey. Don't encourage them!*

She settled for a polite nod instead.

'Hubert, have those levies been raised to send west?'

'They are being assembled as we speak, Majesty.'

'Put Lord Du'Quendel in charge of the expedition.'

'Du'Quendel? I don't believe he has any military experi-ence.'

'Humor me. The generals can run the show, but I want Lord Du'Quendel on his way the first thing tomorrow morning. And send Lieutenant Walthom's unit as well.'

'As you command.' Hubert pointed to the box on their left. 'I see Duke Mormaer has decided to attend this evening.'

Glad for the distraction, Josey followed his gesture to the next box, where the Duke of Wistros was sitting down with an elderly matron.

'Let me guess,' she said. 'That's not his wife, either.'

'No. I haven't any idea who she is. I'm certain his mother is passed. Possibly an aunt or some other relative. Odd, though. Mormaer isn't a regular attendee of the theater. In fact, to my knowledge Mormaer hasn't attended a production in years, but he turns up here tonight.'

Josey resumed her study of the seats below. Armed soldiers walked among the patrons. 'Perhaps he holds the same

154

contrary opinion of my attendance as you and hopes to see me pelted with rotten fruit.'

Hubert turned to her, his brow pinched together. 'You're up to something.'

Josey gave him a bland look. 'What do you mean? I'm simply enjoying this, my first night out of that drafty stone shack you call a palace. In peace, if it pleases you, my lord.'

'You've set a trap!' He leaned so close his nose bumped into her ear. 'You're using yourself as bait to draw out the assassin, and Mormaer is in on it.'

'Keep your voice down.'

Josey grimaced as she glanced over her shoulder at her guards. This was the moment she'd been dreading. Hubert's face was a stiff mask, but she could see the anger bubbling underneath. More than that, there was true resentment. She didn't blame him. That had been the hardest part of the plan for her to accept. But Mormaer had sworn her to secrecy; it was the only way he would assist her. Now, with Hubert sitting beside her, wounded, she wished she had insisted on the need to include him.

'It was Mormaer's idea. He came up with a plan to catch my attacker. The fewer people who knew . . .'

'Fewer meaning not your lord chancellor. Who else knows?'

'Only those who must. We don't know anything about the assassin. He could be masquerading as anyone.'

'Am I a suspect, too?'

Josey met him frown for frown. 'If you were, you would be sitting in a very cold cell right now, and not here beside me. I trust you, Hubert, even with my life. If this fails, you are my last line of protection.'

'Majesty, I cannot protect you if I am not informed—'

A voice called from the hallway behind them. Josey rose as the curtain dividing the back of the box was pulled aside. Lady Philomena stood in the doorway. She wore a long indigo gown that personified her. Plain, but expensive.

The lady made a small curtsy, so small that Josey almost missed it. Josey bent her head to precisely the same degree.

Hubert made a bow. 'I was not aware Your Ladyship enjoyed the theater.'

'I do not.' She looked to Josey. 'I enjoy nothing which distracts me from the grandeurs of the Prophet. But I have come at the prelate's behest, to relate His Holiness's relief that the empress survived the cowardly attempt on her life and our sincere wish that this event will bring Her Highness to a closer relationship with the Church, which is the true source of authority.'

Josey forced herself to smile. 'My lady is too kind. Please convey my thanks to the Holy Father, and ask him to pray for the soul of our servant, who was killed in the attack.'

'Yes,' the lady said. 'Your manservant, was he not? So fortunate for him to be able to give his life for his mistress, the noblest end for a man of such odious birth.'

Josey stared, unable to believe her ears. To hear Fenrik degraded so . . . like he had been a pet or a piece of furniture. Her hands, gripped in her skirts, began to shake. Before she could say what came to mind, Hubert jumped in.

'I believe the performance is about to begin. Perhaps Your Ladyship would grace us with your presence afterward.'

Lady Philomena raised a delicate eyebrow. 'Not this evening, Your Grace. I must be off to vespers.' Then to Josey, she made another minute curtsy. 'Highness.'

Josey said nothing, not trusting herself to remain civil, as the lady departed. Once the curtains dropped back in place, she spat out a string of invectives that made Hubert stare.

'That rotten bitch,' Josey said as she went back to her seat, feeling a little better. 'I'd like to tell her where she can put her wishes.'

'Yes, she's a conniving snake.' Hubert took a deep breath. 'But she is also a powerful force in the Thurim. And she speaks with the prelate's voice. That makes her doubly venomous.'

The house lights went down. The curtain rose, and polite applause sprung from the audience as a woman in a frilly yellow gown and a hat bedecked with long feathers strode to the center of the stage.

'Tonight for your pleasure,' she said in a strong voice that carried through the theater, 'and to honor our patroness, Empress Josephine' – there was a round of enthusiastic applause from the floor – 'we shall perform *The Caliph's Jewel.*'

As the players took their places upon the stage, Josey settled back in her seat and tried to look calm, but her insides were twisted up in knots. She was taking an awful risk. *But it's worth it if the plan works.*

And it would. Through her discussion with Duke Mormaer, she had tried to think about it from the assassin's point of view. Interestingly, her time spent with Caim had come in handy. Although no expert on the art of killing, she had a certain perspective, and Mormaer's scheme made sense. She even thought Caim, wherever he was, might approve of their logic. She tried to find comfort in that thought, but it had been easier when they were back in the palace just talking about it. Actually sitting here, on full display like a target at a carnival game, was quite a different matter.

Josey was just beginning to relax when voices rose in the corridor outside her box. Someone sounded angry, but whether it was one of her bodyguards or another she could not tell. She started to glance over her shoulder. A sound like rustling paper crashed in her ears as something brushed her cheek. Josey froze, her entire body clenched with fear. *No no no! I don't want to—*

Small wings fluttered and disappeared over the roof of the box. Josey inhaled a shuddering breath. It was just a pigeon. *Caim would laugh his head off if he'd seen that.*

She leaned over to share the joke with Hubert, and froze at the look on his face. Mouth open, he was turned around in his chair looking to the back of the box. Josey turned her head. What she saw robbed the heat from her blood. One of her guardsmen had reached over, but instead of fingers, glistening black tentacles extended from his hand to cover the other guard's face and throat. While she and Hubert watched, the stricken guard collapsed to the floor. The killer looked in their direction.

157

Hubert stood up, grabbing for his sword, but a vicious swipe from a fistful of writhing tentacles hurled him over the railing. *Hubert!*

A cry for help lodged in Josey's throat as she slipped off the seat of her chair. She reached into her skirts for her knife, but her legs were tangled up in layers of petticoats. She couldn't breathe. It was all happening too fast.

The imposter's appearance shifted as he advanced. His eyes receded into their sockets, his skin bubbled and darkened like charring meat, and the grotesque tendril-hands morphed into hooked talons. Josey kicked her chair into the assassin's path, and the creature shattered it with a casual slap. Its rubbery lips stretched upward into an obscene grin. Josey dug through the material twisted around her legs. *Someone help us!*

A woman screamed. Relief washed through Josey as the cry was taken up by others. She imagined the people below, standing up in shock and pointing at the imperial box. The assassin stopped and released a ferocious roar that pummeled her ears and drove her to the carpet. She knew the knife was strapped to her thigh, but she couldn't find the handle. As the assassin loomed over her, she looked up, expecting to feel the painful bite of claws.

A flash of intense light blinded her, followed by a burst of heat over her face and arms like the blaze from an oven. A bitter stench filled her nose. Josey blinked away spots of residual brilliance to find the assassin was gone. A dense cloud of smoke hovered in its place. Coughing and waving to disperse the haze, she stood up. In the next box, Duke Mormaer and the old woman were gone. Instead, Hirsch stood in their place, both hands extended toward her. Thin trails of smoke rose from his open palms.

Josey released her skirt and crawled to the railing. Hubert hung by one hand; the other still held his sword. Blood dribbled from a cut across his forehead, but he was alive. Josey laughed in spite of herself and the situation. It had been Mormaer's suggestion for her to pretend to send away Master Hirsch in public. After pretending to leave with

Captain Drathan, the adept disguised himself and accompanied the duke to the performance. It had worked to perfection.

Josey reached down to help Hubert. The floor of the theater was in chaos as people shoved to get to the exits. As she got hold of his wrist, a scraping noise from behind sent a shiver down her spine. Josey turned her head to look behind her. The assassin clung to the roof of the adjacent box section. It looked more monster than man, with a hulking physique and long, veiny limbs. Green flames danced along its hunched shoulders and down its back, but the fiercest fire burned within its cavernous eye sockets as they turned toward her. Gathering its legs, the assassin leapt across the distance and landed on the side of the imperial box. Its claws shredded the lacquered privacy screen.

Though it wrenched at her heart, Josey let go of Hubert. Sobbing, she pulled up her skirt and grabbed for the knife, even though she suspected it would be futile against this thing that had withstood swords and mystical fire and yet refused to die. With a roar, the assassin pushed into the box. The stench of its breath, like putrid rotting meat, made her cringe. The knife in Josey's hand quivered as the assassin stood over her. Blood dripped from its claws. She braced herself, refusing to look away. She had gambled the lives of her soldiers and her friend. The least she could do was face her end like an empress.

A blur of bright steel sprang up beside Josey. As she tumbled to the floor, Hubert appeared and threw himself in front of her. The slim tip of his sword pierced the assassin's side. Its fiery eyes gaped wide, whether in pain or shock Josey could not tell, but the monster leapt back with superhuman agility, dragging Hubert with it. She heard a crackling noise an instant before she was blinded by a second blast of scintillating light.

Josey got up on her knees, wiping her eyes. Through a blurry fog she spotted a huge hole in the side of the imperial box. The edges of the hole smoldered. At first she didn't see Hubert, but then he pushed up off the floor under the wreckage of the partially collapsed ceiling.

'Are you all right?' they each asked at the same time.

He brushed a hand down the front of his evening jacket, the fine gabardine now caked in dust and stone chips. 'I believe my attire has been vanquished.'

'I'm sorry, Hubert.' Tears formed in her eyes as she considered what had almost happened because of her. 'Please forgive me.'

He smiled as he straightened his lapels. 'It is always interesting to serve you, Majesty. And it is my great honor.'

Footsteps echoed in the corridor behind the box. Josey steeled herself for anything, while Hubert looked around for his sword.

Hirsch leaned through the curtained archway. 'Everyone still in one piece?'

'Thanks to your magery, Master Adept,' Josey answered. 'Is it dead?'

Hirsch shook his head as he went over to the railing. 'I merely drove it off.'

Josey's heart sank. They had gone through all of this and had nothing to show for it. Out in the hallway, she could see the legs of her bodyguards sprawled on the floor. Their blood soaked through the short red carpet and pooled between them. *I'm not worthy of such devotion.*

Hubert had gone over to stand beside Hirsch. 'Perhaps it's not dead, but you managed to hurt it.'

Josey joined them. Past the charred partition, streaks of soot and luminescent green slime spread across the wall of the theater, and then ended as if their source had vanished into the air. Hirsch bent over the shattered railing and came back up holding a long splinter of wood. On the tip was smeared a glob of the greenish black stuff.

'Is that—?' Hubert started to ask.

'Yes,' Hirsch replied. 'I may be able to track the beast with this, if the material isn't too badly tainted.' To Hubert he said, 'Come with me while the spoor is still fresh, and bring every soldier you can spare.'

'How—?' Hubert tried to ask, but the adept was gone.

Josey pushed her lord chancellor toward the archway. 'Go with him. Take Captain Drathan and the guards.'

'I won't leave you defenseless.'

A tall figure moved into the archway. 'I will remain with the empress,' Mormaer said.

Josey considered the offer. Hirsch needed help. Whatever the assassin was, she feared the adept would have his hands full if he managed to catch it.

'Thank you, Duke Mormaer.' Josey nodded to Hubert. 'Attend Master Hirsch. Don't let anything—'

'I'm going!' Hubert pressed past the duke and ran down the corridor.

The theater was amazingly quiet in the aftermath of the attack. Below, the audience, orchestra, and players had fled. Josey's hands shook as she clutched the railing. *I could have died here tonight. Now what? I could be attacked again, on the way back to the palace, or while sleeping in my bed. Sleep?* She huffed at the thought. Though she was exhausted down to her bones, she wouldn't be able to sleep as long as the assassin remained free.

'Majesty,' Mormaer said. 'My guards and I shall accompany you to the palace.'

Josey turned. Alone in the dim lighting with him, she was keenly aware of how large he was. If he wanted, he could push her over the side and claim it was an accident. Yet when she looked into his eyes she saw a hint of . . . understanding? Certainly not compassion.

'It was a good plan,' she said.

Mormaer's expression did not change except for a tightening around the eyes, but any warmth she thought she had seen in his gaze froze over.

'We should go, Majesty.'

Josey bit her bottom lip as she walked past him, angry at herself. She had said the wrong thing, as usual. But Duke Mormaer was so damned inscrutable; she never knew what to say around him.

A squad of armsmen in Mormaer's black livery stood in the

corridor. Two of her bodyguards lay at their feet in pools of blood. Josey paused to pay her respects to these men who had died in her defense. Their eyes stared up at the ceiling.

'Duke Mormaer, my cloak, please.'

When he fetched it, she laid it gently over the faces of her bodyguards. Dark spots appeared in the fabric where their blood soaked through.

It was only as she turned away to follow Mormaer, his men falling in behind them, that Josey noticed a detail about her bodyguards. Neither had sported any claw gouges or throat punctures. Instead, each had died from a straight cut across the throat, as neat as if done by a chirurgeon's blade.

A chill ran through Josey. *If not the assassin, then who killed them?*

SHADOW'S LURE

Chapter
SIXTEEN

Caim palmed the hilts of his knives as he headed up the street. The conversation with the old woman had only increased his desire to leave the city. But first he wanted to make sure Liana and Keegan were all right. He realized it was insane, that they were safe with their uncle, but this place – the atmosphere, the tension, the unfriendly shadows – made him anxious just the same.

I'll just stop by for a quick look to ease my mind, and then be on my way.

Coming around a corner, he pulled up quick. Something warned him to drop behind a row of dirty snow mounds. A dozen heartbeats later, a group of armed men passed through the intersection. Soldiers this time, and moving like they had a purpose. Caim rubbed his aching thigh as he crouched on the frozen cobblestones. They were headed deeper into this ward. Liana had said her uncle's shop was in that direction. It could be a coincidence . . .

Caim stayed low as he moved. He didn't believe in co-incidence. Maybe Keegan and his outlaw friends deserved whatever trouble they stirred up, but Liana was there. Damn the girl. Why couldn't she have stayed with her father?

As Caim turned onto a crooked lane, he spotted three look-outs; two loitering on the street and one perched in a second-storey window across from the shop with a hammer-and-nails placard. Spotters. And if they knew what they were doing, the man up top would have a bow . . .

What are you doing, Caim? Just turn around and walk the other way.

But he dipped into an alley three doors down from the shop and followed it to another backstreet behind the storefronts. Peering around the corner, he saw a fourth lookout huddled behind a snowbank. Caim considered his knives, but then put them away. Instead, he reached out to the shadows. They crowded around him as if eager for his summons. He wove a few around him in a cloak and dismissed the rest, who drifted away slowly.

Hugging the wall, Caim moved down the narrow alleyway. The sentry continued rubbing his hands together and blowing into them, but he didn't make a sound as Caim passed him.

When Caim got to the back of what he thought was the right shop, he looked for a way up. One of the second-storey windows was cracked open. Despite protests from his leg and arm, he started climbing. The bottom half of the shop was faced with rough river stones interspaced with deep groves, which made it easier. The shadows stayed with him, concealing his efforts as he reached the windowsill. He eased open the shutters and climbed inside.

Caim sent the shadows away as his feet touched down on the dusty floor of a small room with a sloped ceiling. The shop was quiet. Nudging the door open with his toe, he stepped out into an L-shaped hallway. A cool draft blew across the back of his neck as he slipped around the corner. Voices wafted from the downstairs. A man and a woman. He didn't recognize the male, but he knew Liana's voice at once. He went down the steps without any pretense at stealth.

The ground floor was occupied by a long shop area. All manner of wooden furniture – chairs, tables, wardrobes, chests – crowded the floor. Two shaded windows were set in the front wall on either side of the outside door, with another door in back. Liana and a man about twice her age looked up from a desk in the corner as Caim came down the steps. Liana jerked upright as if she'd seen a ghost. Her hair was damp and glossy in the low candlelight. The man stepped in front of her with a frown.

'What do you want?' he asked.

Caim looked past him to the girl. 'Where is Keegan?'

'Look—' the man started to say, but Liana stepped from behind him.

'It's all right. He's a friend.' Then to Caim, 'What's wrong?'

'This place is being watched. And there are soldiers on the way.'

Liana looked to her uncle. 'They're down in the cellar. Keegan and a few of the others. I can't say they'll be glad to see you.'

'They don't have to be. Collect whatever you need. We're leaving.'

Caim went to the rear door. The back room was a work area cluttered with tables, vises, sealed barrels, and racks of tools. Unfinished pieces hung from hooks in the ceiling over a floor covered in sawdust and hardened puddles of beeswax. There were no other ways out except the doorway where he stood and a single window high up on the wall. Liana brushed past and showed him the trapdoor to the cellar. Trying to ignore the sweet scents of soap and fresh flowers about her, he pulled on the iron ring in the center.

Murmurs wafted up through the square hole. Wooden steps descended between walls of mortared stone blocks. Liana watched as he started down. The stairs came to a short landing before turning into a low cellar that ran the length of the shop above. A few more than a dozen men gathered in the chamber, some sitting on piles of lumber and old crates. They wore city clothes – long tunics and baggy breeches, heavy winter cloaks thrown back over their shoulders. One man was clad in a thick brown robe. Keegan was addressing them.

'—on the way we saw other signs of plundering by the duke's men.'

'We saw the same thing coming down from Prond's Cross,' someone said from the back of the group.

Several others added what they'd heard, painting a picture of destruction all across the region – homes burned, livestock killed, people driven off or butchered. Caim shifted around a wooden support beam, staying out of sight. A board creaked behind him as Liana came down the steps. He motioned for her to remain quiet.

A slight, balding man with a halo of thin gray hair around his oily pate slouched forward. 'Where is Ramon? He said he would be here.'

Keegan clutched his hands together behind his back. 'He was at the meeting spot, but I didn't see him leave.'

'That's no surprise, unless you've grown eyes in your backside.'

'I'm no coward, Grendt,' Keegan mumbled.

His interrogator, Grendt, combed his fingers through the wispy goatee covering his weak chin. 'Just passing strange how you always escape with your hide intact, boy, while others do the dying.'

'What are we going to do about Caedman?' Keegan asked. His voice had a plaintive whine that made Caim wince.

The robed man puffed out his whiskered cheeks. 'He's as good as gone, locked up in that hellhole. If he's not dead already.'

'Caedman,' Grendt said. 'Another good man who stood his ground and fought while you ran off, boy. And now you spin us tales of shadow-men and the Hunt.'

'I'm telling you the truth!'

That's enough.

Caim stepped out of the shadows. Keegan jumped back, his hand fumbling with his weapon. A couple of the men in the audience looked over and then scrambled to their feet. Caim didn't move as they produced an array of knives and cudgels; one man brandished what looked like a boat hook. Caim didn't know whether to laugh or cry. This was Keegan's insurrection? At least the woodsmen had seemed somewhat capable, if disorganized and undisciplined. The men confronting him now

166

were clerks and shopkeepers who didn't look like they could overthrow a produce cart.

Caim showed his empty hands. 'I come with a warning.'

'Caim!' Keegan said. 'You shouldn't be here.' Then he saw Liana behind him. 'Li! What were you thinking?'

'She's helping to save your life,' Caim replied.

The others shouted, some threatening to throw him out and a couple demanding to know who he was.

Grendt looked to Caim. 'You two know this man?'

'This is the one I told you about,' Keegan said.

'He doesn't look like much. If he's so dangerous, why didn't he stand and fight beside our brothers?'

Caim met the man's gaze. 'Why weren't you out there alongside them? Maybe it's easier to sit in another man's basement and complain rather than put your own life on the line.'

Grendt poked a finger in Caim's direction from ten paces away. 'I don't need to answer to you. I've done my share.' He looked around at his fellows. 'We've all done our share and more. I say we bind up this strutting cock and throw him out in the street with the other night leavings. Who's with me?'

Caim dipped his left hand beneath his cloak and produced a *suete* knife. His right hand twitched, wanting to go to the sword at his shoulder, but he kept it by his side. The men shuffled about, but no one made a move. Just as he suspected, they didn't have the heart for a scrap against someone who would fight back.

Keegan looked around, and then back to Caim. 'You said you had a warning.'

'Soldiers,' Caim replied.

That set all the men to talking among themselves. Only Keegan kept his composure.

'Coming here?'

'Looks like it. You need to get out.'

'It's a trick,' Grendt said.

Another man stepped forward. He was short and thickly

built, wearing a long woolen coat and black boots. 'How do we know he didn't lead them here?'

Caim pointed upstairs with his knife. 'Any moment a company of troops is going to burst through the front door. Are you going to let me help you, or are you going to stand around asking stupid questions?'

Keegan surprised him, and perhaps them all, by speaking out. 'We can trust him.'

'Ell's balls,' Grendt said. 'He's working for Eviskine. This is a trap.'

'I'm leaving!' another man shouted as he went over to the wall. He flipped back a sheet of canvas nailed to the brickwork. Behind it was a stout door that looked like it led out into the alley beside the shop.

'Open that,' Caim said, 'and you'll get us all caught. There are lookouts on the street.'

The man froze with his hand on the latch.

'Fine,' Grendt said. 'Then we'll barricade the doors.'

'Then they'll just burn you out.'

'You say we can't stay,' Grendt said. 'And we can't leave. So what do you expect us to do?'

'Disappear,' Caim replied.

A few men muttered in the back of the group.

'We have to vanish,' Caim said. 'And the faster we do, the better it will be for Keegan's uncle.'

'What about my uncle?' Keegan asked.

Caim looked him in the eye. 'What? You thought you could involve him and not make trouble for him down the road? Are you coming or not?'

Keegan frowned, but Liana nodded. 'Yes, we are.'

Caim sheathed his *suete*. 'Then come with me. The rest of you can do whatever you want.'

He went back up the stairs without waiting to see who followed him.

Caim pulled aside the window shade and looked down at the street in front of the store. He didn't like the idea of going back out tonight, which struck him as the oddest thought he'd had since he came to this winter-cloaked land. The night was his time, his home, but the darkness outside held no love for him. But he didn't have a choice.

That was a lie, and he knew it. He had a choice. He could slip away like a wraith. All he had to do was leave these people to their fates. This wasn't his fight. He thought about the pendant around his neck. *I said the same thing about Josey. And where did that get me?*

As soon as his mind touched that sore spot, he threw himself in another direction. The room in which he stood was the bedroom of the owner, Corgan, Keegan and Liana's uncle. It was small and cramped as befitted a carpenter, with only an old bed and a chest of drawers with a hazy vanity mirror, and a stand holding a vase of dried flowers. They might have been carnations, but now they were caked with dust. *Was he married? No, the walls are bare. Nothing on top of the chest except dust and a few coins. Maybe widowed, but long ago.*

Caim looked across the room. Liana and Keegan stood at the bedroom's other window overlooking the alley. The rest of the outlaws were spread throughout the shop's second storey. There wasn't time for a plan, so he'd been forced to improvise, and the odds weren't in their favor. Privately, he thought they'd be lucky if one in five made it out alive. He clenched his right hand into a fist. The forearm throbbed in response.

He studied Keegan. 'What was your plan?'

Liana glanced over. 'What?'

Caim kept his gaze on Keegan, but the young man did not look up from the alley.

'After you assembled your men here in the city, what was the next step?'

'I don't know. Ramon was supposed to be here.'

'What if he's dead? Who's next in line?'

Keegan blew out a puff of air. 'If we lose Ramon, there's

nothing left. We might as well run to the hills and never come back.'

Caim turned back to the street. The front of the shop still looked clear, but he knew better. There was movement in the window across the street.

'Someone's out there!' Liana whispered

But Caim didn't need her warning – he heard the commotion below – but it was good to know the girl was on her toes. He'd pulled no punches when he briefed them on the situation. Tonight might be their last in this world.

Caim lifted the strung bow in his hands. An arrow lay across the shaft, its steel point gleaming in the wan starlight. He pulled back the string until the fletching tickled his cheek. He exhaled. The windows were almost at a level. No wind to speak of. Sixteen paces. An itch prickled the back of his neck as the shadows announced their presence. Despite his misgivings about his phantom allies, he didn't push them away. He would likely need them before the night was through.

There. Another hint of movement within the window across the street. Caim made out the dim silhouette of a shoulder. The tip of the arrow drifted down half an inch and a touch to the left.

He fired, and couldn't tell if he hit anything.

Heavy pounding echoed up from the floorboards. But no sign of movement in the far window. Then something moved in the alley across the street. Caim nocked another arrow as six men converged on the shop, carrying a short wooden ram. Caim took a shot at them, but he rushed it. The missile ricocheted off the cobblestones behind the soldiers. As he reloaded, a second squad took up position around the storefront while the first group applied the beam to the door. Loud booms resounded up and down the street.

'Be ready,' Caim said.

The crash of shattering wood was the signal. Keegan shoved open the window, and Liana clambered through. Brother lowered sister with a knotted bedsheet. Then Caim set his bow aside to lower Keegan. As he swung a leg over the sill,

Caim heard others dropping to the street from other windows. His instructions from this point had been clear: everyone scatter and meet at the rendezvous point, which was another safe house outside the city. Caim wished Kit was here. *Dammit, where is she?*

He didn't want any more surprises. And yet it seemed as if life was determined to keep serving them up. Hanging by his hands, he took a breath and let go. As he fell, Caim realized he had left his bow behind.

He bit down on his tongue as a stabbing pain tore up his injured leg. Limping, he ran as best he could, following the rabbit-fur fringe of Liana's hood down the alley. The next street was empty. All the doors and windows were shut up tight, lending the feel of a ghost town. Caim passed a heavyset outlaw in a bright green vest – *not the best choice of colors* – and almost tripped over a mongrel dog nosing around in the gutter. After he leapt over the pup, he looked ahead and stumbled to a halt. Two blocks away, a line of soldiers was advancing down the street. Caim made out the slender out-lines of long spears. The night was overcast; none of the outlaws would see the trap until it was too late. With a curse, he sprinted after the siblings.

He caught up to Liana first.

'Stop!' he whispered as loud as he dared.

Liana heard him and slowed. Caim accelerated past her to grab the tail of Keegan's cloak. The youth spun around and slashed with his sword. Caim caught the boy's wrist.

'Hold, damn you!'

The youth wrenched his arm free. 'What?'

Liana caught up to them with her uncle in tow. There was no sign of the others.

'Soldiers ahead,' Caim said. 'I'm guessing they've cordoned off the neighborhood.'

'What do we do?' Corgan asked. The older man was panting heavily, but he stood upright, a stout cudgel in his hand.

'We have to tell the others,' Liana said.

Caim picked out distant shouts and sounds of fighting. 'They're already finding out. We need to get off the street.'

He took them down the first narrow alley they found. If the soldiers weren't searching every nook and side street, they might miss this one. He just hoped he hadn't picked a dead end.

Caim went as fast as he could, but they didn't have his keen night vision. After the second time Keegan tripped over something, Caim wanted to bash the youth upside his head. Just as he made the next turn, a bright light stabbed at him through the darkness ahead. Through the gleam he could make out several tall figures coming his way. Their armor creaked and jangled as they marched in loose formation. Caim counted four plus the lantern-holder, but there could be more behind them. He drew his knives as a voice with a thick western accent bellowed for him to hold fast.

'Find another way!' he yelled over his shoulder.

The siblings and their uncle stopped behind him. Corgan and Keegan started back the way they had come, but Liana just gazed at him. It took Keegan pulling her by the arm before she would leave.

Caim eyed the soldiers. The alleyway was wide enough for three men to walk abreast, but the soldiers approached two by two with the lantern-bearer at the rear. They gazed at him over the tops of oaken shields held shoulder to shoulder, their spears overlapped to form a quadrant of sharp steel. A feeling of peace washed over Caim as he shifted into a lower stance. This was what he did best. This was home. The shadows chittered to him from the darkness. They wanted to be let free. *Not yet.*

When the soldiers were within five paces of him, Caim stepped sideways into the darkness under a balcony.

He reappeared behind them, quieter than a whisper. The lantern-bearer dropped with a startled gasp as Caim cut into his back with both *suetes*, their sharp points sliding between the lungs and kidneys. The lantern crashed to the ground and went out. And Caim went to work.

Up close where their spears were useless, he weaved between the soldiers, slashing one across the face and stabbing another low. The men tried to fall back from the sudden onslaught, but their comrades at the front of the formation hemmed them in. Caim ducked underneath a spear swung like a quarterstaff and came up with both knives extended. He wasn't seeking to kill – that's what he told himself – but that didn't stop him from making quick cuts to either side of the soldier's neck. The soldier fell to the bricks, blood spurting between his grasping fingers.

Caim's breath came in short puffs as he fought through his pain, pushing himself to move faster and strike harder. One soldier brought his spear up to block; another dropped the long weapon and grabbed for an axe belted to his hip. The *suete* blades sliced through stitched leather, and the axe-man collapsed against a wall, leaking from twin holes in his stomach. The other soldier stepped back missing three fingers on his left hand. He threw his spear and ran. Caim reacted without thinking. As the soldier was about to reach the next corner, a swarm of shadows fluttered from the darkness. There came a low moan from the end of the alley, and then all was quiet.

Caim stalked down the alley. His forearm throbbed in time with his heartbeat, but the pain was a distant thing. The gloom parted to reveal the fallen soldier, covered by wriggling shadows like a blanket of black maggots. They crooned as they feasted. For a moment Caim felt their hunger and the sweet savor of warm blood. They sucked at the stuff of life like it was ambrosia. The black sword quivered in its scabbard as Caim closed his eyes.

A scream cut through the night.

Caim sent the shadows scurrying back to the nooks of the alleyway with a mental shove as he ran down the alley. He almost missed the entrance to a narrow side street. Inside, the branch avenue ran fifteen paces before it zigzagged. Caim followed it at a run, trusting his instincts and night vision to guide him. Ahead, he heard the clang of steel on steel and saw the steady yellow glow of lantern light. Caim rushed around another sharp turn and almost slammed into Liana, leaning against a wall of the alley. Seeing her hunched over, he thought she was hurt, but there was no blood on her clothes. Keegan held back a line of men with broad swings of his sword. The warriors wore mismatched armor and arms. Mercenaries. A body sprawled at the youth's feet. It was Corgan. A trickle of black wetness oozed through the cracks in the cobblestones. Without pretense or preamble, Caim rushed past Liana and plunged into the melee.

Sword blades and spear points came at him from several directions. Caim used every trick in his arsenal to keep a step ahead of them. His knives slashed out again and again, drawing blood, slicing through flesh and fingers. One merc slipped, and Caim smacked him in the face with the flat of a knife blade. The man dropped back clutching a broken cheek.

He caught them by surprise, but for every warrior he took out of the fight, two more jumped in from the back. The shadows jabbered at him from the edges of the alleyway, but he couldn't risk loosing them with Keegan and Liana so near. A spear jabbed out of the second rank. Caim threw himself sideways, but the point cut through his jerkin and drew a line of fire across his ribs. Backing away, Caim pressed his elbow against his side. He didn't want to give in, but his choices were simple: deny the urge and die, or let loose the blade and maybe have a chance.

It wasn't a choice at all.

He flung his right-hand *suete* in the face of the nearest soldier and reached up. The sword flew from its scabbard. When his palm made contact with the smooth hilt, the alley blossomed to life as if it were bathed in a cascade of moonlight. Every crack in the ground was magnified, every surface gleamed with silvery light. The walls around him seemed higher and straighter. Even the bricks under his feet changed, becoming broad and smooth like sheets of polished obsidian. The sword pulsed in his hand like a living thing, pulling at him. His injuries and aches forgotten, he didn't hold back.

A sellsword – an officer by the yellow slashes emblazoned

on his breast – fell back over his own heels as the black sword knocked off his helmet. A tremor ran up the blade into Caim's hand, and he knew, without fully realizing how, that the sword had pierced the steel-and-leather cap to taste blood.

Two mercs jostled forward to cover their leader's retreat. Caim didn't give them a chance to get set. He pressed hard with sword and knife, slashing at any target within his reach. He sliced open a man's wrist, deflected a sword thrust, and the merc fell against the alley wall clutching his neck.

Everywhere the black sword cut, it left a trail of black-edged wounds. He tried using it mainly for defense, but the ebon blade wouldn't let him rest. It dragged him forward in one brutal attack after another, hardly ever deigning to parry an incoming blow, so that Caim was forced to use his left-hand *suete* as a main-gauche. And then he stopped even that, preferring to use the knife to slit open bellies and cut up bearded faces. Blood spilled over him, ran down his arms, and spattered his face. He forgot about Keegan and Liana, forgot about his injuries. All that mattered was the next kill. When the mercenaries fell back, Caim didn't need the sword to compel him to press his advantage before it dried up. He dipped under a wild slash, lunged, and bulled through their front line. His feet moved of their own volition, taking him back and forth and side to side in a lethal dance where one misstep would be his last. The grind of steel and flesh, bone and blood, shrieked in his ears like church bells. The stones became slick beneath his feet as he rode the cyclone of destruction that was his calling.

The officer stepped up to him holding a hand-and-a-half sword. Caim grinned and lashed out at the warriors on either side, and then launched himself straight ahead. Their swords collided in a sharp clang. Caim beat aside the high chop and almost stepped into a clever stop-thrust to the knee that would have ended the fight right then and there. He leapt back in time to save his leg, but ran into someone behind him. Keegan! The youth was panting as he beat at the weapons of the mercs on Caim's flank. Caim wanted to thank him, but a warhammer swung at his head. He spun away, into the path of a downward-sweeping sword. He deflected the blow off the edge of his *suete*, but the black sword jumped forward despite the precariousness of his position. The officer stood firm. Caim gritted his teeth as the point of the bastard sword sliced through his leather jerkin. He threw himself back before he was skewered.

A warrior fell on Caim's left, and he circled in that direction. Only three mercs remained on their feet. Keegan was doing his best to hold off the others, but he was hard-pressed. The black sword quivered in Caim's hand like a hound on a leash. Shadows crowded the alley's dark places. At the merest thought, they would blanket the alley. And there was something else, an insistent presence on the fringe of his awareness. The shadow beast? He wasn't sure, but he had enough problems on his plate. The first was to end this battle before reinforcements showed up.

Caim feinted and took a merc spearman through the throat with a long lunge. *So much for sparing him.* Before the others could react, Caim launched himself at the officer. His weapons became blurs of black and silver. The officer gave way as his guard began to falter. With a spurt of anticipation, Caim broke through. Blood jetted across his jacket as the tip of the black sword caught his foe below the navel, punching through the scales of his armor and the leather backing underneath. Caim didn't stop until the blade was sheathed to the cross-guard in the man's body. The officer's eyes bulged as they stood, only inches apart. Before he could make a sound, Caim slashed across his neck with the knife.

Caim's whole body trembled as he stood over the dead men. Keegan leaned against the alley wall, breathing hard and studying Caim. His short sword was bent midway down the blade. Liana knelt beside her uncle, but Corgan was dead. Watching these people, Caim knew he should have felt something, but a terrible anger boiled inside him, blighting out every other emotion. His hands tightened around the hilts of his weapons. He wanted more blood; the lust grew into a pain in his chest. Shadows gathered in the eaves of doorways and window bays.

'What did you do?' Keegan dropped his useless sword. His face had become darker and grimmer, the face of a stranger. 'He's dead! Because of you!'

'Shut up!' Caim hissed. 'Do you want to bring more of them down on our heads? Pick up your weapon and see to your sister.'

Keegan knelt and put his arm around Liana. While they embraced over the body of their uncle, Caim chewed on his tongue. The black sword quivered in his hand as tiny voices whispered in his head.

Blood! Blood! Take them now!

Caim drew a ragged breath. A drop of blood fell from the tip of his *suete* knife. He watched it fall. When it hit the ground, he knew he would strike. His muscles tightened, anticipating the sudden explosion of activity. Heat suffused his groin.

The droplet gathered speed. It would make a glorious splash on the grimy stones. The sword thrummed in his hand. He lifted its blade.

Stop! I'm not going to—

A blinding burst of light flared in the alley. Caim staggered back against the assault to his vision. Someone gasped – he thought it might be Liana. A violent sound wrenched at his skull, iron hammers beating on brass kettles. The lights dimmed to the intensity of three small suns, and then the three coalesced into a single star held up by a meaty hand.

Hagan held a lantern over his head. 'Keegan, get up.'

Liana threw herself into the old man's arms. 'Papa! Uncle Corgan . . .'

Caim leaned against a brick wall. It was hard to breathe. He blinked against the harsh light. Blood throbbed in his temple. A shudder ran through him as he realized what had almost happened, what he'd almost done. What was happening to him? Caim stood up straight. He didn't know what had come over him, but he felt like himself again. He turned to face them.

'Stay where you are,' Hagan said.

Caim noticed the seax in the old man's other hand, and suddenly the situation felt a good deal less hospitable. He found his other knife and put his weapons away without bothering to clean them.

'He saved us,' Liana said, still clinging to her father. 'Keegan and I would have died if not for him.'

Hagan looked to Keegan, who nodded wearily. 'All right. Keegan, you go first. I expect your friends have set up a meeting spot?'

With a quick glance at Caim, Keegan headed down the alley. Liana looked like she wanted to stay, but Hagan shooed her on ahead. As he stood there, Caim felt the power of the weapon strapped to his back. He was beyond exhausted, like the life had been drained from him. His forearm ached worse than before.

Hagan held up his lantern as he turned to leave. 'Come on, son. Before my children walk into another muddle.'

Caim gazed down at the slaughter he had wrought. With the shadows gone, he breathed easier. The bodies could have been a jumble of blood-splattered dolls. But they weren't.

He picked up a spare sword from one of the corpses and trotted after the others, following the pale lining of Liana's cloak through the twisting streets.

SHADOW'S LURE

Chapter
SEVENTEEN

Josey shivered as she stood before the sitting room's massive stone hearth. No matter how close she got to the flames, she couldn't get warm.

She was drained down to her toes, but sleep was the last thing on her mind. Hubert and Hirsch were still out in the night, tracking the assassin. Josey instructed the officer on duty to keep her informed if they sent news. That had been almost two candlemarks ago, and still no word.

Her eyes wandered down to the wadded square of parchment in her hand. She started to crush the parchment between her fingers. *He made his choice. We both have to live with that.* She could toss it into the fire and forget about him. Or could she? She looked into the flames, wishing they would tell her where he was.

The door opened, and Josey slid the parchment into her pocket. Her other hand felt for the stiletto hidden under her gown. She pulled it away when Amelia entered. A bitter smell filled the room as her maid placed a silver tea service on a sideboard. She brought over a steaming cup.

'Here, Majesty. This will warm you up.'

Josey took it with a grateful nod and turned back to the fireplace. She'd left the theater in the company of Duke Mormaer and his guards only to find that the carriage house had been set on fire. Though he might have, Mormaer didn't abandon her there. Instead, he formed his guards into a square with her in the center and started marching through the crowd of shouting, torch-waving protestors. Stones and small pieces of wood pattered off the guards' armor, but that was the worst of the violence they'd seen on the long journey back to the palace. The imperial residence had never looked so good. When they reached the gates, Josey tried to thank the duke, but he brushed off her gratitude, telling her in a cool voice, 'What you are trying to do in the east is ill advised.'

She knew at once what he meant. Somehow, word had gotten to him about her plan to end the war with Akeshia. It didn't make her feel any better that one of the most powerful lords in the empire considered it a bad idea. Then again, he hadn't said he would oppose it.

The tea was a bit on the strong side and didn't sit well with her nervous stomach. She must have made a face, because Amelia raised her eyebrows.

'Too hot, my lady?'

Josey shook her head, but set the cup back in its saucer.

Amelia stood beside her. 'They'll be fine, Majesty. Don't worry.'

'I know. I just wish we would hear something soon.'

They both turned as the door opened. Josey let out a deep sigh of relief as Hubert walked in. He looked a mess. His face was slick with sweat, his face and clothes smudged with mud. He went over to the table and poured himself a cup.

Josey couldn't wait. 'What happened?'

Hubert belted back the tea in a single gulp. Wincing, he poured another cup.

'We tracked it all through Low Town. Merchant Ward. Tinkers Avenue. Even through the Gutters. But we lost the trail down by the river near Horman Point.'

'Where is—?' she started to ask, but then spotted the short figure in the doorway. 'Master Hirsch.'

The adept entered with a slight limp. Like Hubert, he was spattered with mud and other, less identifiable, substances.

180

Now that Hubert said something, Josey could make out the smells of the river on them.

'Do you believe the assassin's wounds were fatal?' Josey asked.

Hirsch shook his head as he accepted a cup from Hubert. 'The thing was moving too damned fast to be dying.' He took a sip and made a face.

'We have,' Hubert said, 'something more immediate to worry about, Majesty. We've lost control over several key parts of the city.'

Josey opened her mouth, and then shut it. His words didn't register for a moment. 'What are you talking about? We encountered unruly crowds on our way back to the palace, but nothing the watch won't be able to contain.'

'It's worse than that. All the watch stations south of the Processional have been torched. We don't know how many dead, but the numbers may be substantial. Reports of missing gentry are growing as riots have broken out in several neighborhoods. Fires are spreading in many of the lower wards. Not the docks yet, but it won't be long if we can't stop it.'

Josey imagined the scene outside the quiet palace grounds. The riots that had shaken the city just months ago when she and Caim fought to win her throne had destroyed nearly a third of the city. She'd toured Low Town and seen the aftermath for herself firsthand, and been moved to tears by the plight of her most vulnerable subjects. To imagine that those same people roamed the streets of Othir tonight, taking up arms against her, was like a hammer blow to the heart. She grasped for a solution.

'I could address the people,' she said. 'Explain the situation and ask them to return to their homes until the crisis is over.'

Hirsch stirred a finger in his cup. 'Wouldn't work. Those crowds would tear you and your guards apart as soon as listen to you.'

Hubert frowned at the adept. 'I'm forced to agree, Majesty. It's too dangerous for you to go out in public.'

She swallowed, not wanting to believe what she was

hearing. But she had seen it herself, in the eyes of the crowd. They hated her.

'How long would it take to summon the nearest garrisons?'

Hubert set down his cup. 'That would be Parvia and Wistros, but most of the levies from those lands have already been dispatched to the west. We can send riders to recall them. In the meantime, I suggest that we secure the city gates and the docks. With the granaries still under construction, we need the daily shipments of grain to continue or face the possibility of widespread famine.'

Josey nodded, still numbed by the news. 'Yes, as you say, Hubert. I put this matter in your hands.'

Hubert bowed and left the room. Amelia hovered at Josey's shoulder. The events of the evening – the carriage ride, the attack, the flight back to the palace – came crashing back to her, and her legs trembled as if about to give out.

'Master Hirsch,' she said. 'Thank you for your courage this night. Ask for anything, and if it is within my power, I will grant it.'

The adept hitched his thumbs in his belt. 'Well, lass, I'm not one for collecting payment until a job is done. That creature is out there somewhere, but I'll get it.'

'I trust you will. If you'll excuse me, I shall retire for this evening.'

'Aye.'

Josey peered over her shoulder as she and Amelia walked to the door. The adept stood before the fireplace with a silver flask in his hand. His eyes were almost closed, and his lips moved as if he were praying. Josey couldn't make out the words, but something about his expression unsettled her. Could she really trust him? Or anyone, for that matter? The chimerical killer could be anywhere. What if it was leading her away to her death right now?

With a shiver that had nothing to do with the chill of the hallway, Josey let Amelia pull her from the room.

Stepping out of the interrogation chamber, Sybelle peeled the layers of half-melted skin off her fingers. A rush of cool air rustled her hair as the guards closed the door, shutting out the moans of the prisoners inside.

The session with her other prisoners, though enjoyable on a personal level, hadn't produced the results she desired. She had pried loose the location of several rebel safe houses within the city. *Safe houses.* What a droll phrase. No place was safe from her reach, not within this city, not in all of Eregoth. After sending troops to roust these locations, she set to prying loose the information she needed most of all. Where was the scion? But the rest of her time was wasted. She wiped off her bottom lip and sucked the coppery liquid from her finger. *Well, not entirely wasted.*

The enchantment she had used to break Caedman Du'Ormik's will was irresistible, but it left holes in the memories of its victims, so she had turned to other avenues to fill in the blanks. Yet the captives Soloroth brought in were shockingly ignorant about the long-range plans of their leaders. She didn't know why she had expected more of these half-clothed barbarians.

The clack of boot heels echoed down the corridor as a young man in sleek leathers approached. When he presented her with a cylindrical tube, Sybelle expected news from her commanders about the raids.

Instead, the messenger said, 'From His Highness.' His tone was deferential, but his eyes roamed her body before they settled on her face. 'I am instructed to wait for a reply, Your Ladyship.'

With a look she knew would send the boy's pulse racing, Sybelle broke open the tube. A thin scroll of parchment slid out into her hand. Its message was brief and to the point. Erric had found out she'd ordered raids inside the city without his consent. He wanted her to return to the palace. The last words burned in her mind.

At once.

She crumpled the note into a ball and froze it into ice with a thought. She turned back to the messenger as the note shattered on the floor.

'Tell His Majesty I will return when I am finished here.'

The man departed on swift steps. Sybelle ran the tip of her tongue across her teeth. What was keeping Soloroth? She had expected his report not long after she sent him out with the duke's soldiers.

As if in response to her thoughts, a gargantuan shadow rose against the wall at the end of the corridor. The jangle of metal filled the stairwell as the black peak of a massive helmet appeared. Conflicting emotions quivered inside her breast at the sight of him. Soloroth was the flesh of her flesh, blood of her blood, but something *else* lurked within his steel-clad chest. While he served her dutifully, Sybelle didn't fully trust her son. Someday, he would seek to supplant her, and on that day she would have to kill him. Until then she kept him on a tight leash. But watching him approach now, she had to wonder how secure was the collar she'd fastened around his soul. Dried blood coated Soloroth's metal gauntlets, his breastplate, even the armored plates protecting his legs. It looked as if he had bathed in it.

'What news?' she demanded before he'd even stopped three paces before her.

His metal visor looked down at her. 'The locations were searched and their occupants seized, as ordered. There was insignificant resistance.'

'Did you get them all?'

The face mask moved side to side. 'Some escaped capture in the southern ward. Patrols have been sent out to sweep the burgs.'

'You lost them in the forest, and now they elude you again! Soloroth, I swear by—'

'All the insurrectionists at my site were captured.' He held out a blood-spattered gauntlet. 'Or eliminated. Blame your other captains.'

She slapped his hand away. It wasn't his fault. The outlaws had become devilishly clever of late, but if this persisted, her situation would continue to deteriorate. Her father's patience would not last forever.

'Find the officer in charge of that raid and execute him,' she said. 'Do it yourself.'

Waiting for an acknowledgment that never came, she had an urge to freeze his insolent eyes in their sockets, but she could not afford to be without him. Not yet.

'Is there something else?' she asked.

'The scion is here.'

Sybelle bit the inside of her cheek. Pinpricks raced across her skin. This explained everything – the disturbing portents, the feelings of unease that had settled in her belly like a clutch of serpents.

'You know this for sure? You tracked him?'

'No. As before, the shadows will not cooperate.'

Her nails bit into the tender skin of her palms as she clenched her hands into fists. She expected no better – Soloroth had his uses, but subtlety was not one of them. Still, it rankled. She knew what her master would command if he knew – destroy the last heir of Shadow, of course, and be done with it. But she had other ideas. To take him, to absorb his essence and bind it to her own, that could mean everything, including an end to her filial bondage. The thought made her heart pound.

'Empty the barracks. Send every soldier out into the streets. Your Northmen, too. Scour the city until he is found.'

When Soloroth started to turn away, she stopped him. 'I want him alive. Understand?'

His helmet tipped forward. 'It will be done.'

She watched him march away down the corridor. The chain on his belt creaked like the shackles of the damned. When he was gone, she strode in the opposite direction. She wanted to discuss this new development with Caedman and find out how much the outlaw leader knew. If he had been withholding information about the scion, the punishments she would inflict on his body and soul would fling him screaming into the outer darkness. But first she needed some nourishment to recharge her energies.

With a sensual tingle, Sybelle went back to the cell holding the new prisoners.

SHADOW'S LURE

Chapter
EIGHTEEN

Set on the bank of a sluggish creek outside the city, the abandoned house might have once been a respectable homestead, but time had taken its toll. The wooden porch wrapped around the front of the domicile was warped and sagging, and the yard behind the slumped wrought-iron fence was more dirt than grass. Several holes, some as large as wagon wheels, gaped in the dilapidated roof.

Caim trailed behind Keegan and Liana, who walked with their father around to the back of the house. Although she stole glances at him during the trek from the city, Liana said nothing more, and Caim was content to travel in silence. He was tired, and he hurt everywhere. On the way out they stopped long enough for him to wrap up his sliced ribs, but his leg and forearm had gone stiff. He just wanted someplace he could sleep for a couple years. But he couldn't get what had happened in the alley out of his head. He'd never felt such bloodlust before, so out of control. The sword rested across his back, quiet now, but what would happen the next time he drew it?

Keegan took them to a door at the rear and rapped on the wooden panels. After a minute, it was opened by a young man about Keegan's age. Caim didn't recognize him, but the others apparently did. Keegan shook the lad's hand as he went inside. Liana gave the boy a wave, and Hagan slapped him on the arm. When Caim approached, the young man hurried to get out of his way. *I must look almost as bad as I feel.*

The door led into a large country-style kitchen. A gray-haired woman in a faded blue housecoat and a handkerchief minded a pot on the stove. Broken steps led up to the next floor, but the outlaws bypassed the stairs in favor of a long hallway entering deeper into the house. Caim followed them to a large room. The walls were paneled in dark wood, now pitted and cracked. There was a sizable organ against the south wall, its dusty pipes extending to the high ceiling, and a massive marble fireplace. The meager fire that burned in the hearth looked pitiful within its regal confines.

A band of men stood around the fire. Some were from the store cellar, and others he recognized from the woods, including the big man. Ramon's clothes were ragged, his hair matted with dirt and sweat, and his left hand was wrapped in a crude bandage crusted with dried blood. His nose was flattened as if it had been broken and reset, maybe more than once.

Grendt was speaking when they entered. Caim caught the wary look in the man's eyes. *He's a cold one. No surprise he survived that massacre. If this whole house came tumbling down, he'd be the only one to crawl out alive.*

Ramon saw Hagan and called out his name. A few of the others rushed over to surround the old man, asking where he'd been and how he got here.

Hagan gestured to Keegan and Liana. 'I came to see if my brother had heard from these two.'

'Where's Corgan?' one of the outlaws asked. 'He didn't go back to his shop, did he? The south ward is crawling with soldiers.'

'He's dead,' Hagan said.

A couple of the men glanced at Caim as Liana leaned against her father's shoulder.

'But,' Keegan said, 'Uncle Corgan died on his feet.'

Ramon nodded. 'Like a true son of Eregoth, subject to no overlord, beholden to no king.'

'And no southerlander empress neither!' Grendt croaked from the back of the group with a hard look at Caim.

Keegan broke the uncomfortable silence. 'Where have you been, Ramon? We thought you would meet us at my uncle's shop.'

Ramon shook his head. 'At the clearing I fought for as long as I had breath in my body, but they were too many. So I broke away and made for the low camp. It took me two days, crawling through the bracken like an animal, to get clear of the woods. I stopped at the Malgar steading. Some of you know my cousin Joram. He wanted to join us against Eviskine.'

Ramon pointed a thumb over his shoulder at a tall, raw-boned man in a wool vest who stood near the hearth. A large blacksmith's hammer leaned against the wall by his feet.

Grendt leveled a finger at Caim. 'What about him? He's the one who brought the duke's soldiers down upon us!'

Other voices grumbled in agreement.

Liana looked around with a frown. 'It's thanks to Caim that we're even alive. He saved us! Tell them, Keegan.'

Keegan turned away as Liana shook his arm.

She turned to their father. 'Papa, tell them.'

Everyone quieted as Hagan gazed down at his daughter. 'I saw him, standing over the bodies of a dozen men. Covered in blood. As it covers him now and always will. He is the hand of death, and wherever he goes, death follows.'

Caim could feel the tension in the room. His palms itched. Some men nodded at those words; others shifted from foot to foot and could not meet his gaze. Keegan was one of them. The youth was clearly divided between his loyalty to his cause and his gratefulness to Caim. *Or is it something else? Does he resent the help I've offered, even though it saved his life? What was it that Kas used to say? Never overestimate the depth of a man's gratitude, or the length of his memory.*

He'd learned to heed those words in Othir, and now it appeared he would have to observe them again. Yet despite their disdain for him, he hoped he didn't have to hurt these people. Caim kept his hands by his sides.

'I'll go, if that is what you want,' he said. 'But so should you. Someone told the soldiers where to find you, and more could be on their way here right now.'

'It was you!' Grendt said. 'We all know it.'

'He's no spy.' Keegan stood in the firelight. 'I wasn't sure at first, but he helped me and my sister. He could have left us in the woods, but he didn't. Risked his own life, and I don't think a spy would stick around to see his own goose cooked. That's all I have to say.'

Ramon clapped a hand on the youth's shoulder, making him wince. 'Keegan sees the truth. Besides, the southerner fights too good to be a spy.'

'But he's—' Grendt started to say.

'What do we do now?' someone asked.

Ramon gave Keegan a little shove, pushing him back toward his father. 'We've been mauled by the duke's men, many of us burned out of our homes and separated from our families. I wouldn't cast doubt on any man who wished to leave now and try to find some way to live in peace.'

When scattered cries against the idea filled the room, Ramon raised a hand. 'Then we must return to the castle and save our strength. Come back in the spring when the snows have thawed.'

'We can't leave,' Keegan said. 'Caedman is still in the duke's hands. What will happen to him if we flee?'

'Aye,' a stout man with a gimpy leg said. 'That don't sit right with me neither.'

One of the brothers, Dray, shook his head. 'You're bat-shit crazy. You'll never get close to him.'

Another came forward. The blond-haired spearman. 'I'll go.'

His brother snorted. 'You'll make a fine fucking candle, Aemon. Tied to a stake and set alight by the duke's executioners.'

As the others leapt into the discussion, Ramon shook his head.

'I know what you would do,' he said when they quieted. 'But it's too dangerous. We've lost many of our brothers.

Would you have us all killed? Or trussed up for the sport of Eviskine's witch? We cannot defeat soldiers in armor, nor strive against sorcery and demons with any hope of winning.'

No one spoke. Caim watched as each man struggled with his conscience. Beaten and disheartened, it wouldn't take more than a stiff wind to knock them over. Like Ramon said, they had no chance against soldiers. And against sorcery? It was beyond ridiculous. Liana looked at him with a hopeful expression, like he was the answer to all their ills.

You don't know me. I'm not the solution.

'I'll help you,' he said, not believing the words as they came out of his mouth.

This time when eyes turned to him, he didn't feel the same animosity. Grendt sneered, of course, and muttered under his breath. And Ramon watched with an unreadable expression beneath his dirt-caked beard, but the rest had the look of convicted men who had just been given a reprieve from the hangman's noose.

'But it has to be tonight.'

That evoked a chorus of grumbles and forced laughter.

Ramon quieted them down. 'We need time. To plan, to gather more men. Everyone here is about ready to fall down where they stand.'

'It has to be now. The anthill is already knocked over. We can take advantage of the confusion before they restore order.'

Keegan nodded. 'If they're looking for us in the outer districts of the city, there'll be fewer to stop us at the prison.'

Ramon looked around. Many of the men were nodding to themselves.

'All right. If that is the decision of the clans, then me and my fighters will abide by it.'

Then he left the room with Grendt and a few others trailing after him. Caim could find no reason to be relieved. He had just agreed to a suicide mission in the name of people he hardly knew, and he wasn't even getting paid for it. *What was I thinking?*

Liana whispered with her father off to the side of the room.

She shook her head several times, more and more emphatically, but the old man's frown only deepened. Finally, he gestured toward the door, but she walked past Caim to her brother.

She grasped Keegan's hand. 'Promise me you'll be careful.'

'Sure, Li. I'll be fine. Don't worry. Caim is with us. Nothing can go wrong.'

Caim wanted to vanish into a crack in the wall when Liana swung her gaze to him.

'Look out for him,' she said.

'I will.'

Hugging herself, she ran out of the room, followed by the slower steps of her father.

SHADOW'S LURE

Chapter
NINETEEN

A cold wind blew down the alley on the east side of the city where Caim crouched. Its icy fingers found ways inside his cloak and jacket. Snow fell in thick, wet flakes that lent a placid air to the occasion. He was worried about more than snow at the moment. Specifically, Ramon's plan, or lack of one.

The outline of their destination towered above the skyline. The prison house was a colossal block of stone on the banks of the river that flowed around the eastern flank of the city. Ramon's plan was a full-on charge, or close enough that Caim considered leaving them to their own devices, no matter what he'd said before. But every time he glanced at Keegan, who squatted behind Ramon and the others, pangs of responsibility returned. *So what's stopping you from leaving?*

He didn't know, and that bothered him. Only twenty-two outlaws had volunteered for the mission. A score of men – some of them untrained, others too old to be useful if it came to blows – to assault a fortress that looked like it could hold off an army. The prospects weren't encouraging.

Caim flexed his injured forearm. The pain was getting worse. He checked his knives, keeping his hand well clear of the hilt jutting over his shoulder. The sword had been quiet since the battle in the alley, and he was content for it to remain dormant. The shadows, as always, were nearby, but

192

he wasn't sure if that was a good thing. He opened the bulging pouch at his waist and dipped the fingers of a gloved hand inside. Pulling out a handful of black ash, he dabbed it on the buckles of his clothing, the pommels of his knives, and over his face. He felt Keegan's presence beside him. He could see the youth without looking over, lanky hair that hung past his shoulders, his narrow mouth, the sharp jut of his chin.

'What's with the makeup?'

Caim held up the pouch. 'Put some on your face, and the backs of your hands if you don't have gloves. Cover anything that could reflect light.'

Keegan did as he was told, until he resembled a raccoon with sooty paws.

'Better,' Caim said. 'When we go in, I want you to stay with me. I mean right on my heels. When I turn, you turn. Got it?'

'I don't need a nursemaid. Father's already enough of a pain in my prick.'

Caim snatched the boy's collar and pulled him in close. 'Listen up. A lot of your friends are going to get themselves killed tonight. If you want to see the sunrise, you'll do what I say.'

'If you know something—'

'I know stupid when I see it. I can't save anyone who won't listen, and Ramon isn't about to take orders from me. But I can save you.'

Keegan's mouth settled in a firm line. There was something in the youth's eyes, like he wanted someone to hit him. Caim let him go, and the youth nodded.

'All right. What did you bring in case we run into a fight?'

Keegan touched his belt. 'I've only got my hunting knife. My sword broke back in the . . .' He swallowed and his eyes tightened. 'After we left Uncle Corgan's store.'

Caim reached under his cloak and drew the sword he had taken off the dead soldier in the alleyway. It was a falcata, a curved single-edged blade a little shorter and heavier than a cavalry saber. The steel shone bright in the dim light as Keegan took the weapon with both hands.

'This will serve you better than that bit of tin you were carrying before. Keep it ready, but don't go stabbing everything you see. Things might get confusing in there—'

'Let's go!' Ramon said from the front of the group.

Caim pulled Keegan to his feet as the outlaws filed out of the plaza. 'Just stay close.'

As they joined the tail of the procession, slipping through the dark streets, getting closer to the massive structure, Caim felt a tugging in his chest. He slowed down. It was the same sensation he'd felt at the clearing, right before the armored giant arrived, but stronger. He placed a hand on his chest and took a deep breath as he hurried to catch up with the others. If Keegan noticed the lapse, he didn't say anything. For the next couple of minutes, Caim concentrated on taking slow, even breaths. Gradually the sensation lessened, until it was only a faint throb behind his breastbone. Irritating, but nothing he couldn't work around. While he wondered what had triggered it, for now he could only push it out of his thoughts and focus on the task at hand. If the Beast was here . . .

Caim reached back to loosen his knives in their sheaths.

The thudding of the outlaws' boots on the snow-packed street was loud enough to wake the neighborhood, but the shutters on the buildings remained closed as they passed, the windows unlit. Caim imagined the people huddled inside, afraid to look out of their own homes.

When they reached the next intersection, the prison's outline loomed before them, six stories tall with a twelve-foot-high stone wall surrounding its grounds. Square towers studded the corners of the outer wall; lights burned within their arched windows. The entire compound was surrounded by a hundred yards of wide-open space without buildings or cover of any kind – a killing ground. Had there been a moon out tonight, it would have been suicide for them to even attempt to enter, but black clouds continued to obscure the sky. Their luck was holding.

Without the time for a full casing, Caim scanned the compound and tried to guess the best point of entry. The side facing them was bisected by a small gatehouse; probably the best-defended part of the prison. The western side didn't look much better, but the east bordered the river. There was still a wall on that side, but the sentries might have trained themselves over time to ignore that sector. Caim scanned the walls for signs of sentries, and was both relieved and daunted to find none. Against his better judgment, he reached up to lay a finger on the hilt of the black sword. At once, the night erupted into a vivid palette of colors. Still, the walls appeared clear even to his ensorcelled eyes. The hilt quivered.

Caim slid his hand off the weapon and found Keegan watching him. With a shake of his head, he shouldered his way into the ring of outlaws.

'Listen close,' Ramon whispered, loud enough for all to hear. 'We're almost to the wall. We'll try to take the gate without making too much—'

'The east wall.'

Caim had to fight the urge to reach for his knives as everyone's eyes turned toward him. He wasn't used to operating like this. There were too many of them. If he could take only one or two inside, that would be different. To hell with strength in numbers. Except for Ramon, he doubted any of these men had ever killed before. If they ran into trouble, how would they react? Like they had at the clearing?

'What about it?' Ramon asked.

'That's our best way in.'

Ramon's face was a pale thumbprint in the darkness, his eyes black pits of nothing. 'How do you know that?'

'Call it a hunch. But whatever we do, it needs to be quick. We could lose cloud cover at any time.'

Ramon was quiet for a moment, and then said, 'All right. You're the professional. You can be the first one over.'

'Fine. Does anyone know where your chief is being kept?'

One man – tall, with a full red beard and sharp eyes set deep under bushy eyebrows – raised a hand. He had been at the clearing.

'Maybe I do,' he said. 'My cousin used to work inside.'

A few ribald comments floated in the air, louder than Caim would have liked.

The tall man grunted. 'Yeah. He was a right bastard. Hardly good for anything, but he told me a few things about this place. He said they kept the biggest fish on the top floor. I suppose Caedman fits the bill.'

'That he does,' Dray said. 'The duke's had a hard-on for Caedman since even before Aldercairn.'

'Why's that?' Caim asked.

A grin split Aemon's snarled yellow beard. 'When Eviskine took the city, he offered amnesty to any clan or noble family who chose to join him. Caedman convinced his mother's clan, the Indrigs, to refuse the offer. Even worse, he called for the other clans to ride against Liovard in a show of resistance.'

Caim showed his teeth. 'I'm starting to like this man. So let me guess, the other chiefs didn't show up for Caedman's demonstration.'

'A few did,' Keegan said, softly.

'Not near enough.' Dray grumbled. 'And the fucking witch sent those that did running like a pack of whipped dogs. Then the duke seized their lands for the insult and stripped their families of all wealth and title.'

'So Caedman turned outlaw,' Caim said.

'The duke never forgot who inspired the revolution, and forgiveness ain't in his nature.'

'All right.' Caim rubbed his hands together. 'When we get over the wall, we head for the front gate. Don't try anything brave. Just stick close to me, stay quiet, and don't get lost.'

Heads nodded, their eyes hooded in the gloom. With a deep breath, Caim checked his knives before he started across the long stretch of ground toward the gray walls. Some of his anxiety dropped away once he was out in front. It almost felt like old times: a moonless night, him stalking through the dark streets of the city alone. The only thing missing was Kit's nonstop rambling while he tried to work. *Dammit. What's got into her?*

She'd been gone for days now. What if something had

happened to her? He scoffed at the idea; nothing could harm Kit. Still, he worried. But what could he do? Nothing, except hope she decided to return soon.

They reached the outer wall without raising an alarm. Caim went over first, and was surprised when the outlaws followed without a hitch. Climbing they understood. Being silent, however, was a different matter. Fortunately, a quick jaunt through the interior grounds revealed no sentries, and the towers were spaced far enough apart that Caim was able to lead the outlaws to the prison house without discovery. He peered around the corner of the building.

The prison had only one visible entrance, a large reinforced door set in the southern wall atop a short flight of steps. The six sentries guarding the door didn't appear especially vigilant for trouble, laughing and trading jibes as they leaned on their spears, but they were awake and alert. If they fought like the other soldiers he'd encountered in the duke's employ, Caim was confident they could be taken down quickly, even if the outlaws gave him only scant support, but there was the matter of noise. On a quiet night like this, any hue or cry would be heard throughout the complex, and the outlaws couldn't win a pitched battle. Stealth was the key.

Caim gazed up at the prison walls. Rows of dark windows dotted the smooth stone facing. Little larger than the arrow loops found in castle walls, they were too narrow to allow access, and they probably led into locked cells in any case. Then Fortune smiled down from the heavens. Two of the door sentries walked off toward the gatehouse. They might have been making their rounds or rotating to another post or had just gone to use the latrine. In any case, Caim figured they had at least two minutes before the guards or their replacements came back this way.

'Wolmacks,' Keegan whispered behind him.

Caim kept his voice low. 'What?'

The youth pointed at the remaining sentries. 'They're Wolmacks, the only clan to side with the duke. They come from some backwoods out east.'

197

'You don't sound impressed with them.'

'Nah. They can't fight for shit, so Eviskine gives them the worst jobs.'

'Like guarding his prison.'

Keegan nodded, and Caim went back to his surveying. He thought back to the backwoods boys he had known growing up. One thing they had in common was that they liked to tear it up whenever and wherever they got the chance. He needed to get moving. Those sentries could return at any time. Motioning for the others to stay back, he slipped around the corner.

Caim drew his knives as he sprinted toward the enemy position. The shadows flocked to him, concealing him under layers of darkness. He thought for a moment about how it must look to those behind him, but he didn't have time to be subtle as he closed in on his targets. He only hoped the shadows did as he told them.

The nearest soldier stood with his back to Caim, which was convenient, but the others were more or less facing his direction. He bypassed the easy kill in exchange for added surprise. As he snaked around the first sentry, Caim clubbed him in the temple with the butt of a knife. While the other soldiers took a moment to register his presence, Caim weaved among them. His knives cut silver ribbons in the night. One of the sentries lifted his spear as if to throw it. Caim concentrated for a moment, and a chill ran down his back as the soldier's shadow reached around to seize his neck. The man fell, clawing at the shadowy hands that strangled him. Caim kept moving. He had fought against his baser nature up to this point, but now there was no time for mercy. The clubbed soldier was the only one to make a sound before dying, a grunting croak that had barely begun before the edge of a knife silenced him forever.

Caim dropped to the ground with the fall of the last body and listened for the whistle of arrow fire. All was quiet. He dropped the shroud of shadows and waved for the outlaws to come. He was feeling a little lightheaded, and the pressure in his chest had returned.

Ramon was the first to arrive.

'By Ell,' he breathed. 'I never saw anything like—'

'Check the door,' Caim said, waving the rest onward.

They had no time for chitchat. Every passing heartbeat increased the chances they would be discovered. And once that happened, things were going to get messy.

A few of the men cast curious glances at Caim as they crowded around the entrance. As he'd seen from the corner, the prison door would take a battering ram to bring down if it was barred from the inside. He was tempted to drop to his knees and say a word of thanks to whatever god was watching over them this night as Ramon pushed it open with his shoulder.

'Inside!' Caim hissed.

His forearm was killing him. He pressed it against his side as he waited for Keegan to catch up. The boy looked at the corpses on the ground. With a gesture, Caim steered him inside.

Beyond the door was a plain antechamber. Torches on the walls illuminated a wide corridor that extended through the center of the building; doors were set into both sides all the way down to an archway at the far end. One of the doors was open, and soft noises issued from it as Caim crossed the foyer. He heard men talking, at least two of them. Not waiting for the others, he slid up beside the door just as one man – a soldier with a brown hood settled loose around his neck – exited. The soldier's head was turned as he spoke. Caim let him pass. The man behind him was older, well into his forties, and stockier around the middle. His uniform jacket, with a dozen carmine strips down the sleeve, hung open as he walked behind the soldier. When the officer stepped across the threshold, Caim attacked.

The soldier with his head turned didn't have time to make a sound as nine inches of honed steel pierced the back of his neck. Blood spattered the floor. Before the officer had time to yell, Caim opened a second mouth under his chin.

The sounds of the bodies hitting the floor echoed down the corridor. Caim glanced through the open doorway, saw it was an office – sparsely appointed and empty – and kept moving down the corridor. He stopped at the next door and listened. Hearing nothing, he went on to the one after that. Also silent. No. There was a faint sound like buzzing insects. Snoring. As the doors in this corridor were varnished pinewood and not reinforced, he assumed they led to guard barracks, storerooms, and such. The cells must be in another part of the prison house.

Caim put a finger to his lips and waved for the outlaws to follow. They reached the end of the corridor without incident and found a double set of stone staircases, one going up and the other down. By best guess, Caim figured they were at the center of the building. He waited for Ramon and Keegan.

'You sure your man's on the top floor?' he asked.

Keegan nodded, but Ramon beckoned to the bearded outlaw with the prison guard for a cousin.

'Oak, is that cousin of yours reliable?'

The man shrugged. 'I don't know. I suppose so.'

'Either he is or he isn't.'

A cool sensation touched Caim's ankle. He looked down to see a handful of shadows climbing over his feet. Images popped into his head: the stairs, long bare corridors studded with closed doors, a man in a gray uniform walking down a hallway swinging a stout club in his hand, and a door. Something about the door bothered him.

Oak started to say something, but Caim cut him off with a terse whisper.

'We're going up. Keep your eyes open.'

The outlaws nodded. By the looks on their faces, they hadn't expected to get this far and they were ready for this adventure to be over. Biting his tongue, Caim started up the stairs. He climbed two flights and came to a landing. Four doors branched off in different directions. Caim cracked open the doors and put his eye to each. Corridors led off into the dimness, each with many doors; these doors were rougher and bulkier in construction than those below. Prisoner cells.

By this time, the outlaws had caught up to him. Motioning for them to stay back, he continued his ascent. On each floor, four doors awaited. Caim didn't bother checking them. He tried to calculate how many cells the building contained. Six floors with four wings each, and at least a score of cells per wing. The number boggled him. It spoke of a certain mind-set for the Nimeans to have constructed this monolith of imprisonment back when they conquered the land. Those who resisted were either put to the sword or locked away. *Come to think of it, the True Church held a similar stance on how to treat its adversaries. A simple matter of following a successful model? How many have perished in these dark chambers?*

Caim chewed on his thoughts as he climbed higher. The outlaws inched closer with every step until Ramon and Keegan were practically on his heels. At least their luck held; they didn't see any guards on their climb.

The stairs ended on a wide landing. Here, as below, they found four doors. Caim had been considering how to conduct the search. By the time they reached the top, he'd made up his mind. He didn't like it, but he didn't have much choice. Time was against them. Any moment an alarm could sound.

'All right,' Caim said. 'This is where it gets interesting. I'm splitting you into four groups and—'

As soon as they heard 'splitting,' the men started muttering to each other. The sounds bounced off the stone walls and down the stairwell. Caim's gloves creaked as his hands clenched.

'Quiet!' he whispered, louder than he wanted, but it got their attention.

A noise echoed from behind the west doorway. It was soft, like it came from a long way off. A boot step? Or maybe the butt of a spear striking the floor?

'Listen,' he said, quieter this time. 'We have to move fast. Each team takes a different door. Keegan and I will go west—'

201

A short man with his hood pulled down low slipped through the group. 'I'll go with you.'

'Fine,' Caim said. 'The rest of you, try to stay quiet. If you find Caedman, bring him back here and wait for everyone else to return.'

'What if we run into trouble?' one of the townie outlaws asked.

'This isn't a carnival. Do what you have to do, but don't stop to see the sights. Just keeping going until you've searched every cell.'

Hooded heads nodded to him, and then Ramon took over, dividing the men by some order of his own determining.

Caim went to the door and lifted the door's handle. A sliver of light spilled through the crack. Everyone stopped moving to watch. Although the corridor beyond was dimmer than those he'd seen below, he could see it was empty.

'Come on,' he mouthed, and slipped through the doorway.

The others' boots pattered behind him as he went to the first door on the left. It was a stout portal of old oak secured by a thick beam. As there was no window or peephole, Caim was forced to open it to find out what was inside. He sheathed both knives. The short outlaw hung back a few paces. Swallowing a curse, Caim gestured for Keegan to keep watch as he put his hands under the bar and lifted. The braces attached to the wall squeaked when he applied pressure, but then released the bar without further protest. Caim paused, holding his breath as he listened. Somewhere down the corridor, a dull thud echoed, the same sound he'd heard before, but he still couldn't identify it.

Caim set the bar on the ground and pulled on the door's latch. It opened with just a slight creak. A powerful stench rolled over him as he stood in the doorway, the combined odors of rot, feces, and death. Fighting past the reek, Caim peered into the darkness. Inside was a small stone room roughly four paces by three, furnished with nothing but an empty pewter bowl on the floor. A shape huddled on the far side of the cell. He couldn't tell if the occupant was a man or a

woman. It had something like a shawl draped over its head.
Caim stepped inside. The shape didn't move as he nudged an
exposed, filthy foot.

'Can you hear me? Hello?'

He received no response. No movement, no sounds. Not
even a hushed grunt.

Stooping over, Caim touched the shape's head through the
shawl. It rocked to the side without resistance. Dead.

He left the cell and closed the door. Shaking his head at
Keegan's inquiring glance, he moved to the door across the
hall. They repeated the process six more times, twice more
finding corpses, and just stale air in the other four. In the
eighth cell they discovered a living person.

Living maybe, but hardly alive.

He was a man of advanced age smelling almost as bad as the
corpses they'd found. A long dirty beard drooped across his
shrunken chest.

'What do we do with him?' Keegan asked with a sleeve
pressed over his mouth and nose.

The humane thing would be to put him out of his misery. But
looking at the pitiful wretch curled up on the cold floor, Caim
didn't have the heart for it.

'You,' he said to the short outlaw. 'What's your name?'

The boy hunched his shoulders like Caim had yelled at him.
'Dongo.'

'Dongo, find something to prop this door open. We'll gather
him up on the way out if we have time.'

Caim and Keegan kept checking cells. They found a few
more lost souls, most of them in the same condition as the old
man or worse. One woman of indeterminate age, covered in
dried blood, huddled in the corner of her cell. She screamed
when they opened her door, and went on screaming until
they closed it again. Keegan's eyes were wide as they left that
door, but Dongo crept closer as if he wanted to go inside.

'Leave it,' Caim said. 'We can't save everyone.'

Side passages branched off halfway down the main corridor,

203

but Caim focused on the doors. It made sense that a high-profile captive would be kept somewhere convenient.

As they moved down the hallway, Caim saw there was a door at the end. He thought it was only another cell at first, but as they approached a sense of anxiety began to build in the pit of his stomach. While Keegan and Dongo unbarred another cell, Caim realized what was bothering him. The feeling was the same he'd been experiencing since he came north, a powerful presence that wrapped around him like a ghostly tentacle. Here, it was almost overwhelming.

And it came from the door at the end of the hallway.

Caim went up to the door. On the outside it looked like all the others. He reached for the latch.

'Caim!' Keegan called out.

Caim pulled his hand back. With a long glance at the door, he turned and hurried over to the next-to-last cell. Keegan stood halfway out the doorway. His face was ashen.

'What is it?'

'Look.'

The youth held open the door for Caim to look inside. Dongo knelt beside a lump of tangled rags in the middle of the floor. Caim went over to the young man. He stooped down and reached out to the layer of rags covering the lump's head. Five thick fingers with hairy knuckles snatched his wrist and held it in a viselike grip. Caim yanked hard, but he was held fast. The lump's other hand pulled the rags from its face, and a pair of ice-blue eyes glared at him from beneath bristly red brows. The face was exceedingly dirty, and ugly beyond imagination.

Caim drew his left-hand knife and put it to the lump's chest.

'No!' Dongo cried in a feminine voice.

As Dongo grabbed his knife hand, Caim glanced at him. No, at *her*. Dongo's hood had fallen back in her rush to stop him to reveal Liana's features.

'Li!' Keegan yelled from the doorway. 'What are you doing here? Where's father?'

'He left the city. He's not angry, Keegan. He doesn't like what we're doing, but I think he understands.'

Caim sat back on his heels. Keegan hadn't realized his sister had accompanied them here, and Caim was a little angry at himself for not noticing either. He wasn't sure what to do. Fortunately, the ugly man's grip was faltering. Caim pulled free and stood up.

'You know this man?' he said.

Liana nodded. 'His name is Samnus. He's thane of the Hurrold clan. He was at Aldercairn, wasn't he, Keegan?'

Her brother nodded from his post, but kept his distance.

'He stood up with Caedman against the duke,' Liana continued.

Caim's gaze traveled across the man's torso. Splotches of old blood marred his cloak of rags. His left arm was tucked against his ribs; the right foot looked twisted.

'We don't have time to carry a cripple,' Caim said.

The ugly man growled like a wounded bear. 'I can walk, damn you! Let me up and I'll prove it.'

They stood back, and the man, Samnus, rolled onto his hands and knees. With exquisite slowness, he rose to a kneeling stance, and then got his feet under him one at a time until he was standing before them, albeit with a sway.

'I can help him,' Liana said. 'We won't slow you down.'

'I don't need coddling, girl!'

Caim stepped up to the prisoner's face until their noses were a finger span apart. 'We aren't here for you. If you fall behind, we'll leave you to rot. Understand?'

Samnus grinned and revealed a mouthful of broken teeth. 'Why are you wasting time then, boy? Lead the way.'

'We're looking for Caedman,' Liana said.

The man nodded, and even that simple gesture betrayed the depths of his exhaustion. 'The door across the hall. That's where they've been keeping him.'

Caim headed out of the cell, and Keegan moved aside. Out in the corridor, the dark presence from the end of the hall beckoned, like an echo of a bad dream. Tiny quivers ran up his

205

arms and across his body. He motioned for the others to stay back as he headed for the malignant door.

'Boy.' Samnus leaned in the entrance of his cell. 'You don't want to go in there.'

But Caim pushed open the door.

The room beyond was larger than a cell, but hardly spacious. Its stone walls enclosed several tables, a pair of wooden chairs, and braziers filled with dim red coals. Naked bodies occupied the tables and thrones, strapped into place, six men in all. They had been tortured to death. Though his nose was deadened to the stench by his exposure to the noisome cells, Caim's eyes picked out the worst of the mutilations: flesh peeled away from the faces and chests, hands and feet hacked from their limbs, eyes burned out of the sockets, genitals sliced clean off. A pile of flesh scraps lay on the floor like a dog's dinner. The professional part of Caim's mind had to pause in admiration for the handiwork; it was exquisite in its precision, better than any sawbones he'd ever met could do. But that part of him that could still feel quailed at the sight.

The stench of Shadow was thick in the air, lingering around the bodies like the perfume of a departed lover. Pushing through his anger, Caim examined the corpses one at a time. He forced himself to touch them, turn their heads from side to side, lift their handless arms and peer into bloody sockets. Traces of black residue confirmed his suspicion. The memory of Mathias lying dead, a hole cut into his flabby chest, left Caim cold and angry.

A call from the hallway roused him from his thoughts. Caim turned to find Keegan in the doorway.

'We found Caedman.'

Caim pushed Keegan out of the gruesome chamber and closed the door behind him. Samnus stood in the corridor, looking unsteady. The thane cocked his head toward the open door opposite his cell. Inside, Liana knelt beside a pallet, upon which lay a tall man under a swaddle of stained blankets. She had an arm under his head, trying to help him sit up. Caim went in to help her. Together they wrestled the man upright.

Then the blanket covering his body slid down, and Caim reconsidered.

'This is the right man?' he asked.

'Yes.'

Caim didn't see how she could tell. The captive's face was a mass of bruises; his chest, stomach, and arms were crisscrossed with a hatchwork of incisions and burns. In some places, the skin had been sliced off to reveal the red meat underneath. He was unconscious or dead, and Caim couldn't tell which would be the better deal. Then the man made a low groan.

'Go . . . not here . . .'

Caim looked back. 'Keegan, help me with this.'

Liana made room as Caim and her brother wrestled the prisoner off the mattress, although he couldn't walk. Caim guided them back out into the hall. Liana waited with Samnus, who leaned on her despite his earlier show of bravado. As Caim and Keegan passed them, Samnus spoke up.

'I've seen you before, boy.'

Keegan kept walking, but the outlaw thane reached out and grabbed the back of his jacket, dragging Caim and the captive to a halt as well.

'You were at Aldercairn, right? I don't remember these others, but you were there.'

Keegan yanked free of the grasp. 'Yes. I was there.'

'But you weren't taken,' Samnus pressed.

Caim slid his free hand down behind his back and loosened a knife.

'This is my brother Keegan,' Liana said. 'He escaped the massacre.'

Samnus grunted. 'You ran, huh? Glad you finally found your bollocks, boy. So what is this about? A way to soothe your conscience?'

Keegan winced as if the man had struck him across the face, but said nothing.

Liana dropped Samnus's arm. 'You don't know him! He stood up to fight when others would not.'

Caim winced at the volume of her voice. Down the corridor,

someone groaned in their cell. Samnus watched Keegan with hard eyes. Caim had seen that look in a thousand other eyes; more often than not they preceded an explosion of violence. But the clan leader made no move to attack the youth.

'You'd be talking about your father, eh?' Samnus's mouth folded up in a tight smile. 'Aye, I know Hagan. From long ago. I came to him before Aldercairn. Did you know that? I asked him to come to the peace-meet, to hear what was said, but he refused.'

'My father isn't a coward either,' Keegan said, finally meeting the outlaw's gaze.

The two stared at each other for a long heartbeat, and then Samnus's smile erupted into a full grin, which only made his face more hideous.

'No, he's not, boy. He's just become an old man, and that's not such a bad thing. I can't say the same fate will ever befall me.'

Caim glanced between them, and then at Liana. She seemed agitated, but the moment of violence seemed to have passed.

'Are we okay then?' he asked.

'Good as gold,' Samnus replied. 'So you can take your hand off that pig-sticker, son.'

Carrying the prisoner between them, Caim and Keegan maneuvered down the passageway with Liana and the thane behind them. Caim stopped to peer down the side corridors. The presence of sorcery had touched a nerve in him. He needed to get out of here. More than that, he needed Kit. He felt like a blind man navigating through this labyrinth without her.

A shadow landed on his shoulder. Caim gritted his teeth and fought not to brush it off as a chill bit into his skin. A picture formed in his head. Men climbing the stairs. A flash of metal. Soldiers.

Caim shoved open the door to the staircase with his elbow and listened.

'What are—?' Keegan started to ask.

Caim shushed him. He heard it again, the sound of clomping

boots. He pushed the prisoner into Keegan's arms as the door on the opposite landing popped open. Ramon and his cousin rushed out and slammed the portal shut behind them. Their weapons dripped with fresh blood.

A moment later, loud voices shouted from below. Caim drew his knives and went to the stairs. Company was coming. A lot of company.

SHADOW'S LURE

Chapter TWENTY

Screeching winds blasted Kit from every direction, making her regret every time she'd complained about Caim's choices in women, or his attitude, or pretty much anything. The fear that she might never get back to him had lodged behind Kit's heart as she trudged through this endless nightmare.

She stumbled over a crinkle in the ground and brushed up against the shadow beast. The massive head swung toward her. Kit patted Doggie's shoulder as she righted herself. After their encounter with the monster of the mists, he had rejoined her looking little worse for wear, and they'd come to an uneasy agreement. He stuck around and kept her safe; in return, she tried not to talk too much. It wasn't easy for her, but the alternative was even less desirable, so she soldiered on. And thought about Caim. A lot. Once, they had been best friends, but she didn't know what was wrong with him lately. He was moody all the time. He hardly talked to her like he used to. He was changing, which she had always encouraged on account of his many aggravating habits, but not like this.

It's been getting worse since we left Othir. I know he misses the mud-woman, but this is different. It's almost like the bad stuff that he's done is catching up with him.

Kit let her chin droop to her chest, her eyes half closed against the driving gale. The prickling had gotten stronger, or

210

perhaps she was deluding herself. What if she wound up walking these featureless lands forever? No, she had to get back to Caim. If she did – *when* she did – she had to convince him to leave those northern lands before it was too late, before they changed him for real and good.

She glanced ahead for a moment. Something glimmered in the mists. Kit shaded her eyes as she peered into the shrieking gloam. There it was again! A few points off to the left. *Could it be . . . ?* She glanced in the direction of the tingling itch, and then back to the light.

Slapping Doggie on the shoulder, Kit started running toward the glow. The beast kept pace. Side by side they came upon a circle of light glowing in midair. Another portal. But there was something different about it. The circle was dimmer than the other portal. She glanced at Doggie, but it gave no comment. With a held breath, Kit reached out to the circle. Something moved on the other side of the glow, indistinct shapes in its gold-gray surface. She leaned forward and saw a pale oval. A man's face.

'Caim!'

She rushed forward and yelped when her fingers met a hard plane of resistance. Kit clawed at the portal, but it adamantly refused her. *Damned thing. Let me through!*

But it was no use. Shaking with frustration, she rubbed her fingers and stared through the window at her mud-man. He was walking through a dark place. She got the impression there might be others with him. Was he in trouble? Most likely. He could never stay out of it whenever she wasn't around.

She pounded on the hard surface. 'I'm here, Caim!'

Kit couldn't tell if he responded over the howl of the winds. She turned her head and froze as the portal's view slid sideways. *That was odd.*

She turned her head the other way, and the perspective shifted back to where it had been before, centered on Caim's face. With a little experimentation she was able to move the view in the portal in whatever direction she wanted. She turned the image completely around and tried to get a sense of his surroundings. It was a building of stone. A big building. There were people in little rooms. Her throat closed up for a moment. Caim was in prison! She nosed around for more information. Somehow she was able to expand the picture in a dizzying rush until she was looking at the structure from the outside. The place was even bigger than she had first thought. The night was extraordinarily dark, with almost no moonlight. Then she spotted some light. Torches. She swooped in closer and saw they were torches in the hands of big men. Men with armor and weapons, approaching the prison's main gate. She did a quick count and was confident that Caim could slip away from them. Then the portal's picture rippled. Kit grasped the cool edges, trying to stabilize it. Its illumination flickered. *Not now!*

As she tried to take the view back to Caim, Kit saw something on the periphery that made her stop. A curvy shape wrapped in a dark shroud approached amid the soldiers. The tip of Kit's nose quivered. *Oh, no. Caim! She's coming! Caim!*

Kit forced the portal toward the building. She didn't blink when her viewpoint passed through the gate and into the darkness beyond. All she could think about was warning Caim.

The witch was coming.

SHADOW'S LURE

Chapter
TWENTY-ONE

Caim dove into the front ranks of the men coming up the steps. His assumption – that this was a patrol of jailors, maybe two or three at the most, lightly armed – collapsed when he ran into a squad of helmed spearmen. He barely had time to register this as he plunged into their midst.

He dropped two enemies in his first rush and sent another stumbling back into the men below with a kick to the face. Shouts resounded up the stairwell as Caim cut his way through leather and flesh. His only advantage lay in surprise and sheer ferocity, but that only lasted a few heartbeats before the soldiers discarded their ineffectual spears and drew smaller arms. Step by painful step they pushed him up the stairs until he was back on the landing. Then Keegan and Ramon's cousin were on either side of him. Joram attacked like a man possessed, swinging his hammer with a vengeance. Caim scowled as a sword stroke meant for Keegan almost took off his ear. With another thrust, the soldiers pushed them back another few steps, almost to the wall. Joram didn't retreat with them, but pressed forward by himself. The soldiers fell back before his intensity, but Caim saw the danger.

'Get back!' he grunted between breaths.

But it was too late; the soldiers surrounded the tall clansman, cutting him off from the landing and safe retreat. One moment Joram's hammer rose and fell like he was pounding metal into submission, the next he and it disappeared under the press of bodies.

'Back!' Caim shouted to Keegan.

Keegan retreated into the doorway with his sister, giving Caim some room to maneuver, but three soldiers were already on the landing, with more coming up behind them. Caim glanced around. *How am I going to get out of this?*

There was nowhere left to retreat to – they were on the top floor. No windows in sight. And having seen the results of captivity in this horrid place, surrender wasn't an option. He'd die before they took him alive. *If Keegan loves his sister, he'll kill her the moment my body hits the floor.*

Another option buzzed in the back of his head like an angry hornet. His powers. As the soldiers moved to surround him, that final solution loomed larger in Caim's mind. It was potentially fatal for everyone in the prison – Keegan, Liana, the outlaws, and the scores of men and women languishing in their cells. Then again, some might call it an act of mercy. *Damn yourself if you will, but don't sugarcoat it. Will you kill a hundred people to save your own hide?*

The answer lurked inside him, but Caim didn't want to search for it, afraid of what he might find as the battle-rage bubbled in his chest. The shadows oozed along the ceiling, pulsing with hunger, wanting to be unleashed. Their hunger began to eat away at his concern, and he didn't know how long he could keep the feelings at bay.

Caim froze for a fraction of a heartbeat as a tremendous roar echoed behind him. But it wasn't the shadow beast. Samnus launched himself from the doorway and into the press of soldiers. Seizing them in his bruised arms, the burly thane plunged over the side of the landing and into the empty space between the stairways. Their combined screams dropped like stones down a well. Caim couldn't believe what he had just seen. It was madness.

Caim rushed at the soldiers on the steps. As he deflected a hammer stroke aimed at his face, Caim felt the presence of the sword like a great black bird perched on his shoulder.

He wanted to draw it, but he wasn't sure he could trust the weapon. Or perhaps he couldn't trust himself as the bloodlust sang in his ears.

As he punctured the stomach and inner thigh of the man across from him, the north door banged open. Aemon and Dray exploded onto the crowded landing, plowing into the soldiers with their boar spears. The distraction allowed Caim to beat aside a soldier's guard and put him down with a stab up through the armpit.

When the last soldier was slain, Caim leaned against the wall. His forearm was killing him. There was blood everywhere – pooled on the floor, streaked across the walls. Keegan sat on the floor holding his left hand on his lap. His sister dabbed at the wound with the edge of her cloak. Caim pushed aside his exhaustion to go over to them. Keegan's palm was laid open like a cleaned fish belly. Blood welled from the cut in thick streams. Liana tried to take hold of her brother's arm to get a better look, but Keegan jerked it away and pressed it against his stomach.

'Let it go, Li.'

'Keegan! It looks bad. Let me see!'

'No, Li—'

Caim grabbed the boy's arm and pulled up his sleeve. Long cuts ran along the inside of his forearm. They looked like they had been made with a knife blade. A few looked recent, but faint lines showed where old cuts had healed over. Caim looked up, but Keegan was staring down at his lap, his lower lip pulled into his mouth. Caim moved in front of his find so none of the other outlaws could see.

'Keegan,' Liana said. 'Did you do this?'

His chest shuddered as he drew in a long breath. 'Sometimes I can't deal with it, Li. You know? Father and the war. I just . . .'

Caim sliced a strip of cloth from the youth's cloak. While Liana wrapped the makeshift bandage around her brother's hand and forearm, he gripped the boy's shoulder.

'You did well.'

Keegan winced as his sister tied off the ends of the bandage. 'I could have done more.'

'Any more,' Liana said, 'and we'd be sewing your funeral bag.'

Caim looked Keegan in the eye. 'You did plenty.'

The youth nodded. Caedman was slumped against the wall beside them. If anything, his pallor had gotten worse. *Wonderful. All this to rescue a warm corpse.* Caim turned around. The rest of the outlaws gathered around the landing. Three men held the east door shut, even though the pounding from it had ceased. Ramon strode toward them. 'Where did you come from?' he asked Liana.

'She stowed away,' Caim replied.

Ramon bent down and winced when he got a closer look at the prisoner. 'It's worse than I thought. You think he'll live?'

'I don't know. He's beaten up pretty bad, but he'll stand a better chance if we can get him out of here.'

'The front is the best way out.'

Caim didn't like it, but he had to agree. The presence of the soldiers was a bad sign.

Ramon pointed to a pair of men. 'Take the lead with Caim. Oak and Lumel, you stay with Caedman. Everybody stay tight around them.'

Oak and the other man selected bent down and hefted Caedman. One of the men holding the opposite door shut called over, asking what they should do.

'Wedge it shut,' Caim said. 'With a knife or a spear tip. Anything you can find.'

The outlaws formed up. Those with injuries, including Caedman and Keegan, were placed in the center of the column. Liana scowled when Ramon put her there as well, but she said nothing.

'Let's go,' Caim said, and he started down the steps.

On the way down they passed Joram's body, hacked to unrecognizable pieces. Ramon didn't say a word, but he picked up his cousin's hammer. Flight by flight Caim led them down the stairwell, while the shadows crept overhead. The doors on

216

the other landings were shut and no sounds issued from them, but with each floor Caim's anxiety grew. It was as if some invisible doom hovered above his head. He rode the feeling down to the ground floor.

Samnus lay between the bodies of the soldiers he had carried to their deaths. Blood and pulp were splattered across the floor and up the walls. With a glance at each shadowed corner, Caim moved to the archway leading to the prison's front gate. The long corridor was empty and the doors along its length closed. It looked innocuous, like an easy stroll to the exit, but the feeling nagged at him. Something wasn't right.

'Stay here,' he said.

The word was passed back through the ranks as Caim edged into the corridor. Leaving behind their muted chorus of shifting footsteps, muffled coughs, and clanking metal, he paused at each door he passed, listening for anything untoward, hoping to find something to attach to his heightened apprehension, but they stood like rows of silent guardians watching his passage. He stopped at the edge of the atrium. The sensation had grown to a gigantic weight pressing down on the back of his neck. As he stepped toward the gate, a faint noise reached him. A footstep? He couldn't tell. Maybe it was nothing. They might still get out of here alive.

Caim halted as a tiny voice hissed in his ear.

'Caim!'

Heart racing, he looked around for her distinctive glow. 'Kit?'

'Caim! You . . . door . . . -ow . . .'

It was definitely Kit, but he could barely hear her. 'Kit, where are you?'

'. . . can't . . . you!'

Caim tried to follow the direction of her voice, but it was too faint. He remembered the night he'd fought Levictus on the palace roof, and how the sorcerer's magic had separated Kit from him. He closed his eyes and tried to reach out to her. 'Kit, I'm right here. I need you—'

But she was gone again, leaving him more troubled than

217

before. He only had a moment to process it before a sharp creak of metal against metal whispered through the atrium's still air, and the front gate flew open with tremendous force to clang against the inner wall. A fierce wind, stinking like an opened grave, howled through the gaping doorway. Caim lifted an arm to his face, choking on the horrible stench.

'Dark's blood!'

He looked to see Keegan crouched a dozen paces behind him. How the youth had managed to sneak up behind him, Caim didn't know, but his feeling of dread intensified.

'Get down!'

Caim lunged, but he was an instant too late as something lashed through the doorway. He didn't get a look at it, but he saw its effects as Keegan was hurtled the length of four wagons down the corridor to land flat on his back. Sprawled on the floor where the youth had stood only a moment before, Caim did the only thing he could think of – he rolled to his feet and charged the gate. Something zipped over his left shoulder, as quiet as an evening breeze, but the power of it jangled down his arm from shoulder to fingertips.

Something stood in the doorway. A slender figure framed by the darkness. Something in the way it stood, arms upraised as if supplicating the night sky, reminded Caim of his past. It had to be . . .

The witch.

Caim sprinted with both knives held low for gutting slashes. Then the figure pushed back its hood, and a moonbeam caught her high cheekbones, the slope of a slender nose, smooth smoky-gray skin.

Caim heard sounds beyond the doorway, but all his attention was focused on the woman as her lips parted.

'Scion . . .'

What was that supposed to mean? A warning? There was something about this woman that dug into his brain. Her statuesque beauty called to him. The mysterious folds of her clothing whispered of forbidden secrets. Caim blinked. What was he thinking? He tried to stop his momentum, but an

218

irresistible force drew him toward the doorway. He dug in his heels. His legs shook, but they continued to carry him forward. Caim clenched his jaws as he remembered his battle with Levictus, but there was an allure about this woman he couldn't resist. If he just got close enough to see her better, to smell the sweet musk of her hair, to bend his neck . . . *No! Kill her! Kill her!*

Caim watched his arm extend with horrifying slowness. The point of the *suete* knife shone bright as it reached toward her shadowed breast. Caim warred with himself. He didn't kill women. Not since . . .

He forced his mind back on the witch. She was lifting a hand toward him. Caim braced himself, but nothing seemed to happen. Then a fierce pain flared in the palm of his right hand. Caim ground his teeth together as tendrils of smoke rose from the blade of his knife and the steel began to darken before his eyes. His nerves screamed for him to drop the weapon, but he held on, determined to fight through the pain. All he could think of was completing the last three steps that would carry him to the witch and plunging the smoking blade into her heart.

Two steps.

Caim hissed as his knife inched closer. His legs felt like pillars of wet clay, dragging him along. The wind howled in his ears, the rotting stench filled his lungs. Invisible talons closed around his throat, and the witch's mouth opened in a smile. But the assault only hardened his will.

One step.

Caim looked into her dark eyes, sparkling like pits of oil. Much of her face was still swathed in shade. Then the shadows parted, and Caim saw her in full. His tongue clove to the roof of his mouth, which saved it from being bitten through as his jaws clamped shut. He knew her features as he knew his own. Unbidden, the old dream bubbled up through his subconscious, and he was once again standing in a familiar courtyard illuminated by walls of raging flames.

The frigid wind flogged his small body. The cold slid through his veins like ice water. There was blood on his hands. He wiped them on his shirt, but they wouldn't come clean.

A wail pierced the silent night. Caim's stomach ached like someone had punched him as his mother burst from the burning house, into the arms of the waiting soldiers. He wanted to run to her, to save her, but he could do nothing as the dark men dragged her away, into the fields and the great forest beyond, vanishing like a pack of ghosts.

His mother's face.

Caim's feet almost slid out from under him as the paralysis left him. He halted the impetus of his thrust. His arms, suddenly too heavy to lift, fell by his sides. His mother's screams pierced his skull. Caim opened his mouth, but he stood voiceless before her, unable to move or pull his gaze away. She hadn't changed at all, still as youthful and vibrant as in his memories. But there was a cast to her features, an opacity to her eyes that cut through him. Then she smiled, and he was sure that if he could just look closer, he would see her as she had been before.

The strident screech of metal snapped Caim out of his stupor as rows of iron bars fell across the doorway, separating him from the woman with his mother's face. The impact shook the floor as the heavy portcullis fell into place.

The witch clapped her hands. A cloud of darkness fell over Caim as he was hurtled away from the doorway. A cocoon of shadows enveloped him, protecting him from the icy wind that tore at the skin of his face and hands and stole the breath from his lungs. Despite the protective barrier, he landed hard. Caim rolled up on one elbow as the shadows peeled away from him. Some of them were riddled with hoarfrost and did not move. He glanced down the passage toward the gate. Keegan stood in the atrium, one hand on the gate's windlass. The woman stood in darkness once more, all except for her eyes. They burned into his brain from across the divide. When they flared up, a sudden ache ripped through his chest.

As Caim started to rise, something zipped past his ear.

Outside, a troop of crossbowmen ran up to the other side of the portcullis. Buzzing quarrels peppered the air. One slammed into Caim's shoulder and knocked him on his back. Breathing through gritted teeth, he sat up, and the bolt fell away. Its point had transfixed a wriggling shadow and failed to penetrate his jacket.

Keegan yelled in his ear. 'Come on!'

Caim ran with the youth, missiles speeding past them, and tried not to think about one of those steel-headed bolts punching through his spine. The corridor seemed miles longer than before. As they approached the stairs, he heard fighting ahead. Caim passed Keegan under the stone archway and plunged into pandemonium. Outlaws and jailors were locked in combat on the stairs. There was no time for tactics. Caim jumped into the fight.

Vibrations ran up his injured arm as he stabbed a man holding a truncheon. The jailor cried out and pitched into the arms of the outlaw he had been about to brain, but Caim was already moving past them. The outlaws fought without savvy or technique, but their foes were possibly worse. On the second-floor landing, a knot of Keegan's friends fended off twice their number of guards. Caim sliced his way into the line of attackers. Shadows gathered overhead as if to watch the slaughter, and he had to fight to hold them at bay. The power hummed within him. The black sword rattled against his shoulder, pleading to be let free, and part of him wanted to do it. *What's happening to me?*

He wanted Kit back, but he had no sense of her. She could be on the other side of the moon. Blood ran across the stone under his feet, and bodies piled around him until the remaining guards pulled back up the steps. Energized by this reprieve, the outlaws surged forward and pushed their foes up to the next level. Caim started to follow, but a hand clapped on his shoulder. He whirled, then lowered his knives at the sight of Ramon. The big man's face was masked in blood. An ugly purple bruise marred his cheek.

'What?'

221

Beyond Ramon, several outlaws hunkered on the steps. As the sounds of fighting receded, he heard their painful groans. Caedman sat against a wall. Caim hadn't taken the time to really look at the outlaw captain before. He was as tall as Ramon. His arms and shoulders were strong despite being twisted in angles Caim didn't want to think about.

'I take it,' Ramon grumbled, 'we're not going out the front.'

'I don't suggest it.'

Caim pushed past the big man. Keegan knelt on the floor with Liana's head cradled in his lap. A thick tide of blood ran down her scalp. Caim set down his weapons and touched her gently. The gash on her head looked nasty, but it was shallow.

'She tried to help.' Keegan rubbed the back of a hand across his face, leaving streaks of blood. 'I didn't see the guy behind us until it was too late.'

'She'll be all right,' Caim said. 'But we need to get her out of here.'

He looked around. What options did they have? Fighting their way out the front gate would be suicidal. He might escape, with luck, but with the witch involved he couldn't even predict that with any certainty.

Scanning the outlaws, he spotted the tall man with red hair in the back. 'You. What's your name again?'

'Braelon, but everybody calls me Oak.'

'Oak, did your cousin tell you any other ways out of here besides the front gate?'

Everyone quieted. Downstairs, metal screeched, a violent sound that grated on the nerves.

Oak frowned. 'Orwen never mentioned another exit, and I never really asked. He mainly talked about all the loonies locked up in this place.'

'This is a waste of time,' someone muttered.

'What about the roof?' Caim asked.

In his head he was trying to devise a way to get a dozen people, some of them injured, across the rooftop and down six stories of sheer stone wall. Maybe if they tied blankets together for a makeshift rope . . .

'Nah,' Oak answered.

'I didn't see any hatches above,' Caim admitted. 'And the windows are too narrow to fit through.'

'Wait,' Keegan said.

'What if we make ourselves up like guards?' a man ventured. 'Uniforms and such. Maybe we could—'

'Walk out the door as easy as that?' another finished for him. 'You're crazy. They'd sniff us out sure as—'

'Wait!' Keegan shouted.

'What?' Caim asked.

'If we can't go out the front and we can't go up, what about down?'

'How's that?' Ramon asked. 'We going to turn ourselves into moles and dig our way out? You're as daft as a—'

'What do you mean?' Caim asked.

The boy's face had turned bright red under the scrutiny of his fellows. 'Well, there's tunnels all beneath the city, right?'

'You mean the sewer tunnels.'

Keegan nodded. 'Exactly. A building like this is probably connected to those tunnels.'

Caim ran his tongue around the inside of his mouth, tasting blood. 'That's the best idea I've heard so far. Everyone downstairs. Find an access to the sewers and we might get out of this alive.'

The bulk of the outlaws returned from above, bloodied and exhausted, and Ramon rushed them down the steps. Caim helped Keegan carry Liana. Seeing her unconscious reminded Caim of when he'd carried Josey to his apartment from her foster father's manor. Both were strong, independent women and fiercely attractive. Navigating the gore-slick stairs, Caim shook as the energy that had flowed through him during the short battle drained away, leaving him ragged and worn out. But it wasn't as bad as the debilitating spells he used to suffer after encounters with his powers, for which he was grateful. The last thing he needed was to swoon at the feet of these men just when they were starting to listen to him.

They reached the ground floor to the sound of distant

clanging – the soldiers outside hammering at the portcullis. A few outlaws peered through the archway looking toward the atrium. They held their weapons nervously, but Caim saw something new in their expressions, a grimness he hadn't seen before. *About time. Where was this when we were running for our lives through the city streets?*

Oak came hurrying up and gestured for Caim to follow. Caim helped Keegan settle Liana on the floor, spoke a couple of words of hope, and went after the man. Oak took him down the stairs into the bowels of the prison. They stopped at a narrow landing thirty feet under the foundation. The steps continued downward, but Oak opened a door set in the corner of the landing to reveal a short tunnel. The moist odor of garbage emerged.

'Have you explored it?' Caim asked.

'A bit. There's a tunnel running below us. I sent Billup and Fralk to take a look.'

'Good. Get everyone down there. Head downstream, out of the city.'

Caim went back up and found Keegan. His look of concern had worsened. Liana's eyes were still closed.

Caim hunkered down beside them. 'We found a way out.'

'We need to get her home to my father.'

'We will. You have my word.'

Caim moved to Liana's feet in preparation to move her. The rest of the men had vacated the stairwell, taking Caedman with them toward the sewer entrance. Things were looking hopeful, but something bothered Caim. The feeling of dread had not disappeared. He had forgotten about it during the fight, but now, in the interim, it had returned in full force. They weren't out of danger yet.

A loud rattle echoed from the corridor. Scenarios played out in Caim's mind. None of them ended well. One ended less badly than the others, but it was the one he was most hesitant to attempt. It had been a long time, and he wasn't sure he was up to it. *What choice do I have?*

'Go,' he growled at Keegan.

The boy rose to his knees. 'What?'

Caim jerked his head after the direction the rest of the outlaws had taken. 'Get them out of here. I'll bring your sister.'

'Are you—?'

'Get!'

The youth glanced from him to his sister. A loud crash resounded from the front gate, followed by heavy boot steps. The enemy was inside the prison. With one last look at Caim, Keegan ran after the others.

Caim stood over Liana. Keegan had arranged her arms across her chest, perhaps unconsciously mimicking the pose of death. But she would survive. Caim would be damned if he didn't see to that. Of them all, she most deserved to live. *Just get on with it.* Setting his jaws together in a firm grimace, Caim went to the archway to face the enemy.

The soldiers came at him en masse, two score and change. A crossbow bolt sizzled past his head. The points of their spears and swords glittered in the torchlight.

They didn't stand a chance.

The shadows arrived in numbers he'd never seen before, raining down from the ceiling in an ebon deluge. Torches fizzled out, but Caim saw what happened all too well. He forced himself to watch as the men fell, in clusters of five and ten, succumbing to the crowd of ravenous blots climbing down their faces, crawling inside their armor to devour warm flesh. Not a single soldier made it to the end of the hall.

Gnawing on the evil he had wrought, Caim gathered the girl in his arms. A sharp pain erupted in his right arm as he lifted her, but he didn't have time to dwell on it. He went over to a sweep of shadows draped beneath the staircase. He wasn't sure how this was going to work. In the end, it took less effort than he anticipated.

One moment he stood on a solid floor. Then he took a step, and a tempest of unfamiliar forces lifted him into oblivion.

SHADOW'S LURE

Chapter
TWENTY-TWO

The world righted itself as Sybelle stepped out of the shadow gate and touched down on the cavern floor. She plucked at her sleeves and brushed the front of her gown, seeking out the insidious little deaths, but finding nothing.

How dare *he?*

The indignity burned in her breast. The upstart – scion or no – had sent his shadows against her. In her birth world, none would have dared such an insult. She hadn't expected it, and that had almost spelled her doom as hundreds of the tiny predators swarmed over her. Their bites stung, nothing serious, but only quick action had saved her from worse. Of course, she had left Erric's men behind to deal with the threat.

But the scion . . .

Sybelle went to the orichalcum box and breathed in a double pinch of the yellow resin. The jolt of instant energy washed away her exhaustion, but it did nothing to relieve her aggravation. She shook the box, debating another dose, but the powder was all but gone and there was no way to garner more; the plant from which it came only grew in the Shadow-lands.

She shoved the box back onto its shelf, unable to get the events at the prison out of her head. She had known it was him at first sight. Like a long-forgotten memory, his essence came back to her and stirred powerful feelings. She hadn't been prepared for that. For battle, surely, but not for the volatile combination of resentment and doubt that flooded her mind when they came face-to-face. She had seen him only once before, years ago when he was just a boy. That seemed like another lifetime. Perhaps it had been.

The scion's presence here, though unexpected, was not apocalyptic. Where was he now? Sybelle leaned over her scrying pool and cast forth her vision into the waters. She had tasted a morsel of his essence in those moments they stood eye-to-eye, not enough to wither him with a curse, but sufficient to find him anywhere in this realm. She stirred the waters, but they remained dark. Then she remembered Soloroth's words, how he had been unable to track the scion.

The shadows won't hunt . . .

Sybelle grasped the edge of the pool as a spell of vertigo crashed over her. What was this? She felt . . . distanced from the Shadow, cut off. The sensation only lasted a moment, not even the interval from the release of one breath and the inhalation of the next, but it left her shaken. Never before had she—

No. She *had* felt such a thing before, when she passed through the Barrier to this world. Almost twenty years ago, and now again today. She did not believe in coincidence. She needed an augury. She was consulting her charts of the astral houses when a cymbal chimed in a niche beyond the pool.

Sybelle dug her fingers into her skirt. It was Erric. She toyed with the idea of putting him off. Hunger gnawed at her innards, and she glanced to the passageway leading to the nave. Better for him if she waited until she had assuaged her appetites. But then the cymbal rang again and made up her mind for her. Fine. If he wished to see her now, then so be it. And if he had a trollop draped across his lap when she found him, she would strike them both with a curse to make the gods of this feeble realm tremble.

Sybelle opened a portal in the air and stepped through. Another tremor of light-headedness overcame her as she arrived in the unadorned room at the top of the castle. This was a mistake. She should have fed first. Arrogance, her father called it whenever she overtaxed her abilities. Sometimes she still heard his voice in her head, chiding her for this choice or that, but she paid it less mind than a cockroach scurrying underfoot. She was her own mistress now.

Are you truly?

Sybelle thrust the voice out of her thoughts as she descended the long stairs. She arrived at the great hall to find the duke alone, slouched in his throne, dressed in full regalia with the gold crown settled upon his brow. Despite his sloppy posture, he cut a regal figure. She would make of him a king in truth, if only he stayed out of her way. Like most men, he was willing to be guided by the nose, or the cock, but he had the irritating trait of intruding in her works when he was least wanted. Still, she was . . . *fond* of him. Another word came to mind, but she shoved it away. The Queen of the Night did not know love. Affection, yes. Fondness, surely. But love was as far from her essence as starlight from the day.

Sybelle kept her features neutral as she approached his throne, unwilling to grant him a smile. A petty gesture, perhaps, but no more than he deserved after summoning her like a common servant. Now, if he apologized with sufficient enthusiasm, she might see her way to suggesting a more interesting way to renew her energy. With these thoughts tumbling in her head, she stopped just short of his reach. Her lover's mouth was turned down in a sour grimace. His eyes, though open, looked into the distance as if he did not see her, which brought back her fury all over again. She started to address him and then stopped herself, intent that he should acknowledge her presence first. He tested her patience as the heartbeats stretched into a minute, and then another. He spoke just before she opened her mouth to scathe him.

'The ambassadors from Uthenor and Warmond have left the city.' His voice was thick with lethargy.

'What of it?'

The duke looked up, finally meeting her gaze. 'First, the

mercenaries leave, and now the ambassadors. Who will be the next to abandon me? You?'

She forced a laugh from her throat. It was a small thing, but it took all of her self-control to make it. 'Are you mad? After all I have done in this country, for you, for us, you think I would leave now? Don't be a bigger fool than needs be. I will not leave you, and neither have the ambassadors.'

'No? Then why did they depart at night without so much as a by-your-fucking-leave?'

She swallowed her anger and sat on the arm of his throne. 'They have been recalled to other fronts.' He started to ask, but she cut him off before he could get it out. 'Do not inquire into these matters. Be assured that you still enjoy the benefits of our Master's aegis, and that our plans will go forward without delay. In fact, I want you to—'

He slammed his fist down on the other arm. 'No, Sybelle. No more orders. This is my realm, and you will do as *I* say.'

Sybelle ran her fingers through his hair. 'Is that so?'

He croaked in outrage as she yanked his head back. He started to reach for her, but she placed her mouth over his. She poured all her rage into the kiss, white-cold like the northern winds, bitter as the sun that hovered over this dreadful world. His body stiffened beneath her. Sybelle pulled back and looked into his eyes, which darted back and forth over her face. He was in terrible agony as her sorcery crawled through his veins. She felt herself becoming excited at the thought.

'You do not command here,' she said. 'You are a tool. A pampered one, but in the end just a tool. You can either do as I say and enjoy a long and pleasurable reign.' She traced a finger along his unshaven chin and watched him tremble. 'Or I can find someone else to take your place.'

Sybelle leaned closer, enjoying the play of terror and agony in his eyes. He was so weak, she could kill him with nothing more than a gesture. Sometimes she found it endearing, but today it made her want to grind him under her thumb.

Steel slithered over leather as a sword was drawn. The

229

tendons in the duke's neck stood out like taut cables. Sybelle's smile widened as the blood drained from his face.

'Come in, Arion,' she said. 'We were just speaking of you.'

The voice of the duke's son called from the hall entrance.

'Release him, Sybelle. Now.'

The chamber echoed with the sound of her amusement.

Arion scowled as he barreled through the keep's narrow corridors on his way to the great hall. His father needed to hear the truth from someone, and he was angry enough not to care about the consequences.

He had just left the infirmary, where half of his bodyguards were laid up after an extended march through the western hills behind the witch's hell-spawn son and his pack of wolf-men. Davom and Brustus would mend, but Okin might never be the same again. The doctors called it a brain fever brought on by battlefield vapors, but he knew better. Okin had seen things no man should have to see on this side of the grave. They all had. It was a wonder none of them had deserted on the trek back to Liovard. The gods knew he wouldn't have blamed them.

Sybelle.

This was all her doing. She used men like pieces on a game board. Expendable. But this time he was going to have it out with his father once and for all. The Duke of Liovard would have to choose between his son and his concubine.

Arion paused at the south entrance to the great hall. Voices carried across the stone chamber. His father and Sybelle were arguing. Arion smiled as he inched forward. Perhaps his task would be easier than he anticipated. He might even convince his father to send the witch away. Then something happened. The argument turned quiet.

Arion leaned through the entranceway. His father sat in the ancestral throne of their clan with the witch on his arm. They kissed, and then his father jerked as if he had been struck.

Arion's breath hissed between his teeth. Sorcery, it had to be, for his father did not move.

Drawing his sword, Arion hurried across the flagstones. His gaze focused on the witch. In his mind he saw himself plunging his steel into her breast. She looked up, and her eyes glowed, full of malice.

'Come in, Arion,' she said. 'We were just speaking of you.'

Her greeting set his hands to trembling. His tongue felt like it had swelled to thrice its normal size. 'Release him, Sybelle. Now.'

Her laughter sliced into him like a flensing knife. The clatter of moving metal echoed through the chamber. Arion shifted his grip on his sword as the Beast stepped out from the shadow of a deep alcove. His black plate armor glistened like the scales of a serpent. The challenge was evident in the giant's arrogant stance, the way his massive hands opened and closed within their black steel gauntlets. He made no move toward the mace-and-chain hanging from his belt, but Arion wasn't willing to give him the chance to unfurl its deadly links. He ran at the witch's spawn, swinging his sword with both hands. The blow struck Soloroth square on the crest of his helmet. The Beast staggered back a step, and for one brief moment Arion had hope that he had dealt a lethal blow, but his optimism was short-lived as Soloroth remained standing. Arion wound up for another swing, but the Beast moved with astonishing speed. The sword fell from Arion's numb fingers. He gasped as steel fingers closed around his neck. With the pressure of a vise, they contracted to close off his air and lifted him off the ground. Arion gripped Soloroth's wrist as his head began to ache, but the Beast could have been a statue holding him aloft in its adamant grasp. A gasp hissed from the throne.

'Please . . .' a rasping voice spoke.

Sybelle turned. 'Yes, Erric?'

Arion prayed as the pain in his chest ballooned to block out the world. *Typhon and all the gods that watch over Eregoth, damn the witch and her cursed son to endless night. Let them never see the sun again. Destroy them . . .*

'Spare him!'

Darkness descended over Arion's sight. Consciousness was slipping from his grasp. He clung to it for just one more instant, knowing he would never awake from this slumber. He felt himself falling. His feet struck the floor, but they had no strength to hold him, and he collapsed at the giant's feet. Air – sweet, rich, and intoxicating – rushed into his lungs. He gulped it down like wine. His sight cleared enough to show him that the witch still gripped his father by the hair.

'Remember, Erric,' she said in a sickeningly playful tone. 'You rule by my indulgence.'

With a smile, she released his father and walked away. She stopped beside Soloroth, both of them gazing down at him. Arion wanted to shout at her, to scream his defiance, but the only sound that came from his lips was the shrill whistle of his breath.

Sybelle nudged him with a toe. 'Send this one back to the south to begin the next stage of the invasion. He will be forged into something worthwhile in the heat of conquest.' She shrugged. 'Or he'll cease to be an annoyance.'

Arion closed his eyes as the witch and her son strode away, her mocking laughter ringing in his ears along with the thundering pulse of his heartbeat.

SHADOW'S LURE

Chapter
TWENTY-THREE

Josey yawned as she got out of bed. She hadn't slept well. All night long the problems facing the realm kept her awake, from the riots in the streets to her problems managing the court, not to mention the continual threat of assassination hanging over her head. It didn't help that Hirsch and Hubert had gone out again last night to renew their search for the assassin.

Amelia came in with an elaborate gown from the wardrobe, and Josey began the laborious process of getting dressed. With all that was going on, she had to make an appearance in court this morning even if it killed her. Josey exhaled as the corset tightened around her ribs.

'Not so tight, please, Amelia. I'm feeling a little ill disposed this morning.'

'I'm sorry, my lady. Shall I call for a physician?'

Josey glanced over her shoulder and faked a smile. 'I've told you a hundred times. It's just Josey. And, no. I'll be fine.'

The maid gave another tug on the laces. 'Yes, my lady.'

Josey sighed, but not too deeply, and sat down for her other maid, Margaret, to select her footwear. She declined the knee-high boots with four-inch heels and went with a pair of laced padded shoes. A selection of jewelry – earrings, necklace, golden tiara – and a bit of tasteful makeup completed the outfit.

'Tell them I'm ready,' she said.

As Amelia went to the door, Josey looked at herself in a large mirror. The blush on her cheeks was a little heavy, but she had to admit she looked like an empress, even though she didn't feel it. *Is this how all rulers feel? Are we all a bunch of trumped-up phonies prancing on a stage?* The thought made her feel a little better.

When the door opened and her bodyguards – up to six now, every minute of the day and night – stood aside, Josey walked out into the hallway. The trek from her apartment to the audience was silent save for the clomp of heavy boots on the marble tiles. Josey kept her hands clasped together over her stomach, which fluttered like a bag full of bluetail flies. Decisions needed to be made to restore order to Othir – that was her first priority. She hoped she could find the answers her people needed. Otherwise she would have the shortest reign in Nimean history.

Two of her bodyguards halted outside the Great Hall, and two inside the doorway. The last pair escorted her across the broad chamber. The hall was almost vacant except for a sparse handful of ministers already in their seats. Lord Parmian stood at his appointed place and gave her a commiserating smile as she entered, but the lord chancellor's desk was unoccupied. *Where is Hubert? And where's the rest of the Thurim?*

Her anxiety threatening to burst into a full-blown panic, Josey climbed the steps to the throne. She took a deep breath before sitting down to face her truncated court. When she asked for the day's first order of business, Ozmond started to approach until a side door opened. Quick footsteps echoed across the hall. Hubert, looking uncharacteristically disheveled, hurried over to take his rightful place. After coughing into his hand, he addressed the court.

'My apologies, Majesty. My noble lords and ladies. The first order of the day is the disagreement between our realm and the kingdom of Arnos over the annexation of Mecantia. Lord Gherova has the floor.'

While Gherova, a fussy sophist who had spent many years living in Arnos, stood and read from what looked to be an exceedingly long roll of notes, Josey motioned for Hubert to approach. He climbed the steps with a hung head. She'd meant to show him the sharp side of her tongue, too, but he looked so pathetic she let him go with a stern scowl.

'You look like a bad dream,' she whispered. 'What happened?'

Hubert put a hand inside his jacket and pulled out a parchment packet, which he handed to her.

'Not much, but we found these.'

'By the river?'

'No. We went back to the original scene hoping to discover something we missed before in our haste.' His mouth bunched up. 'The theater is in shambles.'

A pain of sympathy stabbed Josey's heart for the city's loss. 'Was anyone hurt?'

'No one died, which is a miracle.'

Josey opened the packet and spilled out two thin flakes of what she first thought was some kind of leaf. Then she noticed their brittleness.

'Scales?'

'That's what we think. Master Hirsch believes these will help us track the assassin.'

A weight lifted from Josey's chest. 'Thank you, Hubert. This is the first bit of good news I've had in days. Give Master Hirsch whatever he needs.'

'Yes, Majesty. And two new dispatches arrived this morning.'

'News from the north?'

'I'm afraid not. More settlements have been burned along the western border. And the commanders of the Parvia and Wistros regiments have not reported back yet. At best, they couldn't make the march to Othir in less than six days.'

'Six days!' she blurted, a little louder than she intended. Lord Gherova paused, and then continued after a nod from her. To Hubert, she whispered, 'Never mind. Where is everyone?'

Hubert looked away as if he didn't want to answer, but Josey waited him out.

'Some of the ministers are afraid to leave their homes because of the violence in the streets.'

Josey bit down on her bottom lip. *So much for a day of good news.*

'Have the riots crossed into High Town?'

Hubert dipped his chin while he pretended to listen to Lord Gherova's speech. 'Just before daybreak a small mob breached the cordon of night watchmen along the Processional. Some homes were vandalized. No one was seriously injured, but fear is spreading.'

It's already arrived here. Now what shall I do? Unleash more soldiers into the streets? Withdraw until it blows over? She wished she knew. Whatever choice she made, there would be repercussions.

While she stewed, Lord Gherova finished his speech, or so she thought. She watched in dismay as he picked up another scroll and began to unroll it. Josey had heard enough. Her city was tearing itself apart, and this man wanted to ramble about distant problems.

'Please, my lord,' she said. 'A moment's pause.'

The minister regarded her with a jaundiced gaze and then took his seat. Josey looked to Hubert, but he did not move.

'Coward,' she said under her breath. Then, raising her voice, she said, 'We have decided the war in the east to be a wasteful extravagance perpetrated by misplaced zeal, and ultimately unnecessary when more important problems plague us here at home.'

Several of the ministers grumbled at this, but their reactions were no surprise to her. The only lords who had deigned to attend today's audience were the ones most opposed to her rule. Only one person, Lord Du'Quendel, applauded at her words.

'Emissaries,' she said, 'bearing our wishes for peace between our lands, shall be dispatched with all haste.'

'That would be a grave error, Your Majesty.'

Josey looked to the main entrance, half expecting Duke Mormaer. Instead, a portly man in pristine white robes stood in the hall's doorway. Josey started to rise at the sight of him out of long-ingrained habit until Hubert caught her eye and gave a slight shake of his head. The empress did not rise, not even in the presence of the prelate of the True Church.

The holy father entered the hall wearing the full regalia of his office. Josey recognized the emblems from her catechism. The golden staff in the prelate's hand and gold-linked rope around his neck represented the sacred gallows from which the Prophet was hung. Upon his head rested a crown of sharp golden points. The rod, rope, and the sunburst crown – the icons that stood at the foundation of the True Faith.

The new prelate was younger than she expected; his hair was only just beginning to lighten to silver. Though his vestments were simple, their costliness was evident in the cut and lay of the fabric, fine linen with gold and silk stitching. Beyond his luxurious attire and trappings, the prelate didn't strike her as a particularly impressive figure. But as he approached, Josey shifted in her seat under the arresting gaze of his cobalt eyes.

Four hierarchs of the Church and an equal number of underpriests, resplendent in scintillating white robes, surrounded the prelate. Lady Philomena walked beside His Holiness to the center of the hall, where she left to take her seat with the other ministers. One hierarch approached the foot of the dais. Josey recognized him by his slick black hair and hooked nose. Hubert had warned her about Archpriest Gaspar, the prelate's mouthpiece.

The archpriest inclined his head. 'I present His Luminance, Innocence the First, Patriarch of the True Faith, Supreme Servant of the Light.'

Josey didn't know what they expected her to do. Bow to the man? Grovel at his feet? She remained in her throne and tried to present a calm face, but inside she seethed. Just the sight of the man made her relive the harrowing days when she and Caim had been hunted by the Church's minions. She would never trust them again. Hubert saved her by stepping forward.

'The empress greets you, Prelate Innocence. We received no word that Your Luminance would be attending court this day.'

'His Illustrious Radiance—'

The prelate held up a finger, and the nuncio fell silent. Innocence cast a beatific smile at Josey.

'Daughter, I have come this day to forge a new relationship between this body and the True Church of the Holy Prophet.'

Josey cleared her throat and tried to hold back her indignation. 'You said something as you entered, Luminance.'

'Yes, Daughter. It would be unwise to make overtures of peace to the godless heathens of the east.' His gaze slid to Hubert. 'I would caution you not to be guided by the artifices of the Horned One, but to cleave unto the Church as a wife to a husband. Only in this way shall you find the wisdom you seek.'

Josey didn't know whether to be offended or disgusted by his words. Hubert held his hands by his sides, but Josey could see he was agitated, too.

'I beg Your Holiness's pardon,' she said, 'but the empire faces dire threats here at home. The continuation of the war in the east is no longer possible.'

'All things,' the prelate intoned, 'are possible through the Light, Daughter.'

Josey wanted to retch. 'What does the Light say about the thousands of young men who have died overseas and will never see their homeland again?'

Prelate Innocence regarded her with an expression partway between contempt and amusement. 'Sacrifices made in the name of the Almighty are never in vain. We urge you to pray, Daughter, as the faithful pray for the salvation of your eternal soul.'

Josey felt the first strains of an oncoming headache. A fantasy had begun in her imagination, of this flawlessly clean prelate being dipped by his ankles into a vat of pig feces. It brought a smile to her lips, but she missed part of the lecture.

'—people are up in arms,' the prelate said. 'They decry the

scandalous way the True Church has been shut out from its rightful place as the spiritual sovereign of this nation.'

Hubert opened his mouth, but this time Josey didn't give him the chance. This was too much.

'The Church,' she said, pitching her words loud enough to be heard throughout the chamber, 'does not rule any longer.'

If he was embarrassed by her admonishment, the prelate did not show it. 'Daughter, if you do not—'

'Your Majesty.'

Prelate Innocence blinked. 'Pardon?'

'You will,' she said, more firmly, 'address us as Your Majesty, or Your Highness.'

The prelate held her gaze for a long moment. Once, perhaps, she might have bowed before that penetrating stare, but she was not a child anymore. She was the mother of a nation and she would receive her due respect.

After what seemed like ages, the holy man dipped his head a fraction of an inch. 'Yes, Majesty. Have I your leave to continue?'

'You do, Your Holiness.'

'If Your Majesty does not heed the advice of the Church, this city will tear itself asunder.'

That sounds suspiciously like a threat. Be careful, Innocence, lest your visage of impartiality slip away entirely.

'What does Your Holiness suggest?' Hubert asked.

Josey could have kicked her lord chancellor, but she understood the game he was playing. Placate the Church by pretending to consider its position, but continue doing what needed to be done.

'First,' the prelate said, 'the holy war must not be halted, not for a single day. In fact, new efforts must be made to bring the pagans of the east to the Light. Only in this way can the blessings of the Almighty be restored to the nation.'

Josey ground her teeth together until she thought they might shatter.

'Second, the empress must subjugate herself before the Church. Publicly.'

Josey almost jumped to her feet at those words, but Hubert glanced back with a soothing expression. Her nails dug into the wood of the throne's arms. *Why not request that I parade down the Processional naked and prostrate myself before the cathedral doors?*

'Third, an army must be sent north.'

Josey perked up at that pronouncement. She tried not to give away her sudden interest, but it was difficult. Fortunately, the prelate explained himself before she needed to ask.

'There are strange happenings in the northern states,' he said. 'Though they be barbarians, the people of those lands are still children of God and must be protected from the temptations of their baser natures.'

Josey didn't believe the explanation for a minute, but she kept that to herself. She wanted to know what was happening in the north as much as anyone.

'These,' the prelate concluded, 'must be done before the people of Othir can regain their trust in the crown.'

Josey didn't know what to say. She couldn't believe the gall of the man to march into her palace and make such demands.

'Thank you, Your Luminance,' Hubert said. 'Any assistance offered in these tumultuous times is gladly received.'

Josey glared at the back of her lord chancellor's head, but she kept her mouth closed before she said something irrevocable. She continued to fume as Hubert kissed the prelate's ring like a lapdog looking for a treat. When the ring was turned toward her, Josey looked up at the ceiling and pretended she didn't see it. The view of the Church's frescoes above her throne only served to worsen her mood. Fortunately, the prelate took the hint and turned away, leading his entourage out the doors. Josey managed to hold onto her temper. Just barely.

'We shall retire,' she announced to the hall. 'Good day, my lords.'

She descended the dais, and Hubert fell in step behind her. Josey made it all the way to the hallway outside the great hall before she erupted.

'How could you?' she demanded, raising her fist like a weapon. Her temples were throbbing now, which only added to her indignation. 'How could you smile in that pig's insolent face and tell him we would consider his outrageous demands? You might not have any pride left, but you represent me when you stand in that court!'

To his credit, Hubert stood mute and took her assault. He did not flinch, nor did he argue. Finally, Josey ran out of invectives to launch at him. Then, as she stood panting in the middle of the corridor, with her bodyguards studiously looking away, Hubert made a solemn nod.

'If my service fails to satisfy—' he began.

'Don't start that again!' she said. 'Just explain what you were doing in there.'

'Protecting you, Majesty.'

She stared at him for a long moment. 'Yes, of course you were. I'm sorry, Hubert. I've just . . . got a lot on my mind.'

'No apology is required. I understand, and I think you're holding up quite well under the circumstances.'

'Thank you.' She appreciated that. Sometimes she felt she was all alone in this huge stone palace. It was nice to be reminded she had friends close by. All of a sudden, she missed Anastasia.

He smiled, half shy and half roguish, and for a moment the old carefree Hubert stood before her. Then he cleared his throat and the mien of the lord chancellor fell back into place.

'We cannot afford to incite the new prelate, Majesty. Not with the streets in chaos. The Church could make things even more difficult.'

'How?'

'Some citizens have taken up refuge in the churches. The priests . . .'

She began to see the problem. 'They're using this opportunity to say things. Things about me.'

'I've heard accounts of sermons about demons walking the streets and the end of the world.'

Josey glanced over his shoulder to the tapestries on the corridor wall. 'And they blame these things on me.'

'Yes, Majesty. I could go to DiVecci and make your imperial displeasure known to the hierarchs.'

She wanted to let him go, with a hundred soldiers at his back. She would have liked that, but they couldn't afford a confrontation now. Hubert knew as much, but the offer was kind. Josey winced as a sharp pain stabbed her forehead. She staggered, for a moment losing her balance. Hubert grabbed her by the arms.

'Majesty?' He looked to the guards. 'Get the empress's doctor. Hurry!'

'No,' she tried to say, but it came out in a whisper.

She felt queer, as if she had drunk too much wine and couldn't find her balance. The hallway seemed abnormally warm all of a sudden. One horrifying thought shot through her mind. *Have I been poisoned?*

Cool wind rushed across her face as she felt herself being carried. She reached out to touch soft cloth. She tried to grab hold of it and pull herself up, but her fingers wouldn't work. Her world drifted into darkness.

Caim, they've killed me. Caim, come back . . .

The darkness closed around Caim. Here, nothing existed. No pain, no sorrow. Only the dark, and the solace it brought.

A spell of vertigo twisted his insides as he was spat out into the frigid night. A mountain of white flashed before his eyes as he fell. The warm body in his arms started to slip away, but he grabbed tight onto her as his shoulder hit the ground hard enough to make him grunt. Cradling Liana against his chest, he felt the cool cushion of snow against his face.

He opened his eyes with care. They were lying between several evergreen trees. The night sky turned above them, the light from a handful of stars painful to his eyes. He exhaled the breath he'd been holding. *I guess it worked.*

He hadn't been sure it would. The first and only time he'd

tried to transport himself through the shadows had been on the roof of the palace in Othir while fighting Levictus. He didn't know how he did what he did, but it worked. And now again, as easy as falling off a mountain.

Caim blinked as his eyes recovered from their sensitivity. His body ached all over, like he had been sewn up in a canvas bag and beaten with clubs. But after a few deep breaths the strength began to return to his arms and legs. Moving slowly, he laid Liana flat on the ground and slipped his arm from under her. She didn't appear to have suffered any further injury from the abrupt nature of their transportation.

The snow came to his knees as he stood up. Trees extended all around them for as far as he could see through their branches, save in one direction – east if his bearings were right. There, a gentle slope allowed him a view of a great expanse of woods extending to a broad, white plain. In the distance loomed the gray walls of the city. It must have been eight or nine leagues away. *Not quite where I was aiming, but it could be worse.*

But now he had to decide what to do next. Where should they go? Back into the city was out of the question. The streets would be crawling with patrols in force. That left either heading to the old manor house where the outlaws had originally convened, or remaining here and hoping someone found them before they froze to death. Neither option did much to raise his spirits.

Caim knelt beside Liana in the snow. Her eyelids fluttered as one of her hands came up to her head. He caught it before she touched the injury.

'Easy,' he said. 'You've taken a nasty hit.'

Liana focused on his face, and for a moment Caim was taken to another time and place, only he had been the one on his back, opening his eyes to see someone leaning over him. *They're nothing alike, Josey and this girl, and yet . . .*

Biting back on feelings he didn't want to dwell on, Caim helped her sit up.

'What happened?' she asked. 'Where's Keegan?'

'We're safe, a few miles from the city. And Keegan is with the others.'

She looked around, then winced as the movement tugged at the wound to her head. 'I don't see anyone.'

'No, we're alone.'

Should he tell her how they'd gotten here? *Better not. She'd probably run off screaming through the woods.*

'I don't understand.'

'It's okay. But we need to start moving.'

She was shaking. Caim wrapped his cloak around her and started to pick her up, but she reached out to stop him.

'I can walk.'

'Be still,' he said, a little gruffer than he intended, but it worked.

She let him lift her. His arm burned with the effort, but she was light. *Probably undernourished. Times have been harder up here than anyone realized.*

'Point the way back to the old house,' he said.

'They won't go there.'

'Good. Then where?'

She looked up at the sky. They stood like that, her lying in his arms, until his leg started to ache.

'Liana, if you—'

'The castle.' Steam wreathed her mouth as she exhaled. 'That's where they'll go.'

'All right. Which way?'

She pointed west, and Caim started walking through the snow. Crystals of ice flew into his face, and the buzzing had taken up residence in the back of his head again. Northward, it tugged him, always northward. What awaited him there? Whatever it was, it would have to wait. There were mysteries enough right here, and he intended to get to the bottom of them. What had happened to Kit, for one. He needed to find her, but how? Was her disappearance connected to the buzzing he felt coming from the north?

Uncertainties spun around in his head as he marched deeper into the hills with the girl cradled in his arms.

The blizzard came out of the north. The few stars visible in the overcast sky flickered and went out as the snowfall thickened and fierce winds howled through the trees. Visibility dropped to mere yards, and then to nothing.

Caim stopped in the lee of a large oak tree, with the snow piling up around his legs. His arms and lower back ached from carrying Liana for the better part of the night. She had drifted into unconsciousness sometime before midnight, and now he feared for her recovery. With a head wound, out in the cold, her chances were dwindling. And he had no idea where they were. Bowing his head against the oncoming wind, he set off again.

As he trudged through the snow, his thoughts returned to the prison, and the woman at the gate. Eyes dark as the ocean depths, long hair like spun filaments of onyx; he couldn't shake them from his mind. But even as he turned her looks over and around in his head, everything he knew screamed that she could not be his mother. All his good memories from his childhood, all the love he'd felt, revolved around his mother. His father had been a firm influence, a hard man and stern, difficult for a child to understand. But his mother had been his entire world. That she could change so much . . . it was unthinkable.

What of me? Would she recognize the man her son had become? And if she did, would she even care?

He'd made hard choices in his life, choices that had led him down a path of bloodshed and fear. What mother would be proud to call him son? Better to have no son at all than a cold-blooded killer with nothing to show for his life except a parade of corpses.

Burdened by his thoughts, Caim made it another candle-mark or so before he couldn't go on any farther. His legs were stiff, his feet were numb, and he had long since lost his sense of direction. They could be marching in circles for all he knew.

245

He gazed down at Liana, nestled against his chest. They had to get out of this weather.

Looking around, he sought out the tallest tree. He walked about two hundred paces before he found one that would suit. Setting Liana down in a drift, he used his arms to carve out a cave under the lowest branches. He dug until he reached the ground and then he went back out to retrieve his charge. He laid her at the back of the little den and used his body to block out the wind. Caim reached for the pouch at his belt, intending to try to start a fire from the sodden needles, but his fingers were frozen into claws, and he was too tired to make the effort. He collapsed on the cold ground and closed his eyes. Just for a moment.

A voice came to him in the quiet of the night, recalling a voice from a long time ago.

It was late and he was supposed to be sleeping, but the shapes crawling across the ceiling of his room were too interesting. Where was his friend? She usually came around when he was alone, to play with him or sing songs, or tell him stories. He liked her stories best of all. He didn't really understand them, but they filled him with wonder and a desire to see what lay beyond the woods and fields of his home.

The door opened. He heard its creak distinctly even though he couldn't see over the side of his cradle. He listened. Then a mass of dark hair blocked out the ceiling. Its tendrils cascaded over him, full of his mother's smell. He reached up, but she caught his wrists. He giggled, hoping she would pick him up, but a pillow came down over his face. He batted to knock it aside, but his laughter turned to a muffled gasp as the plush surface filled his nose and mouth. He couldn't breathe. He hit the pillow again and again, but it wouldn't move. He was too small. His tears wet the underside of the cushion, mashed against his face. *I'll be good, Momma! I'll be—*

Caim jerked upright, his chest constricting with the need to breathe. He gasped as cold air hit his lungs. The tugging sensation throbbed in the back of his head. He took deep breaths until it faded to a dull buzz.

It was dark. Turning, he looked out through the narrow tunnel. Snow was still falling, but not as heavy as before, and the wind had died down. Then he heard something else. A keening moan, like an animal, or perhaps a woman's cry. Caim froze. *Just the wind playing tricks on me—*

The moan rose again, louder this time, and nearer, as if it came from right outside the shelter. It was definitely a woman. Caim started to poke his head out, but a faint voice stopped him.

'Stay.'

Caim leaned down over Liana. 'What?'

'Don't go.' She swallowed with some trouble. 'The voice. Not real. A lure . . .'

Caim scooped a handful of snow from the wall and placed a pinch on her lips. Liana sucked it into her mouth greedily. As he fed her more, the lonely moan rose again outside the shelter. What awaited him out there? The answer lodged in his gut, even though he didn't want to acknowledge it.

Liana wrapped her fingers around his hand. Her eyes were half closed and lined in purple smudges. Looking down at her, he let his gaze trace the soft contours of her lips and imagined how soft they would feel. Her gaze was frank as she reached up and touched his face. It would be easy to fall for her, to lose himself in her eyes and her body, and banish his personal demons for one night. The passion stirred in his blood, so similar to the killing rage.

Caim eased back on his heels. Liana frowned, but didn't say anything. He was grateful for that, because he didn't know what he would do if she pressed the issue. *Run out into the snow like a coward and freeze to death most likely.*

With a sigh, Caim settled down behind her and wrapped an arm around her middle. She didn't protest, and he tried to think about the snow – cool, cool snow – as she scooted back against him. The wind battered their tiny shelter. He and she were maybe the only living souls for miles, lost in the middle of a trackless wood, but as long as they lived there was hope. He let that thought warm him as he pulled his damp cloak over them. Things were spinning beyond his control. Everything had been simple before he got himself entangled with these amateur insurrectionists, and now he was having a difficult time cutting free of them. Every time he tried to walk away, some new obstacle crept onto his path. *Is this payback for all the evil I've done in my life? Kit. where are you?*

Outside, the voice had ceased its lament.

SHADOW'S LURE

Chapter
TWENTY-FOUR

Caim slapped at the insect crawling across his face and groaned as a pain erupted in the palm of his hand. He opened his eyes.

He was lying in the burrow he'd dug in the snow. Liana curled up against him. The warmth of her body reminded him of the last time he'd been this close to a woman. Moving slow so as not to wake her, Caim scooted away and sat up.

Muted sunlight sketched the inside of the shelter. The ends of the branches poked through the carved-out roof above them. What he thought was an insect in his semi-dream state turned out to be a maddening itch down the side of his face. He probed the skin with careful fingertips. The cuts were healing, but the scars would be bad. Or good, depending on your point of view. Scars kept away bravos spoiling for a fight, and women liked scars. Some did, anyway. The kind that might fancy a roll in the snow with someone like him.

Caim drew his right-hand knife. The blade was charred from guard to tip. He ran his fingers along the length and felt a myriad of tiny imperfections in the metal. It was ruined. A waste of a good knife, and he hadn't even gotten the satisfaction of killing its target. His upper lip twitched at the thought of the witch, whatever she was. He didn't even know, except that he wanted to stay clear of her, for now and for good. He had enough problems already. He glanced over at Liana, but she was still fast asleep.

He put away the knife and held up his hand. The skin of the palm and the undersides of his fingers were red and puffy like he had been burned. While he probed the tender flesh, his forearm began to throb. Caim peeled off his jacket and rolled up the sleeve of his shirt. He couldn't help hissing at what he found. The bandage wrapping his forearm was completely soaked through with yellow and red stains. He smelled it even before he started tearing off the binding. The wound underneath was a raw hole oozing pus and blood. Caim clenched the muscles of that arm, making the wound yawn wider. He was at a loss. He didn't have access to doctors, not even a decent army barber, and he knew next to nothing about healing herbs. If the wound festered for much longer, he might lose the whole arm.

Caim sat back against the snowbank and wondered what to do. He could try to sear out the infection again, but he would need a fire for that. He looked up and was taken aback by the mass of shadows clinging to the roof of the shelter. He hadn't noticed them before, but an idea came to him. It had worked before; it might work again. Caim reached up with his burnt hand and caught hold of a shadow. Chilling cold seeped into his injured hand as it wriggled between his fingers. *This is crazy. I don't have the first notion of what I'm doing.* Before he could stop himself, Caim pushed the little darkness into the mouth of the wound. He gasped as the shadow squirmed inside his flesh. There was a moment of biting pain. Then, just as he started to dig it back out, the pain ceased. Caim sat back in amazement. The bleeding had stopped. He flexed his forearm again. It didn't ache as badly. He grunted in spite of himself, and Liana stirred.

Shrugging back into his jacket, Caim leaned over her. He wondered if the shadow-healing trick would work on her, but under the crust of blood pasted in her hair the scalp wound appeared to be closed. As he touched it, she opened her eyes and looked up at him.

250

'It's quiet,' she said.

He pulled back. 'I guess the storm passed sometime in the night. How do you feel?'

Liana sat up with his help. She let her hand linger in his. 'Not so bad as last night. A little tired. Something to eat would help.'

Caim's stomach stirred at her words. He could use some food himself, but he didn't have high hopes for a decent meal anytime soon. Before he could ask, she was pawing through the burlap sack slung under her cloak.

'I've got this.'

She held up a packet of cheesecloth, inside which was a slab of cured bacon. The smell made Caim's mouth water.

'Now if we had a fire to cook it over,' he said.

'Why?'

Liana bit off a hunk from one end before handing the slab to him. With a smile, Caim took a bite. He tried to picture Josey sitting beside him in a bed of packed snow, chewing on half-frozen bacon, but it was too crazy to contemplate. Right now she was probably still abed, with a long day of dress changes and flower arranging in front of her. Why had he come north again?

Caim shoved the rest of the food in his mouth. Wiping greasy fingers on his jacket, he turned around to the cave entrance. It was almost entirely blocked with fresh snow except for a sliver of open space at the top. Peering through, he saw a curtain of white. Everything was covered in a dazzling patina of snow. He put up the hood of his cloak and started clawing a way out. By the time he had carved out an exit, Liana was finished with her breakfast, and they crawled out-side together.

The air was icy cold after the relative warmth of the shelter. The snow came halfway up his thighs, which was going to make traveling difficult. The hilltops staggered across the horizon before them, their rugged shoulders clad in fresh powder.

'Can you walk?' he asked.

'Yes. I think so.'

'So which way?'

She looked around, her eyes touching on the hills, up and down the range. Finally, she pointed to the centermost peak, which was also the largest.

'That way. Just south of the summit.'

He considered her for a moment. 'The castle?'

She gave him a tight smile. 'I don't know where else to go, and we won't last long out here in the open.'

'Good enough.'

Caim started off according to her directions. He went first, plowing a path through the snow. It was slow going, but he managed to keep up a decent pace. Every few paces he looked back to make sure she was doing all right, but she stayed on his heels, never faltering, never complaining. The only acknowledgment she made to the cold was to pull up the hood of her cloak, leaving just her eyes and nose visible through the circle of fur lining.

As the sun climbed into the brooding sky, Caim focused on his navigation, which wasn't perfect as the forest thickened around them. Whenever he felt they were turned too far south, he adjusted for it. A layer of sweat built under his clothes, but his legs, encased in a coat of snow, became numb as the day wore on.

Caim was pushing through a stand of denuded bushes to get to a broad clearing beyond when his knee slammed into something hard.

'Fuck!'

He reached into the snow. His hands encountered a solid surface. Liana came up beside Caim as he brushed away a section of snow to reveal a low stone wall. On the other side, big snow-covered hummocks rose from the ground all around the clearing.

'This place looks—' Liana started to say, but then her expression changed.

'What?'

Something didn't feel right. Caim reached for his knife as he pulled Liana down into the snow. She pressed a hand to her mouth, and a muffled sound emerged. Shocked, he realized she was sobbing.

'What is it?'

He didn't see any sign of danger, although the scene was deathly quiet.

Liana shook her head. 'This place . . . It was called Joliet. My father and I came here each spring, to trade.'

Caim scanned the clearing. At first he thought she was seeing things, perhaps on account of her head wound, but then he considered the snowy mounds. That one could be the remains of a hut. That one was a little larger, perhaps a store, adjacent to a flat space at the center . . . like a village square. As the pieces came together in his mind, Caim smelled smoke, but it was an old scent. Whatever had happened was now past, days or weeks ago, its ravages covered by the snow.

'We can go around,' he said, to spare her from whatever horrors might lie beneath the surface.

'No. I want to see.'

She started to stand up, but he caught her arm. 'Wait. There's nothing to be done here.'

'Yes,' she said. 'There is.'

She pulled free and swung her leg over the wall. He stayed put as she pushed through the snow toward the middle of the clearing. Then she stumbled over something, and stooped down, clearing the snow away. A wail made him leap over the wall and plunge after her.

He found her kneeling beside something in the snow. It only took him a moment to recognize it was a body. Liana had cleared away a woman's face, her long red hair clotted with ice crystals. The long shaft of an arrow with spiraled yellow fletching jutted from her chest. It looked like animals had gotten to the body. Loose flaps of skin hung from her face, and there were gouges torn from her naked shoulders and arms.

'Her name was Alysse,' Liana said, so low he could barely hear her.

Caim bent down and hooked his hands under Liana's arms, hauling her upright. 'We can't stay. The killers might be nearby.'

'Northmen.'

Caim looked down at the arrow. The fletching was distinctive.

'You've seen this before.'

Liana nodded, a tear running down her cheek. 'They first came two summers ago, down from the mountains. They killed everyone they found.'

Caim gazed around, trying to make sense of it. 'And the duke allows his people to be slaughtered like this?'

But Liana had left, trudging deeper into the ruined hamlet. Caim took a path around the outermost mounds. Coming around a tall hillock of snow, he stumbled onto a scene of carnage the likes of which he'd never seen. Bodies were impaled on stakes, their twisted limbs drooping toward the ground. None of them looked older than ten. Two were mere infants. Their expressions were horrific. Caim could imagine the screams as they died. Then he looked beyond the bodies, and his fingers curled into painful fists. One wall of a longhouse stood a few paces away. Four corpses were likewise pinned to the wall, facing the children. Frozen streams of blood ran down their nude bodies from gory holes where their breasts had been. Long slits across their bellies exposed the entrails. Mothers, forced to watch the murder of their children, and then denied the mercy of a quick death.

Bile filled Caim's mouth. He had witnessed many cruelties in his life, including the murder of his best friend, Mat, but nothing like this. This went beyond raiding, beyond war. *And it's happening all across this land.*

He imagined Kit's voice. *These are your people, Caim. Your father's people. Can you turn your back on them? And if you do, what will you become?*

The horror turned to anger inside him, and then ignited into a full-on rage. He studied every detail of the scene. This was what Liana's people were fighting against.

Snow crunched behind him. Caim intercepted Liana before she saw the massacre. She didn't ask why, but let him lead her in another direction. As they made their way through the clearing, Caim imagined the dead all around him, scores upon scores buried beneath the virgin snow. Come spring, this meadow would become a charnel pit. Swarms of insects would feast and lay their eggs in the bloated flesh of these people who had lived and breathed just a few short weeks ago. As they approached the trees lining the edge of the village, Caim heard a scraping sound half a heartbeat before several dark figures emerged from the vegetation. Snow dusted the hoods of their heavy cloaks. Light glinted off drawn weapons. Seven men in all, unless more remained hidden. Caim counted four bowmen among them, their arrows pointed at him. Liana stiffened at his side.

'Don't move,' he whispered.

While Liana stood as if frozen in place, Caim shifted his weight away from her. If the archers fired, he didn't want them hitting her by mistake. He took a small step and reached back for his *suete* knife.

'Take another step, boyo,' one of the figures said. 'And you'll be food for the crows.'

Caim's hand tightened on the hilt.

255

SHADOW'S LURE

Chapter
TWENTY-FIVE

Josey blinked against the soft light filtering through the chamber's frosted windows as tears slid down her face. She didn't bother to wipe them away. They were a comfort, of a sort. She was the empress. She could cry if she wanted.

Doctor Klav had departed her bedchamber only minutes ago, but he hadn't been able to take his tidings with him. After he left, Amelia looked in on her, but Josey waved her away. The last thing she remembered was fainting in Hubert's arms, which was the first thing on her mind when she awoke. She didn't think anything could be worse than the embarrassment of that memory. Then the doctor had entered, and mortification had turned to fear, deeper and more pervasive than anything she'd ever experienced. The fact that she hadn't been poisoned was no consolation.

With a deep breath, she pushed herself out of bed. She dressed herself, not wanting to be bothered with her maids. She needed time to think, to try to make sense of the shambles her life had become. Instead she got Hubert.

'Majesty,' he began as he entered her chamber, 'I'm relieved to see you up and about. We feared the worst after your spell.'

We? That's right. They hadn't been alone when she swooned. Josey went to her nightstand and poured some water over her hands, using them to pat her face. She looked around for a cup.

'Hubert, about that, I want you to tell everyone that it was something I ate, but I'm fine now.'

'Of course. Your court will be overjoyed to hear it.'

Remembering the last audience session in the throne room, Josey rather doubted they would, particularly in the case of Lady Philomena. She could picture the woman, kneeling in the great cathedral before the saints and angels, praying for the new empress's early demise.

'Speaking of which,' Hubert said. 'Your war council is scheduled to convene this afternoon, should you feel up to attending.'

Josey hardly heard what he'd said. Her head was full of other thoughts, about herself, about Caim, and about what the future held for them. *If anything.*

'I'm sorry, Hubert. Yes, I will be there. I'm still feeling a little . . .'

He leaned forward. 'Majesty, is everything all right? The doctor said you were in fine health, yes?'

Josey bit her bottom lip. She had decided to keep this knowledge to herself and pretend everything was normal. At least until she couldn't hide the problem any longer. Now, standing here, she couldn't keep it in, not from this man who had risked so much to support her since the day she took the throne. She owed him the truth. She took a deep breath and clasped her hands together to steady them.

'Hubert. I'm . . . I am with child.'

She watched the progression of thoughts across his face in quick succession. It started with confusion and meandered into denial, and finally landed in the realm of stark terror. She'd felt the same when she heard the news. She'd questioned the doctor extensively until he assured her with solemn dignity that his determination was beyond reproach. It was only after she'd packed him off with a pledge of silence that she was able to wrap her head around the idea. Seeing someone else go through it gave her a better sense of perspective. *I'm going to be a mother.*

'Uh . . .' Hubert swallowed and tried again. 'Majesty, I know this may seem indelicate, but I must ask. Who . . . ah . . .'

Josey frowned, and then a furious blush exploded across her face when she realized what he was getting at.

'It's Caim's child, Hubert. Who else do you think?'

'Of course. Forgive me. I wasn't aware – I was caught by surprise.'

'It's all right. I was a little taken aback myself when I found out. I think I frightened Doctor Klav with threats of dungeon cells and chain gangs.'

He paced across the length of the room. 'We will have to make preparations, naturally. A governess must be selected. The old salon could be converted into a nursery—'

'Hubert!' She smiled. 'Relax. We'll manage it.'

He nodded as he crossed the carpet going the other way. 'Your ministers must be notified immediately. This child will be heir to the throne. And I hesitate to mention this, but it brings into question once more the subject of your, ah, marital status.'

Josey bit down on her lip, feeling the urge to strangle him. Instead, she found a porcelain cup and filled it with water. 'I warned you not to pursue that subject, Lord Chancellor. And you can tell that to the court if you like!'

'But—'

'Caim!' She couldn't help raising her voice, even though the door was open. She didn't care. 'I will marry Caim and no one else. Understand?'

Hubert's eyebrows rose to a peak. 'Indeed.'

She pushed a loose strand of hair out of her face. 'Good. Now, please leave me in peace for a while. Tell my ladies I wish to be alone.'

He sketched a deep bow and left the room. Josey turned to the window and sipped from the cup. The water was tepid, but it felt good on her parched throat. Outside, gray clouds smudged the sky, but still no sign of snow. She touched her belly. Would Caim be happy? Or disappointed? She thought back to the one night they had shared together, the night he had told her he was leaving Othir. She'd hoped she could change his mind. She cried for days when he didn't. Only Hubert understood why. And now a child grew inside her.

Another thought insinuated its way into her brain and forced her to remember a different night, a hideous night. The night at Kas's cabin in the woods when the Sacred Brotherhood came for her. She saw Markus's face again, mottled with half-healed scars, and remembered his hands upon her. The cup slipped from her fingers. The sound of shattering pottery filled her ears. The room spun before her.

As the door opened and her maids rushed in, one thought hammered at the inside of her skull.

What if Caim wasn't the father?

Caim's heart beat faster as four bronze arrow points centered on his chest. He sank into a lower stance. The hooded figures were spread out in a loose arc. He cast out his senses for the shadows, and a tingle slid down his back. The sword.

'Gaelan!' Liana shouted as she ran toward one of the figures.

Caim started to draw his knife, but she threw herself onto the man. Thick arms came up to seize her in a fierce embrace.

'Caim.' She extricated herself. 'This is my cousin. Gaelan, meet Caim.'

Hoods were pulled back, and hard eyes stared at him. The men reminded Caim of the outlaws who had taken him from Hagan's house: big, rawboned men at home in the wilds. Caim was aware of how he must have looked to them – torn clothing, nasty scars, dried blood crusted all over. So while Liana explained who he was and what they were doing out here, he stayed a few paces away and scanned the landscape ahead. The gentle slope they'd been following continued to rise as it approached the range of hills. The land was pocked with folds and ridges. It would be easy to get lost in this country. Suddenly he felt a new sense of vulnerability. He might have been born in this land, but it was still a stranger to him.

Two of the outlaws turned and started up the hillside on makeshift snowshoes. *Clever. They hardly leave any tracks.*

'They're going to escort us to the castle,' Liana said.

Her cousin raised a bushy eyebrow, but he didn't contradict her.

'Wonderful,' Caim replied. By 'escort' they really meant 'guard,' as in him specifically.

Liana started out walking beside Gaelan, but after a while she dropped back to Caim. 'I asked, but they haven't seen any of the others.'

The anxiety was plain in her voice. Caim tried to sound reassuring.

'That blizzard must have blanketed this entire region. I'm sure Keegan is fine. He's a strong kid.'

Liana nodded as she marched alongside him. A strong woman, fetching in face and figure. She would be a fine wife one day. For someone else.

The scouts took them up the face of a winding ridge and down into a shallow defile. The woods thinned around them, but the snow thickened. By the time it reached Caim's waist, he was half dragging Liana by the hand, despite her protests that she could make it on her own. They crawled up the foot of the center hill in this way for the better part of two candle-marks until Caim was bathed in a cool sweat under his leathers. Exhausted from fighting the snow, he was grateful when he saw their guides had halted up ahead.

When he and Liana reached them, Gaelan nodded his head up the slope. 'The castle lies before you. We go back to our post.'

Liana gave him a brief hug. 'Thank you, Cousin. When will you return?'

'Two days from now, if the weather holds. Otherwise, Killian will use it as an excuse to leave us out there for another turn.'

As the outlaws left, Caim gazed up the way before them.

The defile sank deeper between the ridges on either side to disappear into the hillside. A good place for an ambush. The ridges commanded a view of the entire approach; sentries would spot intruders long before they got this far. His gaze touched on the places on the hill where he would place watchers.

Liana didn't wait for him, and he was forced to follow her. Fortunately, the sides of the defile had shielded it from the worst of the storm so that the snow here was lower than in the surrounding countryside. By the time they reached the summit of the narrow pass, the crust on top of the powder no longer reached their ankles, but Caim hardly noticed as he looked ahead.

The canyon descended into a magnificent valley nestled between the mist-shrouded peaks. Sheer cliffs fell on either side more than five hundred feet to the valley floor. Between clusters of evergreens stretched snow-covered fields choked with the withered husks of rotted brush and stunted trees. A heap of stone stuck out from the canyon like a rocky fist. The outlines of once-proud walls and square towers peeked from under the mantle of snow. A fort, or the remnants of one. It was not as impressive as he'd dared to hope. Swathed in ice and dead ivy, the lone fortification looked centuries old.

'This,' Liana said, 'is what Caedman calls the last bastion of freedom in Eregoth.'

Caim grunted as he followed her down the stony path. Their arrival did not go unnoticed. Before they were halfway down the slope, a group of men came out of the trees and gathered at the foot of the trail. All had spears in hand, with more weapons belted to their waists. He didn't see any women among them, but a small army could have been hidden among the trees.

Caim stopped beside Liana as one of the group, an older man, stepped forward. His long gray hair was pulled back and tied at the base of his neck. Though well into his middling years, he looked tough enough to wrestle a bear. *And I know exactly what that feels like.*

'I see you, Hagan's daughter,' he said in a strong, deep voice. 'But who is this you have brought?'

'This is Caim, a friend.'

The group leader's eyes were the clear blue of snowmelt. 'You know our laws. Strangers aren't allowed here, Liana. And those that find us can't never leave.'

Caim shifted his feet, not liking the sound of that.

'He is no stranger,' Liana said. 'He comes from Nimea to help us in our fight.'

A shaggy mountain of a man standing at the rear of the group hawked and spat on the ground. 'No help comes from Nimea.'

'That's what Ramon believed,' Liana said, 'until Caim fought by his side at Guthern Prison. He helped us free Caedman.'

'Where is Caedman?' the leader asked.

Caim looked to Liana. What to tell them? The truth might get him lynched on the spot, and he hadn't come this far to fight these people. But how to convince them of that?

'He follows with the others,' Caim replied. 'He was injured.'

'Tortured.' The older man worked his jaw like he was chewing something bitter. 'We heard the rumors, though we didn't want to believe them.'

The others looked downcast by the news, and Caim understood. Caedman had been more than their leader; he was their inspiration. Without him, they were just a band of farmers and herdsmen.

'If the weather holds, they'll be here by tomorrow,' Caim said, hoping he was right.

The leader nodded. 'Caim, is it? I am Killian of the Indrig clan.'

Liana put a hand on Caim's shoulder. 'We are tired from the journey. May we enter?'

'Take your ease.' Killian gestured, and the men parted. 'We shall speak more tomorrow.'

As he followed Liana through the gauntlet of outlaws, Caim felt their eyes upon him. Once again he was the outsider. *You think I'd be used to it after all this time.*

Liana took him down a narrow trail through the fir and pine trees. It emerged under the spur of rock and climbed to a gap in the crumbling walls. Inside they found a wide bailey yard. Longhouses of raw timber, roofed in pine branches, were built against the outer walls. A few people, mostly women and a few children, worked and played in the courtyard. Ignoring the glances cast at him, Caim followed Liana to a hut set off by itself in a dark corner of the yard. There was snow piled in front of the door, and the place had an abandoned look to it, but Liana entered without hesitation. The interior was dark. Leaves were scattered across the floor, and a small drift of snow rested against the back wall. Liana set to gathering sticks from a pile.

A short time later, Caim sat beside a crackling fire, holding a wooden bowl to his lips as he shoveled in mouthfuls of hot oats. He hadn't realized how famished he was until Liana started cooking. When the bowl was empty and the hole in his belly somewhat filled, he reclined on the woven reed mats that made up the hut's floor. Smells of earth and smoke filled the air. He could fall asleep right here. In fact, he caught his eyes drooping and forced them open. On the other side of the small room, Liana ate from her bowl. Her demeanor had changed since entering this house. Whereas before she'd been strong and secure, voicing her opinion however she liked, she was now demure almost to the point of acting like a servant girl in her master's house, and he didn't know why. He hadn't done anything. At least, he didn't think he had.

'Who lives here?' he asked.

Liana looked up, but didn't meet his gaze. 'My brother, when he's here.'

The hut had no furniture, just some cooking utensils, a stack of kindling wood, and a few items hanging from the peaked ceiling. One of those items was a bundle of multi-colored feathers tied around what looked to be a bleached animal bone. Caim stared at it while lying on his side.

'He should be here soon,' he said.

She bobbed her head. Caim waited for a few heartbeats.

263

When nothing more was forthcoming, he started to ask what was the matter, but Liana preempted him by climbing to her feet. Carrying the bowls, she went outside.

Sighing, Caim lay on his back. He was too tired to care. He closed his eyes, but instead of soothing darkness he saw a white plain and a row of pale bodies arranged in the snow. He pulled his cloak tighter and inched closer to the fire.

SHADOW'S LURE

Chapter
TWENTY-SIX

Caim tensed as her lips settled over his mouth, but the softness of her kiss coaxed his muscles to relax, and he sank back onto the sumptuous bed.

Her silky hair fell over his face, down his neck. Her fingers left trails of blazing heat on his bare skin. The smell of her perfume filled his head, leaving him incapable of thought or care. This was what he wanted, this and nothing else.

'Caim,' she whispered. 'Be mine.'

The blood coursed in his temples as the answer was ripped from his throat.

'I am. I am yours.'

But her hands left him, and a cold wind washed over his body. He reached for her, but she slipped from his grasp.

'Caim, come to me. Come find me.'

He sat up as a gust of wind tore aside the flimsy silken canopy. A dark fog covered everything. Her voice sounded distant, like she was calling from the other side of the world.

'Caim . . . Come to me.'

'Kit!'

Caim awoke with a start.

It took him a moment to realize where he was. For an instant, the rafter over his head made him think of a cabin in the woods far to the south. Then he remembered the prison, the fighting, the witch.

Bodies in the snow.

He rubbed his eyes as he sat up. Kit and him? Where had that notion come from? Not that it hadn't been a pleasant dream, but still . . . Where was she? He'd thought, after hearing her voice at the prison, that she would return soon, but days had passed and there was still no sign. Worse, he was starting to become used to missing her.

The floor was like a sheet of ice beneath him. The hearth fire had gone out, and there was no sign of Liana.

Stretching, and groaning at the legion of aches throughout his body, he stood up. His arm felt better. A lot better. He rolled up his sleeve expecting to see the ragged hole. Instead, the skin had scabbed over completely. The yellow halo had disappeared. *Crazy. What other tricks can the shadows do?* Then he remembered the feats Levictus had performed with his sorcery, like the ebon serpent that had attacked him in his own apartment. *Maybe it's better I don't know.*

Caim went over to the wash bucket. After breaking the ice film, he plunged his hands into the freezing water and washed his face and his neck, and ran half-numb fingers through his hair. He rooted around for something to eat and could only come up with a shriveled, half-frozen pear. He buckled on his knives as he nudged open the door. The snow had started up again, coming down in puffy flakes. Caim took a bite of the pear.

The castle's bailey was protected from the wind, but a deep chill hung in the air. His breath misted before him in a dense cloud. A woman with two dirty children in tow walked past. Caim looked around, wondering what he should do, when he found Hagan sitting on a stone under a withered crabapple tree with his children. The old man didn't bother with a coat as he puffed on a long-stemmed pipe. Keegan stood a little back from his sister and father. His hand, bound up in white linen, rested on the hilt of his falcata. The blade looked like a part of him now, and Keegan seemed a far cry from the untested boy Caim had first met in the roadside tavern. And smarter, too, staying out of the conversation at hand. Caim only caught a whiff of it as he approached, but it was enough to make him walk slower.

'Why not, Papa? You haven't given me one good reason!'

Hagan shook his head. 'Liana, Liana. I cannot stop your brother, but you at least I can still protect from this insanity.'

'They're *not* insane! They just want a better life for all of us.'

'I cannot allow it, Liana,' Hagan replied, almost whispering. 'I cannot.'

Spinning away, Liana came face-to-face with Caim. She pushed past him and ran back to the hut. The door slammed shut behind her. Keegan grimaced and walked away, down the muddy path toward the other end of the bailey.

Hagan took a pull from his pipe and exhaled a cloud of sweet smoke up through the branches. 'You're up early.'

Caim pulled on his gloves. 'Must be the cold.'

'I want to thank you for saving the lives of my children. I heard if it weren't for you, they'd have been captured. Or worse.'

'They're good kids.'

'They are disobedient and headstrong. Like their mother, Arugul keep her. And being young, they tend to give their trust too easy.'

Not sure what the old man was getting at, Caim tried to change the subject. 'It was no problem. Were you here last night?'

Hagan stuck a finger in his mouth and fished out a sliver of grit. Flicking it away, he shook his head. 'I met Keegan and the others on the trail. We got here before daybreak. Heard some things while we traveled.'

'Like what?'

'Things about you and those knives of yours. And things that might sound to some like sorcery.'

He wasn't sure what to say. Not much use in denying it. Just about all of the outlaws had seen him use some type of shadow-play, at the clearing or in the prison. He should have known they would spawn all kinds of tales. From what little he remembered, there had been stories told about his mother, too.

'What are they planning to do?'

'These folks?' Hagan asked around the pipe's mouthpiece. 'I suspect you'll find out soon enough. But there's something you should know about them.'

'And what's that?'

'They respect strength, but they'll follow a man that's true and straightforward all the way to the underworld and back.'

'Must be what they see in Caedman.'

'I'm talking about you, son.'

Caim shifted his weight from one foot to the other. He wasn't sure how to take that. 'I'd just as soon be on my way.'

The old man nodded. 'You're a lot like your father. Met him once. A few years before his death.'

Caim clenched his jaws together hard enough to make his teeth creak. His mind leapt from one question to the next, but he couldn't get them past his tongue, which was frozen to the roof of his mouth. *Why are you telling me this now? What do you expect me to do?*

'He was a firm man. But he treated his people well, even the dirt-farmers who leased his property and couldn't afford more than a couple of bits for rent.'

'Is that so?'

Hagan met his gaze and held onto it. 'Everyone knew one thing about your father, lad. He prized his family above all else.'

Caim looked away first. All the questions flew out of his head. They didn't matter anymore. None of it mattered.

Hagan took another puff from his pipe. 'But let me ask you something. You got any idea what you're doing?'

'I suppose not.'

'I only ask because I've also heard my daughter's taken a liking to you.'

'I can assure you that—'

Hagan held up a hand to forestall him. 'Liana can take care

of herself well enough. If you weren't treating her the way she wanted, then I reckon you'd be walking funny this morning.'

Caim smiled. 'I believe you're right.'

'But she's got a big heart. Gets that from her mother, too. I just wanted you to know that.'

'I do.'

'Pa,' Liana called from the hut. 'Come inside and break your fast.'

Hagan took the pipe out of his mouth, tapped out the ashes against the stone, and ground them under his heel as he stood up.

'Coming inside?'

Caim sighed. 'No. I'm fine.'

The old man nodded as he strode past. Caim waited until the door closed before he started down the path through the snow. As he crossed the central yard, he saw a gathering of men outside the lichen-clad remains of the old donjon tower. Coils of smoke rose from a fire in the gathering's midst, lifting toward the ominous gray heavens. More people than he would have guessed lived in these old ruins, at least seventy or eighty men in all. A tall outlaw with a tattered cap was speaking.

'—lost a lot of blood.'

'Will he make it?' another asked.

'Who's to say? It's in Nogh's hands. But he's a stubborn bastard. If anyone can survive such misery, it would be our Lord Caedman.'

There was murmured agreement. Ramon stood on the other side of the small bonfire. Grendt was at his side, gnawing on a leg of mutton. *So the slimy rat survived after all? Too bad*. Oak and the brothers, Dray and Aemon, stood near them, and a few others he recognized, but many faces were new to him.

'What will we do if he dies?'

'The Dark take you, you Hurrold mutt!' a big woodsman with a thick brown beard roared, jabbing his finger over the flames. 'Don't you go cursing him with your ill words.'

'We're all thinking it, Malig!' the insulted outlaw replied.

269

'That don't mean you should be—'

'Quiet!'

Ramon stood up to the fire and spoke. 'There's no use fighting the wind. Fralk asked a fair question. The clans are scattered. What's left of our warriors have been winnowed by war and famine. What will we do if Caedman cannot lead us?'

'It's time we made peace with Eviskine!'

When that comment was shouted down, Ramon held up his arms to quiet them, but it wasn't until the wooden door to the tower opened that the gathering fell silent. All turned as a new arrival emerged to join the circle. Caim recognized Killian.

The gray-haired veteran looked around at the faces. 'He has awoken.'

Scattered cheers went up through the crowd, but a few, Caim noted, held their tongues. Ramon and Grendt were among them.

'He wants to see Ramon,' Killian said. 'And Tuan and Vaner, and Keegan, too, if your father won't join us.'

The veteran looked around as if searching for someone. His gaze stopped on Caim. 'And you, Du'Vartha.'

Murmurs sifted through the crowd as Killian went back inside with the selected men following behind him. Caim hesitated. Eyes darted in his direction until he joined the file.

The inside of the tower had been converted into a home. Steps that had once led to the upper floors ended a few feet from the ground. Squares of thatch had been used to fill the gaps in the ceiling. Dry rushes covered the floor. A fire in a low hearth provided some warmth if not much light. On another wall, a shield was displayed. It looked like it had seen some action. Under the many scrapes and scratches lay a rampant bear with golden brown fur. Off to the side, a garland of dried flowers hung from a nail.

Caedman was sitting up on his own, which was a miracle as far as Caim was concerned. The outlaw captain didn't look much better than he had at the prison. Deep purple circles ringed his eyes, which were glazed and bloodshot in the low firelight. His cheeks were swollen and discolored. The white mantle of a clan thane was draped around his shoulders like a shawl.

As they entered, Killian gestured for everyone to come near. Caim joined the others in a loose circle around the bed, which smelled of old sweat.

'Father Ell,' Keegan whispered. 'Is he . . . ?'

'He'll live.' Killian stood by Caedman's head. 'But he's broke up inside. The gods only know if he'll ever walk again, much less hold a sword.'

Caedman watched them as they gathered around him. Caim stiffened as those eyes passed over him. They were filled with pain, but there was also something else, an iron-hard core that could not be touched by misery or fear. The others looked away rather than face their leader. Caim understood. It was doubtful any of them had ever believed in the rebellion until Caedman recruited them. Now, confronted by the prospect of life without his leadership, they doubted once more. The movement could die this very night.

'I have spoken with my kinsman,' Caedman wheezed, his voice slurred by the broken jaw. 'I cannot lead you. It must pass to another.'

'No, Caedman,' Vaner said. 'You are our captain. We will follow only you.'

The outlaw leader shook his head and made what might have passed for a smile. 'Vaner, I value your friendship, but it is Eregoth which deserves your loyalty. I must entrust you to someone who can achieve our goal. A nation of free men.'

Ramon stepped forward, and all eyes turned toward him – all except for Keegan, who rubbed his mouth as he looked away.

'I will lead them,' the big man said. 'You can trust me to see it through.'

Caedman sighed. 'You are the bravest of us all, Ramon. I know you would fight until the end. But you are not my choice.'

Caedman coughed again and grimaced before he continued.

271

'You'll need more than courage to fight the Eviskine. You will need cunning and wisdom. You will have to be ruthless.'

Caim's throat tightened as those stern eyes fell upon him, holding him in place. *What would you have of me? You know what I am, what I've done.*

'Like his father,' Caedman said, 'who came to our land in search of a new beginning, and in the end gave his life for freedom, this man from the south is our brother. He will be the one to lead you.'

Ramon jerked back at the words, snorting like a bull. 'That's your decision?'

The leader nodded, looking tired and old.

'It is the decision of Clan Indrig,' Killian said.

Ramon stepped back from the bedside. 'Those who wish to stay will do it without me, or the rest of the Gilbaerns.'

Without another word, Ramon strode away. No one else moved, though Vaner was considering the patched ceiling as if looking for answers. Caim moved his head from side to side, not sure to believe what he was hearing. *Me? Are they crazy? These people need a leader, not a killer.*

Killian herded everyone outside, but as Caim turned to go, the veteran shook his head. 'Not you. He wants you to stay.'

The others looked at him as they left.

'Caim, come here.'

Caedman tried to sit up higher. Caim watched him struggle, making no move to aid him.

'Why me?'

The outlaw leader winced and settled back onto the cushions of the bed. When he looked at Caim again, his eyes were clearer, but a shadow lay upon them. *He's dying, and he knows it.*

'I'm just a knife for hire,' Caim continued. 'These people don't know me and they don't trust me. Choose Ramon or Killian to take over your rebellion.'

Caedman lifted a hand toward the window. 'This valley is where my forefathers settled when they first came to Eregoth more than seventy years ago. This land was untamed then, and unkind to strangers. The strong survived, and the weak perished.'

It hasn't changed much. I see it in Keegan, the drive to be stronger than his father.

'You're more than just a hired blade, Caim Du'Vartha. Your father was a man of honor. He wasn't afraid to fight, and even die, for what he believed was right. You are such a man, Caim.'

'And if you're wrong, a lot of people are going to die.'

'That will happen regardless. But if they die for a purpose, for something they believe in, then it will have meaning.'

Caim shook his head. There was no meaning in death. Dead was dead. He turned toward the door.

'Caim.' A wet cough made him stop, but he didn't look back. 'Only you can give them the chance they need.'

He pushed open the door and let it close behind him.

Outside, men argued as snowflakes rained down on them. Fewer were standing around the fire than before; Ramon had made good on his promise. Caim estimated almost half of the crowd had departed, among them many of the more seasoned warriors. But Killian had stayed, and a few of the other lieutenants. Still, there were too many young men in the crowd, and too many past their prime. *Caedman is wrong. With or without me, these people don't have a chance.*

'That's it,' the one called Malig was saying. 'Without Caedman, we're finished.'

Oak stood up on the other side of the circle. 'We could stay here. Hole up in the castle until spring.'

'And then what? Don't you get it? We should pack up everything we can carry and move out, to another land.' He made a sour face. 'Uthenor, maybe.'

A man with a bushy yellow beard grunted. 'Go begging to those brigands? You're addled, Malig. They'd as soon bury us as help us.'

'We can't run!' Keegan shouted, but he was drowned out by the others.

Malig put a hand on the butt of his dirk. 'You got a better

273

plan? Maybe you want to die here, but I've had enough. Run and live, or stay and die. There ain't no other choices.'

Caim took a deep breath. The same debate was rumbling around inside him. Stay or go? There was nothing holding him here. *Nothing but ghosts screaming for vengeance. Innocent people. My people. I don't owe them anything. No?*

But thoughts of leaving vanished as Caim moved through the press. Men stood aside to let him into the circle. He felt their gazes on him. Hard looks, gauging him.

Spy. Traitor. Killer.

That's what they're thinking. Lead this bunch? Half of them want to kill me. I don't belong here. I don't belong anywhere.

'He's right.' Caim nodded toward Malig. 'You don't stand a chance against the duke's army, not to mention the Northmen. I've seen what they're like up close. You men are untrained. You're too few. You'd be better off running. Take your families elsewhere.'

'That's what I told you all!' Malig shouted.

The men started murmuring again, a low hum of resentment Caim could feel coming at him. He let it build for a few moments. Keegan lingered on the edge of the crowd, watching with guarded eyes. *Don't dare to believe in me, boy. Not for a single instant.*

Caim pitched his voice to be heard above the noise. 'But there's another choice. You can fight, and maybe die.'

'Is that your idea of a fucking joke, Southlander?' Dray muttered.

Caim shrugged. 'You'll die in any case. You think the duke will just let you leave after this? He has no choice. He has to make examples out of you, until the last man is slain. So you must choose. Die on your feet.' He looked to Malig. 'Or on your knees.'

Malig grabbed for his knife. 'I'll carve out your goddamned eyes before I stand here and let you name me a coward, Nimean.'

Caim walked over to the clansman. Everyone hushed. Fury flickered in Malig's eyes, but he made no move to attack.

274

'Then let me help you,' Caim said.

'How?'

'We will attack.' Caim turned in a slow circle. 'We'll strike swiftly and strike hard. We'll strike where the duke's men do not expect us, where they never imagine we can reach. And as they rush about trying to find us, we'll steal in under their noses and prick them where they feel it most.'

'The duke's got an army,' Yellow Beard said. 'He's got castles and forts.'

'And horsemen,' someone else added.

'Aye,' Caim said. 'The duke has much to protect. And much to lose. But not us. We only have each other.'

Smiles touched some of the faces, faint glimmers of hope where before there had been only dejection and defeat.

Keegan dipped through the crowd to stand before him. 'I will follow you.'

'And I,' Aemon said.

One by one the outlaws affirmed their willingness to follow him. Caim looked around the fire, into the eyes of these men who had been commended into his hands. They were just a band of woodsmen and shepherds, but there was strength here, and courage. That was a start. As for the rest . . .

Only one way to find out.

Caim cleared his throat. 'I only know one way to fight. You'll either learn it, or you'll die trying. Get some sleep. Tomorrow maybe you'll regret this decision.'

As he turned away, someone muttered, 'What if we already do?'

Caim kept walking, down into the valley to be alone.

Arion dropped the empty tin cup and looked across the fire. Stiv sat on his cloak, scraping the last forkful of beans from his cup. The sergeant had never been what the ladies considered a handsome man, but now his face was truly a horror to behold, a mass of black gouges left by the sorcery of the man in black, the one Sybelle called the scion. It was difficult to look the sergeant in the face, but Arion did it without flinching. He owed the man that much, at least.

A driving snowstorm pummeled the army four days out of the city. They stayed in camp while the drovers cleared a path. Arion didn't like the idea of riding south. He had no love for the Nimeans, but he knew the true enemy of his country was back in Liovard, sitting at his father's side.

Stiv put aside his dinner with a curt nod. Arion stood up to stretch. Unfamiliar soldiers sat around the camp. The only men he knew by name were the members of his bodyguard, which was now down to three. Sybelle had made sure his regular company remained behind and had attached him to another unit. And she'd sent a handler to keep watch over him as well.

'Lord Eviskine.'

Arion turned toward the voice. The priest wore a long robe the color of dried blood under a deep black cowl, an over-dramatic touch that only served to make Arion hate him more, as if he needed another reason. A burly Uthenorian mercenary halted a few steps behind the priest and crossed his arms. His gaze settled on Stiv. It amused Arion to watch the big men measure each other. Stiv hawked and spat a mouthful of phlegm into the snow.

'What do you want, Volmer?'

The priest held out his bony hands to the campfire. His fingernails were like chips of white chalk.

'Our mistress sends word. The Queen of the Night wishes you to devise a plan of invasion into central Nimea before we reach the border.'

Stiv grunted.

Volmer glared down at the soldier, apparently unfazed by the sergeant's disfiguration. 'You find our mistress's commands amusing, dog?'

Stiv shrugged and went back to looking into the fire.

'We're eager to be on our way,' Arion said. 'I'll have the plans ready by morning.'

The priest nodded. 'That will do.'

A shout broke above the camp noises. Arion looked across the tops of the tents to a space where several men squared off. Sunlight reflected off bared blades. He couldn't make out the words being exchanged, but their tone was driven by hot tempers. Nearby soldiers started to gather around the noise.

'Miserable curs.' Volmer took a step toward the disturbance. 'They will learn discipline at the end of a lash!'

The priest jerked to a halt as Arion's sword slid between his ribs. As Volmer fell, his Uthenorian protector swore and reached for his blade, and was jerked upright as a massive forearm whipped around his throat. Stiv yanked twice, until there was a soft pop, and then dropped the mercenary's limp body to the ground.

Arion pulled his blade free and glanced around, but everyone's attention was focused on Brustus and Davom as they pretended to pick a fight with each other.

'Put them in my tent.' Arion ducked into his shelter and pulled out their packs.

He whistled loud as he trotted across the snow. Brustus and Davom gave up their game and dipped into the disappointed crowd. They all met at the road. Okin rode up on a courier horse with four steeds in tow.

'Back to Liovard?' Davom asked.

Arion jumped into the saddle. 'That's right. And we don't stop until we reach the palace gates. Not for any reason.'

Receiving a nod from each man, he took off down the snowy road like the Lords of the Dark were on his tail.

SHADOW'S LURE

Chapter
TWENTY-SEVEN

Caim winced as someone's misplaced foot stepped on a branch hidden under the snow. The resulting snap echoed through the trees. The troop leader, Malig, turned around and scowled at the score of men strung out behind him. Caim thought Malig was going to bark at them, but the outlaw held his tongue. With a wave, he motioned for them to keep after him. He was learning. Finally.

From atop a small tor between two sturdy aspen trees, Caim watched the column of outlaws march through the woods below. He had been drilling them for six days straight in close combat, ambush tactics, infiltration, and reconnaissance – all the things they needed if they were going to have any chance against the duke's forces. So far, the results were slow. Each night, exhausted, he fell into a dreamless sleep that was never long enough before dawn arrived, and all the while one unavoidable truth refused to be ignored. He was the leader of a rebellion. *If Hubert could see me now, he'd laugh good and hard. Caim the Knife, leader of rebels and insurrectionists.*

He'd had his chance to skip out, and not taken it. That alone was enough, in his mind at least, to condemn him. But what did he hope to achieve? What would victory look like, and would any of them know if they managed to achieve it? He didn't have the answers.

The daylight was fading. The nights were getting darker as

they approached the new moon. In the old days, this would have been his preferred time to strike. The old days . . . Caim took a deep breath of the bracing air. His need to see Kit was bordering on desperation, not for her talents, but just to see her and talk to her again. He'd wrestled with the question of how to find her, and come up empty. Why didn't she come back? Didn't she see how much he needed her? *Kit, if you can hear me, I need you. I'm sorry for whatever I did. Dammit, just come back.*

Caim exhaled a long sigh that turned to mist in the cold air. He didn't know what he felt about her. She was his friend. Wasn't that enough? Things had been simpler once, though he could hardly remember when. But she wasn't the only source of advice. He'd gone to see Caedman one night after a frustrating session with the men. The outlaw leader sat up in his bed, looking paler and thinner than the day they rescued him. When Caim laid out his problems, Caedman shook his head.

'They aren't soldiers, Caim. They're loggers and trappers.' Candlelight flickered across Caedman's face, hiding some of the scars. 'You can't beat them over the heads with drills and instruction about tactics.'

Caim threw back the last of the crude mead in his cup. 'They don't listen. I spend half my time breaking up fights.'

'You have to show them what you want, Caim.'

'How do I do that?'

'Start at the beginning.'

Then, as he had made his way back to Keegan's hut, he found Hagan sitting on the same stone as before, looking up at the moon. 'You figure out what you're doing yet, son?'

Caim stopped not far from him. 'I'm not sure. Feels like I've been running for days, but not getting anywhere.'

'It's not you they're fighting.' The old man took a puff from his pipe. 'It's the witch. Our people hold to the old ways. They believe stories that the southlands pass off as myth and legend.'

When Caim didn't understand, Hagan explained. 'A long

time ago, before there was a land called Eregoth, or even Nimea for that matter, another empire ruled over the land. An empire of darkness.'

Caim had heard tales of old empires before. They were all evil in the stories. But Hagan told of a dominion that spread its wickedness to every corner of the world, until there were few places of light left.

'And what happened to this dark empire?' Caim asked.

Hagan pulled the stem of the pipe from his mouth. 'Some few found the courage to fight back. And after a long struggle, the few prevailed against the many, and the Dark was pushed back. But now some think it's come back, that the witch and her spawn are the harbingers of a new dominion.'

Caim had walked away shaking his head, but the old man's story had lingered in the back of his mind ever since.

A ragged yell erupted below as a flight of arrows flew from the trees. Some of the padded missiles found targets among Malig's company, but the men hit didn't lie down like they were supposed to do in these war games. Instead, they charged at Keegan's unit descending on them from above.

If Caim hadn't insisted on using sticks instead of real weapons, most of the men would be dead or maimed already. Although he'd showed them again and again how to defend against attacks by employing different angles of approach and a simple system of blocks, but the woodsmen still swung their ersatz swords like wild men, bashing each other over the head, arms, legs, or any part that stuck out.

At least the fights were entertaining. Children perched in the trees to watch; women found reasons to pass by the practice area as they went about their work. Amid the trees, the skirmish had devolved into a brawl with men flinging each other into the snow and falling over each other. Caim nodded to Killian. While the older man hustled down into the melee, separating combatants and shouting for everyone to stand down, snow crunched behind Caim as Liana walked up to him.

She was another problem. He noticed the lingering gazes cast in his direction. Even her father had taken notice. A year ago he would have bedded her and enjoyed it, but with Josey in his head and Kit gone . . .

She handed Caim a steaming mug and watched the fracas below. 'I thought you might be cold.'

'Thank you.'

Liana crossed her arms. She wasn't wearing her heavy coat, just a leather vest over a long-sleeved gambeson and loose leggings. The bandage around her head was gone, the cut now scabbed over.

'Keegan says you talk to yourself.'

Caim swallowed a mouthful of *cha* and spilled a little down his chin. 'What are you talking about?'

'He says at the prison, you called out to someone. Says it sounded like "Cat." Is that a Nimean god?'

Caim thought back to that chaotic night. He and Keegan had been in the atrium when Kit spoke in his head with a warning. Had he responded out loud? 'Something like that,' he said.

She smiled. 'I didn't take you for a pious man, Caim.'

He shook his head. 'I'm not, usually. But the gods know you and your brother have given me reason to pray.'

'I want to ask you something.'

'What's that?'

'We want to train, too,' she said.

'We?'

'Yes. The other women and I. We want you to teach us how to fight so we can stand with the men.'

He looked at her again. She wore heavy boots. Her vest was too big – probably borrowed from Keegan – and her leggings were overly bulky, as if she'd pulled one pair over another for extra padding. *She's serious.*

'No.'

She stood with her hands on her hips, looking too much like Kit in a snit for his comfort. 'Why not? This is our fight as much as theirs.'

'Doesn't matter.'

'Because we're women?'

281

'In a way of speaking, yes.'

'But—'

A loud yelp snatched his attention back to the scene below. Most of the outlaws were wrestling in the snow now, and more than a little blood stained the ground. Caim handed Liana the mug. He had seen enough.

As he trotted down the hill, Caim shouted at Hoon, who held a melon-sized rock above his head as he stood over his foe.

'Put that down. Gently! Everyone else take a step back.'

The outlaws backed away from each other, trading barbs and insults. Caim found Keegan in the crowd, the youth sporting a new bruise over one eye. The scratches they'd found on his arms were disturbing, but Caim saw promise in the young man.

'Good job with your group. You kept the element of surprise and conducted an effective ambush.'

He looked around for Malig. 'You! You started in a good position, but failed to keep control of your squad. As a result—'

'These sods can't fight worth a damn!' the burly outlaw complained, glaring at everyone. He had a bloody lip and snot running from his nose.

'As a result,' Caim continued, 'your group fell apart when the attack came. If this had been a real battle, you'd all be dead.'

That evoked a chorus of contention from Malig's unit.

'They didn't fight fair!' a skinny outlaw grumbled.

Caim walked over and jabbed the man in his bony chest. 'You think the duke's soldiers are going to fight fair?' He looked around. 'You all better wake up, and soon, or your families are going to be digging a lot of graves.'

Caim held out his hand. 'Give me your weapon. Everyone form a circle. Malig inside.'

The outlaws jeered as they made a ring around Malig. The outlaw swung the stout tree branch he had been using as a sword back and forth. Caim looked up to the hilltop. He didn't want to do it, but he had to put this notion out of Liana's head before she did something foolhardy.

He pointed. 'And Liana. Get down here.'

The crowd quieted as she descended the slope. Caim handed her the stick, which she accepted with a nod.

Keegan pushed through the crowd. 'Caim!'

He held up a hand. 'Not now.'

'But she's—'

Caim glared at the boy. 'Take your place and watch, or get out of my sight.'

Keegan shut his mouth, but his hands gripped his wooden sword with white knuckles. Caim understood how he felt. He didn't want to see Liana get hurt either, but this had to be done.

Liana and Malig took up places in the middle of the circle. He was a full foot taller and probably outweighed her by four or five stone. She held her weapon like a carpet-beater, hands gripped too close together, wrists bent at an awkward angle. Caim almost stopped the bout before it began. *No, she needs to see this isn't a game.*

Caim lifted his hand. When Liana nodded, he dropped it.

It was over almost as fast as he anticipated. Malig came out swinging his wooden sword like he was mowing wheat. Liana backed away from his rush and couldn't keep her feet. In a matter of heartbeats she was driven out of the circle and into a snowbank. Malig brandished his weapon to the hoots of the onlookers as he trotted around the ring.

As Liana extricated herself from the embankment, Caim wanted to ask if she was all right, but held back. He owed her the real deal. Amused chuckles arose as she stepped back into the ring.

When both fighters were in position, Caim raised his hand. This time, he didn't wait for Liana to give the okay before he started the bout. His hands balled up into fists as Malig made a side-armed swing that would have ripped off half of Liana's face if she hadn't ducked away. He thought this fight was going to end the same way as the last, but to her credit, Liana darted back in and jabbed her wooden sword at Malig. The tip of her weapon touched his stomach. Then his backhanded swing caught her flush in the shoulder with a loud smack and drove her to the ground.

Keegan launched himself into the circle. Malig barely had time to turn before the youth tackled him. Caim ran over. He and Killian pulled them apart, both a little bloodied and breathing hard, but nothing serious. Caim disarmed Keegan and shoved him toward the sideline. Malig clutched his neck and shot dark glares over his shoulder as Killian walked him in the other direction.

Caim knelt down beside Liana. He expected tears in her eyes. Instead, she grinned as she sat up and rubbed her shoulder.

'Not broken, I take it,' he said.

She lifted her arm to show it wasn't. 'I want another go.'

Caim shook his head. This woman would be the death of him. 'That's not necessary.'

Liana brushed off her leggings as she stood up. 'I can do better.'

'You don't need to.'

'Damn right,' Malig growled. 'I'll knock her fool head off next time!'

Caim looked over at him. 'There's no need to go again because she won.'

'What? You must be blind. I knocked the tar out of her.'

'Yes. Right after she stabbed you through the gut.'

'That fly swat? I hardly felt it.'

'A gut wound is a slow and painful way to go. If those had been real swords, you'd be holding your insides on your lap.'

There were a few laughs from the crowd. Malig scowled at them, but Killian's hand on his shoulder kept him in line.

'He was sloppy, the same as many of you.' Caim faced the outlaws. 'You haven't listened to a single thing I've tried to teach you. You think fighting is about beating down the other man with sheer strength and you're missing the point. It's about staying alive, about killing more of them than they kill of us. I can show you how, but only if you listen.'

They looked around at each other. A few were still frowning, but no one was arguing with him. That was a good start. *I'll take what I can get.*

'All right,' he said. 'Head farther down the trail and try it again, but this time Malig's crew sets the ambush. Killian, get them set up.'

Groans echoed off the valley walls as the men marched off through the brush. Caim suppressed a sigh. *It's going to be a long day. And a long night, too. I'll have Killian set up some night-fighting exercises.*

Liana waited until the men were out of earshot. 'You were trying to embarrass him. I didn't win.'

'You won.'

'I could do better if you gave me another chance.'

Caim sighed and ran a hand over his forehead. He didn't want to get into this with her. *But she deserves to know the truth.*

'Liana, you're brave and you've got more brains than most of these oafs put together, but the men we'll be facing will be bigger, stronger, and crueler than you. What's more, they'll have superior arms and numbers.'

'Yes, but—'

'It takes more than a few days of drills in the woods. It takes years of training and conditioning, and years more experience to know when to fight and when to run. Years we don't have. Teaching you a few tricks and sending you off against the duke's soldiers would mean certain death.'

'What about the men? They don't have years of training.'

He leveled with her. 'Many of them are going to die. Maybe all of them, before this is over.'

She chewed on her bottom lip. 'So what can we do?'

'Go fetch the women. Tell them to cut saplings this tall.' He held a hand about a foot over his head. 'Strip them down to the wood. I'm going to teach you how to use the spear.'

'But the men use—'

'Don't argue! A spear is better than a sword nine times out of ten. Now get!'

With a laugh, she ran off through the trees, back toward the castle. Caim shook his head and wondered what he'd created. He didn't know the first thing about training women to fight. Then again, he didn't know anything about training men either. But now they were here all together, the blind leading the blind.

Gods preserve us.

The pool's cloudy depths swirled and eddied under her gaze, forming patterns that melded and broke away in an endless dance of shadow and light. Sybelle leaned closer and projected her will through the surface to the deeper substance underneath. It was like pushing through a wall of sludge, but then the resistance melted away and a gray void floated before her eyes.

Sybelle released the breath she had been holding. The pool had been acting strangely of late, fighting her with more than its usual tenacity. This was the third time she'd attempted to reach her agent today, and she was determined to persevere until she got what she wanted.

She needed information. Since the events at the prison almost a sennight ago, her entire world had begun to unravel. She had returned to the palace to discover that Erric had gone out to lose himself in the city's sordid pleasure houses. After admonishing herself for the umpteenth time for not putting a geas on the man, she went back to her temple to find her priests conducting a bloodletting rite. Normally, such a ceremony would calm her nerves, but that night she had been beyond consolation. She hadn't been able to summon the necessary hunger to partake fully and had had to content herself with the consumption of a few choice morsels. It was *his* fault.

The scion.

His appearance had disrupted everything. She needed to eliminate him, but that was easier contemplated than done. Again and again she'd sent the shadows hunting for him, to no avail. Now, fortified and rested, she would try another approach.

Sybelle focused her attention on the scrying pool. The one she sought was far away, and his cooperation was involuntary, which made contacting him a more demanding feat. Then, like fog whisked from the surface of a lake by a stiff breeze, the grayness resolved itself into indistinct shapes. Sybelle pushed harder and the shapes became objects. A crude table. A lantern, dark now, its reservoir almost empty. And tendrils of light – the first pale fingers of dawn through a window. She was in a small room walled in old stone blocks. She listened, and was pleased to hear the wheeze of labored breathing. Her servant lay on a wood cot. A fire burned low in a fieldstone hearth. On the opposite wall hung a shield, battered and scuffed. Through the grime she discerned a picture of some furry Brightlands beast.

Sybelle took in a deep breath, feeling it expand the lungs of her real body, and *pushed*. Excitement tickled her stomach as a large hand rose into her view. A man's hand, long of finger and strong despite its wasted appearance. She focused on transmitting her command across the ether.

Turn to the window.

She watched the scene with anticipation, expecting to see the view swivel toward the morning light. Instead, it remained unchanged with only a slight wavering. Sybelle pushed harder. In her own body, the strain sent tremors shooting through her frame.

Turn!

The picture trembled as her minion fought the compulsion, but Sybelle bore down, and with agonizing slowness the view tacked to the left. The morning glow grew brighter as the edge of a window appeared, the aperture covered by a leather flap.

Stand up.

There was a moment's hesitation, and then the view rose to a higher angle. At her direction, the hand rose up again and swiped aside the window flap. Bright sunlight poured into the room. Sybelle squinted reflexively, but the light did not blind her. *Of course not. These are mortal eyes.*

She looked out into a wide courtyard blanketed in snow.

Crude buildings – homes for peasants, she assumed – were built against a backdrop of crumbling walls. Beyond the loose ramparts loomed the sheer face of a cliff, glistening in the sunlight. She compelled her minion closer to the window and lifted his eyes. Sybelle's breath caught in her throat as the startling vastness of the sky opened above the shack. Never had she seen the firmament with such crystalline clarity. Even swaddled in gray clouds, it was incredible.

She pulled her attention back to the task at hand. Her minion was in a canyon or deep valley, but the hills of Eregoth were riddled with gorges and ravines, many of them unknown to any map. She needed a landmark, something by which she could locate this place, but all she saw was stone and sky. She tried to lean out the window.

Sybelle gasped as she was thrust back into her body. Her heart pounded as she drew in several deep breaths. The pool bubbled and thrashed like a boiling kettle. The man had cast her out! She screeched at the walls until mortar oozed down the stone blocks. The shadows flocked around her, feeding off her rage.

As she steadied herself, images flashed through her head. Memories, but they weren't hers. She smiled as the pictures slowed, showing her much of what she needed to see. Then she leaned over the pool and sent forth her consciousness into the cloudy waters again. This time Soloroth's face filled the pool, and for once he wasn't wearing his helmet. Sybelle's anger cooled at the sight of her son's features, his deep black eyes that looked like they could swallow her whole. She had forgotten how much he resembled his father, whom she hadn't thought about in years. One more thing she'd left behind when she came to this horrid world. Sybelle's gaze traced the many scars slicing across his skin, the half-missing ear on his left side. He had suffered in her service. *We all suffer. It is no different for me.*

'Mother.'

Trees moved past him in the background, their white-clad limbs blocking out the dim sky.

'Where are you?' she asked.

'Fourteen leagues west of the city, near the first village. We have begun our first sweep of the—'

'Change direction to south by southwest and go to the Elmerton sentry post. Approach with care. I do not want the scion alerted until you are in position.'

He nodded, though his eyes remained on her. As his image faded from the waters, Sybelle contacted another agent farther west. He answered at once, but his features were unfocused, as if she were seeing him through oily glass.

'I am here, my queen.'

Sybelle allowed herself a small smile. He was one of her favorites, despite his pale skin like an undercooked fish and repulsive blue eyes. 'The rebels are shut up in a secluded valley among the central peaks. Don't stop searching until you find them.'

'Your Darkness, that terrain is treacherous. An extensive search will take—'

She slapped the water with her hand, cutting him off. 'Do not make excuses.'

His shaved pate came into view as he bowed deeply. 'It will be done, my queen.'

'Report back when you are finished.'

As the pool settled into opaque darkness, Sybelle dried her hands on the skirt of her gown and considered her next move. She was tired, but slumber seemed as far away as the stars. Tonight, she would lie in her bower with a stalk of lotus gathered in her arms, inhaling its dream-laced pollen.

The gong in the alcove rang.

Sybelle's fingers froze, dangling over the dark waters. She knew by its tone that the Master was seeking her. The pool bubbled. She jerked away. She was not prepared to face him. *Not now. Not until I have the scion.*

She opened a portal and left the sanctum.

Chapter
TWENTY-EIGHT

K it clutched her hand as something small and flat flew out of the mist and sliced open her palm, but she kept running. With Doggie coursing by her side, she watched the blood well up in the cut and dribble out. It had been so long since she *could* be hurt, she hardly knew what to expect. She showed Doggie her hurt, and his smug expression reminded her of Caim. Still she kept running, until her chest ached and a sharp pain dug into her side. The monster closed in behind them.

After she'd seen Caim through the faltering portal, the circle had collapsed into gray slivers. Stricken with worry, she'd started off across the lifeless plain in the direction of the prickling, hoping to find some other way out. Instead, the monstrous presence had returned. How long had she been running? Days? Weeks? She had no way of knowing. Time flowed differently here. She thought back to the tough spots she had seen with Caim, and how he had managed to survive. She would have given anything to have him here. Or better yet, to be where he was. Even a prison cell sounded nice about now.

Kit rubbed her forehead. The itch was stronger than before, but what was causing it? A flash of yellow light pierced the murky clouds above her. The path sloped upward with grow-ing pitch. After a score of paces Kit was climbing more than running. Sucking in a gulp of desiccated air, Kit forced her tired limbs to churn faster. The light grew brighter, and the hope of finding a pathway back to the Brightlands blossomed in her chest. *I'm coming, Caim!*

The light pulsed, just once and weakly, but the prickling sensation cascaded over her whole body, making her skin sizzle. It didn't hurt exactly, but it spurred her to action. The presence loomed in her wake, but the prickling dragged her onward.

Above in the gloom, the mouth of a cave glowed against the hillside. The sensation became overwhelming, making it difficult to concentrate. *Keep pushing. I'm almost there.*

A sudden gust of wind rushed down the hillside and threatened to hurl her backward. Kit held tight to the rocky ground. Step by step she fought the wind even as the presence loomed behind her. Doggie growled. When the turbulence lessened, she jumped forward. She was reaching for a small knob of gray rock to hoist herself higher when a terrible bellow washed over her. She fell on her belly. Gagging on a fetid stench, Kit risked a peek over her shoulder and shuddered at the sight of the colossus rearing behind her. Hundreds of tiny legs wriggled along the monster's pale underbelly. Rows of curved fangs rasped together inside its gaping maw. *Caim, I'm sorry. I tried. I really tried.*

As the monster arched toward her, another roar clove through the winds. Doggie appeared on the monster's back, clawing up its rubbery flesh. The mist monster didn't seem to notice until the shadow beast's jaws clamped onto a greenish-gray nub. The monster rolled sideways to dislodge the irritant, but Doggie clung fast. Throwing her protector a kiss, Kit jumped for her next handhold and crawled up onto a shallow rock shelf. The cave opened before her. She scrambled inside. Any shelter was better than being out here.

She crawled onto a hard, smooth floor. Soft pads thudded on the floor as Doggie landed beside her. She hugged his wide neck and gave him a peck on the head.

'Glad you could make it! Now where are we?'

291

That was a good question. They stood in a narrow vestibule with a high arched ceiling. The corridor extended as far as she could see. Then she noticed the prickling sensation was gone. Kit kept close to Doggie as she started walking. This place made her nervous. They didn't have to walk far before they came to another oval doorway. No light shone from inside this one, though, only cold darkness. Kit grabbed Doggie's ear for moral support, ignoring the look he gave her.

'Okay, this is it.' Saying it aloud didn't make the decision any more palatable. 'Caim, you better appreciate this.'

Taking a deep breath, Kit stepped through the aperture and tugged Doggie along with her. They entered a rough tunnel. Orange light flickered ahead, but faintly. There was no sound, which only added to the eeriness. The fur on the back of Doggie's neck stood up stiff like bristles. She patted his head.

'It's okay. We're going home.'

Kit moved deeper into the darkness. The light continued to flicker, sometimes dimmer and sometimes brighter. A soft breeze whispered past her head carrying a delicate scent like faded lilies. She stepped through another doorway and halted.

'Oh!'

Kit rose a few inches off the floor and knew instantly she had stepped back into the Brightlands. She hugged herself, so glad to be weightless again. She was in a pyramidal chamber with a slanted ceiling rising to a point several body lengths above her head. There were four windows, one in each wall, but nothing showed beyond their stone frames except eerie darkness.

Something moved in the hazy shadows on the far side of the chamber. Kit drifted back a few paces until she hovered beside Doggie, who sat on his haunches like a trained pup. Then, a voice emerged from the shadows, a voice she hadn't heard in a long time. For perhaps the first time in her long existence, Kit was struck speechless. Doggie lay down on the bare floor while she listened.

SHADOW'S LURE

Chapter
TWENTY-NINE

The outlaws maneuvered across the snow-covered field in complete darkness. There was neither moon nor starlight to guide them. From the slope of a forested ridge above the target, Caim watched as his men began their first live assault since he took over the rebellion.

He'd brought them up close to the fortified settlement, giving last-minute instructions as they crawled through the brush. Then he fell back and let his lieutenants run the show. Fifty-six fighters with painted faces and dark garb took positions around the outer defenses. The attack commenced with hardly a sound.

Caim hissed as an ice-cold tendril touched his ankle. A picture formed in his head, of a half-dozen men in gray cloaks scaling a low palisade wall. It looked like Keegan's team on the east side of the outpost. A second chilling touch made contact with his other leg, and Caim saw another group of outlaws crossing over the wall. Uncomfortable with how well the shadows responded to his wants, Caim started to wish that Kit was here, but then shook his head. She was gone. He had to deal with that. Wherever she was, he just hoped she was safe.

He forced his attention back on the action below. Shouts rose from inside the settlement as a third group assaulted the gate. The wooden doors held. But while the frontal attack held the defenders' attention, the other teams snuck in behind them.

He was studying the maneuvers when Liana came down to stand beside him. She was strapped into a padded leather coat and held a long spear in her hand, a shaft of stripped oak with a butcher knife embedded in the top. He knew what she wanted. They'd had this conversation several times already, but the woman didn't like taking no for an answer.

'Why are we stuck up on top of this hill?' she asked finally. 'While the action is down below.'

Caim grimaced. When they had set out from the castle, the women insisted on coming with them. They had worked as hard as the men, performing the drills he taught them without complaint. Still, he'd hoped to leave them behind. They weren't ready. *Or maybe I'm the one who's not ready.*

'You're the reserves,' he answered.

She thrust her pointing finger down toward the outpost. 'Every man is down below doing what you taught him, while we're left to sit up here like a flock of hens!'

'Keep your voice down.' He chewed on his tongue. Below, the sounds of combat continued. 'Don't be in such a hurry.'

'We trained to fight, Caim. But you're trying to keep us out of the way.'

'I trained you to survive!'

He winced as his voice echoed down the ridge. Liana had a way of getting under his skin. *Like a rash, and no matter how hard I scratch she just keeps coming back.*

'You aren't holding Keegan back.'

'You and the other women have only been training for a few days. You're not ready yet.'

'We *want* to fight.'

Snarling in the darkness, he gave in. 'All right. Move your squad down to set up a screen along the north road.'

'Really?' she asked, excitement peaking in her voice. 'Don't worry. We know what to do.'

'Don't get too close to the walls. And keep your eyes open.'

She turned away. 'Don't worry! North road. Got it.'

'Don't engage unless you have to,' he called after her. 'And don't be afraid to withdraw if . . .'

Caim let the words fall away as Liana ran up the slope. A waste of breath. She was too damned eager to jump into the fray. The others in her unit were no better. Pale moonlight reflected on their spear points as they marched past. Two dozen women, ranging from girlhood to wedded matrons, in homemade armor. He'd given them what training he could in the short time allotted to him, utilizing the first drills Kas had ever taught him: how to make a strong stance, to hold a spear against a charge, to attack and move safely. Was it enough to keep them alive?

The sounds of fighting were dying down, but fires had sprung up inside the compound. Small ones, but he'd told the men not to burn anything until they were ready to pull out. Someone was getting out of hand. As a nightfisher cried out, Caim made his way down the ridge.

The gate was open by the time he arrived. Actually, it was half torn off its posts. Aemon and Dray, their faces bound up in gray scarves, stood sentry. They saluted as he approached; Aemon in earnest, Dray less so. It was something the men had started doing the past couple of days. Caim didn't like it much, but he wasn't sure if he should discourage it, either. At least they weren't calling him 'sir.' Yet.

He found his lieutenants, Keegan and Vaner, in the main yard beside a group of bound soldiers. Caim had wanted Killian with them, but the veteran chose to remain at the castle. Perhaps it was because of his age. Or maybe he could see what was coming. Caim couldn't blame him. Keegan's face was pale in the torchlight. Blood dribbled from a shallow cut across the bridge of his nose.

'Report.'

Keegan started. 'The outpost is secure.'

'Injuries?'

'Only one is serious,' Vaner said. 'Feoras took a spear through the leg, but it's a clean wound. Should heal up fine.'

Caim eyed the soldiers on the ground. 'What about their side?'

'Ah,' Keegan paused. 'Two dead, and another might die before morning. I know you said to avoid that if we could, but—'

'Some things are unavoidable. Go on.'

'Okay. There are a few soldiers holed up in a shack in the southeast corner. We couldn't get inside.'

'So you started fires to smoke them out,' Caim said.

Vaner glanced at Keegan. 'Someone said they saw a man inside wearing Eviskine colors. A couple of the boys went against orders.'

'Have you found their commander?'

Keegan shook his head. 'Only a sergeant so far. He's the one in bad shape. He wouldn't surrender.'

Vaner started to add something, but Caim missed it as a stabbing pain sliced through the center of his chest. For a moment, he thought he had been shot by a crossbow again. His vision dimmed. Keegan and Vaner looked at each other. Caim didn't have the breath to speak. As the agony receded, a harsh tingle ran down the back of his neck. Something bad was coming. Caim glanced northward toward the direction of the disturbance. The sky rumbled overhead, but there was no smell of moisture in the air.

'Are you—?' Vaner started to ask.

Caim bit back against the pain. 'Get everyone back up the ridge now.'

'What about the prisoners?' Keegan asked.

'Leave them!'

Caim pushed past them and staggered toward the north side of the outpost as fast as he could manage. The walking got easier, but it wasn't until he was halfway across the compound that he remembered Liana and her women were stationed on the north road. Right in the path of the disturbance. He broke into a run.

He passed Oak heading back toward the courtyard with a long crate under each arm.

'Caim! I found a whole house full of—'

'Find Keegan and get out of here!' he shouted over his shoulder.

When Caim reached the wall, he leapt without slowing. The palisade was built of sharpened, eight-foot-tall stakes. As his hands closed around the tops of two logs, Caim heaved himself up. What he saw on the other side drove an icy spike into his guts.

The night had come alive. It lapped at the wooden barrier and flowed around it like an amorphous beast seeking entrance. Glints of metal gleamed in the blackness – warriors with swords and spears racing to surround the walls. Caim drew his knives as he dropped down on the hard ground. The darkness swirled with shadows. They approached him like a pack of tame pets, rubbing against him, whispering songs of death and ruin in his ears. He fought the violent urges rising inside him as he moved out into the gloom.

Sounds came at him from every direction. Caim was torn between caution and the need to find his troops before it was too late. He almost tripped over the body of a grizzled soldier, his leather breastplate dotted with a dozen deep punctures. Spear wounds. As Caim moved on, a fierce shout was his only warning as a swordsman leapt out of the dark at him. Caim leaned out of the longsword's path and stabbed the soldier in his side. He twisted his blades free as the soldier slid to the ground and kept moving. Another soldier appeared. Caim glided past a falling battleaxe and smashed the man in the temple with a knife butt. As the soldier shook his head, Caim saw the pale flesh of his enemy's neck exposed above the breastplate. The longing to attack, to kill, sizzled in his brain. He hamstrung the soldier with two vicious slashes and kicked him to the ground. His pulse thrummed in his ears as he stood over the man, who groaned and clutched his ruined legs. *Kill him. They deserve no better.*

A choking grunt turned Caim around. He lifted his knives as a tall, long-limbed man staggered toward him out of the murk. Caim crouched to leap, but checked his attack when he recognized the face. Oak's hands were folded around the spear point protruding from his stomach. Rage, red-hot and steaming, bubbled up inside Caim. He reached out to help until a soldier in an iron cap came up behind Oak and slid the blade of a dirk under his russet beard.

Caim yelled as he knocked the knife from the soldier's hand and slashed him across the face. The man held his face and screamed. Unmoved, Caim punched both knives through the soldier's boiled leather shirt and spilled his steaming bowels onto the snowy ground. The killer collapsed beside Oak's body, both of them curled up like sleeping children. Growling – at the soldier, at himself, at the gods perhaps – Caim turned away.

He found the road and hurried down its hard-packed snow-and-gravel surface. Cries rose to meet him. There was a sinister whoosh, followed by the wet crackle of shattering bones. He sprinted at full speed through the gloom, straight into the path of a galloping brown blur. Caim threw himself to the side and was spun partway around as the warhorse's broad chest barreled into his legs. Something bright and lethal whistled past his head. As Caim regained his footing, the horseman wheeled his steed around and came back for another pass, a long cavalry sword held over his head. Caim leapt before the horseman could close, darting in low on the soldier's left side. His *suete* cut deep into the meat of the soldier's thigh. Intending to swing around to the other side, Caim ran around behind the animal.

Then he was airborne.

The breath rushed out of his lungs as he landed in a shallow ditch beside the road. Pain rippled across his left shoulder and down his ribs from the impact of the warhorse's hooves. The horseman had turned and was closing again. Caim tried to lift himself up, but there was no time. His arm was stiff; his legs felt like boards of lumber. The soldier leaned over in the saddle, his sword raised to kill. Caim hissed between his teeth.

The shadows came from every direction, blocking out the horse and rider with their numbers. A high-pitched whinny sliced through the night air amid a thunder of stamping hooves and human screams.

Caim's breath returned in shallow gasps as he climbed to his feet. A quick examination of his arm and torso revealed that nothing was broken, but he would sport some nasty bruises. He looked to his fallen enemy. The horse lay on its side. Tiny black holes riddled its sweat-flecked coat. The rider had thrown himself clear, but the shadows found him nonetheless. His armor – a shirt of mail – hung in tatters, riddled with similar holes. His empty eye sockets, leaking white fluid, stared up at nothing.

While Caim looked over the scene, cool touches enveloped his shoulder and side. He started to brush the flitting shadows away, but let them be as the pain leached away. Sensation returned to his hand. More shadows crawled on the ground, nipping at his feet, eager for blood. This preternatural darkness was unnerving, even for him, but he plowed ahead. Sounds of fighting echoed deeper in the gloom, and then—

Nothing. The breeze picked up, making eddies in the mist.

He came across the first body lying against the trunk of an ebonwood tree. Bile rose in the back of his throat as he recognized one of Liana's women, but he couldn't put a name to her face. She had died cradling a broken arm. Both her legs were broken, too. He found the second and third bodies face-down in the snow farther up the road. The fourth lay over a rock; blood drenched her chestnut hair from a massive head wound that had caved in half her skull. Caim marched past, fearing what he would find next. His stomach was clenched into a knot of aches. *This is my fault. I shouldn't have let them—*

Lightning flashed behind him, and the darkness lifted a trifle, enough to reveal a line of bodies arrayed across the road. Caim stopped as the thunder crashed in his ears. The women had stood firm, shoulder to shoulder, presenting a strong front to their enemy. Just like he had taught them.

A solitary figure stood on the road beyond them, tides of darkness swirling around his thick, armored frame.

The Beast.

The throbbing in Caim's chest pounded against his breast-bone as the armored giant looked up. A woman slumped at his feet. In one hand the Beast held up her head by a fistful of long blonde hair; in the other, a massive spiked ball hung on the end of a black link chain. Caim's arms trembled as he looked into Liana's glassy eyes. He was too late.

The Beast let go of her hair. Caim was running before Liana's face landed in the bloody mire. He charged past the women, their features streaked with blood. A rattle of metal links preceded the approach of whirling death. Caim's spine quivered as he dived under the ball-and-chain's long arc. He got in close and attacked with all the savagery and loathing he held inside. The Beast was even more formidable up close, an eidolon of metal and darkness. Caim lunged, and both knives struck the ridged midsection of the black breastplate. Jarring tremors ran through the hilts as their points rebounded without penetrating, numbing his hands. Caim caught a glimpse of a black steel-clad fist rising toward him a fraction of a heart-beat before it crashed against his temple. Lights burst in front of his eyes as he staggered back. The chain nicked the top of his head as it passed and knocked him off balance. He put out a hand to catch his fall. *Move! The next pass won't miss.*

Caim heaved himself sideways and scrambled to his feet. The whirl of the spiked ball hissed behind him. He spun around and hurled his right-hand knife. The charred blade turned end over end and shattered against the Beast's breast-plate in a hail of shrapnel. Caim reached up, and the black sword leapt into his hand. In that moment everything came into perfect clarity, the darkness transformed into a palette of vibrant shades. Pulsating sigils were etched into the Beast's armor, including a battlemented tower in the center of the breastplate. Tendrils of shadow curled from his helmet's visor.

Caim followed the sword's lead and felt the point bite into the joint between the Beast's hip faulds and the cuisse protect-ing the thigh. Dark blood trickled from the gap as he twisted the blade, but his foe paid it no mind, bringing his weapon around in an overhand swing. Caim dropped to one knee. The impact of the spiked ball shook the ground behind him. Pulled by the sword, he lunged, but the Beast turned faster than Caim anticipated and smacked him in the chest with the back of an armored fist. Caim rolled with the punch and managed to keep his feet under him. He braced himself for another attack, but the Beast stepped back with a flock of shadows flitting around him. With another step, he was gone.

Caim squinted as he rubbed his chest. A hole had opened in the darkness. It collapsed as soon as the Beast passed through, but Caim could see streamers of shadow left behind. He looked back. Liana lay a couple yards from his feet. Beyond her limp body, the compound was engulfed in an inferno. A file of men ran out of the gate, heading for the ridge, while some waited on the road. Caim made up his mind.

He leapt.

As he jumped, he *pulled* at the space in front of him, and a dark hole appeared in the air. He had time for a quick breath before he tumbled through the gateway.

He fell onto a patch of sharp rocks. As he stumbled over the jagged surfaces, Caim heard a sinister whine and threw himself flat. He dropped his knife as the hard edges of a dozen stones jabbed into him. The spiked ball passed inches from his head.

The buzzing in the back of his skull returned, more insistent than before. Caim reached for the fallen *suete* and rolled away a split heartbeat before the rock in front of him shattered in his face. As he found his footing, he got a glimpse of where they stood, on a narrow section of ground surrounded by plunging slopes on every side. A hilltop. Aside from the scree of broken rocks he had just vacated, there were perhaps a dozen square paces of ground here, and the Beast stood at the center, chain whirling over his head. *Clever. There's nowhere for me to run, but what if I'm not trying to get away?*

Caim rushed in before his better sense could intervene. The

black sword vibrated so fast in his hand he could hear its plaintive whine. It wanted blood, and so did he.

The Beast shifted the trajectory of the spiked ball downward, but the reaction was a hair too slow. Caim got inside the arc an instant before the sphere came around. The Beast leaned away from the sword's black point, but it had been just a feint to get in closer. Caim ripped upward with the *suete*. Its point punched through the mail under his opponent's armpit. Caim expected a groan – something – but the giant made no sound as he knocked Caim back with a forearm smash. Caim set his feet and crouched, sword extended in defense, but all he saw was a huge armored back as the Beast passed through another inky gateway.

With more caution than the last time, Caim made his own portal and stepped through.

Somehow he got turned upside down and landed hard on his stomach. The ground felt like smooth, solid stone under several inches of frozen snow, but when he pushed up with his hands and legs, his feet slipped out from under him, dragging away streaks of snow to reveal a dark sheet of ice. He rolled away an instant before the spiked orb came down and the ice exploded.

Shedding slivers of frost as he stood up, Caim called to the shadows. They swarmed around him, flittering but strangely silent. With a flick of his sword, he sent them at the Beast in a cone of darkness. But the Beast waded through the little darknesses, his armor and his hide intact. Caim circled to his right with short, cautious steps. The Beast followed after him, spinning the chain faster with each pass. Caim angled away, hoping to reach dry land and firmer footing, but his foe's arm shot forward just as he was stepping away. Caim hesitated. Unable to back out of range fast enough, he fell prone.

He landed hard on his elbow. The ice creaked ominously, and then a steel-shod foot slammed into his chest, propelling him across the ice. The shadows flapped around him, unable to help. Gasping, Caim rolled up onto his knees and used the sword to hold himself upright. The buzzing, the pulling, the combat – they sapped the strength from his limbs. He didn't know how much longer he could go on, but the approach of the armored giant across the ice spurred him to stand up once again.

The Beast was unstoppable. Blood leaked from his armor in several places, but still he came on with relentless persistence. Caim shifted to a taller stance as the spiked orb swung nearer. He had to end this soon, before his endurance failed altogether. As the Beast closed the distance between them, Caim rushed forward. At the last moment, he dropped to his knees, and momentum carried him across the ice. Caim slashed with the sword across the back of the Beast's knees. Links of mail parted under the black steel's edge. Blood poured down the blade. Caim kicked hard, and the giant toppled back.

The Beast struck the ice with a resounding crash. He tried to turn over but couldn't find purchase. There was a crackle, and then the lake's surface gave way, plunging him into dark waters.

Caim climbed to his feet. Sweat cooled on his face. It was over. The Beast was gone. But as he turned toward the shore, a terrible grinding roared behind him. He spun and almost lost his balance as a massive black shape rose from the creaking ice. Water dripped from the black chain. Caim ducked, but he couldn't find enough traction. Freezing cold bit into his skin an instant before the spiked orb struck. Only the protection of the shadows, clinging to his back like a second skin, saved him from a crushed spine. As it was, the blow drove the breath from his lungs and hurled him into the snow. Ice and sky whirled before his eyes. His lips shook as he fought to drag in fresh air. On the edge of his vision, the Beast clawed his way out of the water. Flat, black eyes peered from within the slit in the helmet's visor. Chain links rattled as the spiked ball came round again. Forcing his arms and legs to move, Caim grasped onto the first concrete thought that came to mind. A shadowy portal opened beside him.

As the ground shuddered, he plunged into the emptiness.

Caim emerged at the bottom of a trench. A foot of snow cushioned his fall. As he tried to sit up, the pulling sensation flared into a crushing pain that threatened to split open his skull.

Kneeling, he felt rather than heard the portal close behind him. The smells of a forest filtered through his clogged nostrils. His whole body ached – his back, his side, his legs. He just wanted to collapse right here and forget about everything. A faint hiss of sundered air alerted him to the opening of a second portal.

Caim pulled himself to his feet in time to see the Beast stride into view, faint wisps of shadow rising from his armor. Trees stood around them like silent spectators. This was it. He didn't have the strength to run anymore. Caim loosened his shoulders. *All right, bastard. Come and get me.*

The spiked sphere smashed into a tree trunk. Caim ducked inside the blow. Once, twice, three times the black sword rebounded from the Beast's thick armor, each time rushing back eager to draw blood. Caim attacked limbs, joints, even his foe's neck, hoping to penetrate the thin webbing of black mail underlying the gorget, but a near miss from the spiked ball forced him to withdraw. On the next pass the massive sphere came around faster than he anticipated. Caim lost his balance as he dropped into a crouch. Just for an instant, but an armored heel caught him in the chest and flung him backward. He hit something in his flight. It snapped under his weight, and he landed between the broken slats of an old fence. The sword slipped from his grasp. He struggled to right himself, but the Beast's foot stamped down, crushing him into the snow.

Caim searched for the sword, but he couldn't see where it had landed. He tried not to think about the whine of the great chain whirling above him. With his other hand he found the gash in the mail behind the Beast's knee where the black sword had penetrated. He jammed the *suete's* point into the hole as the sphere passed over him, picking up speed. He sawed the knife blade back and forth, and a river of blood poured down to soak his jacket.

Faster, the ball passed overhead.

Caim clenched his jaws shut and shoved on the knife's handle in one last effort. The orb would smash his head like a melon.

Rotten fuck, I hope you're crippled for the rest of your miserable life. I hope—

A ferocious roar shook the night, and the pressure lifted from Caim's chest as the Beast fell to the ground. Caim rolled free, gasping for air. A great mass of shadow sat on the giant's chest, holding him down as its midnight claws ripped through plate and mail.

The muscles in Caim's arm twitched as he pushed himself up. The shadow beast was bent over the giant's throat, trying for a stranglehold. Caim tried to stand. His only wish was that the creature would finish off the Beast, but that hope withered away as a great armored hand grasped the shadow creature by its neck and hurled it away.

Blood pouring from long gashes in his armor, the Beast stood up. He turned, and Caim struck, putting every last ounce of power behind the blow. The *suete's* point pierced the underside of the warrior's jaw, punching up through tongue and palate into his brain. He didn't stop until the knife was sheathed to the hilt.

Caim's breath whistled between his teeth as the Beast's eyes fixed on him. There was no fear of death in the gaze, and no hope for life, only a darkness as deep as the ocean floor. Caim pulled the knife free, and the Beast collapsed in a pile of black steel plates.

Caim sagged against a young tree. The sky was a perfect sheet of black, so close he could almost reach up and touch it. Twin lamps peered at him from the snow and brush. Caim took a step toward the shadow beast. The creature let him take that step, and then it was gone. Like it had never been there. Yet its presence throbbed in his chest, not angry and unrelenting now, but steady.

Like a second heartbeat.

SHADOW'S LURE

Chapter
THIRTY

C aim found the sword's pommel sticking up from the snow. He drew it out. The blade was clean, without a fleck of gore or a scratch, like it had been forged this very day.

Caim turned around. Beyond the crooked slats of the fence he had crushed was a wide clearing. Small mounds rose from the snow, the largest off to his left. He didn't think much of them until something settled in his mind, a piece of a puzzle that had only existed in his mind falling into place. His pulse drummed hard in his temples as the trees hemmed in around him. He had stood here, on this very spot, countless times in his dreams. Now the courtyard was covered by a blanket of snow, but in his mind he saw it as it had been on that fateful night.

There was blood everywhere, pooled in the gravel, splattered across the face of the man kneeling in the center of the yard, running down his chest in a great black river.

Standing over his father, a pale figure in black robes, with a sword upraised in its fist. The sorcerer's face was framed in moonlight, frozen in this instant, the moment the world changed. Caim trembled as the darkness parted. Another figure stood behind the sorcerer, a slender shape wrapped in a cloak darker than black, deeper than death. Long waves of inky hair flowed from under the cowl.

His stomach lurched as his mother burst from the burning house, into the arms of the waiting soldiers. The dark men dragged her away . . . dragged her . . .

Locked in the waking dream, Caim shook as the soldiers dragged his mother over to the body. Her lips moved, but there was no sound. Then her gaze lifted to the figure – not the man who had taken her husband's life, but the woman behind him. The cowl was lifted, revealing features as beautiful and unbreakable as a midnight sapphire. The two women could have been twins save for the glances they cast at each other, his mother's face etched with loathing, the witch's eyes glowing with triumph.

Sisters.

A cool spatter landed on Caim's forehead and left a wet trail down his face. Soft thuds struck the snow around him. The rain felt good on his skin, but it couldn't wash away the blood that stained his blades, his hands. His soul. This was where it had begun. The sword throbbed in his hand. He looked down at the perfect edges of its blade, the sheen of the black metal. This sword had killed his father. He could feel its power flowing through his arteries, surging in his muscles, wanting him to lash out, to kill again and again to sate its abominable hunger. The blade vibrated harder until he slid it back into the scabbard.

Caim's hand shook when he lowered it to his side. As much as he hated the sword, he was bound to it. He gazed across the clearing, to the mound that had been the house where he was born. This place was just a graveyard. It held no answers for him. But he knew where to start looking.

The duke's witch.

Soft light danced on the snow. As he turned, Kit lunged into his arms. He staggered back a step as he caught her. For a moment she felt almost solid. Shocked, and pleased in a way he'd never entertained before, he lifted his arms to embrace her. But she melted into weightlessness, as ethereal as ever.

She looked up, heedless of the gore splattered across his

leathers. He trembled as feelings welled up inside him, pushing through the fury that had controlled him just moments ago. The force of it humbled him. He didn't care where she'd been, only that she was back. He never wanted her out of his sight again.

Then she fixed him with a stabbing glare. 'Do you have any idea what I've been through?'

Caim ground his teeth together, caught between being glad to have her back and wanting to choke her. Then he saw a line of scabbed blood across her palm. She'd been hurt, which stunned him. It had never seemed possible before.

'Good to see you, too, Kit. Where in the hells have you been?'

'It's a long story.' She glanced over at the Beast's remains lying in the snow.

'I'm going after the witch,' he said. 'She knows where my mother is. She was there on the night they took her.'

'Caim—'

'I should have figured it out before, when I saw her at the prison. I knew she couldn't be my mother.'

Kit hovered closer. 'Caim, there's something I need to tell you.'

'People have died, Kit. Liana . . .' He released a deep breath. 'She wouldn't run because I taught her to stand firm. I taught them all. I should have known.'

He looked away, not wanting to see the accusation in her gaze. *I can't help it, Kit. Something is happening to me. It's the sword and this place. It's . . .*

'Caim, I've seen your mother.'

He turned. 'What?'

She was trembling, tears welling up in her eyes. 'She's alive, Caim! I even spoke to her.'

Despite what he wanted to feel, despite what it cost him to admit it, he believed her. He couldn't say how, but he did, and that scared him more than a little. 'Where?'

She pushed a stray lock of silver hair behind her ear. 'That's going to be difficult to explain.'

'Try.'

'All right. When I was taken away—'

'You mean when you left me?'

She frowned, and a bit of the old Kit returned in her eyes. 'When you were fooling around with those farmers at the bonfire, I got this weird feeling. Then just like that' – she snapped her fingers – 'I was dragged back into the Barrier.'

He remembered her mentioning a barrier before, when the shadow-snake attacked him in his apartment in Othir. He'd asked how the creature got there, and she had said something about it needing to cross between worlds. But he must have looked confused now, because Kit tugged on her chin.

'Okay, here.' She put her hands together, palm to palm. 'There are two realms, pressed together like the two sides of a coin. On one side are the Brightlands where we stand now, and on the Other Side is—'

'The Shadowlands.'

'Right. But there is a middle place, too. Sometimes we call it the Barrier, but it's more like a maze of corridors. Or a huge field with different trails. Or, well, it's impossible to describe unless you've been there. But the point is that the passages through the Barrier start in one realm and end in the other, or sometimes they join two different places in the same realm.'

'I think I'm following you.' *Just pray she gets to a point soon.*

'Okay. So I was in this place and couldn't get out. The path that led me into the Barrier wouldn't let me go. And I started to feel this pulling in my head, so I—'

He knew that feeling. The tugging and buzzing that had plagued him since his arrival in this cold land. Was there a connection? Lost in his own thoughts, he missed the next thing Kit said.

'Wait. What was that?'

She frowned at him. 'Your doggie-shadow was there with me in the Barrier. I was a little leery at first. I mean, he's not the most adorable-looking thing in the worlds, you have to admit. But we made a good team.'

Doggie? A team? Caim's head started to ache. He considered

sitting down in the snow, but forced himself to focus. 'But what does this have to do with my mother?'

'She's the one who pulled me into the Barrier, so she could lead me back to her.' Kit leaned closer and peered into his eyes. 'She's been a prisoner all these years, Caim. I'm not sure exactly where. There was too much energy around the place, and then I was booted halfway across the world.' She flicked her finger in the air. 'But she thought you would know.'

He did. The only place that made sense. He looked to the north. She was there. Alive. Waiting for him. He was tempted to start walking, but then he remembered Liana.

Kit was still talking. 'And she told me other things, too. Some of them I don't understand, but the stuff I did scared me to death.'

Caim swallowed, not sure what to think or feel. He had a hard time finding his voice. 'Stuff about what?'

'About your dear auntie.'

Sybelle. The witch. 'What about her?'

Kit looked around as if searching for something. 'How can I explain this? Okay. Sorcery is a product of the Other Side, right?'

He seemed to remember her saying something along those lines. When he said so, she bobbed her head.

'Sorcery is pure chaos. Everything in the Shadowlands is corrupted with it. And it's been leaking over into this world for some time. I don't know why, but it's getting worse. The Barrier is weakening.'

Caim rubbed his fingers together, remembering the silky feel of the shadows on his skin, the rush he felt when they obeyed his commands. It made some sense, but he couldn't shake the feeling that there was something Kit wasn't telling him.

'What about the witch?'

'She's a product of her world, Caim. The people of the Shadow live and breathe sorcery. It's as natural to them as air and sunlight to you. Well, maybe not to you . . .'

'And my mother?'

Kit traced the tear in the sleeve of his jerkin. 'Isabeth was the most powerful sorceress I'd ever encountered. And the kindest. The people of the Shadow are a cruel race, but some are different. Like your mother.'

Isabeth. Invisible hands compressed around Caim's windpipe at the sound of it. *Yes, that was her name.*

Kit hovered closer and lowered her voice. 'But her sister is another tale entirely. She's dangerous, Caim. Dangerous like you've never seen before. She trained Levictus. He was like a puppy next to her.'

Caim looked past Kit to the courtyard. The snow glowed in the faint starlight. It looked peaceful, like he could lie down here and forget about the world.

'It's almost funny in a way,' he said. 'I understand him now.'

'Who?'

'Levictus. He and I aren't so different.'

'Don't say such things! You're nothing like that animal.'

'We're both caught in the same web, Kit. Pulled by strings we can't even see. Killing is the only thing we're good at. If something gets in our way, we cut it down. No remorse. No regrets. Just death.'

Kit placed her hands on both sides of his face. 'Listen to me. You *are* different. You're a good man, Caim.'

Was he? He wasn't so sure.

'There's a dark shadow over this land, Kit. Maybe it started here with my father and mother, but it's gone far beyond this place, and I don't know what to do.'

'Yes, you do. You'll fight. Not because you want to, but because you have to.'

What she said was true, but knowing the truth didn't make it any easier to accept. The rage might have left him, but in its place gathered a more primal emotion: vengeance. Blood to answer for blood. There was no other way.

The sword quivered in its scabbard.

Kit looked up to the blade's hilt jutting over his shoulder. 'What about that?'

'What about it?'

'I don't like it, Caim.'

Yeah? Welcome to the party, darling.

Turning away from the ruins, Caim breathed in the scents of pine and heather. He held that breath as he tore open a hole in the darkness. In its opaque surface he saw his face, drawn and haggard – the face of a dead man. He and Ral, he and the sorcerer, he and the Beast. Dealers of death, one and all. *The only difference is that I'm still alive. Don't follow me, Kit. You won't like what you see.*

Releasing the breath, Caim stepped into the void.

Stone cracked and shattered. Steel was torn asunder, and the air shimmered as eldritch forces shook the foundation of the temple.

Blood leaked from Sybelle's fingernails as she lay on the floor, digging furrows in the cold marble tiles. Her hair was disheveled, her gown slashed and ripped.

Soloroth, her son, was dead.

In the scrying pool she had watched the battle between her child and the scion, seen victory snatched from Soloroth's grasp. Frightened for the first time in many long years, she was able only to gaze on in shock as Soloroth fell at the scion's feet. Then the waters turned dark before her eyes, cutting off her last sight of her son and severing their contact forever.

In the aftermath of her fury, her sanctum lay in shambles. The ancient sarcophagus of Het Xenai, which had withstood the ravages of three thousand years, was reduced to a pile of dust. Her phials and fetishes lay in shards upon the floor along with the orichalcum box, its priceless contents dissolved into the stone. Only the scrying pool remained intact, its black waters as still as death.

A cold wind stirred the debris as a disembodied voice whispered in her ear. *One comes . . .*

Sybelle rose to her bare feet as the curtain leading to the nave lifted. Whichever of her priests was fool enough to disturb her in this, the moment of her greatest anguish, had better have good reason. But the temple was empty. The candles wavered, casting tall shadows against the walls. Sybelle stayed the lethal spell on her lips as the duke staggered across the doorstep. He leaned against the bronze doors, eyes glazed over, his clothes stained with wine and worse. Drunk again, or still. In the past sennight she hadn't seen him any other way. The man had lost his vitality. He was an empty, sodden husk, little better than a corpse. *Like my Soloroth.*

'You killed her,' he said through numb lips.

The words took her by surprise. She had killed many over the years, thousands upon thousands, but she knew who he meant. His first wife. She'd killed the woman not long after Arion was born, and had taken her place at Erric's side.

'She was everything I wanted,' he continued, bracing himself against a wall, staring at her. 'She was my love. And now you've sent my son away to die.'

Sybelle seethed as she looked upon this man she had loved. The sight of him filled her with disgust. She had given him this city, slain his rivals, and still he couldn't tame this one petty realm, so she'd been forced to send her son, her only child, to do it for him. Now Soloroth was dead for it, and the fault lay at this man's vomit-caked feet.

He pointed at her. 'You've ruined my life! Now I'm all alone, all because of—'

'Shut up.'

The duke straightened up, a frown folding the loose skin around his mouth. 'That is no way to address me. I am King of Eregoth, Sybelle. No matter what you and your grotesque ogre of a son—'

The air between them blurred as she lifted her hands. A rush of vigor surged into Sybelle as she drew the essence from his fragile shell. It was wan and addled, but still delicious beyond measure. She could have stayed in this moment forever, content, sated. Then he fell to the floor. As abruptly as it had started, the sorcery drained out of her, leaving her weak and shaking.

Sybelle stumbled across the chamber and collapsed at his side. His eyes stared at her without a hint of accusation.

'My love. My darling Erric.'

She rocked back and forth beside his lifeless body. Alone in her grief, she didn't notice the loud voices outside until the guardian announced the intrusion. Brushing Erric's lips with a kiss, Sybelle stood up as a band of huge men in bestial hides and furs entered the temple. Her son's Northmen. At a barking command from their headman, Garmok, they led a coffle of bedraggled people into the nave, men and women and even two older children. Battered and stoop-shouldered, they were forced to kneel at her feet.

'Prizes for you, Queen of the Night,' Garmok spoke. 'Where is our hetman, your son?'

Sybelle eyed the prisoners, a renewed hunger growing inside her. 'He is dead.'

The Northmen shook their weapons and began to howl. Garmok struck a prisoner with such force that the man sprawled to the floor in a widening puddle of blood. The other captives mewed with terror.

Sybelle smiled, liquid heat spreading through her body as she went down to greet her new playthings.

SHADOW'S LURE

Chapter
THIRTY-ONE

They shambled up the slopes of the foothill under a bruised sky. Bloodied, dragging their wounded behind them on shoddy litters, no one would have guessed they were the victors.

Caim marched at the head of the company. He couldn't face the men, carrying their dead like an honor guard. When he'd returned to the outpost and seen the results of the disaster he'd led them to, he could hardly face himself. No matter what Kit said, he couldn't blame anyone else. He'd forgotten the first rule of warfare – know your enemy – and others had paid the price. He was a killer, not a general. He had no business leading people into battle. Despite that, they followed him, not complaining when he announced they were returning to the castle. Some, he knew, would leave as soon as they were fit, off to join Ramon's outfit or just go somewhere safe. He didn't have the heart to tell them they wouldn't be safe anywhere in this world. What had started here would spread.

Thunder rumbled, sounding like it came from the other side of the hills. It would be daylight soon, but the northern sky was a mass of black clouds.

Keegan's shoulders were hunched as he came up beside Caim. From what he'd heard, the boy had accounted himself well, even leading the outlaws in a counterattack that drove off the duke's soldiers. Caim hadn't known much comfort in his life; fool that he was, he'd left the only woman who had ever tried to offer it. He didn't know what to say. That it got easier? The sentiment sounded hollow even to him, but what else was there to say? The truth? No, better that the boy believed this hurt would pass. *She died a warrior, but that doesn't take away the sting, does it?*

'What's the next step?' Keegan asked.

'Next step in what?'

Keegan jerked his chin back over his shoulder at the men marching behind them. 'The plan. Where are we going next?'

Caim gazed ahead through the tree tops. 'Back to the castle.'

'And then?'

'And then I go on alone. You've done your part.'

Keegan dragged Caim to a halt by his arm. 'Hold on. Caedman chose you—'

'I never agreed to anything.'

'No, but you didn't turn it down either. You owe us.'

Against his better judgment, Caim glanced behind them. The company had slowed to a standstill, the rear elements coming up behind them. His eyes couldn't help finding the four men who dragged Liana's travois.

'I don't owe you,' he told them. 'I don't owe any of you. This isn't my—'

'My sister believed in you.' Keegan's voice was no louder than a whisper, but it hit Caim like a club between the eyes, doing more damage than he wanted to admit. 'So did Oak, and all the rest who died. You owe it to them to see this through. To the end.'

Caim turned away. He wanted to be alone, responsible for no one.

My sister believed in you.

The words dared him to refute them. He couldn't. He was prepared to leave them all, except her. He wanted to growl, to lash out, but a shout cut through the chill air.

'Scouts returning!'

Two figures in brown cloaks approached through the maze of evergreens with long, loping strides. The elder of the two,

Taun, was a man on the downward slope of his middle years but looking quite hale nonetheless. He leaned on the staff of his unstrung longbow as he caught his breath.

'No sign of our sentries up ahead, sir,' the younger said.

'Maybe they were hiding,' Keegan said.

Taun gave a wolfish grin. 'Doubt it. Me and my boy know all the best spots.'

Caim started walking past the men. There were some movements behind him, and then the scouts caught up with him. Taun strode beside him, his son a step behind.

'I can show you where they usually hole up when standing their duty,' the old scout offered.

Caim drew his knife. The sword whispered at his shoulder, but he ignored it. A faint smell lingered in the air. A smell he knew well.

Kit materialized above him. 'Caim.'

'I see it,' he whispered.

The mouth of the defile leading to the hidden valley appeared at the apex of the rise before them. Above it, a column of black smoke twisted in the wind.

Caim ran, through the trees, over the wet snow that slid under his feet and kicked up behind him. Heedless of the danger, he charged into the defile and up its stony path. The smell of burning grew and acquired a gut-churning tinge that quickened his pulse. Hard footfalls echoed at his back as he emerged at the summit of the pass. He stopped and gazed down into a scene of desolation. Gasps rose behind him as the others caught up. A choked sob floated out into the smoke-filled air, growing as it echoed down the valley. Knife in hand, Caim plunged down the trail.

Caim kicked over a charred plank of timber. The features of the body underneath were burnt beyond recognition. It had probably been a woman, but even that wasn't for certain. A tiny mitten lay in the muddy snow beside an overturned pot.

They were too late by more than a day. The settlement had

been attacked by men on foot. There had been no defense. No warning. Caim frowned as he strode down the bailey yard. The outlaws kept a continuous watch over this valley, doubly so when he and his company left to raid. How had they been taken unaware?

He found his answer stuck in the matted roof of a long-house. He pulled it out. A spear, not as long as an infantry lance. Dark whorls marked the steel head, which was affixed to the shaft with tarred gut string. Crude materials, but expertly made. The weapon of a Northman.

'You all right?' Kit asked.

He dropped the spear and looked around. The air was thick with smoke and cinders. 'These were the people who couldn't fight. The old and the young. The injured. They didn't have a chance.'

'You didn't start this war, Caim.'

'No. But they were counting on me to end it.'

Caim started walking across the bailey. Kit was only trying to help, but he didn't want to be soothed. He wanted to be angry. He would feed off of his rage, forge it into a weapon to use against this enemy. Part of him whispered that was the sword talking, but he was past caring.

He found Keegan kneeling outside the ashes of his hut. Two bodies were laid out on the ground; one was Liana's body, wrapped in linen. Caim sighed as he guessed the identity of the other corpse, covered by the youth's cloak. He started to reach out to Keegan's shoulder, but drew back his hand. He knew how the boy felt, to have no one left, but there were no words.

Keegan coughed and rubbed his eyes. 'You're going after them. To Liovard.'

It wasn't a question, and Caim didn't have the strength to lie. Blood to answer for blood. What else did he know?

Keegan climbed to his feet. 'I'm going with you.'

Kit appeared over their heads. Caim didn't look at her. Instead, he forced himself to look at the bodies. *They made their choices. And now I make mine.*

318

'This has gone far enough,' he said. 'I'll finish the rest alone.'

Keegan turned around. His eyes were red, but no tears marred his face. 'You'll have to kill me to keep me from going, Caim. Otherwise, I'll be in your shadow the whole way, because I have more issue with Eviskine and his witch than you'll ever have. This isn't your land. These aren't your family. You don't have any idea—'

The cry of a nightfisher echoed through the keep. Caim held onto the boy's gaze, not sure what to do.

Kit descended to hover by his side. 'They've found Caedman.'

Hearing her so subdued, he knew it wasn't good news.

They had to push through a small crowd of onlookers to reach the tower. They found Caedman inside, tied to his bed frame. His killers had taken their time. His eyes had been gouged out, his tongue sliced off and pinned to his bare chest with a bone-handled dirk in a sign as old as warfare. The mark of a traitor. Killian was laid out at the foot of the bed, his severed head resting upon his chest, eyes staring at the doorway.

The outlaws muttered among themselves. To Caim it made too much sense. Caedman had been a different man after his imprisonment. Everyone said so, but the strangeness they'd all attributed to torture had been, in fact, something more devious. The witch had used him to find them.

Keegan pointed to the man who had started this uprising. 'Now what say you? This needs to be answered.'

Caim gritted his teeth until his jaws ached. 'I know.'

'Then take me with you. We'll kill the duke together. We'll kill every last Eviskine!'

'Aye!' another called out. 'I'll go!'

Caim lowered his head as the voices grew into a chorus. Kit watched him from a corner of the room, not saying anything. She didn't have to.

'All right.'

The crowd grew quiet.

'Come with me if you want.' Caim looked to Keegan. 'But no more playing soldier.'

Keegan made a small, mean smile. 'Aye. Just as you say.'

The others echoed him until Caim lifted up a hand.

'Listen to me. This will be no battle of honor. There aren't enough of us for that. No one will sing songs of valor about us, and the blood you spill will follow you all the days of your lives. You understand?'

They didn't need to say it; he saw it in their eyes. The eyes of men eager to lay down their lives. It was like looking into a mirror.

'Bury your dead. We leave at dawn.'

After a last look at the ruin they'd made of the outlaw leader, Caim left with Keegan, back to help the boy with his family. Then he would try to get some rest, knowing sleep wouldn't find him for a long time to come.

He had murder on his mind.

Shadow's Lure

The house was an empty shell. From where she stood on the dried-up yard, Josey could see into the interior, gutted and charred. Half the roof had collapsed. A shambles that had once been her home.

The parlor where her foster father had taught her to play the harpsichord was charred and ruined, all the furnishings gone. *I wish he was here now. I could use his advice.*

Josey touched her stomach through the heavy coat. A life was growing inside her. Soon it would be plain for all to see, and that would bring questions, for which she had no answers. She'd only ever been with two men, but either could have planted this seed within her. *No! It is Caim's child. Please, lords in heaven, let it be so.*

A shadow came from around the back of the manor and slowly resolved into Master Hirsch. The adept stopped a score of paces away and turned toward the sagging arbor so he could pretend he wasn't watching her. Josey leaned against a decorative fountain and squeezed her eyes shut. *What kind of world am I delivering a child into? Violence stalks the streets of my city. If the riots can't be quelled, I may be forced to flee for my life, for the second time. Is this how my mother felt before the revolution?*

A horseman rode down the street and stopped at the gate where Captain Drathan kept vigil. The captain had been against her coming out so late, but Josey had overruled him.

She needed to get away from the palace, which had begun to feel like a prison. Voices murmured, and then someone entered the yard. She was surprised to see it was Hubert. She'd left him in his office to work out the details of their Akeshian problem.

'Majesty,' he said as he approached. 'I've just received word from the north.'

Josey's stomach fluttered. 'Word from Caim?'

'No, from the unit that was sent to the border. Colonel Restian reports that his company was attacked near Durenstile by brigands, or men disguised as brigands. There seems to be some uncertainty on the matter. But the colonel has retreated to the town to await reinforcements.'

Another horseman cantered up to the gate. *Reinforcements?* She didn't have enough soldiers to keep the peace here in Othir. What could she do for Colonel Restian?

'How long can they hold out?'

'The town is well fortified,' Hubert answered. 'But provisions will become a problem unless we establish a supply line.'

'Send a message to Duke Mormaer. Ask what aid he can send.'

'Mormaer may be reluctant to volunteer additional resources, having just sent a levy of troops to quell the problems in the west. Perhaps Count Dervest of Valia could be persuaded to help. I believe his wife is from one of the border provinces.'

'Ask them both. And draw up a list of other lords who have ties to the north. Maybe we can string together a coalition . . .'

Josey let the words fade away as Captain Drathan rushed across the dead grass, a hand clamped on the pommel of his sword. She couldn't bear any more bad news. Her insides felt as delicate as spun glass.

The captain made a quick salute. 'There is trouble on the Opuline, Majesty. Lord Farthington's estate is under siege by a mob of rioters.'

Anastasia!

Josey fought to keep her voice from trembling. 'Is anyone hurt?'

'Not that we've heard, but the crowd is sizable and determined. The estate will fall if something is not done.'

Josey headed for the gate. 'Captain, assemble the guardsmen to meet us on the way to Opuline Hill.'

'Majesty, I don't advise—'

'Do as I ask, or turn in your commission.'

He saluted and sprinted ahead of her, calling his men to arms. Josey was glad she'd worn her riding leathers as she shrugged off her bulky jacket. She thrust it into Hubert's arms as he jogged to keep up.

'Majesty, this is a matter for the watch.'

'Then why aren't they handling it?'

He grimaced. 'I admit that may be a problem, but your friendship with the Lady Farthington is well known. This attack may be a trap meant to—'

'I'm going, Hubert.'

Hirsch appeared as Josey exited the gate. Her bodyguards waited, their weapons bared. The adept cleared his throat.

'Let me go ahead and check it out, lass. Before you ride out all hot and bothered.'

Josey shot him a look that must have been fierce, because it shut him up without further comment. Hubert opened his mouth.

She held up a finger. 'Don't say it.'

'I'm going with you.'

Josey paused. She could see the vehemence in his gaze. 'I – I'm flattered, Lord Chancellor, but perhaps you should return to the palace. I believe Captain Drathan can handle my protection.'

'Majesty, I insist.' He stammered when she arched an eyebrow. 'I mean, please allow me to go.'

Josey turned toward the horses. 'All right, Hubert. But we must leave at once.'

Captain Drathan waited with a pair of soldiers in battered scale armor.

'We're ready, Majesty,' the captain said. 'I sent word to strip every man-at-arms from their post. These are the men who brought the message. Major Volek and Sergeant Merts. They recently arrived from Mecantia.'

One of the soldiers was quite large, bigger even than Markus had been, while the other was only an inch or two taller than she was. Both had firm, deep-set eyes that reminded her of Caim. Hard men. Not the kind to disintegrate under pressure. Each had a sigil of a jungle cat in red enamel stamped over their hearts.

'I don't recognize your insignia,' Josey said.

'We're Crimson Tigers, ma'am,' the sergeant said. 'Army special tactics and reconnaissance.'

'We would like to ride with you, Majesty,' the major said. 'If you'll have us.'

'Fine,' Josey said. 'Now let's go.'

A trooper stood ready with her steed. Just the sight of the magnificent gray stallion made her blood quicken. True to his name, Lightning had required every ounce of her skill to manage on their short rides around the palace grounds. Now she would see if she had truly mastered him. Stepping onto the box provided, she slid into the high-cantled saddle. As soon as her toes touched the stirrups, the stallion jerked sideways.

'Easy, big boy,' she whispered. 'Don't make me regret this.'

She settled into the seat as the soldier handed up the reins. The stallion's ears twitched, but he stopped fidgeting. With the captain leading, they rode down the Esquiline's broad avenues to the base of the hill, where they met the rest of her bodyguards. Josey looked over them. Three score men, but they looked pitifully few for the task. Major Volek and Sergeant Merts sat apart on tall, broad-chested warhorses.

Captain Drathan approached her. 'At your order, Majesty.'

'Ride, Captain. And let nothing stop us.'

At his command, the soldiers filed past the rows of darkened homes. Josey was afforded a place in their center. Hirsch, his face hidden within the hood of his cloak, rode on one side of her, and Hubert on the other. The Crimson Tigers followed behind. When Josey glanced over her shoulder, Major Volek winked through the slit of his lowered visor.

The streets resounded with the noise of the company, the horses' steel shoes ringing against the hard stones like a continuous peal of thunder. The forward riders galloped ahead to clear a path, even though the streets were empty. Here, where the feet of the five hills of Othir met, the palaces of venerable noble families lined wide boulevards. Beyond the walls surrounding the manors they passed, Josey caught glimpses of expansive gardens and parks. *The city has two faces. This one is like a beautiful dream. And the other, torn by violence and pillage, is a nightmare. Can they ever be reconciled?* She didn't know, and that apprehension created a cold lump in her chest.

The company passed through a string of plazas. As they passed through the largest, the Pleazzo, with its quartet of famous Sighing Fountains splashing in the empty silence, Josey's thoughts went to the emperors who had ruled this city before her. History spoke of the hardships they had faced. Would the line end with her? It was a daunting thought.

They rode out of the Pleazzo and up the Opuline Way. Refuse filled the street. Broken windows watched their passage with jagged stares. A boutique specializing in ladies' hats had been gutted; wreaths of smoke rose from its blackened remains. With a start, Josey recognized the store. She had bought a hat here just months ago, but it seemed like an eternity. That was the day she had met Hubert for the first time, the day her life had changed forever. Josey looked up at the skyline. The hill rose steeply for several blocks before leveling off in a rounded plateau, its summit occupied by gate-lined avenues and haughty manors. When High Town was first built, the richest families had settled here on the Opuline, which offered the best views of the countryside beyond the city's walls.

As Captain Drathan led the company up the boulevard, a wild susurrus filled the air. Josey stood up in her stirrups to see over the shoulders of her guards. Clouds of black smoke blanketed the hilltop. Hubert and then Hirsch urged their steeds ahead, and Major Volek and Sergeant Merts came up on either side of her. She tried to make eye contact with the soldiers, but both men's gazes were focused on the streets, the rooftops, the alleyways. *Just like Caim.*

She remembered watching Caim sleep in their room at Madam Sanya's brothel, how he had tossed and twitched like a man possessed by horrible nightmares. She longed to feel his strong arms around her.

A wail snapped Josey's attention toward the front of the company. Grand mansions clad in marble and granite rose along the avenue. Household guards congregated behind their stout gates, but so far these manors looked to have escaped the wrath of the rioters. The smoke lay farther up. The pall lay thickest ahead, where a massive statue marked the center of Torvelli Square. Fear wrapped its iron fingers around Josey's throat as the vanguard of her soldiers accelerated into a canter.

Josey could see Anastasia's home now. A mob of people surrounded its stone walls; the iron gates heaved back and forth under their press. As she watched, a burning torch sailed over the wall and struck somewhere inside. A moment later, another pillar of smoke added to the haze surrounding the house. At Captain Drathan's command, the company halted a hundred paces from the mob. He turned in his saddle to look back at her. She barely caught his words over the din.

'What are your orders?'

Josey squeezed the reins in her hands until she thought her fingers might break. They had come this far, but now she didn't know what to do. If she unleashed her soldiers, people would die. Her people. But if she held back, Anastasia's family might be killed. Josey searched for a bloodless solution, but after several heartbeats of observing the fury of the mob as it attacked the manor gates she understood the truth: there was no peaceful resolution. She had to decide whether to act and be responsible for the deaths that occurred, or do nothing. Hubert met her gaze; there was anguish in his eyes, which shocked her a little. She'd had no idea he felt so strongly. Still, the choice was hers.

The power over life and death. That is rulership. I've never wanted anything to do with it, but here I am.

Josey pointed forward. 'Advance, Captain! If any oppose you' – she took a deep breath and let it out in a silent gasp – 'do what must be done.'

With a nod, the captain closed his visor and led the soldiers forward. At the first contact with the mob, Josey tried to steel herself, but the screams and shouts that filled the avenue sliced through her defenses. One hand placed over her belly, she flinched with every blow that landed. Her blood cooled with every body that fell to the ground until her insides felt frozen. But with the cold came detachment.

'Caution, lass,' Hirsch whispered at her ear.

Josey nodded, but in her heart she knew there was no such thing. Caim had taught her that. She pictured him beside her now, his mouth twisted into a cocky smirk. The image banished her fears. *No caution and no fear.*

Using her knees, she pressed her steed to follow the soldiers into the swirling melee.

It seemed like days had passed, or perhaps weeks, but in truth the sun's glow through the clouds had hardly moved across the dreary sky by the time they won through to the gates.

Josey, surrounded by five blood-spattered men including Major Volek, sat astride her horse as her bodyguards cordoned off the area around the manor entrance. One of the iron gates had crashed inward; the other stood as a mute observer to the morning's repugnant events. Seven of her soldiers lay dead upon the clay bricks. More than forty citizens were sprawled beside them, their limbs arranged in a mockery of sleep. Josey wiped a hand across her face to hide the wetness gathering in her eyes.

The fighting had been fierce from the onset. One moment her guardsmen were advancing at a steady trot; the next moment the mob turned as if united by a single brain and swarmed. Inside her cocoon of protectors, Josey was afforded the opportunity to watch her bodyguards in action. They remained cool and professional even when the orderly action devolved into sheer butchery. The citizens were armed with clubs and bottles, but soon after the first flush of battle, a group of better-armed men emerged from the crowd, and Josey glimpsed the gleam of mail armor under bulky robes as the mob moved to engulf her position. If not for the ferocity of her bodyguards as well as the relentless efforts of the two Tigers, they would have been pulled under the tide of bodies. In the end, it had not been Volek and Merts or even Captain Drathan who turned the tide, but Master Hirsch, and not in the brutal manner she would have imagined.

As the crowd pressed in around them, with missiles flying over their heads, the adept had inexplicably urged his steed past the ring of soldiers and into the press. Josey was so shocked she couldn't even shout for him to stop. At any moment she expected to see the adept dragged from his saddle or spitted on a pike, but Hirsch tore through the crowd like a hound through a flock of geese. Wherever he rode, people fell back in terror. Josey didn't understand until the adept turned so that she could get a glimpse of his face. It was horribly changed. Instead of his normal features, a demon's visage – gleaming like ruddy brass, eyes glowing, smoke pouring from his gaping nostrils – lurked beneath the brim of his hood. His steed's eyes, too, gleamed like burning coals. The combination of coordinated tactics and sorcery proved too much for the citizens, who broke away by ones and two, and then in greater numbers. Josey wished speed to their footsteps.

Finally, with the battle done and the most immediate wounds tended, Captain Drathan rode up to Josey. The commander sat straight in his saddle, but his eyes showed the toll this action had taken. She started to congratulate him but stayed her tongue. *No, accolades would only twist the knife that has been struck in this man's heart. He has done his duty – may the Gods bless and forgive him – and that must be enough. For both of us.*

The captain saluted. 'The gate is secure, Majesty, but I

suggest we move inside the walls. There is still a danger of counterattack if the enemy is able to regroup.'

Enemy.

The word pierced Josey's breast. She didn't let it show.

'Very good. Move your men inside.' She leaned closer and lowered her voice. 'And do whatever you call it to make sure the manor is safe.'

Captain Drathan's helmet dipped. Turning his mount, he shouted, 'Second and third teams, set up a defensive position inside the gate. Fourth team, sweep the grounds. First team, prepare to breach the house.'

Josey swallowed at the harshness of the words, but at least her nerves had settled. A little. Or perhaps she was in shock. Her hands felt like lumps of cold iron inside their gloves as they gripped the reins.

Major Volek approached, leading his horse. Both man and beast were covered with blood, and worse. The major had removed his helmet. His sandy hair was matted with sweat. He was younger than she expected, perhaps in his middle thirties.

'Shall we accompany you inside, Majesty?'

She pulled the reins to turn her horse; the beast obeyed without any trouble. *Almost as if he feels my pain and understands.*

'Where is Master Hirsch?' she asked.

The major pointed down the street. 'I saw him just a moment ago. Shall I retrieve him for Your Majesty?'

Josey gazed across the expanse of bloodied bricks and the bodies scattered upon them. 'No, Major. Thank you. Proceed.'

Sergeant Merts appeared from somewhere. He and Major Volek led her through the manor's broken gates. The court-yard was a mess. Garbage lay scattered across the lawn; parts of the shrubbery were blackened from fire. Soot streaked the house's façade, and a few of the windows were broken, but it appeared as if the structure had avoided significant damage.

Hubert beat them to the entry, jumping down from his steed with sword in hand. Sliding out of the saddle, Josey hurried up the short flight of steps, the soldiers just behind. The large door opened, and a man-at-arms in leather armor moved aside. As she entered the atrium, Josey started for the double staircase, but a choking sob brought her to a halt. They turned to the parlor, Hubert leading the way. Josey had to run to keep up.

Anastasia was inside. And alive, thanks the heavens! She sat on the same couch where Josey had poured out her heart on a cool autumn day that felt like forever ago, but she was not alone. On her lap lay the white-haired head of an old man, his eyes closed. He wore an antique military uniform from the days of the old empire. The folds of the jacket seemed to swallow him, the pants billowing around his legs. Hubert stood beside the couch, arms at his sides. The only sounds were the dripping of the water-clock on the mantelpiece punctuated by Anastasia's sobs. Her friend glanced up, and the heart-wrenching look in her eyes stole Josey's breath away.

' 'Stasia,' she whispered.

She knelt beside the couch and buried her face into Anastasia's shoulder, both of them crying. Words tumbled into her ears, but it was a long time before she could make them out.

'I'm sorry,' Anastasia mumbled again and again. 'So sorry, Josey.'

Josey lifted her head from the sodden patch she had made on Anastasia's sleeve. 'Hush, hush. Don't say another word. There is nothing to be sorry for—'

'I held it against you, Josey.' Anastasia drew in a ragged breath. 'I held Markus's death against you. I didn't mean to. I know he wasn't the man I thought he was, but I loved him, Josey. I really did.'

Josey touched her friend's cheek. 'I know you did. And I don't blame you for a moment.'

Anastasia smiled, but it was a smile tinged with melancholy. 'When they started throwing things at the house, father's heart couldn't stand the strain.' She smoothed the front of his jacket. 'He hasn't worn this old thing since I was a little girl. I didn't even know he still had it. Doesn't he look handsome?'

'Very handsome,' Josey said, her throat thick with emotion.

In her mind she saw her foster father, the earl, sitting in his bedchamber with a gaping hole in his chest. She wrapped her fingers around Anastasia's hand, needing to feel that warmth.

'I promise he'll have a hero's funeral. But you must come back with us to the palace. It isn't safe here anymore.'

Tears ran down Anastasia's face as she gazed down at her departed father and nodded. Relieved, Josey looked up to Hubert.

'Tell the staff to prepare for the move. Quickly, before the mob returns.'

With a firm nod, Hubert hurried out of the room. There had been an expression on his face when she glanced up, a look of sorrow she wouldn't have expected from him. He returned moments later with a troubled frown.

'Majesty, I think you had better see this. It's Master Hirsch.'

Josey got up and followed him out of the house, to where a squad of bodyguards waited. At a gesture from Hubert, they led the way back to the street. Josey glanced at Hubert, but he said nothing until they turned down the alleyway running alongside the mansion. Two soldiers standing in the narrow lane made smart salutes. Sergeant Merts sat beside them, holding a bloody rag to his side. The other man was partially covered by a muddy cloak. As Josey approached, she saw it was the adept. She pushed through the press of guards to get to him. Hirsch was on his back, eyes closed. His face was such a pale shade for his normally bronzed skin, she thought he was dead. She braced herself as she knelt down and started to lift the cloak, but the adept took a shuddering breath.

'He's alive!'

Hubert eased her to her feet. 'Yes, but perhaps not for much longer.'

'What happened?'

Sergeant Merts shook his head. 'I saw him come down this way, following someone maybe, but when I got here he was on the ground. Looks like someone struck him from behind.'

Josey looked down the alleyway. 'All right. I want everyone

mounted up and ready to leave in ten minutes. Understood, Lord Vassili?'

Josey left with her escort as Hubert called for stretchers to be fashioned. She was beyond tired. She wanted to collapse where she stood. Instead, she steeled herself and headed back to the mansion, to her friend, and to all the problems piling at her feet.

Brilliant light flashed in the oriels high above the great hall, casting stark shadows across the walls as Sybelle lay upon her back, one bare foot resting on the leg of the throne. The thunder soothed her nerves. Distant shouts and occasional screams whispered in the stone beneath her head. She smiled at her lover.

Erric, my love. So strong. So handsome. Why don't you smile for me?

She sat up with a pout, and then the memory crashed down upon her. He was dead, and she was alone. She'd been alone as long as she could remember, growing up in a palace of cold black ice where no one ever sang or cried, in her father's court where she'd been expected to play the role of the silent princess. Everyone abandoned her eventually. *Just like Erric.*

When a voice in her head whispered that the Duke of Liovard had not left her, that she herself had slain him, she clawed it to pieces and tossed it to the winds. She would never harm her sweet love. She had brought him to this chamber where they often sat in state together. He even had an audience – palace servants, rebellious prisoners, and even her son's Northmen. The power of their blood thrummed in her arteries as their dripping heads orbited around the throne on sorcerous tethers. She did not know how much time had passed save that the torches around the room had gone out. The shadow play on her lover's face gave the illusion of life. She could almost believe . . .

Sybelle crawled up the throne and climbed onto Erric's lap. Ignoring the strange way his legs shifted beneath her, she

332

caressed his face. His whiskers tickled her palm. She closed her eyes and pressed her lips to his mouth. Though his flesh was cool, there was fire enough inside her for both of them. Tears ran down her cheeks and into her mouth.

Sybelle did not notice the pressure in her chest until the pain was almost overwhelming. She looked around to see the shadows of the chamber oozing forth, gathering in the center of the floor. They spun in a spiral, faster and faster, until a hole formed in the air. Her blood chilled. With Erric and Soloroth dead, there was only one who would contact her.

She slid down from the throne as a figure appeared in the window. Her lord and father, seated on his basalt throne. His stern voice seized hold of her heart.

'Sybelle. You have not made contact in days. Tell me why.'

She let out a shuddering breath. 'Great lord, my son, Soloroth – your grandson – is dead.'

The image blurred, and Sybelle realized she was crying, something she hadn't done since she was a child. It was a strange sensation, almost like rage but wrapped around a core of hopelessness.

'Compose yourself and tell me whom you allowed to slay your progeny.'

'The scion, Lord.'

There was a long silence before he spoke. 'Why have you not told me of him before? I am disappointed in you, Sybelle.'

She bowed her head, fighting back a sob. 'I had no choice. I knew your lordship would intervene.'

'You were correct. I would have taken steps. Perhaps I could have prevented this. But now I leave it to you. Eliminate this threat to our plans, Sybelle.' His face loomed larger, his refined features daubed in shadow and starlight. 'Do I make myself clear?'

'Yes, my lord.'

As the aperture darkened, the pressure lifted from her chest, but the intoxicating tang of sorcery remained in the air. The shadows continued to spin, extending outward with dark tentacles until they formed a circle of darkness ten paces across. Sybelle stepped back as figures emerged from the gateway, six warriors encased in suits of dark armor. She knew them on sight. The Talons were her father's personal cadre of assassins. Said to feel no pain and no emotion, they were completely loyal to the Lord of Shadow. The last time she had been in their presence was nearly two decades ago, when a squad had accompanied her and Levictus on the night they retrieved her sister from the mud-lord's estate.

Sybelle trembled as the portal snapped shut, and the mordant wind of its closure ruffled her hair. The Talons watched her, their eyes impenetrable behind black steely masks. One came forward. He did not bow or acknowledge her, but merely held her gaze. She frowned, but he could have been carved from obsidian for all he reacted.

'What are your orders?' she asked.

'To serve the daughter of House Tenebrae.'

A warm sensation ebbed in her stomach as she considered the one desire that lay tantamount in her mind: to track down and kill the scion.

The lead Talon turned his head to the side. 'Intruders have entered this structure.'

Sybelle stretched out her senses through the stone walls. At the entrance she tasted coppery blood and the sweet savor of death. With a smile, she flicked her fingers. The Talons melded into the darkness, leaving her once again alone. Soon her son's murderer would pay for his crimes. And then there would be nothing and no one to stop her.

Smiling, Sybelle sauntered back to her lover.

SHADOW'S LURE

Chapter
THIRTY-THREE

Twenty-fourth day of Circept, 1143

*Levictus has been absent these last three nights since I sent
him to Ostergoth. Although I am confident he will perform the
tasks I have laid out for him with his usual precision, I find
myself less willing to trust him. These past weeks and months he
has become at turns more sullen and secretive. I do not know
what I will do if this pattern of volatility continues.*

*The pact into which I entered with the Power in the north has
been costly, both here and abroad, and produced little in the way
of results, but it is too late for regrets. I have sown my crop, as
they say, and I will abide by its harvest. Still I cannot keep from
wondering if this was not a miscalculation.*

Caim leaned closer to the flames burning in the large
brick hearth as he turned the page. The wind moaned
through the gaps in the conservatory's tall windows.
The timbers of the old mansion creaked in protest with every
gale.

Coming down from the hills, they had taken shelter in the
outlaw rendezvous to await nightfall. While the others kept
watch, Caim sat inside by himself and perused Vassili's journal. The flames of the funeral pyres burned in his memory.
Liana in a borrowed dress, her copper hair brushed out in
waves around her face. She looked like an angel on the verge

of waking, forever young and beautiful. Beside her lay her father, a cudgel of oak by his side. Caim could only watch in silence as Keegan spoke the words of passage into Arugul's realm. Too late, they both understood what the old man had been trying to tell them, that in this conflict there would be no victory, no satisfaction. Only devastation.

Blinking from the sting of the hearth's smoke, Caim turned the page, and a square of parchment fell out. Its stamped golden seal glimmered at him from the floor.

'You miss her.'

He didn't answer as Kit passed through him and appeared in the fireplace. Yes, he missed Josey, but it was like missing a dream, only half there to begin with and nothing but mist come the morning. She was back in Othir, and he was here. He threw the parchment into the fire without opening it and watched it burn. He followed it with the journal.

'I missed you, too.'

Kit seemed different after her travails in the Barrier, more reserved. He wasn't sure how to take that.

'People are coming,' she said with an impish smile.

That didn't surprise him. He was ready. He just had to do this thing, and then he'd be free. *Free to do what?*

Kit blew him a kiss as Keegan entered the room.

'We've got—'

'People coming.' Caim stood up. 'I know.'

'It looks like Ramon and his crew. And they've brought friends.'

Caim wanted to sigh, but he held it in. He had enough enemies already, but anyone who got in his way tonight might not live to regret it.

'Pull in the outer sentries and make sure everyone is ready to go.'

Keegan returned with two men in damp cloaks. Ramon was more bedraggled than the last time they met, face caked with sweaty dirt, his white fur mantle muddied and stained. The other man was built like a young bull, though he hardly came up to Ramon's shoulder. He had a harsh, unforgiving face with eyes harder than cold steel, and a glistening shaved head. He, too, wore a white mantle under his cloak.

'—hear me, boy?' the smaller man was saying as Keegan led them into the room. 'Watch your mouth or there ain't nothing to stop me from stringing you up by the yarbles and bleeding you like a harvest lamb!'

Caim tugged on his gloves. 'There's me.'

The shaved man glared across the room. 'And who the fuck are you?'

A little chill went through Caim as he spoke his full name aloud, something he hadn't done in longer than he could remember. But it was time to own up to his past.

The grizzled warrior walked across the room. 'I'm Angus, thane of the Allastars since Jevick's murder. I've been hearing your name of late.' He jerked his head back toward Ramon. 'From them. They say you're some kind of warlock. I came to see for myself.'

Angus had a dirk sheathed on his left hip and a waraxe on the other side, but he made no move toward them.

Caim stepped to within arm's length of the man. 'I'm worse than that. I killed the Beast and left his body to freeze in the snow. I've got more blood on my hands than you and all your clan together. And tonight I'm going after the duke.'

Angus nodded slowly, and a crooked smile broke open his face. 'I like that. My boys and I have come to help.'

Caim looked to Ramon. 'You heard what happened at the castle?'

'We were holed up with the Allastars when the news reached us. We came as fast as we could.'

'How many warriors did you bring?'

'Almost sixty, most of them blooded fighters.'

'Where's Grendt? I don't see him lurking behind you.'

Ramon spat on the floor and stomped on it. 'He ran off as soon as he heard we were coming back here to finish the job.'

Caim forced his mouth to turn upward in a smile he didn't feel in his heart. 'So what did you come to do? Torch a few granaries?'

'And the armory, and mayhap a few houses in the old city. Want to join us?'

Caim glanced to Keegan. The youth was wound tight enough to chew wrought iron. 'We're going to the palace.'

Angus gave a barking laugh. 'That's as good as cutting your own throat, boy.'

Caim shrugged. 'Still, we're going. You could join us. We'd be a good-sized band if we joined forces.'

'Aye. Enough to bloody the duke's nose good. There's rumors he sent the bulk of his men south.'

Caim pressed his lips into a firm line. South could only mean a push into Nimea, and with the border in shambles Josey wouldn't know until the invaders were deep into the heartland. Then it would be a long, bloody affair to dig them out.

'That only makes our job easier. Are you with us?'

'Who leads?' Ramon asked.

Caim hooked his thumbs in his belt. 'Keegan Haganson.'

Ramon's mouth twisted as if he had bitten into something sour. 'He's no thane.'

'My father is dead,' Keegan said. 'By right I take his place as loreman of the free clans of Eregoth. And I call upon Caim to lead us until the duke is overthrown or we all lie dead.'

Ramon started to shake his head. 'He's no war—'

'Show them, Caim.'

Caim untied the laces and pulled his tunic aside. On his shoulder glistened knots of fresh blue ink in the ancient trefoil pattern. Angus grunted, but he held his tongue. Ramon took in a deep breath that strained his deerskin jerkin, but finally he nodded.

'So be it. For my brother and my cousin, and everyone else who's died at Eviskine's hands. You have a plan?'

Caim took out his knife and knelt on the floor. By the firelight he started cutting lines in the hardwood.

Arion pressed a hand to his hip as he leaned against the corridor wall. The combined stenches of blood and puke and shit clung to the back of his throat. He looked over at Stiv and Brustus, catching their breaths. This wasn't the reception they'd expected.

They had reached Liovard after an exhausting ride to find the city in shambles. People fought in the streets, burning, looting, and killing indiscriminately. When Arion and his men forced their way through to the barracks, they found Yanig and Okin barricaded in an arms locker. But the joy of the band's reunification was short-lived as Arion outlined his plan.

Passing through alleys littered with corpses and abandoned plunder, they climbed the hill to the castle and found the gates unguarded. The watch towers were unlit by torch or lantern. They moved through the vacant outer bailey and entered the donjon, not sure what to expect. It wasn't this.

The keep's chambers were scenes of carnage. An odd light filtered through the high windows and tinged the bodies stretched out on the floors with a sepia patina. Paintings and sculptures had been defaced, excrement smeared on the walls. The attack came as they entered the series of corridors that led to the great hall. A door opened. Half a dozen foreign mercenaries carrying wine casks, and a rolled-up carpet spilled into the chamber. The melee was swift and furious. While Arion concerned himself with staying alive, Brustus and Davom put on displays of bladesmanship such as he had never seen. Their performance was so inspiring he didn't notice the stablehand with the pitchfork sneaking up behind him.

Arion pulled away his fingers. The puncture wasn't crippling, but it bled like a rainspout. Others had paid a higher price. Okin had taken a butcher's cleaver to the neck. Yanig slipped on the floor and split open his skull.

They laid out their brothers on the floor. While Stiv mumbled some kind of a prayer, Arion looked down at the men he'd known, for more than ten years in Okin's case.

Davom rolled over a body with his foot. 'I know these guys. Pavel here owes me six nobles.'

Stiv shook his head. His short beard was matted with blood

and spittle from a split lower lip. An ugly red gash on his temple dripped down his cheek. 'What in the Dark's name is going on here?'

'They've all gone mad.' Brustus wiped the blade of his sword with a discarded cloak. 'Toe-curling, shield-biting, bark-at-the-moon crazy.'

'This is Sybelle's doing,' Arion said. 'She bewitched my father. Now she's done something to the city. When we find her, we'll find the source of the problem.'

'So what's the plan?' Stiv asked.

Arion looked down the corridor. 'We don't stop until we reach the throne. Kill anyone who gets in our way.'

Stiv reached inside his mail shirt and pulled out a small gold amulet. Arion was surprised when he saw the sunburst design. He hadn't known his right-hand man was a follower of the True Faith. Since Sybelle's coming, there weren't many believers left in Liovard. At least, not in public.

The sergeant shrugged. 'It can't hurt.'

Brustus grunted. 'If we get out of here alive, maybe I'll let you convert me.'

'If we get out,' Davom said, 'I'll build the biggest temple you've ever seen. Maybe even set myself up as the high priest.'

Arion let out the breath he'd been holding. 'Form up.'

They moved with purpose. When they reached the doors to the great hall, Stiv lifted a hand. But the sergeant halted in his tracks as the portals swung open before them, revealing a tableau straight out of a nightmare. Arion tried to swallow, but couldn't.

The light of a single lamp high above the chamber illuminated his father's throne. Headless bodies slumped on the floor in pools of congealing blood, and shaggy orbs floated in the air around the throne.

'Bugger me,' Stiv swore.

'Easy.' Arion tried to exude a confidence he didn't necessarily feel, but then he saw the figure slumped in the throne. 'Father!'

He started to run forward, but a willowy shape emerged from behind the throne. Her inky gown devoured the light. Seeing her, with her hand upon his father's arm, Arion halted at the edge of the ring of floating heads.

'What have you done?' he demanded.

Sybelle lifted his father's arm and dropped it, and Arion's heart lurched to see the limb flop lifelessly. He couldn't breathe. He took another step and batted aside a hovering head. Stiv cursed in earnest as the macabre trophy spun away into the darkness.

Arion pointed his sword at the witch's chest. 'I always knew you would be the death of him. From the start I saw you for what you are, witch.'

Her laughter played down his spine. 'And I knew you from the first moment, Arion. As a fool too weak to live up to your father's legacy, and too stupid to leave when you had the chance.'

With a shout, Arion charged, but Sybelle stepped into the gloom before he could reach her. He looked around his father's throne, sword raised, but the witch had vanished.

'Arion,' Stiv said.

He looked up. Sinuous figures moved in the darkness, weaving closer. Arion adjusted his grip on his sword as his men took up positions. Davom stayed low, knife weaving back and forth, almost taunting the enemy to approach. Brustus struck a classic dueling stance, sword extended perfectly still. Stiv unleashed a string of vile curses as he caught a floating head and hurled it into the shadows. They were good friends, better than he deserved.

Mocking laughter filled the hall as the lamp above began to dim and near-silent footsteps whispered across the floor. Arion lifted his blade within the diminishing circle of light.

SHADOW'S LURE

Chapter
THIRTY-FOUR

Josey closed the door and held onto the handle as lightning flashed in the palace windows. A heartbeat later, thunder crashed amid the steady staccato of driving sleet.

Inside the room, Anastasia was resting after the doctor dosed her with something to help her sleep. Hubert remained at her bedside with the nurse. His devotion no longer surprised Josey. All the way from Opuline Hill, he had refused to leave 'Stasia's side. Josey smiled, warmed by the thought of Hubert's gallantry. He couldn't hide his feelings for Anastasia from her, much as he tried. But it made Josey miss Caim all the more; she could use some comforting herself. Before Anastasia drifted off, Josey told her friend about her delicate state. Anastasia had been ecstatic and promised to help. Josey fought back the sigh that gathered in her chest and turned away from the door.

Four bodyguards in full armor stood at attention in the hallway. The sight of them, with their gleaming halberds held high, caused a lump to form in her throat. She would never be able to look at them the same, these men who had risked their lives for her. She was bound to them now, and they to her, but it wasn't the comforting thought she might have wished for. She'd sent men into battle and watched them die. That knowledge sickened her. *That's part of what I accepted when I put on the*

342

crown. Soldiers die. It's regrettable, but I'd be a fool to think it would never happen again.

Josey addressed the ranking subaltern. 'I want a guard at this door at all times, day and night.'

The officer saluted with a sharp snap of gauntlet to helm. 'Yes, Majesty.'

He directed one of his subordinates to remain and then followed her down the hall with the others. They met Captain Drathan as he rounded a corner.

'Majesty,' he said. 'I was coming to report.'

The captain looked beyond exhausted, deep into a realm of fatigue that showed in the lines in his face and the dark circles around his eyes. Yet he held himself upright. While she suspected he had not taken the time to bathe since their return to the palace, his armor had been cleaned and his face washed to give a semblance of suitable presentation.

'How are my men?' she asked.

'Eleven are in the hospital ward, Majesty, including Sergeant Merts. There are some bad cuts and a couple broken bones, but the physicians believe everyone will pull through.'

'And Master Hirsch?'

Captain Drathan's frown pulled the corners of his eyes downward. 'He lives, but I'm told it will be a miracle if he survives until morning.'

Josey's hands trembled. They were losing this fight for the soul of her city, and now her most potent weapon hovered on death's doorstep.

'I want funerals for the fallen, Captain,' she said. 'With full honors. What arrangements have you made for the defense of the palace?'

'I have increased the sentries on the walls and inside the palace proper. Your personal bodyguards' – he looked past her and frowned at the subaltern – 'should have been doubled.'

'I will do as I wish with my guards, Captain.'

'I didn't mean to imply—'

Josey held up a hand. 'My apologies. I'm tired and short of temper. Please forgive me.'

'There is nothing to forgive, Majesty. I meant to say that the situation has grown decidedly more precarious. I can vouch for the mettle of every man in your guard, but I fear we are too few to protect you. If the assassin strikes again—'

'If the assassin strikes,' she said, keeping her fear from rising to her voice, 'we shall deal with it in due time.'

'Yes, Majesty.' But by his expression he was not convinced. 'I also came to inform you that Duke Mormaer has arrived with a request for an audience.'

'At this time of night?' It had to be almost midnight.

'He seems . . . intent.'

A sudden burst of thunder rattled the window frames. Josey sighed and put a hand to her temple.

'Are you feeling all right, Majesty? Shall I fetch a—'

'I'm fine. Lead on.'

Josey was exhausted. Not just physically, but mentally and emotionally. It felt like huge fists were grinding against the sides of her head. She tried to shut it out, but the rumble of the soldiers' boots on the marble floor only made the pain worse. Gritting her teeth, she descended the broad staircase to the ground floor.

Despite the hour, Lord Parmian and Major Volek waited in the throne room. Both men bowed as she climbed the dais and settled on the throne. The main doors of the chamber were open, and through them she could make out Mormaer's broad frame in the foyer. She nodded for Ozmond to issue the summons.

Duke Mormaer's footsteps rang out on the hard flagstones. His usually impeccable ensemble appeared slightly rumpled, as if he, too, had not slept in some time. His eyes, though, were fierce as ever as he strode up to the foot of the platform. His bow was stiff and perfunctory.

'What could not wait until morning, Your Grace?' she asked.

'Empress Josephine, the messengers you dispatched to Parvia and Wistros never reached the garrisons. They were murdered.'

344

Josey stood up. 'How did you discover this?'

'I sent couriers of my own. My men came across the bodies of two imperial envoys on the road. Their assailants didn't bother to hide the evidence.'

Josey struggled to breathe. Without those garrison troops, she could not save Othir. Sinking back onto her throne, she gazed up at the ceiling. The tiny eyes of saints and Church hierarchs looked down at her from the paintings above. For the first time she noticed that none of them, not even the Prophet of the Light, was portrayed with a smile.

'Duke Mormaer,' Ozmond said. 'How far from the city did your men find the bodies?'

'About two days' ride.'

Josey drew in a deep breath and was mindful of the tautness of her belly beneath her gown. *Two days. How long before we would have begun to suspect? The city may have fallen before we sent new messages.* Which, of course, was her enemies' plan.

'Was the assassin responsible?' she asked.

'I do not believe so,' Mormaer said. 'My men reported the envoys both died of wounds to the stomach and chest, possibly the work of daggers.'

'Close-up work.' Ozmond turned to the throne. 'Majesty, those who killed the messengers were able to get within arm's reach of them without drawing suspicion.'

Mormaer cleared his throat. 'Empress Josephine, twenty of my best men await outside this chamber. If you will permit, I would add them to your guard for the time being. I personally vow as to their loyalty, each of them having served me for many years.'

Josey rose to her feet. 'Duke Mormaer, I am honored, but a fortnight ago you might have gladly stood by and watched as I was toppled from this throne. What, may I ask, has brought on this change of heart?'

Mormaer nodded. 'It's true that we have different views on how this nation should be ruled, but I will not suffer the throne to be bullied. Not by anyone. Now if you will accept—'

A terrifying howl sliced through the air of the chamber.

Josey fell back against the throne. Captain Drathan and his men drew their weapons as everyone gazed up at the ceiling. Ominous darkness cloaked the balcony overlooking the hall. Josey's breath froze in her lungs. *Gods protect us. It's here.*

Mormaer placed a foot on the bottom step of the dais. Shouting for his men, he looked to Josey. 'Majesty, you must be away now. My men and I will hold this chamber.'

'But—'

'Majesty!' Captain Drathan shouted. 'He's right. It isn't safe here.'

With a frown at Mormaer, Josey hurried down the steps. Major Volek strode up behind them as Ozmond, the captain, and a pair of guardsmen surrounded her.

'With your permission, Majesty,' the major said. 'I would accompany you to safety.'

'Of course,' she replied as they hurried her away.

Her last view of the throne room was of Duke Mormaer drawing a huge sword from an ornate scabbard while his soldiers fanned out with weapons readied. Josey's silk shoes made a soft patter on the floor as she jogged to keep up with her escorts. Their flight reminded her of the night she had been whisked through these corridors by Ral and Markus during their insane bid for the throne. That feeling was re-inforced as they turned a corner and passed through the wide chamber that had once been a trophy room. Even though the room had been converted into a sewing nook with cushioned chairs and placid arrays, she breathed easier when they were well past it.

Captain Drathan took a lamp from the sewing room and led them into the east wing of the palace. Scaffolds and tarps covered the walls, and crates were stacked in the available niches – all part of Hubert's pet project to turn this wing into new apartments for the palace's many servants. As they came to another intersection, Ozmond and Captain Drathan turned down opposite corridors.

'This way,' the captain said. 'There is a postern leading to the north bailey.'

Ozmond gestured down the other hallway. 'We should get the empress back upstairs to the imperial suite. There are stairs this way.'

Captain Drathan shook his head. 'Upstairs is no good. For all we know, the upper levels are in the hands of the assassins.'

'There is only one assassin,' Ozmond said, 'and he is occupied in the throne room with Duke Mormaer. The empress would be safer—'

'Gentlemen.' Josey cut them both off. 'I'm right here.' When they quieted, she said, 'Ozmond, I appreciate your concerns, but this is the captain's area of expertise. Captain Drathan, if you would—'

'Pardon,' Major Volek said. 'But if I may interrupt.'

Josey looked past the tall officer. The corridor they had just come down was pitch black and silent. Gooseflesh prickled her forearms. 'Yes, Major?'

Major Volek pointed down the opposite hallway. 'If we proceed straight, I believe we will arrive at the east guard tower, where more reinforcements may be found.'

Captain Drathan nodded. 'He's right.'

'Let's go, then,' she said.

Captain Drathan sent the two guardsmen ahead while he and Ozmond flanked Josey, with Major Volek bringing up the rear. They navigated the corridor around several turns, and then stopped before a blank wall. Blocks of chiseled granite lay beside buckets and trowels, and other masonry tools. The bitter odor of lime hung in the air.

'I don't—' Captain Drathan began, only to have his words cut off by a grunt.

Josey turned. The lamp clattered on the floor, somehow staying alight as the captain fell to his knees. He turned away as he collapsed, revealing the back of his uniform, drenched with blood. Major Volek's helmet bounced off into the darkness as he crumpled beside the captain. The two guardsmen pushed past Josey to take up positions between her and the unseen source of the attacks. Something flashed in the lamp's feeble light, too fast for her to see. One soldier collapsed where he stood; the other was jerked into the darkness as if he were a puppet. Horrible screams filled the corridor, and then died away.

Josey stepped back from the corpses. The fallen guardsman had rolled over onto his back; ribbons of bloody sinew trailed from the gap where his throat had been. She put both hands on her stomach. Terror coursed through her as she considered the fate of her child. *No! I will not allow this to happen. Caim, why aren't you here when we need you?*

Fingernails biting into her palms, Josey held her breath. She almost sobbed as Ozmond drew the rondel at his hip and stepped in front of her. When he made to approach the darkness, Josey grabbed his arm.

'Don't!' she whispered.

'Majesty, we cannot remain here.'

'I know. Just a moment . . .'

She let her words drift away as a shape moved at the lamplight's edge. At first she thought it was Duke Mormaer, but even a brief glance revealed that the figure was far too large. Its shoulders spanned the width of the corridor. Yellow flames danced in its bulging eyes. It was coming for her.

Josey didn't have time to be frightened. One moment Ozmond stood before her. Then talons flashed, and he was slumped against the wall, blood pouring from a row of parallel slashes ripped down the front of his coat. His mouth moved, but no sounds came forth. She read the words formed by his lips.

Forgive me.

Tears filled her eyes. This was her fault. She had no right to put these brave men in danger. She was nothing, no one. . . . *I am the Empress of Nimea.* The words rose from the depths of her soul. She wanted to cast them aside and reject them, but she couldn't. Not even in the face of death. Josey met the assassin's glowing eyes as she reached under her gown. Her fingers closed around the handle of the knife strapped to her thigh. *I am descended from kings and warriors, queens and protectors of the people. If you desire my death, come seek it.*

She drew the knife, and almost dropped it as a brilliant glow banished the darkness. The blade shone like a white-hot iron. Josey lifted the knife as the creature shambled toward her, and it paused. She was shocked. She had expected it to knock aside her tiny weapon and take off her head. Yet it held back. *As if troubled by the knife . . .*

She advanced a step. The monstrosity held its ground, but did she see a hesitation in its manner? She didn't know why her knife was glowing, but she wasn't going to give up any advantage she could find. If the creature was bothered by the strange light, then she would use it. Josey took another step. The assassin swiped at her with its curved claws. She lunged behind the point of her blazing stiletto, but a gust of hot air buffeted her to the floor an instant before a crackling burst of blue-white light filled the hallway.

Huddled against the newly constructed wall, Josey smelled powdered stone and quicklime. Two dark shapes loomed over her. She didn't cry out, not even to spit in the face of her enemies. *Two shapes?*

Her vision cleared over a span of several heartbeats to reveal Hubert and Hirsch standing over her, the adept leaning on her lord chancellor. Beyond them, Captain Drathan and the major sat against a wall. There was no sign of the assassin. Josey placed a hand over her abdomen. Was the baby hurt? She wished she could know. *Please be all right, little one. Everything is fine now.* But was it? She felt like this nightmare was never going to end.

'Where is it?'

'Gone,' Hirsch answered. His voice was wan, and he looked terrible.

Josey's palms stung a little where the skin was scraped, but otherwise she felt fine. Then she saw Ozmond. Both hands pressed to his bloody chest, he looked over at her and smiled. Before she could make the order, Major Volek stood up, shook himself off, and volunteered to find a physician. Once he was gone and Ozmond had been made as comfortable as possible,

Josey looked over as Master Hirsch picked up her knife from the floor. The blade shimmered in his hands.

'My knife . . .'

'I enspelled it,' Hirsch said, 'using the skin samples we obtained by the river. I wasn't sure if it would be effective against the creature. Evidently, it is.'

She had trouble focusing on what was being said. 'What?'

'Majesty,' Hubert said. 'Are you hurt?'

'No, I'm all . . . fine. Where did the monster go?'

Hirsch shook his head. 'It got away. I gave him a blast in the hindquarters he'll not forget, but the thing has more lives than a Hestrian moorcat.'

'You,' Josey said, 'should be abed yourself, Master Hirsch. Your wounds are serious.'

'My impending demise was exaggerated,' he answered with a wink. 'Did you happen to strike the creature, lass? Did you draw blood?'

Thinking she would have to have a long talk with the adept about keeping secrets from his empress, Josey found the knife on the floor. The glow remained, but the point was clean.

'Powers be damned,' Hirsch muttered.

Josey opened her mouth to chide his blasphemy, but she didn't have the energy.

'You need blood?'

Steel scraped across the floor as Captain Drathan lifted his sword. An oily fluid stained the end of the blade.

With Hubert's assistance, Hirsch hobbled over to the captain and reached for the weapon. He held it up to the light. 'It's arterial blood.'

'What does that mean?' Josey asked.

Hirsch laughed. 'It means we've got the beastie right where we want it.'

'We do?' Hubert asked.

Hirsch held out the blade. 'With this, I can follow the blasted thing anywhere.'

Josey's heart beat faster. 'Master Hirsch, are you certain?'

'Aye. But we must track it down right away.'

'First we have to get these men to the hospice, and you are in no condition to—'

'I am able to continue,' Captain Drathan said, standing up as if to prove it.

'Captain, you are in no condi—'

'We must finish this,' Hirsch said with a rasp that turned into a cough.

Josey was getting tired of everyone interrupting her. 'You need to rest, Master Hirsch, and my guardsmen . . .'

She looked down at the soldiers on the floor, their blood mingling with the thick dust. *Two more deaths at my feet.*

The adept's frame trembled, but his gaze was steady. 'We must do it tonight, before the creature has a chance to recover. Before it can harm anyone else.'

Josey heard the wisdom in the adept's words, but she hesitated. It would mean ordering more soldiers into harm's way, and she was already holding so much misery inside. Any more and she felt she would collapse.

'All right,' she said. 'But I'm going with you.'

Hubert opened his mouth to protest, and Captain Drathan sputtered. The adept's lips turned down into a sour frown, but Josey put on her 'empress' face and he said no more. She was terrified, especially for the life growing inside her, but she had to be strong.

'Lord Chancellor, conduct a search of the entire palace, including the outer grounds. I am guessing the assassin has fled, but we need to be sure.'

Hubert nodded and made way as Josey walked past him. Holding up the glowing knife, she led them down the darkened corridor, back to the inhabited portion of the palace.

Chapter
THIRTY-FIVE

Caim blew into his cupped hands to warm them. He stood with his fighters in a dark alleyway off Trepmire Avenue, a corridor of furrier stores and taxidermists in the city's upper west end. The street had one shining feature: it gave a clear view to the citadel at the heart of the city. He was following his instincts at this point. They had gotten him this far.

Kit huffed. 'It's a mark past midnight already. What are we waiting for?'

In defiance of the cold, or perhaps just to tweak his nose, she wore a slinky white dress. *Past midnight.* Caim counted days in his head. *Gods above. Today is Yuletide.*

Hoping the holy day wasn't a bad omen, Caim leaned out of the alley. The contrast with Othir couldn't have been starker. In the south, Josey's city would be festooned with lights and holly wreaths. People were still out this late, visiting with family and friends. But here, the frozen streets were empty. No people, no lights. But there were plenty of bodies to be seen as they infiltrated the city. It looked like a war had been fought inside the walls, and he couldn't tell who had won. They'd heard the roar of battling mobs in distant streets and seen the glow of fires erupting all across Liovard, but with Kit's help he'd been able to steer his men around the trouble spots. It reminded him of the riots in Othir, but these people seemed almost crazed, some half naked as they attacked everything and everyone around them.

Once inside the old city, Ramon and Angus had taken their men and split off on a different track, something to which they were well suited and prepared. Waiting for their signal, he hoped they knew what they were doing.

Keegan came up to stand beside him. The youth was wrapped in his cloak. His hands were gloved, his face blackened with soot. Caim told him before they embarked not to hold back. Tonight, they hunted in earnest. By the look in his eyes, the boy had taken that to heart.

'Well. What are we waiting for?'

Caim looked from Kit to Keegan, then ignored them both.

'Caim,' Kit whispered.

He felt it, too. A bizarre undercurrent in the city, stronger than before, setting his nerves on edge. Then distant bells began to ring, and a new glow lightened the east side of the city. That was the signal. Caim took a deep breath and unclenched his fists. It was time for the next phase of his plan. The idea was simple. He'd done it before without trying, but never on such a scale. True, he had been fighting for his life in those moments, but if he did it by accident, he could do it deliberately. *So why are my hands shaking? Stop stalling.*

He pictured a place. He'd never been there, but he had a rough description. That would have to be enough. An image formed in his mind, an empty courtyard paved in broad stone blocks surrounded by gray walls. He added battlements and defensive towers. When the picture was as real as he could make it, Caim reached out with his mind. Whispers chattered at his back as an empty hole appeared in the air at the mouth of the alley. It remained steady for a pair of heartbeats, but then the edges began to ripple. The strain of holding the gateway open was more than he had anticipated.

Caim beckoned the men standing behind him. 'Move! Quick!'

Keegan was the first in line. With only a brief glance at Caim, he ducked his head and jumped through the portal. For a moment, Caim thought the rest might balk, but one by one they entered. By the time the last of his team had crossed over, his entire body was shaking, and the edges of the portal wavered. Hoping Keegan remembered his instructions, Caim dove through.

Darkness closed over his eyes, and the air froze in his lungs as he passed through the void. A tearing sensation pulled at his flesh. It might have lasted for one heartbeat or a dozen, but then the night sky reappeared before his feet struck hard-packed earth. It took him a moment to gain his bearings. As his sight cleared, Caim made out the battlements atop a massive barbican, stone walls studded with square towers, and the keep squatting within their embrace. He had expected some kind of reception – a few sentries on the walls, at least – but there was no one here. That bothered him more than a little. It didn't seem possible Ramon's diversion had attracted every soldier in the citadel.

A soft glow surrounded him as Kit appeared. Instead of a quip and a grin, she greeted him with a frown.

'I don't like this.'

'Me neither,' he said under his breath.

'This place has a bad aura. Like a lot of people died here recently.'

'Just get inside and poke around. We need to find the duke.'

'Be careful.' She leveled a stern glance at him as she vanished.

The outlaws hunkered against the base of the nearest wall. Caim found Keegan standing over one of the men, who was writhing on the flagstones and clutching his knee.

'What happened?'

Keegan looked up. 'Iain slipped coming out of that circle thing and broke his leg.'

'I just twisted it,' the outlaw said.

Caim could see the knee joint was dislocated. This fighter was no longer of use to them. He told the others.

'I can make it,' Iain argued.

Caim shook his head. 'You'll slow us down.' To Keegan he

said, 'Put him someplace out of sight. Make sure he stays quiet.'

He didn't say they would come back for him. Everyone understood the risks and accepted them. While a pair of men carried Iain to a dark corner of the courtyard, Caim beckoned to Keegan, and they both went over to the gate that separated them from the keep. Like the sallyport across the bailey, the inner gate was open and unmanned. There was a guard station on the other side, but it was dark. Caim listened for a dozen heartbeats, but heard nothing. The post was abandoned.

He stepped closer to Keegan and kept his voice down. 'Once we get inside, keep everyone close on my heels. If we get separated, remember what I taught you. If someone falls—'

'We won't let you down.'

Aye, but what if I can't hold up my end of the bargain?

Caim swallowed his anxiety while Keegan gathered the outlaws. When everyone was ready, Caim drew his blades. The black sword shook in his hand. Blood pounded in his temples. The faces of the men around him appeared leaner and grimmer. With a deep breath, Caim dipped inside the doorway and sprinted across the pavestones.

The inner keep was a vast square with angled walls to provide for enfilading fire. Caim stared down fifty arrow loops as he ran across the courtyard. There could be a company of archers behind them, waiting to feather him. He didn't slacken his pace until he reached the door. Finding it ajar, he swung it open with the knife. No guards here, either. The worry that had begun as a tickle at the nape of his neck was now stomping up and down his spine.

No sentries. Unguarded gates. An unlocked door leading into the central keep. Why do I feel like an undertaker digging his own grave?

Caim waited ten breaths for the others to get across the bailey. Then he eased inside the doorway. Two armored figures waited inside. He started to attack the one to his left, but checked the sword's arc before it landed. These men were dead. Both slumped against the walls; one with a broken

355

sword blade jutting from his chest, the other missing the top half of his head. As Caim's eyes adjusted to the gloom, he saw more bodies farther in, all slain in a vicious brawl within the past couple candlemarks, judging by the wetness of the blood on the floor and walls, and sprayed across the ceiling.

When the first outlaws reached the door, Caim held out a hand to forestall them. Moving down the long atrium alone, he reached out to the shadows. In a dark place such as this, he expected them to come flocking to his call, but there was only a faint chitter. He could feel them around him, but they weren't eager to come out. He made the summons more demanding, and after a few moments coaxed a pair of small shadows to his side. He needed spies, at least until Kit returned from her reconnaissance excursion. He urged the ebon blobs to go out and gather intelligence as they had done before, but they just crawled up his ankle and clung to the fastenings of his boots. *What the hell?*

With a growl, Caim started ahead, trusting Keegan to follow. He moved down the entryway into a taller room, a killing chamber in typical fashion. Arrow slots lined the chamber walls, all angled downward to fill the space below with lethal fire. But they watched silently this night. Three stout doors faced him, one in the wall straight ahead and one on either side. Caim had seen the inside of enough fortifications to have a general idea of where they needed to go. The keep would be built around a central hall. The upper floors would be occupied by storage, kitchens, and living quarters. He expected to find his primary target on the top level, but every castle was unique, and this one was big enough to sport a variety of changes. He had already decided to start with the great hall.

Not waiting for the outlaws, Caim stole up to the door on the left and nudged it open. Inside was a dark corridor, likely leading to the servants' wing which might have its own staircase to the higher floors. But something drew him to the door at the end of the chamber. He crossed the room, mindful of the arrow loops above, but stopped short of touching the door. A presence loomed on the other side. *All right, Kit. Anytime now.*

Keegan entered the chamber, his falcata held high as if expecting an attack at any moment. 'What happened here? Why'd they kill each other?'

'I'm not sure,' Caim answered. 'Something's not right—'

Kit popped into view in front of him. 'Caim, they're coming!'

'Who?' The question spilled from his mouth before he remembered he wasn't alone.

Keegan frowned. 'Who what?'

Caim grimaced as the presence returned, much stronger, coming from behind him. He jumped in front of Keegan and the brothers as the right-hand door swung open and a dark shape exited. The intruder wore a suit of exotic armor, black metal plates sliding soundlessly over ebon mail. Caim recognized the design at once as a slimmer version of the Beast's protective shell. The figure raised a long curved sword with a night-black blade as it advanced.

The shadow warrior was fast. Damned fast. Before he took a full step into the room, two blurs shot from his off-hand, and two outlaws in the middle of the chamber crumpled. Caim leapt forward and made a lunging parry in front of Keegan, but before he could launch a counterattack, the shadow warrior spun out of the engagement. Another outlaw, Siman, went down missing half his face. Caim rushed at the shadow warrior from the side and swung his sword in a wide swipe that didn't come close, but it caught his opponent's attention. The shadow warrior ignored the outlaws as he turned to Caim with a vicious series of attacks. As he circled away, Caim remembered fighting Levictus, and the speed of the sorcerer's movements. The shadow warrior's quickness forced him to fight by intuition. He tried to stay in close where he could use his knife, but the shadow warrior kept him at bay. Every time Caim thought he spotted an opening, the black scimitar was there to cut him off.

Keegan slammed shut the door behind the shadow warrior,

placing himself in the path of the enemy's retreat. *Brave boy. I hope it doesn't get you killed.*

Caim hissed as the point of the ebon scimitar twisted past one of his parries and sliced across the top of his left wrist. He hopped back a pair of steps and clenched both fists tighter around his hilts. The cut burned like red-hot iron across the skin. The shadow warrior followed him, curved sword moving in constantly changing patterns. Beads of sweat trickled under Caim's shirt as he blocked a double thrust. The tension in his chest, rather than alleviating, was growing stronger. Then he realized he could feel a second presence, coming from . . .

Caim turned as the other side door opened and another shadow warrior appeared. The outlaws were too busy watching the duel to notice, and two of them fell to a black staff before they even realized they were in danger. Caim jumped clear of the sword wielder and, with a snap of his wrist, sent his knife hurtling across the room. It sailed straight, but the second shadow warrior batted it aside with his staff and moved to engage the others. Caim was there an instant before he could enter the room.

Caim heard shouts from behind him, but he put all his focus on this second warrior. His opponent's staff had sharp blades at both ends. They were everywhere, spinning, slicing, darting back and forth. It was all Caim could do to keep from getting spitted on the agile weapon. The sword's hilt warmed in his palm. He made a desperate thrust, aiming for the upper thigh. Just before it connected, the shadow warrior stepped back and vanished into a pocket of darkness.

Growling in frustration, Caim snatched up his knife. The other shadow warrior was surrounded by Keegan and the brothers, Dray and Aemon, and a short outlaw with a hood over his features. For a moment, Caim thought it was Liana. Then he remembered helping Keegan scatter her ashes in the hills above the castle, and his thoughts turned dark.

The shadow warrior slipped past Aemon's spear and cut his legs out from under him. As the brother fell, the enemy launched himself at Caim. Their swords met with a screeching clang, sprang apart, and rushed at each other again. Keegan ducked in low from a flank and tried to score a hit, but with a deft move the warrior whirled out of the path of the attack. Caim lunged and caught on the flat of his blade the blow that would have disemboweled the youth.

The others retreated as Caim pressed the shadow warrior. The enemy's attacks, which had seemed so quick only moments ago, had slowed to a more manageable speed. Or maybe he was catching up. The black sword seemed lighter in his hand, like he was wielding a reed cane instead of a blade. Caim blocked a stroke aimed at his side and tied up the scimitar long enough to dip inside the warrior's guard. The *suete* knife flashed. Once, twice, and found flesh in the armpit joint on the third punch. The shadow warrior hissed and backed away. A moment later, he was gone in an eddy of dark shadows.

Caim let his arms fall to his sides as he fought to catch his breath. Kit came up through the floor.

'Are you all right?' she asked.

He stepped back from the outlaws where they huddled around their fallen comrades.

'Where did they come from?'

'I don't know.' She reached out to touch a tear he hadn't noticed across the breast of his jacket. A couple inches deeper and . . . 'But they aren't alone. There are a bunch of creepy things crawling through this place.'

As he considered that, Caim called out to Keegan. 'Gather up everyone to move. Take out some of the torches we brought and get them lit. We don't have much time. More will be coming.'

'What about the wounded?'

The outlaws stood over the fallen men with dour expressions on their sooty faces. Caim looked down at Aemon, sitting against the wall with a pained expression as Dray tied a tourniquet around his leg. *They're useless to me, all of them.* He bit his tongue to still the bloody thoughts colliding inside his skull.

'Leave them.'

'No fucking way,' Dray said. 'I'm staying with him.'

Caim squeezed the hilts of his weapons. The presence had returned. Four presences, actually. The strongest was behind the door at the far end.

'When is this going to end?' he whispered.

Feathery tickles ran down his arm as Kit laid a hand on his shoulder. 'Be careful what you ask for, love.'

With a grunt, he called Keegan over. The left-side door, heading west, felt like the direction of least resistance. 'Take everyone through there. Look for a way around to the main-hall.'

'Where will you be?'

'I'm aiming to be there before you. If not, you know what to do.'

Keegan frowned, but he began ushering his people to the doorway. Caim watched the outlaws exit. When they were gone, he turned to the north. The black sword thrummed in his hand. It was hungry.

'What's through there?'

Dray looked over, but then turned his attention back to his injured brother. The men had their weapons arrayed on the floor close at hand. Spears, knives, a bow and a brace of arrows.

Kit hovered close. 'I don't know. It's one of the places I can't see. I'm sorry, Caim. I can try again. It's just . . .'

'No. We'll go together.'

'Are you sure you want to do this? It's not too late to change your mind.'

Oh, but it is, Kit. It's been too late for a long time.

With a grim smile, he kicked open the door.

SHADOW'S LURE

Chapter
THIRTY-SIX

They rode through the foggy streets while chunks of hail shattered on the cobblestones. Huddled under the hood of her cloak, Josey shivered and kept her eyes on the street. Between the freezing rain and the howling wind, speech was next to impossible. Not that she had much to say to the men surrounding her.

Somewhere out in the storm, the assassin was headed for a safe place to lick its wounds. And they followed.

By the light of her soldiers' lanterns, she could see Hirsch, astride his steed in an intersection of three streets. The adept leaned over in the saddle, his face nearly touching the soaked ivory mane of his little steed. Every few breaths he would look down at a glass case in his hand while the rest of their party – pitiful as it was – waited a respectful distance away. Josey sat between Captain Drathan and Hubert. The captain had wanted to bring more men, but Hirsch had insisted on fewer. As they argued the merits of strength versus stealth, Josey sided with the adept. Enough of her men had died already.

The Crimson Tigers, Volek and Merts, made up the rest of the small company. The two sat on their fierce-looking horses a few paces from the group, no doubt conversing about stratagems. After the assassin's attack, Major Volek had refused medical care despite the nasty bruise on his forehead. Josey supposed he was ashamed for some perceived failure, but she didn't see what he could have done differently. They had been caught ill prepared and paid the price.

Likewise, the sergeant, insisting that his injuries were negligible, had also asked to accompany them. When he stripped the sling from his arm and flexed it to prove his readiness, Josey didn't have the heart to deny him.

After what felt like a short lifetime, Hirsch turned his steed northward and took off down a narrow street at a canter. Josey choked up on the slick reins as she headed after him, her protectors keeping pace on either side. She couldn't help thinking about what they would do when they finally cornered the assassin. Under their oilskin ponchos, each guardsman carried a crossbow with steel-headed bolts designed to penetrate heavy armor, but so far mundane weapons hadn't proved effective against the assassin, and Master Hirsch didn't have the resources to enspell them. For the thousandth time in the last couple days, Josey wished Caim was here.

A strong smell cut through the rain. It took only a moment's concentration to identify the combination of distinct odors – mud, fish, and garbage – that was the river. She clenched her thighs together, which made Lightning toss up his head in irritation. Patting his neck, Josey forced herself to relax. She trusted in the adept. She had to.

The street climbed to the top of a steep embankment. The river, swollen with rainwater, rushed past on the other side. Josey steered her steed away from the edge and tried not to think about what might happen if she were to fall into those turbulent waters.

They passed a row of houses on the bank's landward side. The storm and the dark made getting her bearings difficult, but Josey guessed they must be getting close to the Processional, which meant they were approaching the city cemetery. Josey had too many memories of that place to suppress them all. The most recent, and the hardest to dismiss, was the day she had 'buried' Caim. The mere thought of it produced a twinge in her breast. *Damn you, Caim. Will I ever see you again?*

Josey reined up. The adept had halted before a decrepit brick building.

'Is this it?' Captain Drathan asked over the clamor of the storm.

Hirsch nodded weakly, and Josey was seized by a pang of regret. Master Hirsch had spoken to her alone before they left the palace.

'I forged the letter, lass,' he'd said to her with pain in his eyes, not all of it physical. 'My order didn't send me. Truth be told, they banned me from coming.'

When she confessed she didn't understand, the adept bowed his head. 'But I had to come. Too much rests on your success. Earl Frenig was a great man. A great friend. I should have done more . . .'

In that moment, an image popped into Josey's head, of a small ivory plaque bearing a face. Hirsch's face. He'd been one of her foster father's coconspirators.

'Master Hirsch—'

'He loved you, lass. I couldn't live with myself if I let you be torn down by the same bastards who took his life.'

Brushing raindrops from her eyes, Josey dismounted. The building the adept had indicated looked like an apartment home. The brick was worn, showing traces of a distant white-washing. The windows were empty holes, their canvas panes torn or nonexistent. Sleet rattled on helmets and armored plates as the guardsmen threw back their ponchos and checked their weapons.

Captain Drathan, sword in hand, peered at the building through his visor. 'Majesty, this situation gives every advantage to our enemy.' He pointed to the gaps on either side of the building, at the windows and roof. 'They can come at us from any direction, and it would take an entire company to secure all the ways in and out.'

Josey helped Hirsch climb down from the saddle. 'Forget about securing it, Captain. We're going inside.'

He opened his mouth, but she didn't give him a chance to argue.

'All of us. Make it happen.'

As Captain Drathan turned away to instruct his men, Josey studied Hirsch. The adept's condition was deteriorating. His face was as pale as a fish belly, and he shook as he leaned against her.

Hirsch gave her a wan smile. 'Not as bad off as I look, no doubt.' His voice was barely audible over the storm. 'Anyway, it's got to be done and there ain't no one else to do it.'

Josey tried to smile. Hubert saved her the awkwardness of having to mouth an encouragement that the adept neither wanted nor needed.

'Majesty.' Hubert leaned close to be heard. 'Major Volek suggests we move inside quickly. Something about too many places for hidden eyes to watch us out here. I can't say I disagree. This place makes my skin crawl.'

'I agree, and this weather isn't making things any easier.'

'We could burn the place down,' Hubert suggested. 'Safer than entering the spider's lair.'

'No. We don't know who's inside. There could be innocents. Have Captain Drathan find us a way in.'

Hirsch lifted his hand, his index finger pointing to a cellar door set against the side of the building. With a nod from Josey, Hubert hurried over to the captain, and together with the guardsmen they approached the entrance. Josey helped Hirsch over the muddy ground. The soldiers pulled open the cellar doors as Josey and the adept came over to stand beside Hubert and the captain. The light of their lanterns showed worn stone steps falling away into darkness. Before the freezing rain washed them away, Josey saw wet patches on the steps. Footsteps.

While Josey shivered against the adept, Captain Drathan selected two to remain outside with the horses, giving them strict orders to ride back to the palace for assistance if the party was gone for longer than a candlemark. The other two he sent down the stairs first. As the soldiers descended, crossbows held ready, the circle of their lantern's light pushing back the darkness, the captain looked to Josey.

'Majesty,' he said. 'I would prefer that you return to the palace.'

She shook her head, sending droplets of icy water flying from the ends of her hair. 'No, Captain. We will all go in together. Lead the way.'

With a nod, Captain Drathan took up a lantern and went down the steps. Hubert and Josey each took one of the adept's arms. Although Josey had the feeling Hirsch didn't want the aid, he didn't complain. The major and Sergeant Merts came last, both men wearing grim expressions beneath the half-visors of their helmets.

They went down a dozen steps to emerge into a crude root cellar. Strange smells filled the place. The brick walls were pocked with holes, possibly to hold shelves, and the floor was littered with dirt, tree branches, and withered leaves. Hirsch paused at the bottom of the steps to catch his breath, and Josey felt ashamed. The adept was pushing himself too hard. *Don't crumple! Honor his loyalty with strength.*

More wet patches formed a trail across the cellar. Leaving the adept with Hubert, Josey followed Captain Drathan and his men to investigate. As she came up behind the soldiers, she realized Major Volek and the sergeant had come with her. She'd grown so accustomed to the presence of bodyguards that she hadn't registered the footsteps behind her, which was a little unnerving. She smiled to the major, and he returned a brief nod.

Her guards stood around a hole in the wall. Bricks and chunks of mortar were piled on the floor in front of the aperture, which was big enough to accommodate a man. Beyond the hole extended what looked like a tunnel through solid rock extending as far as she could see. Josey's mind boggled to comprehend the amount of labor that must have been required.

'This can't be the work of the assassin, can it?' she asked.

Captain Drathan held his lantern higher. 'This would take a team of engineers months to dig out. It's . . . I don't know what to make of it.'

'—combs.'

Master Hirsch shuffled up to stand beside Josey.

'What did you say, Master Hirsch?' she asked.

The adept coughed into his hand. 'Catacombs. Carved from a system of caves under the city.'

'Who made them?'

'*Why* did they make them?' Captain Drathan asked.

Hirsch wheezed as he inhaled through his nose. 'Predecessors of the modern . . . Church found the' – he coughed again – 'caves and used them to meet in secret. Later . . . they enlarged them to bury their dead where they would not be . . . disturbed.'

Josey remembered from her catechism that the Church had been outlawed by the empire at one time. Tolerance came eventually and the True Faith had spread, but this was the first she'd heard of catacombs under Othir. It bothered her that something like this could be hidden from common knowledge.

'Why would they believe that their dead were not safe in the boneyard?'

'Your ancestors.' The adept nodded to Josey. 'They ordered the remains of those who worshipped the upstart Prophet to be removed from their graves, wherever they were found . . . and thrown into the Memnir. A heinous desecration in those times.'

Josey peered through the crack. The walls of the tunnel were unfinished, as was the floor. 'Master Hirsch, are you well enough to lead us?'

'My men and I can go first, sir,' Captain Drathan said.

'Thank you, Captain. But no, this falls under my purview.'

Holding onto the rough edges, Hirsch stepped through the hole. The palace guards went next, with everyone else following. Their footsteps echoed down the tunnel like the march of a gigantic, shambling beast. Josey stayed near Hubert and his lantern. The closeness of the stone walls didn't bother her as much as she had thought it would. In a way, the tunnel reminded her of the terrifying voyage through the city sewers with Caim, him bleeding all over her. But she had survived that nightmare and found strength in it. She wanted to think she wasn't the same sheltered little girl she had once been.

Then Josey muffled a yelp with her hand as something skittered over her foot.

Captain Drathan spun around with his lantern over his head. 'Majesty?'

She swallowed. It was just a rat. 'I'm all right, Captain. Proceed.'

With a nod, he quickened his pace to catch up to Master Hirsch. The tunnel forked ahead of them. Without pausing, Hirsch headed down the branch to the right. As she passed the split, Josey glanced down the other direction. It was an identical tunnel as far as she could tell, running as far as the lanterns could reach. She shivered as she hurried after Hubert, who waited for her with a tight smile. It was cold down here, especially as they were soaking wet, but it wasn't the cold that made her tremble. The thought of being trapped down here alone, without a light, jangled her nerves. To take her mind off it, she focused on the captain's back.

They passed a smooth stone face set into the tunnel wall. Josey paused a moment, and Hubert stayed with her. It took her a moment to grasp that it was a grave marker. Dust filled the indentations of rigid characters carved into the stone. Hubert brushed away the accumulation, and Josey recognized the script as old Nimean. It listed a score or so names, and a number had been chiseled at the top of the stone – 816. Josey reached out to trace the date. *So much history, lost for centuries. What other secrets hide down here in the dark?*

'Stirring, is it not?' Major Volek asked, standing beside her. 'To think that on this spot, more than three hundred years ago, men and women who didn't know if they would live to see another day gathered to mark the passage of their brothers and sisters into the Prophet's arms.'

'Are you a religious man, Major?'

'Without the Light, how could we find our way in this dark world?'

Josey was surprised to hear such words from the stoic soldier.

367

Sergeant Merts watched the exchange without reaction, as impassive as the stone around them. Josey and Hubert continued on, followed by the heavy trod of the soldiers' boots.

The tunnel split again, and then again fifty paces or so after that. Each time, Hirsch chose the right branch, and Josey began to worry that the adept had lost his sense of direction. *No. He's gotten us this far. Have faith.* But faith was an expensive commodity down here.

A few steps farther the tunnel widened, and Josey heard a sound in the darkness. A rhythmic plinking.

'Water.'

Hubert turned his head. 'What?'

'Listen. It's dripping water.' She reached out to the wall. The stone was slick with moisture. 'We must be under the river.'

Hubert tapped his toe in a small puddle on the floor. 'How far do these catacombs extend? Majesty, we should send a team down here to search for hidden ways into the city.'

Josey gave him a short nod, hiding her smile as she looked down the tunnel and began to hope that they were coming to the end of it. She stood on her tiptoes to look over Hubert's shoulder. For a moment she thought she saw something in the shadows. A brief flicker of movement, too quick for her to be sure. She was about to forget it when a loud yell echoed from the front of the party.

Josey tried to push past Hubert, but she jumped when something from the ceiling bounced off her shoulder. She looked down to see a small rock on the floor. She looked up and didn't have time to shout a warning before the world collapsed.

Chapter
THIRTY-SEVEN

The corridor zigzagged as Keegan shepherded his men through the castle. He waited until the last person entered the hallway before hustling back to the front.

You're not fooling anyone, Keegan. They all know you're not the leader type. They're just humoring you, but when the shit storm hits you'll be left all alone holding your pecker.

For the life of him, he couldn't understand why Caim had chosen him to lead this mission. There were plenty of fighters here with more experience, like Vaner or Taun. Even Malig could do a better job, and he hardly talked except to complain.

Keegan thought about Dray, staying back with his brother. Would he do the same if it had been Liana? Just the thought of his sister shoved a burning spear point through his heart. He nodded to the men as he passed. *Act like you know what you're doing.*

He was almost back to the head of the group when a shout reached him, followed by a fierce war cry. Keegan pushed through the press until he burst into a small room furnished with little more than a wooden table and chairs. One chair lay on its back beside the sprawled figure of a large man in a dyed cloak. The rest of the outlaws held back, looking in all directions. Only Vaner had the guts to approach the open door on the other side of the room, torch in hand.

Keegan went over to the fallen man. Blood leaked from a

puckered gash across his cousin Gaelan's throat. Even knowing he was too late, Keegan tore off his cloak and tried to stanch the flow, but it seeped through the material and kept running.

'What happened? Bring me more light!'

Men clustered around. They tried for more than a minute, but by the end Gaelan was dead. Keegan sat back on his heels. His arms were drenched up to the elbows in blood.

'Damned thing just came out of nowhere and cut him down.' Yosur pointed across the way. 'Then it flew out that way like the Dark One himself.'

Vaner hadn't moved during Gaelan's ordeal, but kept staring through the open doorway. Keegan snatched his sword and stood up.

'Was it one of those shadow men?'

'Maybe.' Vaner raised his torch higher. 'I think I see it. There. Standing against the wall.'

Keegan couldn't see anything down the dark hallway, but he backed up to the others while keeping his eyes on the doorway.

'Okay. Caim said don't stop for nothing. When I give the call, everyone rush through that door. If you see something that ain't us, kill it. Otherwise, keep moving.'

Everyone nodded. Keegan was surprised no one argued with him. His forearms itched. The urge to scratch was almost overpowering, but he pushed the thought aside. Caim was counting on him.

Keegan raised his sword. Just before he gave the signal, something detached from the gloom in the corner of the room, like a black cloud with arms and legs sheathed in black metal. He started to yell a warning, but his voice froze in his throat for a fatal heartbeat. That was all the shadow man needed to slip his sickle-shaped knife across Yosur's stomach and rip out his guts. Lumel was the next to fall, split open like a side of beef. Then old Taun collapsed near the back of the group. Keegan spun as another figure in black darted through the darkness.

The clansmen backed away, but Keegan stood his ground. The sickle glinted dully in the torchlight; the shadow man swung a length of thin chain in his other hand. Keegan took a wide stance as Caim had taught him and tightened his sweaty hands around the handle of his sword. When the spiked end of the chain rushed toward him, he expected to die. But something urged him not to give up. He stepped out of the way and smacked the chain with the flat of his sword. An awful tone rang from the contact, but Keegan got the satisfaction of seeing the chain fall limp to the floor. Before he knew it, he was running *at* the shadow man, who seemed a little confused himself. At least Keegan hoped it was confusion, but he didn't have time to think about it. He launched an overhand cut with all of his strength. The shadow man slid out from under the attack as neat as anything he had ever seen. The sickle came up and across in a slash that would have sliced out his liver, but Keegan shoved his heels into the floor and fell straight back, not gracefully by any measure, but the sudden change in direction saved his life.

He rolled onto his stomach as the chain swung over his head. He pushed himself up, knowing this was it – he was about to die – and hoping it wouldn't hurt too much, when a quiet gasp sounded from above him. Keegan jumped up to find his enemy standing like a tree, head tilted oddly to the side.

Vaner stepped from behind him, bloody sword in hand, and the shadow man collapsed. Others ran forward to chop at the slumped body, spattering the floor with dark ichor. Keegan's legs shook as he tried to comprehend that he wasn't going to die. *Don't speak too soon. We ain't out of this yet.*

'Where's the other one?' he asked.

A few men looked around.

'Gone.'

Vaner's left arm hung limp at his side, the sleeve drenched in blood, but he was alive. Keegan started toward the man, but stopped when he noticed a wedge of darkness bulging from the wall behind Vaner. As Keegan opened his mouth to warn him, something ice-cold wriggled down the collar of his tunic. He looked up, and the cry lodged in his throat.

The falcata fell from his hand as thousands of tiny black leaves rained down from the ceiling.

Nine bodies lay on the floor.

Silence reigned in the gloomy chamber. The seven men and two women sprawled across the floor were a medley of soldiers and common folk, but all had met with the same savage violence. A few had bite marks on their faces and necks. He had come too late to find out which side they were on, if any.

The shadows swarmed nearby as Caim walked to an archway on the other side of the chamber, so close he could hear them chittering. The black sword thrummed, warm in his hand like a living thing. The point hovered over the corpses he passed as if sniffing for new foes to battle. The sword craved blood, and while he held it he shared its dreadful lust.

Before he reached the archway, Kit emerged from a wall. Her outfit had changed to a chiton of hunter green belted with a silver sash to match her flowing hair.

'What did you see?'

Her eyes narrowed to purple slits as she floated before him. 'There are a few bodies scattered about. It looks as though the people living here went mad and started killing each other.'

He glanced around. Blood was everywhere.

'I think *she's* here, Caim. I can't be sure, but there is something ahead. I can feel it, but I can't get close.'

Caim started to walk through her, but stopped himself when they were face-to-face. The touch of her nose played like foxfire along his lips.

'Get away, Kit. This is only going to get worse.'

She laughed. It was the most beautiful thing he could imagine right now. 'What? And miss the chance for you to finally get what you've got coming?'

Same old Kit. Never misses an opportunity to kick me where it hurts.

'You ready for this?'

She drew back to arm's length. 'Are you?'

He strode through her, savoring the sensation as their bodies melded, and passed under the archway. The sword pulled him through the corridors beyond. The shadows crept in his wake. Every so often he would see a flicker of Kit's luminance ahead of him. He followed, hoping she knew where she was going.

A staircase appeared on his left, spiraling upward into the dark. As he turned toward it, a dark blade slashed at his face. Caim jerked back and swung his sword up to meet the attack. The black blades met and rebounded in a clash of phosphorescent sparks. He riposted . . . and the shadow warrior was gone.

When the Beast shadow-jumped away during their fight, Caim had been able to see a wispy residue that gave him something to follow. But these fighters just vanished. *No, hold on.* Looking closer, Caim saw a web of filaments – no wider than strands of hair – shimmering in the dark. They faded before his eyes.

Caim put his foot on the first step and spun around as something disturbed the air behind him. The thrusting black knife got past his sword. Only a quick jerk of his *suete* kept the point of the curved blade from piercing his chest. As silent as death, the shadow warrior lunged with a second knife. Caim deflected it and counterattacked with a slash to the neck. But the shadow warrior had vanished. Like before, only a handful of gleaming skeins gave any evidence that the shadow fighter had ever been there.

'Kit.'

She appeared beside him. 'What? I was trying to find you a way out, but this place is a labyrinth.'

Caim grunted. That was a good word for the warren of corridors running through the palace. It had become evident that the rulers of Liovard had added new passages and chambers to the castle, probably over the course of a couple generations. The result was a royal mess.

'What did you find?'

'The stink of sorcery is thicker on the floor above you,' she answered.

That made sense to him. The great hall would be on the next level, with the residential chambers above that.

'Will these stairs get me there?'

'They'll get you to the second floor, but you still have a bunch of halls to cross.'

The sword jerked in his hand, in the direction of the staircase. Caim followed the blade's lead, and Kit followed him up the winding stairs. The steps ended on the next floor, opening into a dark corridor. He turned left. The pressure grew stronger inside him as he moved down the drafty passage. He didn't fear it anymore. The feeling was a part of him, as familiar as the fit of his clothes or the weight of his knife.

The shadow warriors struck again at the intersection of two hallways. The sword-staff slashed back and forth, lightning-quick, blocking his way. Caim started to meet the attack, but Kit's sudden cry alerted him to the second threat. He fell to his chest and rolled as twin blades cut the air above him. Caim regained his footing with his back to a wall. Kit floated over his attackers' cowled heads, then flew up through the ceiling. The shadow warriors came at him side by side, eerie twins in matching suits of black armor. The sword shook in his fist. *Yes, I agree.*

Caim catapulted himself at his foes. The shadow warriors split apart, smooth as watered silk. Caim feinted at the knife wielder on his right, then pivoted and blocked a thrust from the sword staff. He used his *suete* to tie up the longer weapon long enough for him to dart underneath. The black sword dipped under the warrior's breastplate and met ebon mail underneath. Caim shoved harder, extending himself to his full length, knowing he presented a prime target to the foe at his rear. The blade's point bit into black steel links.

374

And the staff wielder leaned back, disappearing into a cloud of shadows.

Biting back his disappointment, Caim threw himself forward. Not fast enough. Two lines of blazing fire cut across his lower back. He rolled and came up on his feet and deflected a black knife inches from his throat. The second blade came in low. Caim kicked it away and slashed high. The shadow warrior ducked under with both blades whirling. *Just what I would've done.*

Caim should have retreated and regrouped. He was tiring fast, and defensive actions would only preserve him for so long. Instead, he charged. Black knives cut into his arms and shoulders. He ignored the stinging cuts, hooking his sword arm around the warrior's wrist and pulling him closer. His *suete* slashed upward, not at the adamant black armor, but across the eye slit of his enemy's helmet.

The shadow warrior lurched backward, tearing free of his hold, but Caim jumped after him. As a dark portal opened behind his foe, he lunged. Hardened mail burst open, and his sword bit into flesh. Dark blood bubbled forth. Caim didn't pull up. He kept pushing and sent both of them stumbling through the gateway together.

Into darkness they went, as the portal snapped shut.

SHADOW'S LURE

Beams of light swung back and forth as the ground pitched beneath Josey's feet. Colliding with the tunnel wall, she clung to the stone with both hands as chunks of the ceiling rained down on the men in front of her. Hubert fell against her, his lantern almost bashing her in the head, and they tumbled to the ground. Huddled beneath him, she shook with the fear that threatened to overwhelm her. The cave-in seemed to last for several minutes as cries of pain were cut off by the crash of falling stone, and then . . .

Silence.

Hubert crawled off her, holding his elbow. Josey coughed as she sat up.

'Are you all right?' she asked.

She glanced at the ceiling, wondering why the river hadn't deluged the tunnel, but it looked like only a portion of the rock above their heads had fallen. Then she saw the heap of dirt and rubble filling the passageway. Hirsch and Captain Drathan had been walking just a few paces in front of her, along with Sergeant Merts and her guardsmen. Now they were gone. Josey crawled to the rock pile. Shards of stone ran between her fingers as she started to dig. They might still be alive underneath, trapped in a pocket of air.

Hubert's hand settled on her shoulder. Josey tried to shake

him off, but he pulled her away. He was saying something, but it took a moment to sink in.

'They're gone, Josey. They're all gone.'

She leaned against him as heavy sobs shook her body. More people dead, because of her. Life had been so simple once; she longed for those days with a thirst like she'd never known. Wiping her eyes, she stood up straight. They weren't out of this yet.

One lantern remained, sitting upright on the floor. A minor blessing. She picked it up as Volek climbed to his feet. The major's armor was dusty and pocked with dents, but he seemed unhurt. Another piece of luck, but she would have traded a score of Crimson Tigers to have Hirsch back.

'All right, gentlemen.' She forced her voice to steadiness. 'This is what we're going to do. We're heading back to the last fork and taking the other tunnel. We'll keep working our way back until we find the other side of this blockage.'

Hubert glanced at the major. 'Majesty, what if there is no way around?'

'There is. And we're going to find it.'

Volek picked up his sword and brushed the dirt from its guard. Hubert nodded with a sigh of resignation.

The major led them back down the tunnel. The silence seemed more oppressive without the others, the darkness more ominous. Josey couldn't keep herself from glancing over her shoulder every few steps. The emptiness behind her pulsed like a living thing. At any moment she expected an ambush.

When they reached the split, the major turned into the unexplored branch, but Hubert drew Josey aside with a glance. His left arm was pressed against his side.

'Majesty, I believe we should leave. We can return later with more—'

'No. We are going to find the others, and then we'll all leave together.'

His eyes searched her face. 'They're dead. No one could have survived.'

'We're going to make sure, Hubert. That's the least we can do.'

With a small nod, he followed after the major. Josey quickened her pace to keep up. Major Volek waited at the next fork. Josey pointed to the right-hand tunnel, hoping it led in the right direction.

After a few dozen paces, Josey caught a whiff of an unpleasant odor, faint at first, but it grew fouler the farther they walked. Wrapped up in her thoughts, Josey didn't notice Major Volek had stopped until she and Hubert came up beside him at the entrance of a long cavern. The floor sloped away from the entrance, its contours smoothed as if by the passage of countless feet. She looked down where the major's gaze had settled.

Two bodies lay at their feet, a woman and a young boy. If not for their pale waxen skin and perfect rigidity, they might have been sleeping, but Josey knew they were dead at first glance.

When did I become an expert on death? Is this Caim's doing, or the price for wearing the crown?

The stench was overpowering. Josey held a sleeve across her face and breathed through her mouth as she looked deeper into the cavern. Horror crawled up her throat at the sight of more bodies. Scores of them. Men and women, many of them stripped nude, their limbs tangled together like a jumble of discarded dolls. Her insides quivered at the sight. *So many people. My people.*

Hubert bent down over the nearest corpse. 'This must be the assassin's larder.'

Feeling like she was observing from miles away, Josey watched Hubert inspect the body of a young woman. Long strands of brassy hair lay tangled around her slender neck. She couldn't have been more than thirteen or fourteen, still in the bloom of youth. Scraps of a red dress clung to her torso. Ragged gashes shone against the alabaster of her throat.

Major Volek gestured with his sword. 'We should keep moving.'

Josey started to agree, but then Hubert lifted the girl's hands. They were bound with rope, as were her feet. He turned the girl's head to the side. A ghastly mark had been seared into her cheek. Josey knew the mark – a rounded upside-down teardrop. The demon's horn. A cold spot formed in Josey's chest.

Hubert fingered the red fabric. 'She was a whore.'

Josey tried to imagine what the girl's life must have been like to sell her body at such a tender age, and then to be marked like livestock and murdered in this fashion. It was unbearable.

'How did she come to be down here?' she asked, more to herself than anyone else.

Hubert stood up. 'Exile is still a common punishment for those convicted by the Church's magistrates. Perhaps the assassin hunts outside the city and brings his victims back here to feed.'

Josey took off her cloak and draped it over the girl's corpse. 'From this day on, no citizen of my realm shall be punished by the canonical courts without the crown's consent.'

Hubert nodded, but his eyes were deep in thought. The major grunted. Holding up the lantern, Josey walked past the men. She wanted this to be over. The sooner, the better.

As she picked her way through the charnel pit, Josey searched out the dimensions of the cavern and any possible exits. Chalky rock formations studded the ceiling in several places. While the left-hand wall was relatively straight, the wall to her right curved away. Deep shadows swathed the area beyond.

Hubert came up beside her. His face was paler than before and covered in sweat. She nodded forward, and he moved ahead while she held the lantern's light on him. A faint sound whispered in the dark. Josey turned and spied something emerging from around the bend of the wall. A person. Invisible hands closed around her windpipe. She lifted the lantern higher. Broad, coarse features came into focus. Scuffed boots and a shabby coat. *Could it be . . . ?*

Josey rushed over to Hubert as he raised his sword and put a hand on his arm. 'Master Hirsch?'

With a rasping sigh, the adept staggered into the light. His coat was covered in rock dust. He had lost his hat. Dirt matted his hair, and his left eye was swollen shut.

Josey pushed past Hubert. 'Where are the others? Captain Drathan? His men?'

The adept shook his head as he shuffled closer. 'Gone. Your Majesty.' His voice creaked with the strain of saying even that much.

Josey froze. Something was wrong. The adept's gait was choppy and slow, which was to be expected. He looked like the entire city had fallen on his head. His shoulders were bent forward like an old man's, but there was a strange cast to his eyes.

Josey handed Hubert the lantern, which he took with his bad arm. 'A tragedy, Master Hirsch. But thank the heavens you survived.'

A stale odor emanated from the adept's clothes as he staggered up to her. Josey lifted her arm in an embrace. His breath was hot on her neck as she pulled him close.

When you're faced with danger, don't wait for an opening. Strike hard and fast, because you won't get a second chance.

Josey punched upward. The adept went rigid against her. She staggered into Hubert, who hissed through his teeth as he caught her. The adept swayed, his features running like melted wax as he clawed at the glowing stiletto lodged in his throat. Josey looked into eyes turned jet black, and panic seized her limbs. But the assassin collapsed on the uneven floor. Gasping and mewling, it retreated to the wall, where it stopped, no longer resembling Hirsch at all. It had shrunken to a rail-thin frame wrapped in glistening gray-black flesh, with tiny ears close against a hairless scalp, a flat nose with a single nostril, and gaping jaws filled with curved fangs.

Hubert pulled Josey away. 'How did you know?'

She released the breath she had held pent-up inside her.

'Master Hirsch never called me by my title. And the smell. He reeked of death.'

As Hubert started to turn away, he fell to his knees in front of Josey. She thought he had tripped until she saw the dark stain spreading across the back of his jacket. A large boot lashed out of the darkness to kick the lord chancellor to the ground.

Josey backed away as Major Volek loomed before her, his face half in shadow. The illuminated half was as grim and gray as the stone of the cavern. He had donned a tabard over his armor. Its deep crimson cloth was almost black in the dim light, the golden circle emblazoned on the breast shimmering like a sullied halo. A spasm seized Josey's chest. *We've been a pack of fools.*

Volek said nothing, but the truth stared at her from his eyes, mirror-smooth orbs devoid of emotion. His sword, dripping with Hubert's blood, swung toward her. Josey retreated faster.

'This was all a trap,' she said. 'Does the prelate know?'

The major approached with measured steps. Josey looked around for something, anything, she could use as a weapon. Her knife, still stuck in the jerking assassin, was on the other side of the chamber. There were no rocks in sight larger than a robin's egg.

'How much is Innocence paying you?'

She flinched as her back touched the wall. There was nowhere to go. Her mind devised a dozen stratagems and rejected them all. She needed a weapon. She needed Caim. *This is your fault, damn you, Caim. You left me and you left our baby.* Rage poured through her, mixing with the terror. She had to fight.

'I won't insult you by offering money. I just want to know the truth before I die.'

He stopped a pace away from her. 'It isn't a matter of money.'

'What then, Major? What gift or favor is worth the life of your empress?'

Volek's cheek muscles twitched. 'You are *not* my empress!

The True Church is the only authority in this world. You're just a petty despot dragging this country into the sewer.'

She clenched her fists. 'I am the lawful heir of Emperor Leonel. I—'

'You are a harlot and a usurper!'

'And you will be a murderer, Major.' Josey looked around for something to help. But there was nothing. She was alone. 'Is that how you want to be remembered? As a common criminal?'

'I will be the greatest patriot in history.' Flecks of spittle clung to his lips as he raised his weapon. 'You have betrayed the Faith and your countrymen. And for that you shall di—'

A flash of incandescent brilliance filled the cavern an instant before the floor tilted under Josey's feet. She shielded her eyes and fought to stay on her feet as a colossal roar battered her ears. The major stooped over her, his sword swinging back. Then he was gone, swept aside by a barrage of crashing boulders.

When the earthquake stilled, Josey coughed and waved her hands to clear the air before her eyes. There was no sight of the major beneath the landslide of stone and gravel. A vast hole gaped in the far cavern wall. Hirsch stood on the other side, lowering his hands as he leaned on Captain Drathan. The two of them looked like hell, but she'd never been happier to see anyone.

Then Josey remembered Hubert. Peering through the pall, she lurched across the rubble-strewn floor.

Chapter
THIRTY-NINE

Caim's knees slammed into the floor as he and the shadow warrior landed in another corridor inside the ducal palace. He rolled away and put his back to the wall. Quick glances in both directions indicated he was alone.

The shadow warrior was dead.

Caim scooted over and lifted the helmet's visor. In the long, narrow features underneath he could see a vague resemblance to the witch. And to his mother. But the dusky skin paled before his eyes, becoming thin like old paper. Shadows flitted in the hollows of the warrior's eyes, deepening as his body melted away, the armor crumbling into flakes, until only a patch of greasy ash remained. Caim got up. A handful of shadows wriggled up his arms, their touch cooling the burning cuts.

The corridor arrived at another intersection. To either side were smaller hallways, but Caim ignored them for the set of wide double doors in front of him. Heavy oak with hinges set into the frame. If they were barred, it would take a team of men with a battering ram to break through. Caim didn't have a team anymore, and he was short on siege weapons. But he had something else.

The sword pulsed as he pointed it at the portals. Before he could form the command, the shadows poured down his arms and along the length of the blade, and flew at the doors. They washed across the wooden panels in a great black wave. Holes appeared in the wood; brass handles and hinges fell to the floor with heavy bangs.

The black sword nearly yanked Caim off his feet. He dug in his heels, and the blade's hum rose to a whine. *All right. Just this once.*

The pull lessened for a moment. Taking that for acquiescence, and wondering at his own sanity for trying to reason with the thing, Caim allowed himself to be led through the doors.

Eerie cold enveloped him as he stepped across the entryway. His breath misted in the frigid air. The walls of the octagonal great hall were buttressed with thick wooden pilasters at each corner, rising to a vaulted timber ceiling. In the center was a wooden throne. Caim assumed the man in fine regalia sitting in the chair was the duke – the late duke, for he was clearly dead. Dozens of bodies lay around the throne, male and female, all headless. Caim had seen many awful things in his lifetime, things that had made him doubt the inherent goodness of mankind, but the severed heads floating in lazy circuits around the throne turned his marrow to ice. Lord Arion lay at his dead father's feet. What had brought the young lord to this end? Then Caim saw the cocoons hanging on the walls, more than a score of them, shaped like men wrapped in black shrouds. He spotted the tufts of Keegan's unruly hair sprouting from a casing. Some of the men moved, a little, but many remained still. Caim took a step toward the nearest cocoon and halted as four dark shapes glided from the shadows of the room. A voice whispered from the darkness.

'All these years, I thought you were dead.'

Caim braced himself as the witch walked out from behind the throne, radiating power like a miniature black sun. She strode over to the nearest cocoon and paused a moment to touch it. Muffled cries issued from the bubble of shadows. The man within the grim prison struggled for a moment, and then hung still. Her fingertips came away reddened with blood, which she put to her lips as she smiled at Caim.

He tried to take another step into the chamber but found he could not move as the cold infiltrated his body. His limbs were locked in place, his lungs frozen in midbreath. Everywhere the chill spread, sensation vanished. He didn't want to know what would happen when it reached his heart. Caim strained with every muscle, but the paralysis held firm. And the shadow warriors circled nearer.

The witch gave him a smile that bordered on seductive. 'And when Levictus reported your presence in the south, I hoped he would kill you and save me the trouble.'

A soft glow sparkled beside him.

'Caim,' Kit whispered, almost too soft to hear. 'It took me forever to get through all the energy laced around this place.'

He wanted to tell her to get away before it was too late, but he couldn't talk. He widened his eyes as far as he could and darted them back and forth between her and the witch, but Kit just hovered in place. *Think of something, Kit. Distract her – anything!*

Kit flew up next to him and ran her hands across his chest, like she was swatting at cobwebs, but nothing happened. There was a flicker of shadow, and then the witch was standing before him. Her eyes were so black he could not tell where the pupil ended and the iris began. They seemed to yawn wider as she placed a finger on his chest. A stabbing pain cut through the layers of his clothing to penetrate his skin.

'I warned Soloroth about you, but he was always too headstrong to heed me. Sickening, how he allowed himself to be conquered by an untrained half-breed like you.'

Kit ducked out of sight. Caim hoped she had some kind of plan.

'Pathetic,' Sybelle said. 'But my sister was a weak-minded fool, always adopting helpless creatures. And here you are, a stain on our family. One I intend to cleanse away for good.'

A cloud of tiny darknesses descended from the ceiling. Caim tensed as their minuscule fangs chewed through his clothes.

He strained harder against the power holding him in place. If he didn't escape, he was going to die, slowly, painfully. He tried to bite down on his tongue to elicit some feeling, anything.

'Fight her, Caim!' Kit whispered, as if he weren't.

He called to the shadows. He felt them along the walls of the great hall, lining the cracks in the high ceiling, but none answered his summons. He tried again, and the sword quivered in his hand as a sudden pressure filled his chest. His heart thudded, once. And then again, sending warm blood flowing through his body. The cold retreated for a moment. If he could just move an inch . . .

A roar tipped through the chamber. The shadow beast. Caim pushed harder and felt a crackle along his spine. Something bit him on the shoulder, but he didn't stop. With a final push, the paralysis shattered like a crust of ice covering his skin. The moment his arm was free, Caim swung at the spot where the witch had been standing, but the black blade cut only air. Then his grunt became a hiss of pain as the shadows tore into his flesh. He tried brushing them off, but they were everywhere. He stomped on the ground and swung his blades. Then the stinging bites vanished and the darkness lightened. Hundreds of shadows – maybe thousands – fluttered in the air like demented moths, colliding in the air and falling to the floor. His shadows had come to him after all.

As the pall lifted, Caim looked around. Kit was nowhere to be seen, and neither was the shadow beast, but he didn't have time to find out why as four shapes glided toward him. He ducked under the curved blade of a sword-staff rushing at his throat. Rolling across his shoulders, buds of agony blossomed from the wounds along his back, but he was alive. For the moment.

A line of fire traced down his left arm. Caim spun around, but the shadow warrior had drifted out of range. He started to follow until another warrior advanced on his right flank, forcing him to turn in that direction to deflect blinding-fast cuts from a pair of black-bladed axes. Caim parried and circled away, never stopping, but the four warriors had him pinned. Every move he made put him in range of one of them. A twisting thrust from the scimitar broke past his defenses to jab his upper thigh. Caim smacked aside the midnight blade and riposted with a long lunge. The scimitar wielder parried his thrust, and Caim followed up with a combination of high-low attacks. The tip of his *suete* slashed across the cuisse plate covering the warrior's thigh, but it didn't penetrate. Caim jumped back as the other three closed in around him. But even that much success bolstered his resolve.

He wove around a slash from the sword-staff and rushed in low, dropping to his knees and sliding under the shadow warrior's guard. His knife rose to ward off the sword-staff while he thrust with his other hand. The sword's point dug between armored plates and punched through the mail underneath. Caim pushed until the blade's length sank into the shadow warrior's guts. He was up on his feet and turned around before the body hit the floor.

The remaining warriors pressed him harder than before. Caim backed away under their barrage of attacks, trying to keep one shoulder to the wall. The axe-man wandered half a pace too close and took a deep cut across his elbow. But before Caim could follow up, a jet of cobalt fire lit up the hall. Caim dropped to his belly, and a blanket of frosty air draped over him as the blue flames washed against the wall. Hoarfrost spread up the wooden paneling, which split under the intense cold.

Caim jumped up. The shadow warriors were gone. No, he felt their presence in the room, moving through deep patches of darkness even his vision could not pierce. The witch was gone, too, and that worried him more. Caim edged farther into the chamber. A draft of cool air wafted across the back of his neck.

Caim dropped to one knee and swung his sword as he spun around. The axe-man fell back, blood streaming from the stump of his severed wrist. His other hand came up. Caim blocked the overhand chop. The sword lashed out again and again until the warrior lay on the floor, his legs drawn together and one arm folded over his chest.

As Caim stepped away, a mass of dark webbing caught his left hand, its fibers clinging to his wrist. He turned with the pulling of the net and parried a spear thrust. As the weapon flicked out at him several times in rapid succession, Caim gave up trying to pull away and instead yanked himself closer to the spearman. The scimitar sliced the air behind Caim as he swatted aside another spear thrust. He made two quick counterjabs and the spear clattered to the floor, followed by the shadow warrior's body, pierced through the throat under the chin.

Caim sliced through the net holding his wrist and flung himself over his crumpled opponent. He turned as soon as his toes touched the floor, but the remaining shadow warrior held back, watching him from several paces away. Caim trembled from the exertion even as the sword's hunger pulsed through him.

A snarl cut through the quiet, and the scimitar wielder collapsed facedown on the floor. The shadow beast perched on the warrior's back, its jaws locked around his neck. Caim looked around, expecting to have the flesh blasted from his bones at any moment, but the witch was gone.

Heavy thuds sounded all around the chamber as the outlaws fell from the walls, their shadow-wrought cocoons evaporated. The men were covered in bloody marks, and they moved a little slow, but it looked like they would live. Caim thought he should feel some relief at that; instead he just wanted to be gone. Across the hall, he spotted the lingering remains of a gateway. He could see the direction it led, but not where it arrived.

It was a trap, of course. He thought of the many reasons why he shouldn't follow, but then the sword sent a jolt of pure hatred spiking up his arm. He needed to end this now, while he had her on the run.

As Caim sprinted across the slick floor, someone spoke behind him, but he was listening to something else, a faint buzz at the edge of his hearing. His heartbeat thundered in his ears as a black hole split the air.

For Liana and Hagan. For my father, my mother . . .

He took a deep breath and plunged into the portal.

Caim swayed as he landed on hard flagstones. He reached out, thinking he was going to fall, but then his balance snapped back.

He had an idea he was still inside the city, but beyond that he was lost. The place was dark, though he could see well enough with the sword in his hand. High stone walls enclosed him on all four sides, decorated with bizarre pictograms, some of which might have been words but in a tongue he had never seen. A massive throne of black stone towered on a pedestal in front of him. Above it, something carved into the wall had been defaced and smeared with soot. Two smaller seats rested before the platform. The place had an odd smell, dry and acrid like a tomb. *Or a temple.*

A chill ran across his scalp. There was no sign of Kit, not that he expected any. He hoped she was smart enough to stay away. Caim tensed as something stirred beside him, and relaxed a hair when the shadow beast padded out of the dark. It sat on its haunches a few paces away, watching him like a tame hound. Caim didn't know if he entirely trusted the creature; his dealings with it had been haphazard at best, but it had also saved his life. Whatever it was, wherever it came from, he was glad for its presence.

He found an open doorway behind the gigantic throne. The corridor beyond ran straight as far as he could see. The shadow beast entered, but the hairs on the back of Caim's neck stirred as he followed.

He held the sword before him as he advanced. He saw movement down the corridor and made it out to be a shimmering sheet suspended across the passage like a black curtain stirring in the breeze. The shadow beast stopped and growled. Caim reached out with his sword. The curtain's surface yielded before the tip, stretching like skin. Then the point pierced the membrane. Too fast for Caim to follow, the curtain detached from the corridor walls and slashed at him with curved ebony claws.

Caim lifted his knife to block, but the claws passed through his *suete* to score stinging furrows down his arms. Fluid as quicksilver, the rippling creature struck again, scoring on his thigh and hip; shallow cuts, but they burned under his skin. He jumped back to make some space between them, but it harried him with rapid swipes. Caim managed to deflect one with the flat of the sword, but the thing was more powerful than it looked, and the parry almost tore the hilt from his grasp. The creature dipped under his guard, and Caim braced for another set of fiery cuts, but before it could strike, the shadow beast jumped onto its back. The two creatures rolled across the floor. Then, with a sound like tearing leather, the shadow beast tore a hunk of material out of the creature's center. A keening wail filled the corridor as pieces of silken flesh fluttered in the air. Caim prodded the curtain to make sure it was dead.

The shadow beast sat a couple paces away. It didn't lick its paws or pant with a lolling tongue; it didn't do anything a normal animal would do.

'You ready?'

The shadow beast started down the hallway, and Caim followed. Another fifteen paces brought them to an ornate archway that marked the end of the corridor. Intricate scroll-work was carved into pillars of pale limestone and across the arch above. Beyond the aperture there was only blackness.

Well, I've come this far.

Caim called, and the shadows gathered around him in the hundreds. Their tiny voices hissed in his ears. With their bodies wrapped about him like a second skin, Caim stepped through the doorway. A moment of panic gripped his chest as the temperature plunged. A bitter wind snatched at his clothing. Once he was through, he looked back and saw only a wall of bare stone behind him. His breath curled in the air as he tapped the wall with the butt of his knife. *Solid. At least a foot thick. What did I do?*

He was in some kind of chamber. It had a subterranean feel. A shroud of shadows obscured much of the walls and vaulted ceiling. The place stank of alchemy and death, quicklime and camphor infused with the rot of the grave. Caim couldn't see Sybelle, but he got the impression she was here, in the dark that ebbed and flowed around him. His skin prickled from more than the cold. He had stepped into the viper's lair.

At least the shadow beast had come with him. It stood near his feet, its broad head swinging side to side, nose to the ground. *That's it. Sniff her out.*

Without warning, the beast leapt into the murk. Caim froze, listening for sounds of fighting, but all was quiet. The shadows clung to him as if afraid to wander from his person. A lilting chant whispered in the dark. Caim looked around, trying to pinpoint the source, but the song came from multiple directions. The words were alien, but also somehow familiar. Had he heard something like them before? It almost sounded like . . .

Caim dove sideways as a stream of bitter cold rushed past him. He came to his feet with both weapons extended. A throaty laugh tickled his ears.

'I remember that night.' Her voice filled the air, like she was speaking directly into his head. 'When we came to crush the worm who dared to abduct my sister.'

Caim slunk forward, straining every sense to locate his quarry. The floor was covered in something like gravel or broken glass. He strived for utter silence, but he'd only taken a few steps when the sword's point struck a wall and rang like a gong. He jumped back, and another jet of freezing air hurtled past the spot where he'd been standing. The shadows on his back squirmed while Caim listened. Obviously Sybelle couldn't see him either, or this hunt would have ended already.

'Your father was twice the fool,' she said. 'First, to think he could abscond with a daughter of the Shadow, and then to believe he might live the rest of his days in peace.'

Caim kept his ears open as he traveled along the wall.

'The truly absurd thing about it,' Sybelle continued, 'was that my sister didn't resist once we got her away from that sty where she'd been living. I think she longed to return to proper civilization almost as much as I did. If we hadn't come for your mother, she would have left on her own in time.'

Caim bit his tongue as he worked his way around the edge of the chamber. His fingers found the splintered remains of a cupboard or bookcase, and he avoided the debris. But as he crept onward, it became increasingly difficult to concentrate. The urge to lash out built inside him, as palpable as physical lust, until his blood was pounding and sweat ran down his back. The sword thrummed with fury, as if the blade had its own vendetta against the witch. He saw his father again. Dying.

He knelt at their feet, with a sword's pommel jutting from his chest.

Caim shook his head, but the image refused to leave. The sword's vibrations shook him from his thoughts. The witch's voice had moved again.

'The conceit! To think he could keep her,' she said. 'Mud-born aristocrats. Grant titles to a nest of *vretch* and it would mean as much. Even my Erric, for all his beauty, is still only . . . was . . .'

She sounded nearer now, but Caim still couldn't pinpoint her. He decided to leave the safety of the wall and strike out into the unknown middle reaches of the chamber. He held the sword up to his chest so it wouldn't give him away again as he probed the area for Sybelle, but she had fallen silent. When he reached a point he judged to be the center of the room, Caim stopped.

'A shame about your fair duke,' he said. 'Whose handiwork was that?'

Caim threw himself flat to the floor as furious shrieks assaulted him from all sides. Blasts of ice-cold air exploded above him. Rubble showered the floor. Confined to the darkness, he imagined titanic sorceries gouging holes in the walls and ceiling.

When the clamor died down, he crawled to his feet. Deep sobs sounded in various spots around him. Then he realized what she was doing, and a plan came to him. It was risky, maybe even fatal, but he didn't see that he had many options. *Let's see how you enjoy it when I play your game.*

Opening his mind to the Shadow, he formed a portal and stepped through. It snapped shut the moment his feet touched down on the other side of the room. The vertigo lasted only a heartbeat or two as he stood still, listening for any sign he might have been heard.

'I will make an example of you.' Her voice had dropped to a whisper. 'For what you've done to me and my family, I will feed your soul to demons of the Outside, bit by screaming bit.'

Caim turned to his right. He thought he had a bead on her now. When she dropped the volume of her voice, the reverberation was lessened and the source seemed to come from a far corner. He kept low as he circled toward her position.

'Would you like to see her again?' the witch asked. 'One last look upon your dear mother before you die? I could make that possible.'

Caim halted in his tracks. The shadows trembled against him, and the sword swung back and forth regardless of how he fought to hold it back. He growled as something inside him refused to remain silent.

'She's dead.'

'No.' The witch's voice echoed around him. 'She lives.'

Before he could draw it back, the sword sliced through the space beside him. But it met no resistance and quivered in his hand at the end of the arc. The witch's laughter filled the chamber.

'Put down your sword,' Sybelle commanded. 'Kneel and bow your head to me. Then perhaps I will let you see her.'

Caim's fingers tightened around the hilts of his weapons as

the craving to feel the witch's blood on his hands gnawed at him, but he had to know what she knew. It was a hunger deeper than rage, fiercer than vengeance. He hadn't fully appreciated it before, but a gaping hole had yawned inside him his entire life, ever since that fateful night. He'd tried to fill it with money and women, with discipline and death, even with Kit, but the only thing that could make him whole was the sure knowledge of what had happened to his family. And the witch would tell him, one way or another.

Sybelle's laughter floated past. This time Caim was ready. He opened another portal. As soon as he landed, he swung both weapons, low cuts at the height of a woman's knees. An invisible punch slammed into his chest out of nowhere and knocked him back a couple steps, followed by a second clout, and a third. Caim dipped and wove, but the rain of ethereal attacks battered his body and face with the force of mule kicks. The shadows encased around his body absorbed some of the impact, but enough got through to leave him shaky. A punch caught him flush in the midsection and flung him against a wall. He landed on his knees and rolled through another gateway.

He collided with another wall when he emerged. Face smarting, he turned around and put his back to the surface. *You're cutting it close, Caim. Next time you might land inside one of these walls.*

His chest burned where he'd been struck, and it took a few breaths before his lungs stopped aching so bad he wanted to throw up. *That was stupid. You might have known she would be better at this than you.*

But what else did he have? Her sorcery was superior, and he couldn't get close enough to strike. He didn't even have Kit to help him out. Thinking of her, Caim felt a soreness inside him that had nothing to do with the bruising he'd suffered. There was too much left unanswered between them, as usual.

Caim stalked the darkness with a sense of resolve. Before he took more than a few steps, a thunderous growl broke the stillness. Caim spun to his left as the witch shouted – only a single Word, but the sound of it stopped up his ears and stung his eyes. Caim jumped in the direction of the noises. One moment he was moving through the dark, and then the veil lifted. He emerged to see the witch huddled against the wall, dark blood pouring down her arm from a vicious bite. The shadow beast was crouched to spring.

Stop! He wanted to shout, but the beast was already pouncing.

The point of Caim's sword pierced its side. The beast yowled and twisted around. Caim launched a series of stop-thrusts. To his shock, the creature retreated. He waded in closer, forcing it back, but even as he did so Caim felt bad for the creature, which looked confused by this treatment. The shadows wriggled up and down his body as if in protest. What would Kit say if she saw this? He pushed the thoughts out of his head as he pressed forward, driving the beast away from Sybelle and the answers he needed.

Step by step, he pushed the shadow beast back into a corner. Caim's knee connected with something low, a retaining wall of dark gray stones, but he focused on keeping the beast at bay. The creature snarled and snapped, but it would not come within range of his sword.

Caim started to turn away, but a grip like solid ice closed around his head. The witch's fingers, cold and caressing, clamped onto his temples. A wave of bitter cold closed around him, locking his muscles. The shadows shrouding his body shivered and spat as Caim struggled to break free, but she turned him with inexorable power until he faced the low stone wall. A still pool lay inside, its waters dark and impenetrable.

'Look,' Sybelle whispered.

The waters roiled and bubbled, but no steam rose from the pool. Then the gray miasma cleared, and the chamber – along with the witch and everything else – fell away. When the gloom rolled back before his gaze, Caim was soaring high above a bleak wilderness. The land below was cracked and pitted, devoid of any vegetation he could see. A pallid splinter of the moon hung above the dark horizon, where jagged mountains rose against the night sky. His perspective raced toward them at a terrific rate, though he felt no sense of movement.

This is a dream.

Yet by the clarity of the vision, he was sure it must be a real place. Was this the Shadow realm? That didn't seem right. For all its depressing monotony, the scenery appeared ordinary enough. As the mountains rushed closer, his vantage plunged toward the ground. The view wavered for a moment. When it cleared, he hovered before an enormous construction perched on the desolate plain. Its construction was foreign. The angular black walls were riddled with silver veins and pockets of polished crystal. Gargantuan towers rose like titanic fingers, topped with dagger-sharp spires. As his view flew over the outer curtain wall, Caim felt a presence before him. Even though he knew this wasn't real, a kernel of anxiety opened in his gut. The vantage slowed as it approached a massive structure at the center of the cyclopean city, a pyramidal building of the same black stone. A window yawned in the side of the structure, and Caim's perspective halted before a narrow balcony. A man wrapped in a loose cloak stood looking over the city. Shadows cloaked his face, but his eyes shone with the dark majesty of a new moon. Caim forced himself to meet those haunted eyes without flinching. There was something about him . . .

Caim's gaze was wrenched away, to another window near the top of the building. A slender figure was silhouetted in the lighted space, with long dark hair hanging down to her waist.

Wake up, Caim! This isn't real. Wake up!

The mountains and the vast citadel were gone. He was flying again. The sky had lightened to a sheet of purple; the orange patina of dawn's arrival glowed in the distance. The rooftops and walls of a great city spread out beneath him. He knew its winding streets and high rooftops at once. Othir.

'Look,' the witch crooned in his ear. 'And see what the future holds.'

Dust and smoke wafted from fallen gatehouses as packs of large, brutal men roamed the city streets, their fur cloaks thrown back over brawny shoulders. The dead were piled in alleyways and against buildings like stacks of cordwood. Caim turned his gaze to the highest point in the city. The sight of the Luccian Palace, reduced to a pile of slag and rubble, hit him like a hammer to the forehead. Columns of black smoke rose from the ashes.

The pool darkened, returning Caim to the chamber. Despair crushed his windpipe. Was all this for nothing? Supple hands massaged his temples.

'Give your life over to me, Caim. I can be merciful. Take my son's place and save the ones you love.'

His weapons were like lead weights. He didn't want to fight anymore. He saw his mother in his imagination, standing in a field of summer grass, her gaze turned longingly to the northern woods. To see her again, to touch her hand, to smell the lush perfume of her hair. Just one more time . . .

A faint sound buzzed in the back of his mind, but it was hard to hear, and he was so tired.

Fight her, Caim!

The words filtered through his consciousness. Fight? A shudder raced through his hand.

His small hands gripped the hilt of the sword and pulled. The wound made a sucking sound as the blade slid free.

Caim shook his head. His father had died rather than relinquish his freedom. Caim understood now. There was another side to death, a noble side. To die in the pursuit of justice was not to perish in vain. The muscles in his right arm trembled.

'You were born of the Shadow.' Her cool breath rustled the hairs at the back of his neck. 'You cannot deny your blood, Caim. Accept it and claim your birthright.'

Caim opened his eyes. The shadow beast crouched before

397

him, its bright gaze locked on him. He felt like there was a question in its look. *What do you want from me?*

But the answer shivered in his hand. The sword twitched, wavering before Caim, and he saw the blade for what it was, a weight around his neck dragging him down. Killing had become easy, convenient. How long before he started to enjoy it? *Or is it already too late?*

Caim flung out his hand. The hilt stuck to his palm for a moment, and then the blade sprang free with a tearing sound. Before it touched the floor, the shadow beast leapt.

Caim opened his arms as the creature struck. Instead of knocking him down, the beast plunged into his chest. Not through him, as Kit had done countless times, but *into* him, into his flesh. The pain was beyond anything he'd ever felt, worse than the bear mauling. It tore all coherent thought from his brain. He saw his mother again, leaning over his bed. The pillow came down . . . No!

She sang to him as she touched his chest. For a moment he could not breathe. It felt like he was underwater. And then . . .

With a small, sad smile she pulled away. In her hand was a ball of darkly shining light. For a moment it looked like a little animal, all black and glossy, curled up in her palm. He sat up as she left the room. Don't go, Mommy. I'll be good. I'll be . . .

Caim grunted as the witch's icy nails dug into his skull. Caught between the twin torments of the beast and her touch, he could only hold onto the tattered edges of consciousness and ride the pain, hoping to see the other side of it. He heard the sound of breaking glass, and then he was splintering into a thousand pieces. *I'll be good. Just come back.*

The agony faded. He was whole again. Not just in body. Something pulsed inside him, filling a space he had never known was vacant. Before he could plumb the new feeling, a furious hiss erupted behind him.

Caim turned, faster than he expected. His body moved with a speed and a grace he had never known before. Sybelle glared at him, holding up her hands as if they had been singed. Her lips parted to speak, and Caim opened a portal before him. As he passed through, a sudden inspiration made him split the gateway's path into two forks. He didn't know quite how he did it, but when he exited the portal, another empty hole yawned on the other side of the room. He hurled his *suete* knife as Sybelle turned to the wrong one. A pair of shadows flew up to deflect the missile. She reached out to Caim, and a shaft of pitch-black energy leapt across the distance between them.

Caim thrust out his empty hand without thinking. The air shimmered in front of him as the bolt of energy vanished. *How in the hells did I . . . ?*

But he was too busy to think as the witch launched a volley of spectral attacks at him. Some he saw coming, but others he could only defend by instinct. Time and time again he neutralized them. He took a step toward the witch. Her features changed as he closed in, from rage to frustration to the first inkling of apprehension. When she hurled another bolt of black lightning, Caim focused his attention on her motions. The energy dissipated into the air before it reached him. Sybelle curled her hands into white-knuckled fists. Something passed behind her eyes. A portal opened beside her. Caim traced its path through the darkness; it led outside the chamber to somewhere in the north quarter of the city. Before she could step through, he slashed the air with his hand.

Sybelle emerged from the portal only a few yards from where she had entered and jerked to a halt before she collided with the wall. She turned to him with an expression of astonishment. She opened her mouth as if to speak, but he didn't give her the opportunity to bewitch him; he lashed out with every shadow at his disposal. He lost sight of her in the vicious whirlwind of darkness. When she fell to the floor, he lifted a hand.

The shadows parted to reveal the witch propped against the pool's retaining wall. Her skin had taken on a pale sheen.

Rivulets of blood trickled down her face and neck, and leaked from the many rips in her diaphanous gown. She looked nothing at all like the imposing sorceress she had been before. But Caim didn't care.

'Where is she?' he asked.

Sybelle coughed, and winced as her upper body convulsed. Her hand reached down to caress a shadow shivering at her side like a despondent pet. Caim dropped to one knee and grabbed her by the shoulders.

'Tell me where she is!'

Her lips turned upward in a crooked smile. 'You have her eyes.'

Caim shook her hard. 'Where is . . . ?'

Her hands latched onto his wrists. 'Find Erebus. Your moth—'

Caim jerked away as a curl of smoke rose from her mouth. Stumbling to his feet, he could only watch as green flames erupted from her clothes. Even as she burned, the witch did not cry out, but only watched him with her midnight eyes, eyes he had chased across leagues and decades only to see her end like this. A word whispered from her smiling, charred lips.

'Erric.'

Her body collapsed into itself, the fire's greedy fingers licking the air, until only a pile of gray ash remained on the floor.

Find Erebus. Was that a person? It sounded more like a place. Caim recalled the black fortress from his vision, and the man on the balcony.

Across the chamber, the black sword lay against the wall where he had thrown it. It was quiet now, showing no sign of its earlier zeal. For an instant, the urge to pick it up and turn it upon himself was overwhelming.

'Caim!'

Kit appeared out of nowhere and jumped into his arms. Her touch was a mere tingle on his skin, but it had never felt so good.

'I thought you were dead,' she murmured into his chest. 'I was shut out. I couldn't feel you. I thought . . .'

'I'm all right.'

She looked at him, her features drawn up in an expression more earnest than he had ever seen on her before.

'I love you,' she said.

'I know.' He tried to swallow, but his mouth had dried up. 'I love you, too.'

The words were true before he spoke them, but saying them aloud had a power all its own. There was no taking it back. He tensed as she floated up and kissed him. Electric tingles ran through his lips and across his tongue.

'I've been wanting to do that,' she said, not nearly as breathless as he was, 'for a damned long time.'

He was still enjoying the rush when she held him close and asked, 'What about Josey?'

'I don't know.'

Over her slim shoulder, he stared at the pile of ash.

'I don't know.'

Chapter
FORTY

'Is everything all right, Josey?' Anastasia called from outside the door.

Inside the water closet, Josey braced herself for another painful upheaval. The morning had begun rather tamely as she arose and sat at the table in her chambers, where Anastasia joined her for breakfast. But when she started to eat, something about the consistency of the eggs on her breakfast dish had—

She shuddered as a mouthful of bile slipped from her lips and down the noisome hole. The close air inside the stall made her feel worse. Dabbing her mouth with a cloth, Josey pushed open the door.

Anastasia stood outside with Amelia and Margaret, all three of them wearing looks of concern. Of course, 'Stasia had told her maids about her condition. Now they fluttered about her like mother hens, clucking and giving her all manner of unsolicited advice. *I suppose it's better than having them in mortal fear that I've been poisoned every morning.*

Indeed, they took the news well enough, neither giving her a sour eye nor shirking from their duties in the slightest. *Which well they might, being among the few who know that their empress is carrying the bastard child of a self-exiled assassin. That's if it's Caim's child at all. Of course it is! Don't even think about—*

'You don't look well, my lady,' Margaret said. 'You should try to eat something.'

Amelia nodded as she arranged Josey's hair. 'At least a piece of toasted bread. And a posset to settle your nerves.'

Josey folded her hands over her belly. Just the thought of spiced wine mixed with curdled milk made her queasy. 'Please don't talk about food.'

Her maids looked to Anastasia, who shook her head with an insanely darling pout.

'Josey, you must—'

Just as Amelia started explaining that she must eat to keep up her strength, a loud voice called from the doorway.

'Majesty!'

Josey swallowed the sour taste in her mouth as Hubert rushed into her bedchamber. *What is it the man does not understand about personal privacy?*

But she was willing to forgive him, as the cane he leaned upon reminded her of the sacrifice he had been willing to make on her behalf. The events in the catacombs had been a nightmare, one she would be glad to forget. But Hirsch had gotten them out alive – another debt she owed the adept. Sadly, not everyone had emerged from those tunnels alive. Two more of her guardsmen were dead. *A bad affair all around.*

After the bodies were retrieved, she'd ordered the tunnels sealed. The soldiers were laid to rest with full honors beside the tombs of other national heroes; Merts and Volek were buried in unmarked graves outside the city.

'Shouldn't you be abed, Lord Chancellor?'

Anastasia gave Hubert a sideways glance. 'Yes, I believe Her Majesty is correct.'

Josey watched the exchange with a smile. She had worried about how Anastasia would recover from her father's death, but this morning her best friend seemed to be past the worst of it – with a little assistance from the lord chancellor. She wished the best for them both.

Hubert glanced at Josey, and then to the open water closet. Margaret nudged the door shut with her foot.

'The delegation has arrived,' he said.

Josey sighed. *And it started off as such a lovely day.*

'I still have my doubts, Majesty,' Hubert said. 'I wish you would reconsider.'

'We've already had this discussion. More than once. This is my decision. If you will not—'

He bowed as low as his injuries would allow. 'Of course I will. I'll see to it personally.'

Struggling not to beat him over the head with the nearest object, Josey shooed him away. Then she allowed herself to be stripped, sponged, powdered, corseted, and draped in a shapeless sack that her seamstress claimed was the height of fashion in Brevenna. Only when her hair was arranged, her face made up, and her entire body misted with citrus perfume did her maids allow her to leave the boudoir. Anastasia watched the whole affair with an amused smile.

'I'll see you later,' Josey said to her friend.

Anastasia performed a deep curtsy. 'Yes, Your Majesty.'

Josey stepped into the corridor with mincing steps. She was beginning to feel a little better. *Don't think about your stomach. Think about what you're going to do. Hubert has everything arranged. All I have to do is play my part and everything will go fine. So why do I feel so wretched?*

She knew why, but knowing didn't make her feel any better. She was on the cusp of a decision. To act or not, and either choice presented its own dangers. *Why couldn't being an empress be all about wearing nice clothes and knighting handsome heroes?*

With her bodyguards in tow, she descended the broad staircase to the ground floor. The Grand Hall was lit with hundreds of white candles, lending the chamber a ghostly ambience that made the time feel more like evening than midmorning. Hubert and Lord Parmian stood beside the dais. Ozmond greeted her with a firm nod. He wore a new chain signifying his elevation to the rank of viscount.

Most of the Thurim's members had taken their seats. Every head turned as Josey entered. Concentrating on not tripping over the hem of her gown, she crossed the floor. She glanced up, and then looked again when she noticed blots of fresh color on the ceiling. Where the Church's propaganda had once glared down, now traditional scenes of Nimean history were beginning to emerge. Although the restoration work had just begun, she could make out the faces of emperors and empresses in their fine regalia. The largest figure, occupying a central position, was a face she knew.

Smiling, Josey climbed the steps of the dais and turned to the hall. She took a deep breath and let it out. With a nod to Hubert, she sat down. The guardsmen flanking the main entrance opened the tall doors. A dozen men stood in the atrium. Eight were soldiers in the uniform of the Nimean army. The first units from the nearest garrison towns had arrived late last night. By morning they had secured High Town and begun the task of reinstalling the rule of law in Low Town. The soldiers surrounded four men in clerical raiment. The man at their forefront wore a dour expression.

Not the honor guard you were expecting when next you returned to the palace, Prelate?

Josey kept her expression neutral as the soldiers escorted the Church leaders into the hall. Instead of his former raiment, Innocence wore only a white cassock belted with a sash of crimson silk. As the delegation halted, the prelate looked up at the ceiling, and his expression hardened.

Lady Philomena stood up from her seat among the Thurim as the hierarchs were led before the throne. 'This is preposterous! How dare the court summon Our Holy Father in such a disgraceful fash—?'

'Be silent,' Josey said.

The lady stared, her mouth agape. She sat down with an unladylike grunt. Josey's eyes never left the members of the delegation.

'Lord Chancellor, the next person who speaks without our consent is to be taken outside and flogged.'

'Yes, Your Majesty.'

At Hubert's signal, the soldiers turned inward to face the

clerics. Josey waited to see if any of them would be fool enough to test her. But none did. *Too bad. It would have made for a fitting example to the others.*

'I have summoned Your Holiness to this court,' she said, 'to hear defense against the charges laid against yourself and your ministers.'

One of the hierarchs, a venerable priest in white vestments, shuffled forward to speak, but the prelate stopped him with a clearing of his throat.

Prelate Innocence worked his mouth around before muttering, 'Have I permission to speak?'

'You do.'

'Then we demand to know the whereabouts of Archpriest Gaspar. The unwarranted seizure of his person is cause for—'

'You will answer the charges put before Your Holiness.'

'The True Church recognizes no authority invested in this court.' The creases of his brow wriggled back and forth as he spoke, animating the upper portion of his face. 'Furthermore, the seizing of our person is an act of defiance against the Prophet Himself. It is you who shall be judged, and not I.'

Hubert stepped forward and dropped a bundle at the prelate's feet.

Josey pointed, 'Whether you acknowledge our authority or not, you will answer for this.'

At a gesture from his master, the old priest bent down to pick up the bundle. He opened it to reveal two torn and bloodstained tabards in crimson, each bearing the golden circle of the Sacred Brotherhood.

'Those surcoats, Your Eminence,' Josey said, 'were found in the possession of two agents who were, we believe, aiding the assassin seeking to end our life. Agents of your Church, Eminence.'

'This is lunacy!' one of the younger hierarchs barked. 'A pair of old shirts, no matter where they were found, does not constitute evidence against the Holy—'

Josey nodded to Hubert. Two guardsmen seized the archpriest and hauled him from the chamber. Voices erupted from the Thurim. Josey allowed them a few moments to digest her words. The prelate said nothing. His eyes, though, glowered at her with pure venom.

'Holiness,' she said. 'Do you deny the Church has encouraged demonstrations against the crown throughout the city since the day of my coronation?'

'There is no proof of that,' Innocence replied. 'I, myself, have issued proclamations condemning such—'

'The uniforms, the demonstrations, and the assassin. They are all connected to the same plot to overthrow this government and seize power. A plot traced back to the Church. To your office.'

The prelate swallowed and glanced at the soldiers surrounding him. 'That is absurd. You don't have the proof. The faithful—'

'Archpriest Gaspar has made a full confession.'

Ozmond extended a roll of parchment. One of the remaining arch priests took it and handed it over to the prelate. Innocence glanced at its contents.

'A confession made under considerable duress, no doubt. Worthless.'

But there was something new in his gaze. Was it fear?

Josey stood up. 'If there are any further demonstrations, or should my ministers unearth additional plots against the throne, I will dismantle the True Church piece by piece.'

The prelate's chin trembled. 'By the Prophet, you shall live to regret your audacity, child.'

'That may be.'

She inclined her head, and the prelate started to leave. But she gestured before they reached the doors, and her guardsmen stopped their exit.

'*Majesty*,' she said. 'You will address this throne properly for all the court to hear, Your Eminence.'

The prelate turned, his face hardened into a stony mask. He cleared his throat. 'As you wish. Majesty.'

Josey held out her hand. The imperial seal flashed in the sunlight as she and the prelate stared at each other for several long heartbeats. Finally, Innocence shambled over to climb the dais and touched his lips to the ring.

'Well done,' she whispered. 'Now get out of my sight.'

As the delegation hurried from the hall, Josey swallowed several times to clear the taste of bile from her mouth. She glanced over at the Thurim to see how Lady Philomena was taking the prelate's public humiliation, but her seat was vacant. *I should have had her flogged.*

Settling back in the throne as the tension eased from her body, Josey presented a composed face to the court. The ministers watched her with what she hoped were benign expressions. *Well, they haven't denounced me yet. So there's hope that I won't be the shortest-reigning monarch in Nimea's history.*

A side door opened, and Captain Drathan stepped through. He looked in her direction and made a shallow nod before leaving. Relieved, Josey jumped up, almost forgetting to dismiss the court as she hurried down the steps. She was out the door before anyone could say a word.

A candlemark later, Josey came down a secluded staircase in the west wing of the palace. She was hugged in a suit of comfortable green leathers and heeled riding boots. Her hair was pinned up under the hood of her cloak. Despite the pangs in her stomach, half nausea and half excitement, she was excited. *I'm actually doing it!*

Hirsch waited by the postern door. The adept leaned as he stood, favoring his left leg, but he had made a remarkable recovery. He met her eyes with a frank gaze.

'That was well done, lass. Not many people could take the Holy Father to task like that. There's a lioness in that heart of yours.'

Josey allowed herself a little sigh. 'I wish I felt like there was, but what I really feel is . . .'

'Uncertainty,' he offered.

'Yes.'

Hirsch coughed into his hand. 'Someone once said that leading a nation is like walking through a dark wood on a moonless night; you never know what's coming.'

'That's how I've felt ever since I put on the crown. Who said that?'

'Your father.'

Josey's breath caught in her throat. 'Thank you.'

Offering the adept her arm, she pushed open the door. The outside air was laden with the crisp smell of winter. After weeks of rain and sleet, the stones of the courtyard were covered with a blanket of fresh snow. It had begun falling sometime after midnight, and judging by the fluffy clouds overhead, it was going to continue for some time. The flakes fell upon the shoulders of her palace bodyguards as they stood in sharp formation. She'd asked for volunteers, and every man who could ride had insisted upon coming, even the wounded in their bandages; she didn't turn away anyone who could sit on a horse. Behind her bodyguards stood four columns, a full company of hobelar infantry with their mounts. The golden griffin fluttered on their chests, but they seemed too few for the task she had in mind.

'They aren't enough,' Hubert said, coming over to her.

Josey pressed her lips together, barely managing to stifle a pointed retort. The man was entirely too good at reading her thoughts. Anastasia accompanied the lord chancellor, the two of them standing rather close. A few paces away, Duke Mormaer talked with Captain Drathan. Mormaer hardly seemed the same man who had stormed into her throne room. Where he had been rigid and prickly, he was now almost genteel. *Or perhaps I just understand him better now.*

'We will acquire more,' Josey said, loud enough for everyone to hear. 'On our journey north.'

Hubert nodded, but the frown remained on his thin lips. 'I must restate my opinion that this decision is unwise.'

Duke Mormaer grunted. 'Give it a rest, Vassili. She's doing what needs to be done. What the Empress of Nimea must do in times like these.'

'Thank you, Your Grace.' Josey turned to Hubert. 'All is ready?'

'Yes, Majesty.'

'Good. Has the Watch been reestablished?'

'Numbers are low, but some of the deserters are starting to slink back into the ranks.'

'Don't be too harsh with them. We've all been through a rough time.'

Hubert tapped the ground with the tip of his cane. 'There is a spot of good news. We have received missives from some of the nobles involved in unlawful raids against their neighbors. One and all state their undying fealty to the crown. Furthermore, Lords Devring and Karstan are coming to Othir to prove this in person.' He leaned closer. 'And I have managed to convince enough of your ministers that we might send an envoy to Akeshia to introduce a truce and begin discussions on a trade agreement. Money still poses a problem, but I believe it can be done.'

Josey suppressed a smile, wondering how the man could keep track of it all and still find time to court a lady. 'Anything else, Your Grace?'

'Well, rampant banditry still plagues the western border, and a diplomatic mission has arrived from the kingdom of Arnos. I presume they wish to discuss the status of Mecantia.'

'I trust you to handle the matters, Lord Regent.'

'Majesty, I don't—'

Josey pulled a scroll from under her cloak and passed it to him. 'I'm leaving you in charge. You are hereby named the imperial regent of Othir in my absence.'

He handled the order gingerly. 'I'm not—'

'There's been no word from the northern border, and none of our envoys have returned. That can only mean one thing.'

'War,' Mormaer said.

Josey nodded. 'There is a foreign army on our soil, Lord Chancellor, and I intend to send it back to where it came from. Master Hirsch' – she glanced at the adept, who was watching the discussion quietly – 'will accompany us.'

Hubert finally gave a hesitant nod.

Anastasia walked to take her hand. 'Josey, I'm going to be worried every day until you return. Promise you'll be careful.'

Josey kissed her cheek. 'I promise, 'Stasia. And try to keep Hubert out of trouble, will you?'

Anastasia blushed, and Josey had to laugh, but there was a note of sadness in it. She might never see these people – her friends – again. But somehow, instead of making her fearful of the future, it urged her to go forth with courage.

'Hubert, keep an eye on Lady Philomena and the prelate. They will not forget the slights we served them this day.'

As the lord chancellor bowed, a groom brought Lightning over. Josey didn't wait for the stepping stand, but climbed into the stallion's tall saddle on her own. As she settled into the stirrups, a cheer went up from the troops in the courtyard. It was echoed by the sentries on the palace walls. Josey's face was hot in the chilly air as she took her place at the head of the formation alongside Captain Drathan and the army commander.

Hubert came over to stand beside her. 'Take every care, Your Majesty. Your country needs you.'

Her heart swelled to the point of breaking, Josey pointed to the open gates and shouted, 'Forward!'

Caim traced the outline of Josey's pendant under his shirt as he stood on the crest of a flat ridge. The midmorning sky was clear and blue, but the brittle air carried the scent of snow. Stern hilltops crowded the western horizon. To the north rose the beginnings of the great forest, dark and forbidding even in the daylight. The tugging in his head was clear as crystal; he could have pointed to its source far beyond the northern mountains, but his thoughts ran in the other direction, to Josey and the vast distance between them.

Below the ridge, wild brush and weeds choked what had once been the grounds of his family estate. Low mounds crested the snow where buildings had once stood, including the house where he was born. He'd left the city in the early morning, slinking out with the rest of the bad memories, while the townspeople snored away the effects of the drunken celebrations from the night before. Some part of him had considered staying, just to see what they would make of their newfound liberation. But it was better he left before they remembered what he was.

Assassin. Sellsword. Killer.

As always, victory came with a price. Caim recalled the names of the fallen in his head: Liana, Hagan, Caedman, Killian, Oak, Vaner, and more. Too many. Ramon's tale was being told throughout Liovard, how he'd met his end holding off a legion of foreign mercenaries while his men set fire to the city barracks and the homes of ducal sympathizers. Already his name had joined Caedman's in the pantheon of martyrs to what was being hailed as a new era of freedom in Eregoth. But Caim remembered another man, long ago, who had also died following the banner of his nation's freedom. His gaze touched a spot at the center of the estate's courtyard. The black sword was finally back where it belonged. He didn't want it. Its vengeance exacted too high a price.

A finch soared across the fields to settle on a green sapling rising through the snow and greeted him with a bright chirp.

'You'll catch your death out here.'

Caim dropped his hand from his chest as Kit materialized beside him. The scandalous cut of her dress at the bodice and thigh was in a garish contrast to its somber purple hue. Her silver hair wafted against the breeze.

'Who would notice?' he asked.

'You're in a glum mood this morning.'

'I haven't slept in three days.'

She wrinkled her nose. 'Nor bathed, evidently.'

Caim looked to the north, to the leaden gray sky above the ocean of trees.

Kit floated around until she was looking into his eyes. 'How are you feeling?'

'I'll live.'

The rage was gone from him, buried with the sword. Or so he hoped. All in all, a fair trade. But something was different. He could feel it inside him, like an itch he couldn't scratch.

The shadow beast.

It was a part of him now. Kit said it always had been, but he just didn't know it. Caim wasn't sure what that meant. The dreams of his mother still lingered in his mind. She had sacrificed herself for him. That much he knew. As for the rest, there was only one way to find out.

'So you're still intent on going north?' she asked. 'And I suppose trying to talk you out of it would be a waste of breath.'

'Something like that. You coming with?'

She gave him an ethereal peck on the cheek. 'What are we waiting for?'

But he saw the other question in her gaze, the one she'd asked as they held each other in the witch's lair while the tiny electric pulse of her heart tickled his chest. *'What about Josey?'*

He still didn't have an answer, but he was saved by the clop of hoofbeats.

'You're a damned hard man to track down, Caim.'

Dismounting from a fine gelding, Keegan walked over to him. The youth was wearing the same bloodstained clothes he'd worn the night before. Aemon, Dray, and Malig rode behind him on similarly upscale steeds. Aemon's leg was wrapped in bandages, but the brothers had both survived the night of chaos, which was amazing. If Caim were the pious sort, he might have called it a miracle. But he was content to chalk it up to dumb luck. *Where would any of us be without it?*

'Maybe I didn't want to be found,' he replied.

Kit snorted.

Keegan looked at the others. 'We don't want you to leave, Caim. In fact, we'd like you to stay as—'

'No, thanks.'

Keegan's grimace pulled at the black smudges under his eyes. The eyes of an older man. 'You don't know what I was going to say.'

'Sure I do. But I'm not the man for the job. Did you burn everything in her temple?'

'We tore the whole rotten place down,' Dray answered. 'And I personally pissed on the ashes.'

Keegan flashed the ghost of a smile. 'We did like you said, but there's trouble in the city. Some of the celebrations have gone out of control. People are burning down buildings, fighting, and drinking themselves stupid.'

'You'll figure it out.'

'But you're nobility,' Keegan said. 'That's something none of the rest of us can claim. Eregoth needs—'

'This country needs a new beginning.' Caim looked down over the ruined estate. 'Not another reminder of the past. Let the people work off their anger in debauchery for a day or two. When they're done, they'll be looking for a leader. A man like you.'

Keegan studied the snow between his feet. 'But how can I lead a nation, Caim? I'm not even a thane. I don't know . . .'

Caim felt for the boy. He was stepping into a new world he'd never dreamed of before these past couple days. Caim placed a hand on Keegan's shoulder over the knots of blue ink.

'Remember the ones who have fallen to make it possible. Let their memories guide you. Being a leader isn't about giving commands and making men kneel. It's about winning their hearts. You've got your father's strength, Keegan, and your sister's heart. That's a good start.'

Keegan bit his bottom lip and nodded. He took a long dagger from under his cloak and held it out, hilt-first.

'I want you to have this.'

A knot inside Caim's chest loosened. He had seen the weapon before, from the other end.

'That's your father's knife. I can't take that, Keegan.'

The youth pushed it at him. 'He would want you to have it. It's good Eregothic steel, not like that flimsy slag they make down south.'

Caim took the seax knife. The hilt felt good in his palm, and it had a nice weight, but the blade was half a finger broader than his *suete* knife. That would take some getting used to.

'You won't reconsider?' Keegan asked.

414

'Not a chance. Go on before I get arrested for cuffing the new duke, or whatever they're going to name you.' Caim lifted his chin toward the others, still on their horses. 'And take these old war dogs with you.'

Keegan laughed. 'I wish I could, but they're not here for me.'

The men watched him like they wanted a piece of him in the worst way.

'What did I do this time?'

But Keegan was walking away. As the boy mounted up, Caim cupped his hands around his mouth and called out. Keegan looked back.

'You can trust the Empress of Nimea! She's got a good heart, too.'

Keegan made a final salute as he started down the trail back to Liovard. The brothers and Malig waited until he was gone, then they urged their steeds forward. Caim waited in a neutral stance, hands resting by his sides.

Malig leaned over as they stopped a few paces away and spat into the snow. 'We figure you're headed out of here. Out of Eregoth, at least.'

Caim looked from one face to the next. 'I might be.'

Aemon broke into a broad smile. 'We want to come with you.'

'Fucking right,' Dray said. 'It's going to be damned boring around here, now that Eviskine and his witch are gone.'

Caim started to shake his head, but when he searched for reasons why not, he came up empty.

'All right.' He walked between their horses. 'Let's get moving.'

'Where we going, boss?' Aemon asked.

Caim looked past the men, to the dark forest bordering his father's lands and the mysteries beyond. His mother was alive, somewhere out there.

'North,' he said.

With a shared smile, the outlaws clicked to their horses and trotted up the trail ahead of him.

Caim looked over his shoulder. 'Are you coming?'

Kit reappeared beside him with a lopsided grin. 'Trying to get rid of me?'

'All the time. But you keep coming back.'

She patted his cheek. 'That should be a lesson for you.'

'All right, then. Lead the way.'

With a laugh that drove away the clouds in his heart, Kit sped off toward the woods like a shooting star. Caim spared one last glance for the snow-covered ruins and the spot in the center of the overgrown yard that the daylight seemed to avoid.

Then he swung his satchel over his shoulder and set off after her.

ACKNOWLEDGMENTS

I would like to thank . . .

Jenny, for always believing, even when the going got rough;

Logan, for showing me the whole new world that is fatherhood;

Eddie, for making the right calls at the right times, for the right reasons;

Lou, for putting me in the game and letting me throw deep;

Chris, Fred, Jen, and Gillian, for making me work harder;

And all those who have inspired and supported me.

Up the Irons!

ABOUT THE AUTHOR

J on Sprunk lives in central Pennsylvania with his family.
He received a bachelor of liberal arts degree from Lock
Haven University in 1992. He has worked at a variety
of jobs, including fourteen years as a juvenile detention
specialist. His first novel, *Shadow's Son*, was published in 2010.

For more on his life and works, visit www.jonsprunk.com and
his blog, Fear of the Dark (http://jonsprunk.blogspot.com).